An
I-NOVEL

An
I-NOVEL

MINAE
MIZUMURA

Translated by
Juliet Winters Carpenter
in collaboration with the author

Columbia University Press
New York

Columbia University Press wishes to express its appreciation
for assistance given by the Suntory Foundation
in the publication of this book.

Columbia University Press
Publishers Since 1893
New York   Chichester, West Sussex
cup.columbia.edu

An I-Novel from Left to Right
Copyright © 1995 by Minae Mizumura
First published in 1995 by Shinchosha Publishing Co., Ltd., Tokyo
English language translation rights arranged with Minae Mizumura
through Japan Foreign-Rights Centre

Copyright © 2021 Columbia University Press
All rights reserved
Library of Congress Cataloging-in-Publication Data

Names: Mizumura, Minae, author. | Carpenter, Juliet Winters, translator.
Title: An I-novel / Minae Mizumura; translated by Juliet Winters Carpenter in
collaboration with the author.
Other titles: Shishōsetsu from left to right. English
Description: New York: Columbia University Press, [2021]
Identifiers: LCCN 2020021822 (print) | LCCN 2020021823 (ebook) |
ISBN 9780231192125 (hardback) | ISBN 9780231192132 (trade paperback) |
ISBN 9780231549660 (ebook)
Classification: LCC PL856.I948 S5513 2021 (print) | LCC PL856.I948 (ebook) |
DDC 895.63/5--dc23
LC record available at https://lccn.loc.gov/2020021822
LC ebook record available at https://lccn.loc.gov/2020021823

∞

Columbia University Press books are printed
on permanent and durable acid-free paper.
Printed in the United States of America

Cover design: Julia Kushnirsky
Cover art: Japanese woodblock print, c. 1880s.
Photo © GraphicaArtis / Bridgeman Images
Book design: Lisa Hamm

CONTENTS

——Yes.

　私は答えたあと、つけ加えた。

——In Japanese.

——Ho-ho!

　「Big Mac」は驚きと揶揄をこめて腹から笑った。そしてその
あともわざと笑いをかくさずに訊いた。

——Can you write Japanese? I mean, good Japanese. After
all, you weren't educated in Japan, Minae.

　例の食前酒のシェリーをもう二三杯はやったあとなのか、ふだ
んより御機嫌である。

——I know. But I've been reading Japanese all these years.

　And writing letters in Japanese と続けようとしてやめた。
これではかえって馬鹿馬鹿しく聞こえるにちがいない。

——Well, I suppose you can give it a try.

　かれはそう応えたあと、まだからかいを含んだ声で訊いた。

——Do you know what you'd write about?

——I don't know yet.

——Your experiences in America?

——No. I think that'd be too boring.

　私はまた笑われるのを覚悟で続けた。

——I do want to write like Sōseki.

——Ho-ho!

　「Big Mac」は案の定また腹から笑った。私も笑った。彼は笑
いやまないまま言った。

——Well, try not to mix up your Japanese with English.

——I'll try not to.

　そう応えながら、ふいに私はこの期に及んで私を悩まし始めた

324

▲ Page from the original novel

TRANSLATOR'S NOTE

An I-Novel was originally published in 1995 under the title *Shishōsetsu from left to right*. The word *shishōsetsu* designates a confessional autobiographical genre—the "I-novel"—that has played a key role in modern Japanese literature. The original, based on the author's experiences growing up in the United States and Japan, freely mixes natural American English with Japanese. In a break with age-old tradition for Japanese novels, the book was written and printed not vertically but horizontally, from left to right, so that readers would not have to crane their necks or turn the book around every time they encountered an English word or phrase.

As the English translator of a book that was promoted in Japan as the nation's "first bilingual novel," I faced the seemingly impossible task of capturing the bilingual format and sense of the original in a monolingual context. Mizumura herself has addressed that challenge:

> Any writer writing in a language other than English can reasonably expect her readers to understand some, if not most, of the English words she might happen to throw in. It would therefore be possible to replicate the bilingual form of *Shishōsetsu from left to right* in any

language in the world—be it Korean, Bengali, or French—by translating the Japanese and leaving the English parts as they are. The only language in which this wouldn't work would be English. . . . Indeed, the very impossibility of maintaining the bilingual form while translating the work into English, and the singularity of that impossibility, are clear testimony to the linguistic asymmetry we now face in this world. (*The Fall of Language in the Age of English*, p. 65)

The solution I devised, in consultation with Mizumura, was to use a different typeface for words that appear in English in the original and occasionally insert Japanese writing when a specific expression in Japanese is the issue. Even readers with no knowledge of Japanese will glimpse some of the language's richness. Other typefaces are also used as needed to reflect Mizumura's concern with the visual aspect of written language.

An I-Novel is Mizumura's second novel. Her debut novel, *Zoku meian* (Light and Dark continued), created a huge stir among readers in Japan when it came out in 1990. This is because it picks up where Natsume Sōseki's (1867–1916) unfinished last work leaves off, finishing the story and brilliantly recreating the master's idiosyncratic language and style. How might Sōseki have finished the novel, had he lived? Legions of novelists and critics had mulled this question and made conjectures, but then a nameless woman came out of nowhere and dared to step into Sōseki's shoes. The revelation that the writer had moved with her family to the United States at age twelve and received her education there only deepened everyone's shock and admiration.

An I-Novel, which came out five years later, makes clear how and why Minae Mizumura would have chosen to write a work like *Zoku meian*. At the same time, it also demonstrates her ability to write a very different type of novel in her own style. From the time of its publication, her status as a writer was assured. She has continued ever since to write at her own pace, steadily expanding her oeuvre and winning accolades in Japan and around the globe. Besides English, her works have been translated into many languages, including most recently Slovenian and Polish. The girlhood dream of the narrator-protagonist of *An I-Novel* has come true many times over.

Minae is not the only character in *An I-Novel* with literary aspirations. Minae's mother declares in a letter her intention to take writing classes and write her autobiography, and in real life Mizumura's mother, Mizumura Setsuko, did exactly that. After ten years of writing, in 2000, at age seventy-eight—five years after *An I-Novel* came out—she published *Takadai ni aru ie* (The house on the hilltop), the story of her colorful life in prewar Japan. The book was warmly received, with reviews in leading newspapers and magazines, and it enjoyed brisk sales. Mizumura not only achieved her own dream but helped her mother to achieve hers by participating in the final editing of the work. And so the literary longings of both the fictional daughter and her mother were happily fulfilled in real life.

Mizumura's own works are, without exception, the fruit of her meditations on words and language. One nonfiction work with a particularly strong connection to *An I-Novel* is *The Fall of Language in the Age of English* (2008, trans. 2015 by Mari Yoshihara and myself), a wide-ranging rumination on language and the act of writing. Its core ideas are present in *An I-Novel*, showing how a highly personal novel that Mizumura wrote early on continued to reverberate and percolate within her, leading to an influential work that became a must-read for Japanese intellectuals and the wider reading public.

Two more novels followed, both of which I had the privilege of translating into English: *A True Novel* (2002, trans. 2013) and *Inheritance from Mother* (2012, trans. 2017). They continue

Mizumura's exploration of and homage to the ambitions and traditions of her predecessors—the "true" or orthodox novel and the serialized novel, respectively—while showcasing her remarkable storytelling ability and, ultimately, her celebration of life.

Finally, I must point out that in the course of translating *An I-Novel*, as often happens in literary translation, a variety of changes to the text were made as, working closely with Mizumura, I tried to keep, paradoxically, to the truth of the original novel.

Juliet Winters Carpenter

Before I knew it, I was standing in front of the tall oak bookcase on the opposite wall from the **computer**, *looking up. On the top shelf was the set of books with vermilion bindings, untouched for a while. I reached up and pulled a volume down. I opened it, and the familiar musty smell rushed out. The past twenty years—and many more— were contained in that smell.* ✀

Friday, December 13, 198X

Twenty years since our . . .

"Our exile"? No. That sounds too ordinary. How about "the Exile"? No . . . "The Exodus"? Oh yes, "the Exodus"! Yes, let the word be "Exodus."

Twenty years since the Exodus.

And what if I start with "Alas!"?

Alas! Twenty years since the Exodus.

And another exclamation mark at the end.

Alas! Twenty years since the Exodus!

How about three exclamation marks to really mark that pang I felt.

Alas! Twenty years since the Exodus!!!

No. That looks too vulgar. Take out the last two. Delete and delete and, wait, do I hear a siren? Yes, I hear a siren—Yes, definitely, I hear a siren in the distance . . .

The faint sound came closer, threading through the darkness. A sound to rouse the loneliness of the dark winter night—*somehow resembling and yet so very remote from the siren I used to know as a child.* Not the long wail of an animal howling, but an electronic *ee-aw* alternating from high to low, no way to tell whether it was the police or an ambulance. A sinister sound, bone-chilling.

Somebody's been killed . . . shot, maybe. A student? A prostitute again? *No. It's the snow.*

Snow.

The snowstorm was fierce. The first snowfall of this winter had begun in the afternoon and gradually picked up in intensity until now, late at night, the snow was coming down hard, blanketing everything.

Must be a car accident.

I got up from the **computer** and ran to the bay window. I hadn't been outdoors all day, and not only today, yesterday and the day before too. I hadn't set foot outside, hadn't so much as opened a window. The sudden movement made the stagnation of the room feel heavy, thick with heat and dust. The siren kept coming closer and closer but then, instead of turning onto my street, continued straight down the main avenue toward the center of the college town.

Good-bye. Farewell, ma belle Sirène.

I remained at the window.

Below, circling the streetlamp, infinitesimal snowflakes danced, shimmering in the cold. The double-paned window rattled in the wind.

How deep was the snow now?

Tarō o nemurase	Snow piles deep on Tarō's roof
Tarō no yane ni yuki furitsumu	putting Tarō to sleep.
Jirō o nemurase	Snow piles deep on Jirō's roof
Jirō no yane ni yuki furitsumu	putting Jirō to sleep.

And this was the only poem he could recite by heart.

One night Tono had stood here at this window, looking down like this at the falling snow, and recited those words, rather shyly. **And how I wished and wished I had that snowy scene in front of me.**

Snow . . . snow falling heavily . . . heavily and silently, piling ever deeper. Not these dry snowflakes flying in the wind like desert sand, but 牡丹雪 *botan yuki*, "peony snow," flakes full of moisture, falling like heavy round flowers. I still remembered the chill of them landing on the palm of my hand—*so I think, at least. Or is my memory only an illusion of a memory?* And as I remembered or tried to remember that chill, amid the hush of large flower-flakes falling heavily I could make out a line of snow-covered thatched roofs stretching back and back and back, blending into distant white mountains that merged in turn into a sky lit white by the snow. Such a rustic winter scene might now be forever lost, existing only in folklore or on travel posters of the national railroad company, and certainly I myself had never seen anything like it; yet as I imagined the scene spread out before me, snowy mountains in the distance, my chest tightened with nostalgia.

What I saw now through a veil of powdery snow was the big brick **Afro-American Student Center** across the street and next to it, the **University Cabaret**.

How very quiet . . . and to think it's a Friday night.

Through the double-paned window I should be hearing the music and laughter of black students from around the campus, clapping and punctuating the patter of the **DJ** with husky cries of **"Oh, yeah!"** as they danced into the night, their bodies moving to the rhythm with a suppleness few if any Japanese could match. Every time I heard those sounds of life, I felt a surge of self-pity: *Oh, they're having so much fun, and here I am, so miserable. . . .* But tonight the **Afro-American Student Center** was as quiet as abandoned ruins, and the **University Cabaret** doors with their Gothic arches were shut tight.

Between the two buildings was a narrow twisting alley where two black prostitutes had been killed that summer. Usually, even in winter, prostitutes lingered in front of the worn stone steps of my apartment building, hopping into a car whenever one pulled up, but tonight there was no sign of them. On a night like this there wouldn't be any customers. One prostitute, noticeably taller than the others, was always nice to me—but, come to think of it, I hadn't seen her in a long time. Could she have been one of the victims? *Poor soul! Such a friendly girl that she was. She'd shout things like "Hey China! I like your coat!" and I'd answer, "Thank you" . . . always timidly, of course.* Like the other prostitutes, she would stand with her coat open, revealing the flimsy garment she had on underneath, wearing boots with vertiginously high heels. In the alley where the murders took place there used to be faint blood stains, but after a snowfall like this, that alley would be covered till spring with layers of snow, dirt, and grit.

Farther down the alley, for once nobody would be working late in the editorial office of the university newspaper. On a night like this there'd be no way to get home. No cars were driving by, no one was out walking. In the distance, hazy fluorescent lights shone from the high-rise architecture building, tall and immobile in the swirling snow.

The lingering echo of the siren now gone, the night was totally silent.

I rested my head against the window, mesmerized by the snow until I lost all sense of time and place . . . there was only the soundless dance of the snow, gleaming like frozen sparks . . . glittering bits of frozen fire . . .

. . . and then through those glittering bits, from beyond those distant snowy mountains in my mind, running barefoot through the blizzard came a horde of *yamamba*, crones kicking and prancing. These mountain women of Japanese folklore had risen from their graves to run madly in the dark of night. Wild hair streaming behind them in the gale, they sprinted over the ridge and down into the valley. That one was my grandmother, that one my great-grandmother, over there was my great-great-grandmother . . . before me I saw these women from the past, women with whom I shared a bond of blood. They were singing a rousing *nagauta* refrain:

A-ara omoshirono-o yamameguri . . .
Oh, how thrilling is this mountain journey . . .

"Come join us, come, hurry, come," they urged. From all around, their voices rang in my ears.

My whole being responded to the call of these women of the Rising Sun, my blood and theirs part of a stream that had flowed uninterrupted with bewildering consistency going back hundreds—no, thousands, no, tens of thousands of years. Their noiseless footsteps echoed through the hills. The wind roared . . . *Yes, I'm coming! I'm on my way, Grandma!* Soon I too would race across hilltops. My hot soles would melt the snow and my feet would kick up rich fragrant black earth. I would then kiss the ground and cry, "Oh, my beloved country, my homeland, I have come back to you!"

No, no. *Make it sound more classic:* Then shall my voice cry out, "O my beloved country, land of my birth, now have I returned to thee!"

"Kiss the ground"—where did that come from? Strange how easy it is to slide into translationese.

The first thing the pope did when he visited a country was to kneel down and reverently kiss the ground, not minding if his splendid white robe got soiled. No Japanese person would do such a thing.

An act of great humility. But only from the viewpoint of people who used a mop with a long handle to clean the floor and would never dream of getting down on their hands and knees with a hand-stitched cloth. My ancestors turned their gaze downward at all times. They were on intimate terms with the ground underfoot, lived with minimal resistance to the force of gravity. Whether cleaning house, planting rice, or pulling weeds, they kept their noses close to the floor, the field, the ground. One day when I was spending my summer in Tokyo, I'd seen women squatting on the ground pulling weeds. They were wearing bright-colored jogging suits and white sneakers, old-fashioned indigo-dyed towels tied around their heads, and when they moved to a new spot, instead of getting up they would pivot on one leg, moving dexterously like a crab. But whenever I saw **George**, the building superintendent who was black, standing by the back steps with mop in hand, he'd be holding himself erect, chest thrust out. "Hi, George!" I'd call, and he'd wave with his free hand, face wreathed in smiles, and call back **"Hiya!"** No lowering of his head toward the ground; rather he'd lift it a smidgen. Only when such a *Homo erectus* kissed the ground was it **an act of great humility**. And yet . . .

. . . *and yet none of that matters in the least, now does it, Minae?*

No, none of those things mattered.

The problem had always been simple: **to return or not to return.**

I'd been drinking **Jack Daniel's** ever since I started typing today's diary entry, and the cold window pane felt good against my hot forehead. I could hear the low rumble of the snowplow slowly making its way through the night.

Perhaps I had dreamed a long dream—a shatteringly long dream—yes, *that has to be it, I've only been dozing at the kotatsu in our Tokyo house and Grandma is shaking me awake.* "Come, come, be a good girl, you've got to sleep on your futon." *I rub the sleep from my eyes and hold out my arms to be picked up.* . . . But in truth the days had passed with cruel finality. I had been living in real time, time that could never be reclaimed. ***And what have I learned from all these years I've spent living in my own shadow?*** What I had learned from all those irredeemable years, what I had had to learn, was that the connection between having Japanese blood in one's veins and

being Japanese was at best tenuous, more slight than a strand of
spider silk.

*And so, Grandma, just having your blood in my veins should never
have been enough to make me want to go back*—to make me long des-
perately to go back, as I always used to do. And yet now I am about
to go back. After having reached the promised land, I am going to
leave it behind and return home to Japan.

As I kept my forehead pressed against the window, the slow
progress of the snowplow below took on the menace of a tank rum-
bling through occupied territory. Where I was and what I had been
doing came back to me, and I returned to the big desk that used
to be Tono's and faced the **computer**, which also had been his; he
had taught me how to use it and then left it as a farewell gift. I was
proud of it, proud I could use it. No one else on campus studying
literature, I was sure, possessed such a high-tech machine—the one
ultramodern item in my apartment. Too bad it knew only English.

I saw what I had written and typed another line.

Alas! Twenty years since the Exodus!
9:45 a.m. A call from Nanae.

I sighed, picking up my glass of whiskey, and found it watery
with melted ice.

Oh, there goes that sound again.

What could be making that sound in the radiator?

The noise hadn't seemed so loud during the years when Tono
lived here with me. And how odd to be reminded of my old boyfriend by a banging radiator, especially as 殿 "Tono," the name I'd
teasingly given him, was the term of address for a Japanese feudal
lord. Tall and fair-skinned, Tono looked the part, though his origins were hardly aristocratic. After he went back to Japan, I'd had
to cut corners in order to stay in this apartment that was, though

in a bad neighborhood, spacious and elegant with high ceilings and wooden floors. Here, things like the heat conking out in the middle of the night never happened; even now, the *clang! clang!* in the wall was followed by the vigorous *whoosh* of steam in the radiator. The rooms were almost too hot, in fact. On nights when nothing moved but my own shadow, listening to the sounds of the radiator brought home how alone I was.

The bespectacled Tono was brilliant and a thoroughly good person, honest and conscientious almost to a fault. After finding a position at his alma mater in Japan, he had proposed, running his fingers through his hair the way he always did when he was nervous. When I declined, explaining that I couldn't think of marriage until I'd finished my ever-elusive PhD, a look of relief flooded his face and his stooped shoulders relaxed. Seeing this, I was glad I'd had the sense to turn him down.

But then—**but then I was suddenly faced with my own solitude.**

After Tono left, it occurred to me that had I known I'd feel this hopelessly alone at night, alone on a winter night in a snowstorm, I might better have taken advantage of his conscientiousness—or rather, since that sounded awful, embraced it and married him. His father having died early on, his mother had raised him singlehandedly, and he would expect us to live with her—**oy vey!**—but surely if I had tried I could have survived, like any ordinary Japanese woman with a mother-in-law in the house. If so, then . . . *yes, since he said theirs was a traditional home where they eat sticky rice with adzuki beans on festive occasions and scatter salt after funerals, by now they surely would have the* kotatsu *out, and I'd be sitting tucked under the quilt warm and cozy, although with his mother there I couldn't very well nod off . . . I'd be sipping a fresh cup of tea so hot I'd have to blow on it and maybe peeling a tangerine, snug in the palm of my hand. Outdoors there would be the hush of peony snowflakes falling heavily and silently, deeper and deeper, till all was bright in the reflected glow of the snow. . . .*

My determination not to make my sister Nanae's mistake kept me from chasing after him. The image of her standing disconsolate in **Kennedy** Airport haunted me, even though the incident had happened long ago. With our parents looking on anxiously, Nanae had slipped her **carry-on luggage** from a pathetically thin shoulder and set it down on the ground. "Here you go, this is what you asked for." She handed me a boxed set of picture cards inscribed with classical *waka* poems. "People must no longer play that game at New Year's, because smaller stationery shops no longer carry it," she said. "I got it at Takashimaya. I didn't take anything else on the plane to read because I thought I'd be too worn out. That's why the box is open. I'm sorry, I couldn't resist." Then she turned to our parents. "I'm afraid I didn't bring you anything. I'm so sorry." It was, for her, an amazingly proper sort of apology. Was it her unconscious way of containing Mother's ire by first enlisting her sympathy? Predictably, Mother responded, "That's all right, we don't need anything, let's get you home." They walked her to the parking lot, supporting her on either side as if handling an item of great fragility.

Anyway, it's finished. No point in dwelling on it anymore. It's all finished.

After Tono left, bottle by bottle I had polished off the liquor in the cabinet, ending with the **Jack Daniel's**. Ever since, I only ever bought **Jack Daniel's**, perhaps because that way I could feel as if I were still on the last bottle and so ignore the passage of time. I had a limited capacity for alcohol and could never tell the good stuff from the bad anyway, so whatever I drank was fine with me.

Glass in hand, I turned on the kitchen light, and there was the usual flurry of movement in the sink as a dozen or more tiny pale cockroaches sought to escape the sudden brightness. Every so often when I got up for a drink of water in the night, I would see roaches and spray them with insecticide in a sudden frenzy. Could that have caused mutations? For lately it seemed the baby roaches were all albinos. The sight of the little white things swarming gave me the willies at first, but I got used to them. Now I calmly opened the refrigerator, dug out a few ice cubes from the tray, and dropped them into my glass. The refrigerator was smallish, the corners rounded, an ancient model that was a relic from prewar days. The door of the freezer compartment was missing, broken by some previous tenant, and the walls were coated with a layer of ice so thick that hardly anything would fit inside.

Time moved slowly in America. The four-story brick building itself was a remnant of the gaslight era. Willfully deceived by this capsule of time, I had somehow let things get to this point.

I returned to the **keyboard**.

What would Nanae be doing now? I was aghast, thinking of all the time we had spent on the phone today—and without my achieving my objective. *Was it two hours? No, no, much more. Maybe three.* How would she survive without such phone calls?

I tapped the keys.

Nanae called first thing in the morning to remind me that today marks the twentieth anniversary of our Exodus.

※ ※ ※

The telephone rang at 9:45.

As the morning poked through cracks in the blind, I reached out from the mattress on the floor and inserted the telephone plug into the wall jack, wearily cognizant that another day had begun. No sooner had I done so than the phone rang, giving me a start. Fear shot through me. It might be the French department office.

"Is this Minae Mizumura?"

"Yes, it is."

"What on earth are you doing?"

If they asked me that, what could I say? I could not explain it even to myself. And I was terrified that somehow the way I was living—holed up in an apartment that was dim all day long, like a snail coiled tightly in its shell—might become exposed to the light of day.

Every night, as hopes of an overseas call from Tono faded, I'd fallen once again into the habit of unplugging my telephone. Apart from the practical desire to avoid being awakened by my sister, the main reason was fear. A neurotic fear, of course. Every graduate department had one or two delinquent students on its rolls, so why should it matter to my department that I kept putting off my orals on the pretext that my **main advisor** was in and out of the hospital? And for that matter, in the whole vast United States was there anyone apart from Nanae who was aware that I even existed? And why should they be? Still, I was full of fear. From the time I woke up in the morning till five in the evening when the office closed, I lived in fear that the telephone would ring and I would be given final notice—"**Your time is up!**"—and stripped of my graduate student identity.

The news that **Rebecca Rohmer**, of all people, had suffered a meltdown at her orals had unnerved me to the core. In literature departments hardly anyone ever flunked their orals, yet unbelievably, **Rebecca**, a top student from my **high school**, had failed hers. Unable to cope with the stress, she'd started shrieking in the middle of the exam.

The telephone went on ringing menacingly.

Wait. It might be a wrong number, someone trying to reach the **Social Security Office** *first thing in the morning.* This often happened, as my number was just one digit off theirs. I picked up the receiver, now faintly anticipating an old lady's gravelly voice.

"**Hello?**"

"**Hello. Hi there.**"

Immediately things fell into place: it was my sister, Nanae. Along with relief, I felt irritation at her calling so early in the morning and setting my nerves on edge. Nanae's calls were never over in a minute or two. I had been lying on my stomach, propped up on my elbows, but now I flipped over flat on my back and pressed the receiver to my ear.

Nanae was a telephone addict. Adding up all the hours we spent on the phone together might lead one to the logical conclusion that I was no less of an addict, but that was only because she called so often. If two days went by with no communication, she would call and ask, "Still kicking?" Mostly she called late at night, since after eleven the rates went down by more than half. The night before, she'd talked on and on about some trivial matter until my right ear started to hurt. I had to transfer the receiver to my left ear and then back again. I certainly hadn't expected to hear from her first thing in the morning.

The telephone had rung the moment I plugged it in. She must have been on the edge of her seat, waiting impatiently to get through. This happened generally when she had some distressing tale to relate, such as how her old clunker of a car had been stolen from the street (only to mysteriously reappear in the same space a few days later), or how the new plumbing had broken down, or how one of her two cats had been taken sick. Her problems were never the kind that calling me would fix.

Nanae's voice was low, with distinct variations: often it would be dark with resentment and malediction, distraught with loneliness, or hollow with fatigue, but once in a while it would be full of cheer or even, on rare occasions, effervescent. Fortunately, today's "**Hello.** Hi there" sounded fairly upbeat. I could feel my irritation dissipate.

"What's going on? You're calling early."

"You unplugged the phone again, didn't you?"

"Well, last night after we talked I was up till all hours."

"**Jesus**, how can you study all the time like that?"

"I *don't* study. That's the whole trouble."

Nanae never took my complaints about myself seriously. Her self-pity had no room for mine. Being on her own in **Manhattan**, she could not imagine how I, embedded in the university system with a proper identity as a graduate student, a scholarship to pay my living expenses, and university health insurance too, had any problems whatsoever. If she caught a cold, she would call and cough into the receiver and say: "Do you know how lucky you are? I can't afford to go see a doctor. **You have no idea what kind of money they charge for your first visit!**"—as if the injustice were my fault. And naturally, she believed that the loneliness she endured was far worse than mine, when in fact she had several other people that she talked to regularly on the phone or had lunch with and a place of work that she went to, however sporadically, so she at least had a social life, unlike me. She also had a pair of cats that she lavished affection on. For the past year, I had rarely left my apartment and hardly had a real conversation with anyone other than her. Even so, she was convinced that she was more to be pitied than me. Strange to say, I felt the same way.

Mother always used to say what a demanding child Nanae had been: "If I left her alone even for a minute, she'd howl and carry on. I couldn't even go to the bathroom!" This was her stock response whenever I complained about some inequity in how we were brought up. "You, on the other hand," she would go on, "always played happily by yourself, so without really meaning to, I left you more on your own. Children are born different, what else is there to say?"

Somewhere along the way my sister and I had switched roles. Although she was the elder, Nanae unloaded her problems on me with a kind of helplessness that forced me to feel responsible for

her well-being whether I liked it or not. Out of all our telephone
calls, she originated four or five to my one.

"I woke up early," Nanae went on. "Well, actually it was almost
nine, but ever since then I've been punching **redial** every five
minutes. I knew the phone was **unplugged**, so I was just waiting
for you to **plug** it in again."

"Sorry about that," I said, though I wasn't particularly sorry.
Her midnight calls were what had started me unplugging the
telephone in the first place. I wondered what this call was going
to be about, if something had happened. From her tone of voice,
I doubted it was anything serious.

"The package came. **Finally.**"

"Glad to hear it."

For some time she'd been after me to send her any extra Japanese novels I happened to have, and the week before I had finally
mailed off the lot. Some had belonged to Tono, others to friends
who had since moved away; for the most part they were dupli-
cates of books I had gotten when Mother sold the house. Nanae
had taken the records and cassette tapes, but ever since she'd been
going on about how starved she was for Japanese reading material.

"It arrived this early in the morning?" I was mildly surprised.

"Yes, lucky thing I happened to be up and dressed. Thanks."

Normally she was irritatingly slow in the morning.

"Did you open it?"

"Yes. I can't believe how many there are. **How am I going to read
all these?**"

"I know. They were heavy to lug to the post office. I don't have
a car, you know."

"Thanks so much. Where should I start? **Gotta tell me what to
read, sis.** Some of them I've already read."

Asked point-blank, I wasn't sure what to say and just reeled off
the names of several Meiji literary giants.

"I've read most of the **big names.**"

"But you've never read Higuchi Ichiyō properly, have you?" Ichiyō, who had died at twenty-four nearly a century ago, still ranked as the greatest Japanese female novelist in the last thousand years. I was in awe of her.

"Ichiyō? **Gee, thanks. I've read her, I even liked her.** I liked her so much I even read her diary. **Didn't I tell you?**"

A bit surprised, I said no, I didn't know that. After listening to Nanae chatter on day in, day out, I could only marvel that there were still things I didn't know about her.

"**Well, now you know. I'm not as ignorant as you think I am.**"

"When was this?"

"Ages ago."

"Ages ago when?"

"Ages and ages ago. Maybe in **high school.**"

"Interesting. Why didn't I know that?"

"Probably because you were too much of a child at the time."

I was only two years younger than Nanae, but definitely there would have been a time when she found me "too much of a child."

"But why didn't you tell me later?"

"**You know, I don't tell you *every*thing.**"

"Anyway, if it's been that long, you should reread her."

"Reread her? Why?"

Nanae did not share my habit of returning to books again and again.

"Reading Ichiyō when you're an adult is an entirely different experience."

"**Well, let me think about it, hon.**"

"That's why you called?" I had been anticipating something more urgent.

Nanae said that she'd been planning to call anyway when the package arrived, but this morning she had another reason.

"Can you guess what it is?" Before I could answer, she added, "When you woke up this morning, didn't you feel like there was something kind of, you know, special about today?"

"Not particularly . . ."

She giggled. **"You really don't know. Poor thing."**

"Know what?"

"Take a wild guess."

Nanae used ten times more English in her speech than I did, and her English was more colloquial than mine. In Japanese she sounded like a well-brought-up young lady, whereas in English she often liked to play at sounding tough.

I responded halfheartedly. "Um, you won the lottery?"

"*Ha ha*. I wish. Thanks for rubbing it in." This was followed by the sound of a long exhale; she must have lit a cigarette.

The lottery. **"All you need is a dollar and a dream."** So Nanae thought, *Sure, I have a dollar and lots of dreams—sure, why not?* That's how she got started last spring.

When she told me what she'd done, I didn't know how to react. *So it's finally come to this*—pity and wretchedness washed over me, a feeling I couldn't convey to her. Maybe I was wrong, but I had always assumed that people like *us* did not buy lottery tickets. But perhaps this unexpected action was an indication that eventually she would be capable of managing on her own. I should have looked at it that way and felt some relief, but more than anything, I felt despondent as I reflected on the path she'd taken. We had grown up with multiple layers of protection—protection we accepted as a matter of course—and now it seemed as if she was standing alone in a valley of **Manhattan** skyscrapers, the wind howling as it whipped between the buildings. (The cold is so intense in winter that New Yorkers love to tell the story of the Eskimo who came to the city only to turn right around and head back to Alaska, teeth chattering.)

Of course there was no need to make a fuss over my sister's purchase of a lottery ticket; it wasn't an earth-shattering event. But I could remember how when we were children in Tokyo, she was too shy to step first into the stationer's shop and would nudge me over the threshold from behind so I'd be the one to go in first and say hello. It amazed me that someone once so shy was now lining up at the corner **grocery store** with **hot dog vendors, cabbies, welfare mothers,** and whomever else to purchase a lottery ticket, telling herself, *Sure, I have lots of dreams—sure, why not?* The tagline for **Virginia Slims,** the brand she smoked, came to mind: **"You've come a long way, baby."** Lately when a man took her out to dinner she'd say to me, **"That was one free meal right there"**—sounding not spirited but mean-spirited. Compared with the timid Nanae of our childhood, the change again left me forlorn.

She called me the last time she bought a lottery ticket, when after a record number of weeks with no prizewinner, the **jackpot** had grown to such unprecedented size that everyone in the state, according to her, was in the grip of lottery fever. She called again later that night, her voice foggy, as if she'd spent the intervening hours wandering between fantasy and reality, yet lucid enough to sound a bit embarrassed at being so obsessed. If she won, she said, she would of course buy a spacious condo in Minato Ward in Tokyo as a *pied-à-terre*, but as for a place in **Manhattan,** rather than a co-op across from the **Metropolitan Museum** fit for a **Jackie Onassis,** she felt she should stay in **SoHo** if she had any serious intention of continuing as an artist. What did I think?

I was silent for a bit, then ventured the opinion that if she won the lottery, she might feel more at ease mingling with fellow millionaires. I said this rather as a joke, sadly aware that her chances of winning the lottery were even slimmer than her chances of making it as a sculptor. But she had taken my response straight, without irony, and said in a strangely thoughtful tone, "That's true, and now that you mention it, I remember reading that if you hit the **jackpot** it's better not to stay in the same neighborhood."

Now she moaned, "**I wasted one whole day going crazy over that stupid lotto.**"

"Who won?" I asked out of idle curiosity.

It was a group of **assembly workers** who bought tickets together, she said. "People like that buy tickets all the time, so in the end they're the ones who win."

Awakened from her dream, she spoke of "people like that."

"They had an agreement that regardless of who **drew** the winning number, if one of them won, they'd all share the winnings."

"I see."

"**So, nobody got very rich . . . Too bad, babies . . .**" Her voice was now a purr. She had to be talking to her cats. "You missed your chance to be filthy rich. **We've got no luck.**" Her **babies**, as she called them, were a brother and sister.

More inhaling and exhaling as she smoked. I visualized her long, slim fingers, a source of pride with her, holding an equally long, slim cigarette, smoke rising in languid swirls. She had learned to smoke in her musical days, while at the conservatory, and was unable to quit even in this age of antismoking zealotry. "**Quitting smoking is real easy,**" she liked to say. "**I've done it many times.**" She had also learned to drink alcohol and smoke marijuana, mimicking those around her, but cigarettes were the vice she could never shake. They were a link in a chain of events that had changed her life and altered the family's fortunes, and that, I suspected, might be all the more reason why she couldn't give them up.

Nanae hadn't come upon the idea of buying a lottery ticket by herself. Credit that to the Polish refugee she'd been living with until last New Year's. After years of leaning on Mother while at the same time rebelling against her, Nanae one day found herself cut off. With Father in no condition to offer support, she'd been reduced to crying and cuddling her newly adopted kittens. One day she discovered that *Lady and the Tramp*, the **Disney** classic that our family had seen together back in Japan when she was little, was playing in her neighborhood. She dried her tears, put on some eye makeup, and set off for the cinema. That was where she met **Henryk**. He was from Gdansk, he said, where he'd been a member of the labor union **Solidarity**, which later became the base of operations for the Polish revolution.

Nanae by no means took **Henryk** to be a gentleman of breeding. **"Can you believe we actually met at the movie Lady and the Tramp? Me, such a lady and him, you know what he's like . . ."** Henryk, around thirty but already missing teeth, was scruffy and unkempt, but she declared him to be a saint, someone so selfless that he might be "the second coming of Prince Myshkin." I wondered if she knew she was saying that in effect he was the second coming of Christ. He did have a certain unworldly quality, I had to admit. Of all her boyfriends, he may well have had the noblest heart. The trouble was that his selflessness signified not just unworldliness but an inability to comprehend middle-class proprieties. Life with my sister, who was after all the daughter of a corporate executive, was beyond him. Scornful of work and indifferent to penury, he made alcohol his best friend. He would fall into a deep, angelic sleep fully dressed, wherever and with whomever he happened to be, and he would eat anything, of any shape or color or flavor, that was put before him. When he was paid on a Friday, he set aside the rent money and then drank the rest. He had no bank account. He often forgot about his bills until the electricity or the telephone was cut off.

Two years before, **Henryk** had disposed of his **Brooklyn** apartment and moved into Nanae's **SoHo loft**. Since I had expressed opposition to this from the first, Nanae, who normally would bombard me with complaints as soon as the glow of a romance started

to fade, restrained herself and only muttered her dissatisfaction
from time to time. Her mutterings were nonetheless appalling.

In Poland, **Henryk** had studied philosophy and theology at a
Catholic university considered subversive by the Communist
regime—his former professor was now pope—but in the United
States, where even immigrants qualified to teach at a university
often had to drive a cab, he was at a loss. He didn't know how
to drive, he had no other skills, and his English was broken. He
seemed unable to hold down a steady job. One day Nanae let drop
that she couldn't keep liquor in the house. Then she grumbled that
on weekends he slept literally all day; that he had again lost his job
but instead of looking for work, he drank; and that even though
they had no spare bed, refugee friends of his would stay for weeks
at a stretch. Finally she let on that he had lost his temper and broken dishes that she cherished, and that once, worst of all, he had
hit her in the face—"in the face, Minae, my precious face!" This was
no Dostoevsky novel but a taste of a world that she and I happened
to know nothing about, a world that was everywhere, once you
lost your footing and slipped down the social ladder: a world of
alcohol and idleness and disappointment and violence and tears.
While the two of us had long since ceased to be amazed at things
that would have astonished proper young ladies in Japan, seeing
Nanae barely scandalized by the life she was leading, putting
up with it even while grumbling about it, was deeply troubling.
I could only wonder how much lower she was willing to descend.
But at last her tolerance was exhausted, and a year ago, last New
Year's, she had thrown him out.

Henryk used to buy lottery tickets with his Polish immigrant
cronies—they all had dreams—whenever he had a spare dollar. "If
he wins, he says he'll give everything to me, down to the last cent.
And he means it, too. He's definitely someone who would do that,
I really believe he is," Nanae had burbled to me on the phone.

I did not doubt that there were people that generous in the world, nor could I deny the possibility that **Henryk** might be one of them, yet given the statistical probability of his ever hitting the **jackpot**, Nanae would have been better off living with a man who, even if he was only half as generous, faithfully paid his share of the bills.

I thought that in the interest of financial stability Nanae ought to increase her hours of part-time work rather than stocking up on lottery tickets.

"You know those tickets never win."

"I know."

"Why don't you quit buying them then?"

"Yeah. But I still have a dollar and a few dreams. A person can't live without dreams, after all."

"I suppose not."

"Anyway, nothing good ever happens in life." She sighed.

This was her constant refrain. I gave my stock reply: "No, it doesn't. Good things just don't happen."

"I'd have been satisfied with something small. I don't need **a million dollars. I'd have been very happy with a hundred thousand.**"

While Nanae had never sold a piece of sculpture to a museum, she had participated in several group exhibitions and had sold several pieces to private collectors—but sculpting didn't put food on the table. She made her living, or tried to, working part-time at an architectural design office where she constructed architectural models on a scale of one hundred or two hundred to one. She was good with her hands, and her work was highly valued for being **"very Japanese,"** detailed and meticulous, so the hourly rate was more than decent; but in the end it was just a part-time job, and she never knew how much work would be coming her way. For a major project she'd go in every day for weeks at a time, but between projects she'd have nothing. She really ought to have combined that with some other job, but as she pointed out, (a) not many jobs paid as well as that one; (b) since she wasn't physically strong, it was ridiculous to think of taking a crummy, low-paying job; and (c) if she economized, she could manage fine on her earnings.

The upshot was that Nanae made no effort to find other employment, apart from an occasional interpreting job. Mother had given us equal shares of the proceeds from the sale of the house, with the warning that this was "really and truly the last time," and with her share Nanae had made a down payment on the **loft** in **SoHo** where she now lived quietly with her cats, no man in her life, working on her sculpture. Sometimes she played her **Steinway**, a relic of her piano-playing past, bemoaning how "fat" her fingers were getting. She had purchased the **loft** for a good price, but making it livable cost a surprising amount of money, and now, with **Henryk** gone, she had to be responsible for all expenses. By the end of summer she could no longer make ends meet and was reduced to begging me for a loan. (I hadn't touched my share of the money from Mother.) The monthly **maintenance** on her **SoHo loft** was itself considerable, and she talked about how she should move to a cheaper place in the **East Village**. She had a big, old, beat-up car, one that our parents had bought for her long ago, and she said that when it broke down she would give up driving. I didn't want to know more, so I didn't ask.

Nanae had become just another struggling artist in a city full of them. New York, like Vienna or Berlin or Paris of old, still attracted swarms of aspiring artists from all over, despite the diminishing dominance of the United States on the world stage. Leaving aside those lucky few who could rely on wealthy parents, artists survived for the most part by taking on **small jobs**, holding their hours to the bare minimum. Those serious about their art could be hard to distinguish from those who simply wished to avoid taking on a regular job. Objectively speaking, Nanae was now one of this ambiguous crowd, neither well off nor in dire straits. Given that many artists lived across the river in **Brooklyn** or **Queens**, unable to afford **Manhattan** rents, perhaps she was doing well just to have her own **loft** in **SoHo**, which had undergone thorough gentrification.

But I refused to take comfort in this view. I somehow felt that her living alone with her cats in **Manhattan** must be part of a crazy, interminable dream of mine, and the real Nanae must be off in a Tokyo suburb raising not a pair of cats but a pair of children in grade school. Instead of rising just before noon and reaching for a hand mirror, then lifting her chin, closing one eye, and applying glossy jet-black eyeliner, she was up early in the morning amid the clamor of Tokyo rush hour, hair a mess, putting breakfast on the table and shouting to her children to hurry up and get going. I wished—no, I prayed that this was the reality, because otherwise, I had a hard time imagining how she would live out the rest of her life. If she could make a living as a sculptor that would be one thing, but few people in the world did. The bar was especially high for someone who was a woman, and Japanese.

Time brings most artists to some sort of turning point. Many of Nanae's friends had switched course to earn a living, moving on in different ways. Some refused to the end to **"sell out,"** but even they were forced at some point to make the transition from promising artist to *artiste manqué*. I wouldn't have been bothered in the least if Nanae **sold out**. She tended to look down on people who went into solid professions, but if she would just go ahead and get a job telling at the **Bank of Tokyo** or somewhere, I would quietly have thanked whatever gods prompted her to do so.

"Come on, **be serious**," Nanae said. "Why do you think I called?"

"**MoMA** bought one of your pieces."

"Ha ha."

"You had a nice dream."

"Wrong."

"An old boyfriend called you in the middle of the night."

"Wrong again."

"**Claudia** called and woke you up."

Claudia, an Italian woman Nanae had known since her piano-playing days, was now married to an American and had two children. She would sometimes call Nanae on a sudden impulse and wake her up; Nanae would then call me, waking me up, to complain. Unplugging the phone had solved the problem.

"**Nope.** She hasn't called lately. So fortunately I haven't had to listen to her *tatahta tatahta*." This was her imitation of **Claudia**'s Italian-accented English. "She goes on and on. Sometimes I feel like telling her, Enough, *punto e basta!*"

"I give up."

"You still can't guess?" Nanae then addressed the cats. "Auntie Minae says she doesn't get it. **Your aunt isn't as smart as she thinks. You know that, babies?** Oh, oh, are we hungwy? I'm a bad mommy. Mommy will get you some num-nums just as soon as she hangs up, okay? Good babies."

It had happened entirely unexpectedly. Nanae had gone to visit our old friends and neighbors the Murakamis—Mr. Murakami, like our father, was the overseas representative of a Japanese company in New York—and returned home to her **loft** with two kittens. Accustomed only to dogs, I looked upon felines as a species that had no place in our household and reacted nervously. The kittens had caused Nanae's maternal instincts to kick in hard.

This was shortly after the loss of our parents' house on the North Shore of **Long Island**. Located in a leafy suburb, the **Colonial-style** house looked typically American from the outside. Inside, however, was a world where we sisters could chatter away in Japanese from morning till night and feel as if we were back in Japan, our names written not **Nanae** and **Minae** but 奈苗 and 美苗. The **breakfast nook** next to the kitchen was crowded with familiar, homey items from Japan: the rice cooker and thermos with a stupid floral

design; the pair of tea canisters, large and small, covered in rice paper with slightly better traditional patterns; jars of roasted seaweed and brewer's yeast tablets for intestinal disorders; a **Japan Airlines** calendar; an unglazed teapot and a set of small containers for soy sauce, Ajinomoto, and toothpicks. As Nanae and I grew more accustomed to the look of American homes, the tacky clutter embarrassed us and we used to gripe about it, but looking back, I am certain that the very clutter made the **breakfast nook** a cozy place to relax. Mother and Nanae and I—how many hundreds or thousands of evenings did we three spend sitting around the table deep in conversation while sipping tea with less and less flavor because we were so engrossed that none of us bothered to change the leaves? But in the end, two years ago in the spring, the house was put up for sale. Though it was hardly big by American standards, the amount of stuff we had collected through the years was near-overwhelming—a fantastic jumble of odds and ends. Three large trucks were needed to haul away all we threw out, two more to cart the rest to storage. The sheer bulk of our accumulated possessions told the story of how long we had lived there. And so we lost the family house; and at the same time, before anyone quite knew what was happening, the family itself fell apart.

It was around this time that the kittens had made their sudden entrance into my sister's life. "Having two of them," she said, "makes us seem like a family, doesn't it?"

Soon after, Tono, whom everyone liked, went back to Japan.

"**Hey, Wagahai, will you stop bothering me?**" Nanae was clucking at one of the cats, named after the feline narrator of the Natsume Sōseki cat novel. "Shoo! Leave Mommy alone!" Then to me she explained, "I was holding off fixing their food until after I called you. They're hungry."

"So what? They're a couple of butterballs anyway."

"It's true. Lately even the little one here can't stop eating. **Oh, why are you two such pigs?** And your mommy has such a good figure. You know what? Mommy can fit into her old **Jordache** jeans. . . . Come on, why do you suppose I called?"

"I have no idea."

"Well, what day do you think today is?"

"Today? Gosh . . ."

"You can't remember?"

Was something supposed to happen today? Had I forgotten a promise of some kind? But she sounded too upbeat for that. She went on in a teasing tone.

"*Ha*, you did forget! **Now, think hard.**"

"Has it got something to do with me?"

"That it does."

"And you too?"

"Yes, the same as you. I woke up this morning and it hit me."

We were into December, but what was today's date? I must have written the date in yesterday's diary before going to bed, yet now it escaped me. I didn't even know the day of the week. Hardly surprising, as I spent my time lounging around in complete inertia. Groggily, I searched my memory. Then I had a glimmer of suspicion.

"Wait a second. You don't mean—" A strange sensation prickled my skin, and the world surrounding me momentarily froze.

"**Thaaat's right.**"

"Don't tell me it's twenty years today!"

"**Thaaat's right.**"

"No! I'd rather be dead."

"I knew you forgot." She sounded pleased.

I had indeed forgotten. The awful thought had occurred to me once in the summer, but I had pushed it out of my mind.

A vivid image of a black-and-white photograph of the three of us rose before me. Too old to hold Mother's hands, my sister and I were standing leaning against her, pressed up to her on either side. Under a silk coat she was wearing a formal kimono, and Nanae and I had on dressy wool suits. My skirt came to my knees, just like Nanae's, but below the hem were the legs of a child, two sticks—a reminder of the grade-schooler I'd been just six months before. In one arm I was holding a little brown stuffed dog that Father had earlier brought me as a souvenir from **Hawaii**. Nanae and I both had on pearl necklaces, something unusual for little girls, because Mother took seriously what someone had told her—that if U.S. Customs found Mikimoto pearls in your luggage, they suspected you of bringing them in for sale and made you pay duty on them. At the time I'd felt only an incoherent mix of excitement and nervousness, but the anxiety in our expressions was unmistakable. The photograph was taken by our Uncle Yokohama, who came to Haneda Airport to see us off.

Twenty years ago today, my mother, my sister, and I had left Haneda on our way to join Father, whose company had appointed him to head their fledgling U.S. branch in **New York**. Two years ago we had marked the eighteenth anniversary of that day, and a year ago the nineteenth, so this year was the twentieth. *The twentieth anniversary.* The idea that it had been twenty years since we had left Japan seemed impossible, bizarre.

Ever since finishing the coursework for my doctorate two years before, I had been telling myself I would wait until I passed my orals and then finally go back to Japan for good, but while I lived in anticipation of that day, time drifted aimlessly. Lately I was gripped by the fear that instead of drawing nearer to my goal I was seeing it recede farther with each day, that I was traveling away from the light, stepping deeper into darkness—and now it felt as if my fear was in danger of becoming a reality. Unless I acted, I would be stuck forever in this dingy American college town, a mummy slowly desiccating in a spacious and elegant apartment where the radiator worked overtime.

I was shocked, more so than Nanae could have suspected. "I mean it. I'd rather be dead."

"I know. **And to think it's Friday the thirteenth again.**"

On the first airplane ride of our lives there had been just a handful of other passengers. Only much later, after I had lived in the States for a while, did it occur to me that this might have been because our departure fell on, of all days, the one widely held to be the unluckiest day of the year. Our anxiety accentuated by the near-empty plane, Mother, Nanae, and I had sat dutifully in the seats indicated on our boarding passes and put our three black-haired heads together, staring out the tiny window as the night view of Tokyo vanished into the distance.

"What have I been doing all this time?" I said. No doubt Nanae had been expecting to hear me say those words. Every year when this day rolled around I would bewail my fate in this woebegone fashion.

I had stayed closer to Japan than she had. I yearned for Japan, Japanese food, Japanese people; I loved the Japanese language and, more than anything, Japanese literature written with the three distinct systems of Japanese writing: graceful *hiragana* ひらがな, spartan *katakana* カタカナ, and dense *kanji* 漢字. Someday soon I was to return to Japan, to the country that held all things dear to me, and when I did, then at last I would awaken deep, slumbering yearnings and embark triumphantly and ecstatically on a new life—my real life. Yet that day never came, and I had ended up spending an unconscionable portion of my one-and-only life on foreign soil, far from where I was meant to be.

What *had* I been doing all this time? . . . This year I felt the usual lament transport itself to a different level. I was frightened, aghast. I felt as if my disembodied soul were looking back on my life from the edge of the abyss.

"Well, never mind. **Think about me, honey.** Compared with me, you're sitting pretty. With a PhD and all, your future is assured."

"When did it hit you?" I said, ignoring her last comment.

"I woke up and was lying in bed wondering if I should forget about getting a **Christmas tree** this year since there'd be no one here to share it with, or if that was all the more reason to get one, and out of nowhere it just came to me. Then I thought *Oh, I've got to tell this to my little sissy* and picked up the phone."

Dazed, I listened vacantly. Tonight she was going over to the Murakamis', she said, and before that she would stop off as she sometimes did to visit Father in the nursing home.

"I just wanted to tell ya."

The higher rates always kept Nanae's daytime calls relatively short. We hung up.

I remained still for a while with my eyes closed. Then I got up off the mattress-bed, mechanically put on socks, slipped into the bathrobe hanging on the door, and went into the living room. It was full of gloom. When the sky was heavily overcast, the large windows served only to darken the room. In one corner was the big red vinyl armchair that Tono had always favored, and I fell into it. From both the south and north windows, the sky was a block of pale gray. The apartment heat always made me wake up thirsty, but I could not summon the energy to go into the kitchen for a glass of water.

When did it start?

When did I start wanting to go back to Japan? So many years had passed with me haunted by the longing to return that the wish seemed to have been there from the first.

Even for a Japanese, Father had been especially fond of cameras, and the family pictures he took through the years filled dozens of albums, starting with Nanae as a newborn. Around the time she was clapping her hands in glee at a birthday cake as tall as she was—a gift from some officer at the American base where Father worked—I made my appearance. If you kept turning the album pages, following the progress of the young mother and her two children, along the way you encountered the photo of the three of us at Haneda Airport. Turn that page, and all of a sudden there would be bright color pictures marking the start of our sojourn in America.

"Aloha! Welcome to Hawaii!" With these words, a travel guide had greeted us and snapped our photo. Against the backdrop of the blue Hawaiian sky, Mother and Nanae and I had colorful leis draped around our necks.

On the next page were pictures of us in California at Disneyland, standing alongside Alice in Wonderland, an actual blonde, and the March Hare. Mother was wearing the same formal kimono that she had worn when we left Japan. The camera caught her looking perplexed at the sight of America, the land that movies had long inspired her to dream of, especially after the war. Behind her was another sky of astonishing blue. The next page showed scenes of snow. The season hadn't changed; rather, we had arrived in New York. Nanae and I were in the backyard of our house with big shovels, shoveling snow for the first time in our young lives. The small white building with a red roof in the background was our garage. I remembered pointing at it when we arrived and exclaiming, "We could live there, it's so big!" This tickled Father, who was delighted to have brought his family to America. Expecting to join the ranks of the curly-haired, Nanae and I had been given permanents just before leaving Japan; they were still fresh, the curls too tight. Our collie Della, dead these many years, had just arrived on a separate flight and looked young and lean. I was smiling in the photos and so was Nanae.

What had been going through my sister's mind? I suspected that I, for some unknown reason, already wanted to go back to Japan. And from then on, for the longest time, my waking reality had seemed but a semblance of life.

How many times did I dream the same dream? I would be back in Japan, surrounded by the faces of my playmates. "Oh wow, it was this close all along!" "Yeah, what took you so long?" "I didn't know it was this close." *All this time, I was making a mountain out of a molehill. Geography never was my strong point. I got mixed up and thought that to go back to Japan I'd have to cross a huge ocean. But getting here was a snap! All I had to do was change trains and buses.* For a junior high school student in those days, the cost of traveling by air or sea was astronomical, but getting around by bus or train was a different story. I could go back with the money I'd saved from **babysitting** the little boy next door. Sometimes Japan was a two- or three-day train ride away. Sometimes it was less than an hour away on a suburban train. And sometimes it was within walking distance. Take the right road and I could be there in twenty minutes. *Why didn't I ever think of this before? How could I have forgotten this road?* All I had to do was go straight down the road by the tracks, crowded with stores on either side. Turn right at the end of the road and when the stores began to give way to houses, turn left, then right again, and I'd come out on a higgledy-piggledy road I knew very well. Going past the kindergarten, the fire station, and the little factory, I'd come to the area where my house and school were. If I turned left, toward home, there would be the narrow crossroads where I always played; at twilight, out of nowhere the *clunk* of water from a tap hitting a tin sink and the *clink* of jostling cups would come to my ears, and soon a yellow light would glow atop the leaning utility pole, deepening the surrounding darkness. If I turned right, toward school, I would end up at the grounds of the local shrine, where towering pines blocked the sunlight—the shrine where Grandma used to take Nanae and me to play on the swings. In my dreams the shrine grounds appeared darker, cooler, and more mysterious than I remembered, as if in my dreams I were dreaming.

But when I woke up, I was always in America.

Dear God, please, please let me be in that town, just for a moment.

How ironic that that Tokyo suburb should have been my home-town. The Japanese word for "hometown," 故郷 *furusato*, was poetic, suggestive of old temples and picturesque scenes with hill-sides where children chased rabbits and streams where they fished for minnows. But my hometown wasn't, never had been, poetic in the least, and after the war it was marred by unsightly spill-over from Japan's rapid economic growth. Year after year fields and rice paddies were converted to cheap housing. Zigzagging narrow roads were covered with bumpy pavement to accommo-date three-wheeler trucks. A pair of huge gas tanks went up in the distance. Utility poles shot up everywhere. This wasn't devel-opment—it seemed more like a lack of vision exposed by develop-ment. And yet that town and none other was my hometown. Off in an affluent New York suburb where tall, leafy **maple trees** lined the streets, I dreamed endlessly of that sad, ugly, dull hometown.

Of course, when it was decided that we were going to America, I was on cloud nine. Defeat in the war was still fresh in everyone's mind, not yet reduced to a page in history, and people turned for hope to all things American. My family, Westernized to start with, was caught up in that fever more than most. The very sound of "America" was magical to me, out of this world, like "candy house." The time in my life when my heart was closest to America was surely the span of months between the decision to move there and our actual departure.

They were unsettled months. Father went to New York ahead of us, the house was put up for sale, and Mother fell into the throes of packing. When the house was sold, Nanae and I stopped attending school, and we accompanied Mother on a visit to Kyoto and Kobe to bid her relatives good-bye. Then, until the time of our depar-ture, Mother stayed with her best friend and former employer, whom we called "Aunt Utako," in Ogikubo, a suburb of Tokyo, while Nanae and I went to live with relatives known collectively to us as "Yokohama." Grandpa Yokohama, now retired, used to be the captain of an ocean liner. Uncle Yokohama, his son and Mother's cousin, was Nanae's piano teacher.

What dreams of America filled my mind then?

"Yokohama" lived on a hill near the port of Yokohama. Nanae and I, with leisure on our hands, would gravitate to the park across the street from the house. As we sat on a bench, out of nowhere would come the drone of a ship's whistle, and the words to a children's song would spring to my mind: *A girl in red shoes was taken away by a foreigner at Yokohama Port . . . she must have blue eyes by now.* The awareness that I was about to leave for America would flood through me. I happened to own a pair of red shoes, hand-me-downs from Nanae. They were stylish with pointy toes, and Nanae had faithfully kept them polished so the red leather was still pretty. I would listen to the ship's whistle and think abstractedly of my fate, being taken away to America not by a foreigner but by my own parents. "One day you can study in America," Mother used to tell us, but I had never believed her, not really, since our family so clearly lacked the financial wherewithal to make such a thing possible. Yet, somehow, a miracle was about to occur.

One day a police officer came up to us in the park and asked, "Why aren't you girls in school?" Nanae and I answered as one, full of elation: "We dropped out of junior high school. We're getting ready to go to America, that's why!" "Well, well, America, you don't say!" He sounded doubtful, scrutinizing first the one of us and then the other. Not far away, observing this interchange with interest, were several aproned housewives—undoubtedly it was they who had reported us as delinquent. When the officer asked where we lived, we told him the name of the family we were staying with, and his attitude underwent a quick change. It was a family of local distinction.

Really, what were my dreams then? All I can be certain of is that the moment we crossed the Pacific and the word "America" took on tangible reality, any dreams I may have had began imperceptibly to evaporate amidst the heat of my longing for Japan.

"How long are we going for, Mama?"

"I don't know, five years maybe."

That exchange took place before we boarded the airplane. Then, as we grew accustomed to breathing the air of America, somehow all talk of returning faded and our life overseas stretched on and on, no end in sight. At first I wrote regularly to friends in Japan and took pride in American abundance as if it were my own, but as six months, then a year went by, I wrote fewer and fewer letters. Meanwhile, to avoid the possibility of being sent back to Japan at a moment's notice, Father arranged with the company to be reclassified as a local hire. This was not an option taken by many Japanese employees, because it meant a lowering of status.

"Neither of you is ever going to get into a Japanese college," Mother would declare. "The educational systems are too different." Father would chime in, "Cramming for entrance exams is ridiculous anyway." And so without realizing it, we began to assume that we would attend college in America. Eventually Mother, a woman of extravagant tastes and abundant energy, began to work outside the home, as she used to do under Aunt Utako—owner of a lucrative fashion business—and her paycheck helped us to enjoy a life even more comfortable than when we first started living in America. On the mantle, the potted fern that our "American uncle" Jesse had brought over as a welcome gift upon our arrival put out new fronds every year. Nanae and I grew bigger too, and our dog Della got happily fat.

How long had our parents actually intended to stay in America? At that time, the country's affluence allowed even those passing through a taste of the **American Dream**. That was surely one reason why our parents lingered. Nanae and I, uprooted during our growing years, were too young to appreciate and enjoy the privileges America offered. But for our father and mother, moving to America must have felt like being transported to a better world, a world they were prepared to savor to the full. They each did so in their own way.

Father loved going for walks with Della in our parklike neighborhood. "In Tokyo you can hardly walk down the street without getting run over and killed," he used to say. In the spring, as leaf buds started to swell, gardens would burst into bloom with lilies-of-the-valley, **dogwood**, violets, **azaleas**, crocuses, hyacinths, tulips, and **alyssum**. In the autumn, as the grass started to wither, golden leaves from the **maples** lining the street would tumble down to form a thick carpet. Father would stroll amid springtime's abundance of flowers and autumn's bright dancing leaves, murmuring with satisfaction, "Fantastic! Do this in Tokyo and you'd get run over and killed."

Mother relished more costly outings, for which we dressed up. She would take us to a **Broadway theater**, **Carnegie Hall**, or **City Center**—until she discovered the **Metropolitan Opera House** with its spectacular ascending chandeliers at **Lincoln Center**. That magnificent place became her favorite destination. During **intermission** at a performance by the **Royal Ballet**, she would look down from the balcony on the people milling around the fountain in the plaza and declare: "Japan has nothing to equal this. And no Nureyev." She was entranced, perhaps imagining herself as **Margot Fonteyn**, who moments before had made a graceful bow and disappeared on **Nureyev**'s arm behind the heavy curtain. Mother would be wearing a floor-length dress topped by something she could only have dreamed of wearing in Japan: a mink coat. Proud of being tall for a Japanese person and of having "un-Japanese" features— though to her credit she refrained from saying so out loud—she felt confident that such clothes looked good on her. Kimono that she

Sidewalk ▶

had acquired at considerable sacrifice she stowed in the basement without a pang of regret.

Still, our parents had no intention of living in America forever. In that land of immigrants, we were an aberration. None of us had the least doubt that one day we would go back to Japan. They just kept putting off the day, secure in their belief that, come what might, Nanae and I would remain Japanese. But my sister was fourteen when we landed there, and I was only twelve. That we would remain Japanese was far from a given. We were the only Japanese students at school—the school newspaper featured an article on us as the first in the school's history. Of course, we were in New York, and there were quite a few Japanese expats in the area; Father's colleagues would visit our house, and once in a while there would be somebody with daughters our age and our two families would do things together. But having my family and other Japanese people to talk to, Japanese food to eat, and Japanese books to read was no substitute for being in Japan.

All through my girlhood, I was consumed by thoughts of the homeland I'd left. I longed for it with an intensity that words like "yearning" or "nostalgia" could not convey. I felt I was someplace I didn't belong, where I should not be. Japan steadily grew to near-mythic dimensions in my mind, transfigured into a place where life transcended the smallness of the everyday. Since these were the years that shaped me, I was never again to be free—not even when I finally did return for a visit.

My first trip back to Japan took place the summer when Nanae was twenty-two and I was twenty—eight years after we'd left. She had just graduated from the conservatory, and I had completed the first two years of art school—which was, from my family's perspective, merely a kind of finishing school. After that first visit,

I would cross the Pacific Ocean with increasing frequency, and my memories of the Japan I came to know as a traveler eventually were so jumbled that it was hard to say what happened when. But memories of that summer I was twenty, of seeing the Japanese sky and treading on Japanese soil, have always remained distinct in my mind, as if preserved on a separate roll of film.

"Ladies and gentleman, we will soon be arriving at Tokyo International Airport."

Tears rose dangerously near the surface the moment I heard the words "Tokyo International Airport"—the official name of Haneda Airport. I was on the verge of crying when the wheels of the airplane landed on the tarmac, again when the aircraft came to a full stop at the gate, and again when music started up in the cabin and the tension eased. But when the heavy door was opened and a uniformed airline official came in and greeted the passengers in Japanese, a hand raised to his cap in salute, my eyes started burning and the tears poured down my cheeks. This short, unassuming official was not a Japanese man in America but a Japanese man *in Japan*, someone who worked in Japan, ate Japanese food, and spoke in Japanese without thinking twice about any of it, doubtless without any special awareness of being Japanese. It was eight years since I had last laid eyes on a man like that. I looked down and pretended to be gathering my carry-on luggage, sobbing to myself while the other passengers inched forward in the aisle. The man in uniform was standing by the door, still greeting passengers, unaware that he had made a young woman burst into tears.

It was not the sight of an almost unrecognizable Tokyo that brought home to me how long I had been away. No, it was the sight, a few days later, of Nanae as she emerged from the crowd, her face moist with perspiration, declaring, **"I didn't know Tokyo was this hot. Did you?"** She had arrived a bit earlier, as soon as she had graduated, and we had arranged to meet at Shibuya train station on my third day in Tokyo.

"Is Japan really in the temperate zone?" she went on. "Not the subtropics?"

Nanae herself had appeared the most changed of all, and she stood out like a foreigner from some unknown subtropical land. Even in Boston, where we shared an apartment, I had been unsettled not by how Americanized she was but by how indeterminate her nationality had become, an impression that was strengthened now that we were here. Her flashy miniskirt made people stare. Was her boyfriend from Boston really serious about marrying her? She had come to meet his parents.

"Thank God, I can finally breathe," she said, sitting across from me in an air-conditioned coffee shop, holding a **Virginia Slims** cigarette in her left hand, about to sip **Coke** through the straw she was holding in her right. As usual her eyebrows and eyes were carefully made up. With her head bent down, I could clearly see the multiple layers of her eye shadow and her jet-black eyeliner. Her forehead, never pale to begin with, had a deep **Coppertone** tan, the fruit of her labors. For most Japanese women, skin whitening is the basis of cosmetics, but Nanae proudly showed off skin that went beyond tawny to teak. What set her apart in Japan was not just her miniskirt and makeup, though; her carriage and features were different too, also her way of opening her mouth—actually everything about her. I was annoyed with her for being so un-Japanese and at the same time so determined to marry a Japanese man. I was annoyed with Mother too, for pushing the whole marriage idea. But Nanae, not yet having met her boyfriend's parents, was still in good spirits.

"Look what I found!" she declared, rummaging in her purse. She produced an envelope small enough to fit in the palm of her hand containing multicolored sheets of paper-thin soap, the kind we loved when we were children. She pulled out one translucent sheet, and a cheap, sweet scent emerged. **"Aren't they cute?** They still sell them. Maybe it's been revived. I got some for you too, see . . ."

Never did I dream that two months later, abandoned by her boy-friend, Nanae would attempt suicide. All I did in that period was to use her selfishly as a mirror in which to study my own reflection.

The previous day, at Aunt Utako's house in Ogikubo, I'd stepped indoors without removing my shoes, provoking titters and a high-pitched reminder: "Shoes, Minae, shoes! This is Japan, you know!" If I attracted attention for an air of sophistication acquired in America, that would be one thing, but I had no wish to stand out as something alien, something that needed to be expunged. I did my best to stay within the bounds of acceptable Japanese behavior.

"Hard to relax in somebody else's house, isn't it?" Nanae groused. She was staying with "Yokohama" so she could have piano lessons. I remembered that when we stayed there before we left for America, she slept so late that the maid couldn't open the shutters of the verandah by our bedroom. Try as I would to wake Nanae up, she would only brush me away and roll over. One day I overheard Grandpa Yokohama remark, "Poor Minae, with a lazybones sister like that." I hoped Nanae was behaving better now.

She and I sat in the air-conditioned coffee shop sipping our **Cokes** and marveling that after life in America, neither the Yoko-hama house nor the one in Ogikubo seemed the least bit stylish or grand. It was as if the spell they'd cast on us as children had worn off.

By the time I took a suburban train to visit the town where we'd grown up, much of the summer had passed. I walked down the street that had figured so large in my dreams, the spot where I used to pray, "Please, dear God, please let me be in that town, just for a moment"—only to be confronted by an utterly unremarkable, unenchanting sight, a town bleached by the summer sun, even more prosaic than I remembered. It had grown; there were more paved streets, more tiny houses, more two- and three-story apartment buildings. I was disappointed, yet somewhere deep inside, I wasn't. I had put off coming to my hometown precisely because I knew that it would be this way. I also knew that nothing in this world could satisfy the craving I had so obstinately nurtured.

Nanae and I only got together a few times that summer. On the rare occasions when we did, we shared our gripes about Japan like untraveled Americans: the suffocating crowds, the diminutive size of everything, the chaotic jumble, the inane music inside every coffee shop, the sticky heat . . .

"I got groped on the train again today. What's with that?"

"I know. Me too."

And toward the end of summer I went back to America, leaving my ever more morose sister behind.

My recurring dream of Japan didn't stop. As if the trip home had never been, the same dream came back to me again and again. It didn't go away until much later, after years had passed and plummeting airfares meant going back was no longer an epic journey or a special treat. Even then I could not rid myself of the crazed obsession with my homeland that had eaten away at me in adolescence. From my perch in America, I still thought *This isn't where I belong, my real life is over there*—feeling as trapped as a cloistered nun or a languishing exile yet never making the obvious choice to return to Japan for good.

Mainly this was because our parents kept extending their stay. The idea never occurred to them that I might leave by myself, and I too could only conceive of going back to Japan permanently *en famille*; I lacked the resolve to pack up and leave on my own.

After that first summer in Japan, I took a leave of absence from art school, went to Paris to study French, changed schools, and went back to Japan for summer vacations, blithely maintaining the in-between status of someone who was and wasn't a student. In America, students were expected neither to finish college in four years nor to take a job as soon as they did finish, so campuses were full of hangers-on; in that sense, though a foreigner, I fit right in. Staying in limbo allowed me to hold down the cost of living, and I managed well enough thanks to part-time jobs and help from my parents—in fact my parents, being Japanese, gave me more financial help than I deserved, perhaps making up for all they had lavished on my piano-playing sister. In my late twenties I had even gone on to graduate school simply as a means of prolonging my life in limbo. But I was powerless to halt the stream of time.

Awareness of how much time had gone by hit me all of a sudden, as if one day I, like Urashima Tarō, the Japanese Rip van Winkle, had opened a jeweled box and been greeted with a puff of smoke and jolted to the present. Was it because of the unfamiliar ring of the words "thirty years old"? Or the disappearance from my living room of Tono's back hunched over his big desk? Or was it because the **Colonial** house in **Long Island** was suddenly gone and my parents became such different people from who they had been before? To my astonishment, I myself was no longer a young girl, and neither was Nanae. And for the first time I realized what I had always known deep down: I was *afraid* of going back to Japan. My crazed obsession had shaped me so profoundly that—like an invalid fearful of being cured—I was terrified of losing the thing that defined me.

How else to account for the state I was in? For months—no, years—I had passed my time doing God knows what. Though most of my fellow students had moved on in their studies and were starting to write their theses, I, after having postponed my orals more than a year before, so unreasonably that the French department secretary's eyebrows had shot up, had postponed them twice again this year—all because, it had grown patently clear, I was petrified of having finally to go back to Japan. I was also tortured by apprehension about leaving Nanae on her own. My fellowship would soon run out and I would have to drop out of grad school, but still I was immobilized. Once again spring came and went, summer came and went, and here I was staring at the end of the fall term, trying my best not to notice the passing of the seasons.

No wonder the strangely aged visage of **Rebecca Rohmer** had begun to flicker before my eyes. It was just a year since she'd contacted me.

A little past eleven at night the phone rang, and I turned over in bed to reach for the receiver, thinking *Oh dear, this will be Nanae again, after that long talk yesterday*; but the **"Hello"** on the other end was from someone else: it was **Rebecca**, my high school classmate who by chance, three years before me, had come to the same graduate school to study German literature. **"I'm so glad you're still there,"** she said cheerily, though it was something I felt decidedly uncheerful about. She was coming to town the following week, just before the school shut down for Christmas break, to talk to her advisor about retaking her orals and could she possibly stay with me? She spoke fast, rattling on, her linguistic gifts pouring out in long, grammatically complicated sentences. I gripped the receiver in a daze, murmuring an occasional polite **"Uh-huh."** I rarely saw anyone anymore, and now for a full two days I would have to put up with someone who spoke rapid-fire, convoluted English? The prospect was less than thrilling, but I could not say no. She was after all a friend and also someone whose intellectual capacity had always left me in awe.

Rebecca arrived at my apartment late at night and sat down in the red armchair, drinking **chamomile** tea that I'd made after she said she needed to calm herself before bedtime. She reenacted the scene at her orals when she went crazy, ending her narrative with a short declarative sentence: **"I just started yelling and couldn't stop."** Her free hand described circles in the air.

"Oh no . . ."

"The next thing I knew I was lying in a hospital bed." She shrugged. The last time we had stood chatting on **campus**, several years before, she'd still looked as pretty and alive as she had in **high school**, where she'd excelled in field hockey, but now she seemed to have aged a generation. Her dark straight hair was streaked with gray, her skin was dry, and her figure was dumpy, the way I remembered her mother used to look. Emotional instability caused her weight to yo-yo, she said, and she was dependent on tranquilizers that caused bloating. I could barely hide my shock at the state she was in.

"Was it a nervous breakdown?"

"Yeah, sort of."

She put her face in the steam rising from the tea and breathed in the fragrance. I watched as the lenses of her glasses clouded over. They, at least, were the same as in the old days, with red frames.

The long regimen of self-discipline imposed in graduate school was more than some people could abide. Stories of people flipping out weren't unusual, and it was widely recognized that foreign students were particularly vulnerable. As I tried not to fixate on **Rebecca**'s gray-streaked hair, I thought of the slim Arab grad student I had seen in the library over the past several years, at all hours of the day. He had a heavy black beard out of keeping with his thin frame. What sent him over the edge no one knew, but he spent all his time roaming the library basement where no ray of sunlight penetrated, muttering and clutching prayer beads. The gray pallor of his smooth, porcelain skin, framed by that black beard, was pitiable. Not once did I see him in conversation with another human being. Also, Tono used to know a Southeast Asian doctoral candidate who after nearly twenty years still hadn't finished his thesis; one day he was found dead in his small apartment, whether from a stress-related attack or suicide, who could say? And I had heard many a story of Japanese students becoming deranged and having to be whisked home by distraught parents. But Rebecca, raised as a child of New York's Jewish intelligentsia, should have been used to the pressure cooker. That she would have a mental breakdown was something I could never have imagined.

Fear of the same thing happening if she retook her orals had haunted **Rebecca** for years. Again and again she had tried to retake them, always telling herself that *this* would be her year, but it never was. "You know, the fear builds up, day after day, month after month, year after year. It just becomes more and more insurmountable." She laughed nervously.

Now, a year later, her voice still sounded in my ears: *"You know, the fear builds up, day after day, month after month, year after year."* I got up from the red armchair and, trying not to think about what I was doing, went down the hall into my study, where mechanically I began pushing the buttons on the phone, dialing the number listed in my notebook. Friday afternoons the office emptied early, so I couldn't put it off any longer.

"This is Minae Mizumura."

"Oh, yes."

She did not say, "What on earth are you doing?"

When I informed the department secretary that I wanted to go ahead and take my orals on the planned day whether or not my **main advisor**, now in the hospital, could attend, she responded in a calm, disinterested tone: "Fine. I'll note it down. You'd better inform the members of the orals board yourself."

The call was over in seconds. I felt let down. My fingertips were ice cold.

In another month I would have no further need to stay in this college town—no further need or excuse to stay in America. Faces of former classmates, some of them in Europe writing their doctoral theses, flashed in my mind. Another month and I too would be free to go where I pleased—except that Nanae would still be here, in New York.

After hanging up the phone I went to the kitchen for a drink of water. The hands on the wall clock pointed to just before eleven.

%. %. %.

The snowplow moved off someplace far in the distance. Then I heard a slight sound I hadn't noticed before: a low hum emanating from the **computer**. It wasn't very late at night, yet the hush of the heavily falling snow engulfed the sounds made by all living things.

Everything is so quiet. So dead.

The **computer** screen shone, the sole evidence of life.

Nanae called first thing in the morning to remind me that today marks the twentieth anniversary of our Exodus.

She could not have known how seriously the news would affect me. I remained sunk in that big red armchair . . . just motionless. It was after an hour that I finally said to myself: "Now or never." 11:00 a.m. A call to the department.

The call was over in ten seconds. It was so easy. Shockingly easy. The secretary only said with her usual detachment, "Fine. I'll note it down. You'd better inform the members of the orals board yourself." And to think I had dreaded to make this call for such a long time. . . .

I knew I had to talk to Nanae again. I had to tell her that
things would no longer remain the same once I took the orals.
I had to confront her with the inevitable.

12:00 noon. A call to Nanae.

// // //

I called Nanae nearly an hour after talking to the secretary of the
French department.

First, I took a shower. The hot water pelting my face dispelled
the strange floating sensation I'd had since hanging up the phone,
and reality returned. I felt the rough surface of the worn enamel
beneath the soles of my feet. Would I really be bidding farewell
to this old-fashioned tub soon? It must be nearly a century old.
Water trickling from the faucet had left a greenish stain and,
though I had no desire to soak in the tub, the four lion's clawfeet
were classically beautiful. The first time I laid eyes on them, they
had seemed somehow familiar, as if I'd seen them in a previous life.

From the first, I had been attracted to this apartment in the old
brick building because everything from the bathtub with the lion's
clawfeet to the high ceilings, white plaster walls, and dark hard-
wood floors, not to mention the workmanship of the brass window handles, seemed somehow detached from the here and now.
To find things that would match that atmosphere, Tono and I had
gone scrounging in secondhand stores that were **antique shops**
in name only and in junk-filled **thrift shops** run by the Salvation
Army, finding cheap, dusty old furniture that we repaired or
painted. With antiquated furniture scattered around the apartment, the place had seemed even further detached from the here
and now. It was perfect for me, convinced as I was that I had no
place in the present time or in America. After Tono left, I would

sink into the big red armchair that he used to occupy and while away the afternoons, feeling, as I looked around in the stillness, more and more left behind by everything. And now, soon, I in turn would be leaving everything behind.

After my shower I changed into a **sweatshirt** and **sweatpants**, really not much different from pajamas. College students paid less attention to their appearance than the young people of the town, and graduate students even less. Yet few graduate students were as careless of their appearance as I was. The thought came to me every time I threw on these truly basic clothes and felt the rough texture of the cotton against my skin. When I went out, I made some effort to look presentable, but that became more bothersome by the day. When was the last time I had put on a dress over a lacy satin slip and lustrous pantyhose, applied makeup, and gone out in a pair of high heels? The memory of ever having done so—or of how satin felt against my skin—was so remote that it didn't feel possible. The lacy satin slips were tucked away in a chest of drawers along with a lavender **sachet** that I couldn't bring myself to toss out though its scent had faded. All sorts of other feminine things—the shiny, see-through, and fluffy apparel I self-consciously dubbed **"vanity items"**—were buried deeper down, as lifeless as if slumbering beneath gravestones. Would they awaken and return to life in Japan?

I went into the kitchen and had my usual **breakfast**, a bowl of **granola** with milk and a banana. Then, after sipping a **mug** of tea, I went back to the bedroom, lay down on the mattress-bed on the floor, slowly put out my arm and felt for the receiver, allowing my fingers to slide along its all-too-familiar shape before finally lifting it to my ear. The time was twelve o'clock.

It took her forever to come to the phone. Her **loft** was spacious, so I let the phone ring. I was just about to hang up when I heard her voice.

"Hello?"

"It's me."

"Well, well. What a pleasant surprise! What's the occasion?"

"You're still there. Good."

"Sure. I don't go out to **Long Island** till later. Mrs. Murakami always says come at dinnertime."

"How nice of her." I was especially grateful to hear of such kindness today, knowing I was going to inform Nanae of the call I had made to the French department. She was not likely to take it well.

Unsuspecting, she imitated Mrs. Murakami's effervescence: "My husband positively walks on air Friday nights, Miss Nanae, knowing you're coming for a lesson!"

"That's how she sounds?"

"Yes. I'm actually on good terms with her. They're both so kind."

The Murakamis had stayed on longer than they originally intended, though not as much as we had. They lived two blocks down from the house where we'd grown up, and, even after moving to **Manhattan**, Nanae had continued going there to teach piano to their two daughters—though lately she seemed to spend less time doing that than talking with the girls about their budding adolescence. Despite their life in America, they still maintained the bashfulness of Japanese girls their age. All in all, it was a very nice arrangement—Nanae had the chance to enjoy Japanese cooking with a regular Japanese family, and she earned welcome pocket money.

"Feels like the first snow's on the way," I remarked, putting off what I had to tell her.

"Oh, shit. You think so? Did you listen to the weather report?"

"Why would I do that?" Since I never went out, I had no need of weather reports. There was no radio in the apartment anyway, just a fourteen-inch black-and-white television that Tono had inherited from a Japanese grad student friend of his; it had a wire hanger for antenna, so only two channels came through, and those had diagonal lines running through the picture. After Tono moved out, I stuck it under the kitchen sink to gather dust. Whenever I got out a large pan, I would catch sight of it looking bedraggled.

"I wonder if Father will say he wants to eat rice again," I ventured. Nanae and I often took him home-cooked food on our visits, hoping to inject a bit of pleasure into his dismal life.

"It's all so hard to bear."

When we lived in Japan, he had always preferred Western-style food, and if we were having a typically Japanese meal of, say, grilled fish, miso soup, rice, and pickles, he would make a great show of loading his rice with butter and ending the meal with slabs of cheese—then an expensive delicacy. In America, he had indulged himself all the more. And then, of course, he came down with diabetes; only now, when his eyesight was failing and his mental powers declining, did he develop a craving for simple Japanese foods.

"Did you make him rice balls?"

"The rice cooker's on now. I was using the **belt sander** while the rice was cooking. That's why I couldn't hear the phone."

She had to be getting ready for her group exhibition next spring. As she hadn't gotten many calls from the architectural office lately, she'd been working harder than usual on her artwork. Still, she never sounded peeved at being interrupted when I called, although I would have felt better for her sake if she did.

"**I'm glad you called,**" she said brightly.

"Why, did something happen?" Even if I originated the call, we always ended up talking about her. This could be irritating, but today I didn't mind.

"I wanted to call you, but I already called once this morning. And it's really no big deal . . ." Her voice trailed off.

"**Don't tell me you've got some other bad news.**" For once I spoke in English.

"Ha ha. **The news this morning was quite a shock to you, I guess. Don't worry, sweetie.** This doesn't concern you. A little while ago I got a letter from Kanae, special delivery."

"Special delivery?"

"Yes."

"Wouldn't she phone if it was an emergency?"

"Yes, but it's not. Japanese people send letters by special delivery all the time. They think it comes across as more polite."

"Kanae's not all that Japanese."

"Way more than we are. Or maybe she's quickly turning Japanese now that she's back in Japan. I don't know."

Kanae had graduated from the conservatory one year ahead of Nanae and, like her, had stayed on in **Manhattan**—unlike her, she went on to **Juilliard**—but the year before last she had finally gone back to Japan.

"Say, **can you wait a sec? I want to go get a ciggy, okay?"**

She said this so rapidly I had no time to react and was left waiting. Whenever she could tell from my tone of voice that the conversation had a chance of stretching on, she would go get her cigarettes and a **Diet Coke**. It used to be regular **Coke**, but at some point she had switched to **Diet**. After a minute I could hear the clink of ice as she came closer. "When I'm busy in the office and I hear that clinking sound, I know she wants to drag out the conversation. It's so aggravating." That's what Mother used to say—before she disappeared from our lives to go off "in search of myself," as she put it.

When Nanae returned, she sounded even more upbeat. "Listen. I remembered this just now when I opened the freezer. It has nothing to do with anything."

"What?"

"Ready?" There was laughter in her voice. "You know the old saying, 'gold coins before cats'? Like **'pearls before swine.'** Well, here's a twist: 'Catnip before cats, gold coins before *ojorō.*'"

"Before what?"

"*Ojorō*. **Prostitutes—you know.**"

The proper *kanji* then came to mind. "Oh, お女郎." The quaint Japanese word evoked an image of women in kimono with long ornamental hairpins in their chignons, their faces painted white, sitting on display in the pleasure quarter. Not a word anyone ever used anymore.

"**Did you get it?**"

"I understand what it means, sure."

"**Did you ever hear that expression?**"

"Never."

"I'm not surprised. Every time I open the freezer door I think, 'Oh darn, I forgot to tell her again' . . . **I have two little mice in my freezer. Very cute. All wrapped up in plastic.**"

"You're kidding me."

She giggled. "**Not the real thing, of course.** Stuffed toys. A pair of them, with catnip inside. **They're Christmas presents for my babies.**"

"What, you went out and bought them?"

She didn't answer this. "Anyway, I thought it was funny. 'Catnip before cats, gold coins before *ojorō*.' They both mean giving someone exactly what they want."

"I get it, I get it."

"Isn't it funny?"

"I guess."

"I think it's a hoot. Mrs. Murakami heard it from that nisei lady."

"That nisei lady" was the original owner of Nanae's cats.

Those two felines were supposedly descended from a long line of cats originating in the Japanese American community on the West Coast, the very first ones having been brought over at the end of the Meiji era by a Buddhist priest accompanying a group of farmers across the Pacific Ocean. The Murakami daughters,

who had been begging their parents for kittens, were given a pair
by an elderly nisei lady, but as it turned out, the older daughter was
severely allergic to cats, and when the Murakamis asked Nanae to
help them find someone to take them, Nanae responded, "*I will
take them!*" She promptly put them in a cardboard box and took
them home to **SoHo**. At the time, the kittens were small enough to
fit in her cupped hands.

Just the week before, the nisei lady had driven to the Murakamis'
to deliver a pair of toy mice.

"For the young lady who took in the **kittens**, she told Mrs.
Murakami."

"The 'young lady'?"

"That's what she said. **Do you mind?**"

Apparently Mrs. Murakami had politely accepted the trinkets,
while thinking how cheap they looked, and then the nisei lady had
said, "They're filled with **catnip**. You know what they say, 'Catnip
before cats, gold coins before *ojorō*.' " Unable to share the joke with
her daughters, Mrs. Murakami had held in her laughter until her
husband came home.

"The nisei are more out of touch with Japan than we are,"
Nanae said.

"They certainly are," I said, and added, "That lady gave you
something for the cats last **Christmas** too, didn't she?"

"Yes, bonito flakes to perk up the cat food."

The nisei lady, whom Nanae had never met, was in her six-
ties and had lived in the area since the days when if you wanted
Japanese food you had to make it yourself, unlike these days,
when everything from packs of bonito sprinkles and jars of pickled shallots to Kagome catsup and Kewpie mayonnaise—not to
mention Kanebo or Shiseido hair gel—was available at the Yaohan
supermarket in **New Jersey**, where Japanese expat wives pushed
shopping carts up and down the aisles, husbands in tow, reveling

in Japan's prosperity (and America's decline). The nisei lady must have felt bewilderment at the topsy-turvy changes she'd experienced. I was no stranger to such bewilderment myself.

Nanae chattered on. "Listen, **by the way, you're coming for Christmas, *n'est-ce pas*? Henryk's gone, you know.** So you can stay the night. I was thinking I'd put up a **Christmas tree** after all. When I went out for cigarettes, they were selling trees on the corner, and they had that irresistible piny smell. **I'll get a small one. They're a lot cheaper.** I don't think it's a good idea to not have a **Christmas tree** just because you don't have a man in your life."

"Certainly not."

"I don't want my life being determined by whether or not I happen to have a man anymore."

"Certainly not."

"I'm old enough to have reached that awareness by now."

"Yes, you are."

"I mean it."

"Well, I should hope so."

"Gee whiz. Thanks for the encouragement. Anyway, come on over. You haven't been to the city in a while."

When Tono was still here, we often took the train to **Manhattan** to see some dull film with the **European chic** he admired and then we'd have dinner with a couple of our few American friends. Conversing in English made Tono self-conscious and he would always say: **"Ai amu sori mai Ingurishu izu so puah."**

"Oh, no no. Your English is very good, Tono."

"No no," he would protest.

"Oh, yes."

My American friends were always fond of Tono. And **Sarah Bloom,** an aspiring novelist whom I'd gone to **high school** with— and who used to be **Rebecca's** best friend—actually found my stoop-shouldered, droopy-eyed Tono handsome. **"I find him better**

looking than Toshiro Mifune." One time she said this when we
visited her in the **West Village.** I must have expressed disbelief,
because she added, while gracefully pouring tea, **"No, I'm serious,
Minae."** Tono raised his arms high and whooped in delight.

I hadn't seen **Sarah**, that lovely soul, in quite a while now. When
I made the trip to see Father, I didn't even take time to stop off and
visit Nanae but transferred at **Grand Central** to **Penn Station** and
took the **Long Island Railroad** straight out to the nursing home. On
the way back, too, I would just change trains in the city and head
north. Living in a constant state of idleness had made me impatient,
and I never felt like taking the time to run any sort of errand on the
way. Nanae assumed I was busy with my studies, and anyhow we
talked nearly every night on the phone, so she never complained.

Nanae went on talking. "Come for a visit. It's pretty here now.
The **Christmas** decorations are going up. **Manhattan looks its best
during the Christmas season.** Do come."

I sighed.

"What's wrong?"

I couldn't think of words to explain my sigh.

"Oh, come on. What is it?"

"It's just—here we are, at **Christmastime** again." I sounded
sentimental even to myself.

Twenty years earlier, when we first arrived in New York, the
Christmas season had been in full swing. The sight of **Christmas**
decorations in tropical Hawaii and sunny Los Angeles hadn't
aroused any strong sentiment, but from the moment we landed in
New York, the very air had smelled Christmassy, a feeling that only
intensified as we stayed in a hotel in **Manhattan** for several days
while waiting for beds to be delivered to our **Long Island** house.

When I stepped outside the hotel's revolving door, the jingling
I heard on every street corner, borne on air that was piercingly

cold against my cheeks, came from men and women in Salvation Army uniforms standing beside iron kettles, ringing hand bells to urge passersby laden with Christmas presents to remember the less fortunate. "Mama, I want to give something too!" I squealed, wheedling a **quarter** from her. Clutching the coin tight, I walked up to the red iron kettle and let it clatter through the slot in the lid. **"Thank you, young lady,"** the man boomed. Sometimes Salvation Army officers would play carols on dispirited trumpets and a loose drum. Among them was always a middle-aged woman with stumpy legs showing beneath the skirt of her navy-blue uniform. Nearby there'd be a fellow wrapped in sweaters and a scarf, calling out, **"Chestnuts! Chestnuts!"** as he stirred the nuts roasting in a shallow pan, the air rich with the smell, and when Mother yielded to curiosity and bought some, they turned out to be not as sweet as Tianjin-roasted chestnuts but tasty enough that we all clamored for more. I also had my first encounter with salty **pretzels**, which I found vastly inferior to rice crackers. It was the first time I got to go to **FAO Schwarz**, the toy store where Father used to buy expensive dolls for Nanae and me as souvenirs of his trips, and the first time we went to **Macy's**, "the world's largest store," where Mother bought us each a proper little dress, mine trimmed with white lace at the cuffs and the hem. We also ventured into a cheap diner called **Chock full o'Nuts** and sat at the counter eating vegetable soup that was more like stew. Father wasn't with us, and I remember Mother murmuring that she wasn't sure how one left a tip. Those few days marked the last time I was able to enjoy America like any other tourist.

"It was **Christmas** when we first came here, so of course it is now too," I said, trying to mask my sentimentality.

"That's right. We got here just before **Christmas**." Nanae sounded no less sentimental.

And from then on it was a family tradition to set out for **Manhattan** every year before **Christmas**. The freezing cold, ordinarily all but unbearable, added to the festive mood. The center of attention was the gigantic **Christmas tree** at the skating rink at **Rockefeller Center**, seemingly tall enough to pierce the clouds. Every year we went to see the tree, making the same exclamations every time: "Look how big it is!" "Isn't it gorgeous?" "How on earth do they get it here?" There would always be a performance or two of the *Nutcracker* and even more showings of Christmas-themed movies, including classics. The windows at **Saks Fifth Avenue** would draw huge crowds straining to see mechanical dolls enacting nostalgic **Christmas Eve** tableaux. The bells of **St. Patrick's** rang sonorously to announce mass, and the ubiquitous jingling of Salvation Army bells filled in the gaps. Those were the sounds and sights of Christmas as people rushed around shopping for presents, their noses bright red with cold. Later I would learn how intellectuals frowned on the season's rampant commercialism, but America's lingering Puritan heritage meant there were few festivals during the year, unlike the way it was in Japan, and I always liked **Christmas** as a time when Americans would let go and feel merry, their spirits dancing and full of excitement.

"Remember the first time we saw the town we were going to live in?" Nanae now asked. "I could hardly believe it was real."

By the time we had checked out of our hotel in **Manhattan** and set off for our new home in a car driven by someone from Father's company, Christmas was just days away. We got off the highway on **Long Island** and traveled north a short distance down an avenue running through the center of town, then turned right. The scene that met our eyes through the fine, bright snow was straight out of a picture book. Large, old-fashioned houses lined either side of the street, with myriad tiny colorful lights twinkling on porticos with towering columns and around wide windows with curtains

Christmas tree at Rockefeller Center |▶

open to showcase the decorated Christmas trees within. Even the tall trees in the yards were wrapped with twinkling lights. We later learned that we had moved into a town where the majority of residents were Jews, many of them wealthy, but in this one neighborhood wealthy Christians clustered together and competed in putting up elaborate Christmas decorations.

"I know."

"It was so unreal. Just too beautiful. I thought it was like a dream."

"It was."

"The huge houses were amazing, remember?"

Farther on, where the houses were smaller, had been our family's house.

After a short silence, Nanae said again, "Come to see me. We can go visit Father together for Christmas."

"Right."

"I could take **Bing Crosby.** *I'm dreaming of a white Christmas, lahlala lala lalalah . . .*"

"Father was always happy at Christmas, even in Japan."

"Yes, but he hated Japanese New Year's."

"His generation had an aversion for things Japanese, because of the war."

"And a love of all things Western."

Every year around this time, Father would go down to the basement, get out the box marked **"Christmas Tree"** in Mother's round English handwriting, and in a corner of the living room set up a tall, American-style artificial fir tree with plastic trunk and needles. When that was done, he'd go back to the basement and bring up another cardboard box, this one marked "Christmas decorations" in Mother's round Japanese handwriting. Carefully packed inside were gold and silver stars; felt Santa Clauses with wire-frame reindeer; ornaments shaped like candles, bells, and

candy canes; red, green, and blue glass balls; gold and silver tinsel; miniature lights; and white cotton for snow. We would take them out and festoon the branches of our artificial tree, happy because unlike the real but skimpy trees we used to have in Tokyo, here no matter how many decorations we hung on the tall tree, there was always room for more.

Schools let out before Christmas, and, as most families spent the twenty-third, twenty-fourth, and twenty-fifth together, this was understandably the cruelest time of year for the lonely. Our family would invite people from the company where Father worked, and later on my sister's boyfriend and maybe mine would join us, and we would all sit around the extended mahogany dining table loaded with a **Christmas dinner** of American and Japanese dishes, eating with knife, fork, and chopsticks. All through the dinner, various records of Father's choosing would play on the hi-fi, with **Bing Crosby's "White Christmas"** the favorite. On evenings when it was just the four of us, after dinner we would go into the living room and get out Mother's old sheet music, and, while Nanae accompanied us on the piano, Mother and I would sing and sing— everything from Japanese children's songs and simple *lieder* to old *chansons* from Mother's youth. Mother had taken voice lessons after graduating from girls' school, and that training plus the natural richness of her soprano was enough to drown me out. Nanae kept up with us at the piano, while Father, his face pleasantly flushed from the small amount of wine he'd drunk, wandered around the room contentedly, Della padding along at his side.

The image of the blank walls of Father's room in the nursing home suddenly came to mind. *At least back then he was happy. As were we all.* Who was better off, someone with memories of former happiness or someone without them?

Nanae seemed lost in her own thoughts. For a short time neither of us spoke.

The year before, I had gone to see Nanae just before Christmas, but with **Henryk** around I hadn't wanted to stay, so I'd come right back. Several days after that **Rebecca Rohmer** had shown up at my apartment, and she and I had gone to hear the university choir sing sacred music.

Shaking off the ghost of Christmas past, I changed the subject. "So how's Kanae?" I asked. "Is she okay?"

"Oh. Yeah. Kanae." Nanae too sounded as if she had just come back to herself.

"Are you still sending her music?"

Not long ago, Nanae had complained to me, "Kanae asked me to send her some music. Like it's no trouble at all. **I take the subway and do this and that for everyone and what do I get? Nothing. Absolutely nothing in return.** Miss Nice Guy, that's me." This time she sounded unexpectedly cheery: "Yeah. Some more music but also some of the **Germaine Monteil** products she loves. Can't get them in Japan, she says."

"What products?"

"**You don't know? My God, you really are out of touch with the trifles of life. Germaine Monteil cosmetics.** They're expensive. Department stores here carry them."

"Sounds like a lot of trouble."

"It is." I expected her to say just how much trouble it was, but she didn't. Instead, she went on, "She's been surprisingly good about sending things to me, you know. Her letter said that a parcel was coming by sea mail." Nanae was genuinely happy when people gave her things. "Japanese food. Really basic stuff, the kind of thing you can get here if you're willing to pay, but those things come in the handiest, after all. **Whatchamacallit** curry, instant noodles, bonito flakes for my **babies.** They developed a taste for bonito last Christmas . . . **I told you they went absolutely nuts!** I figure it's the DNA of their Japanese ancestry. Wagahai hates turkey, but if

I sprinkle it with those flakes, he'll eat it. Kanae told me she'll send some more when she gets a chance. That and some **pantyhose**. I have to say, **pantyhose** is one thing where you get better **quality** for your money in Japan. Shipping probably costs more than the **pantyhose** are worth, but, oh well . . ." Then, lowering her voice, she said, "Remember I told you she got a few pupils?"

"Yeah."

"Apparently things are going really well for her." She paused to exhale a long stream of cigarette smoke. After another short space she added glumly, "She's earning enough to pay her way."

"Really."

"She now has more pupils but that's not all. **She might possibly get a teaching job at a college, too. Now what do you say to that?**"

I heard her take a drag on her cigarette and blow out another stream of smoke.

Nanae had heard about Kanae, an overseas student from Japan, on her first day at the conservatory. **"Are you Kanae's sister?** I must have been asked that ten times on the first day alone. *My goodness, how could there be someone with a name so much like mine—* I wondered who she could be, and at suppertime I looked around the **cafeteria** and there she was, a dark-skinned Japanese girl who actually looked a lot like me. *Oh no, it can't be her!* No way, but **sure enough, that was Kanae all right.**"

Kanae looked more like Nanae than I did; anybody seeing them together would have taken them for sisters. But, for whatever reason, they resisted having been thrown together by fate and saw little of each other in school. Kanae had a rather fraught family background and, choosing not to go back to Japan, had applied herself, was accepted at **Juilliard**, and continued to study the piano, meanwhile going out with plenty of men, never marrying, and supporting herself by giving lessons. As time went on, she and Nanae found they had more and more in common, finally growing quite close, meeting for lunch and calling each other to pour out their woes on the telephone. The year before, Kanae had announced she was worn out from living in America. The winters were cold, the streets weren't safe, and just shopping for food was so much trouble she could cry; and, besides, if she was ever going to live in Japan she had better not wait. "So, Nanae, hang in there and do your best for me too. Say hi to your sassy little sister." And with that she had hopped on a plane home.

"So apparently now she's making enough to afford top-of-the-line cosmetics. **Maybe I should send her a congratulations card. Why not?**" Nanae made no effort to hide her jealousy.

Though she herself had given up the piano, Nanae had followed Kanae's progress with interest even before they became friends. When Kanae graduated from the conservatory, her playing had been at about the same level as Nanae's, but after **Juilliard** she had won an international competition and succeeded in coming out with a recording. Around then Nanae began to sound glum when talking about her. But as years went by, with Kanae still just teaching piano, she was relieved. That's when they began spending time together. **"Let's face it. I mean her playing is . . . all right. It's nothing great. But it's all right. And her credentials are fine, too. The fact of the matter is, there are zillions of people like her in New York.** Well, maybe **zillions** is stretching it. Anyway, people like her are a dime a dozen, so for someone like her to stand out in New York is pretty much impossible, **poor girl.**" She had sounded at once sympathetic and gleeful. When Kanae announced that she was going back to Japan, Nanae had said to me a bit scornfully, "She's going back home with her tail between her legs." And when Kanae worried that her carefully trained ear might lose its edge in Japan, Nanae had been unsparing: **"Tough! That's her choice. She's made a decision. She has to take the consequences."**

Kanae had never attended a music conservatory in Japan, or even a high school affiliated with one, so she had no network of contacts. Moreover, Japan's era of piano fever—a time when everywhere you looked, little girls whose feet didn't reach the pedals were practicing Czerny, their fingers tripping over the keys—was long gone. Kanae had left New York not knowing whether she would be able to make ends meet teaching piano in Japan. Six months ago, she had written that by installing soundproofing and whatnot to set up a studio, she had gone through her savings and feared there was no choice but to go back and live a constrained life in her parents' house in Kobe. At the time, Nanae and I had nodded in agreement that she should count herself lucky she at least had someplace to go back to. Then about three months ago she had called Nanae to say that things were taking a turn for the better, that she had picked up several pupils, and would Nanae please send her certain sheet music that was hard to come by in Japan? While grousing **"What nerve!"**—a stock expression of hers—Nanae had still been generous enough to add, **"I hope everything works out for her."**

According to Kanae's special delivery letter, things were looking up yet more: she'd gotten to know an eminent teacher of piano who was making a slow recovery after surgery for uterine cancer and who fortunately—if one could use the word under the circumstances—was cutting back on her teaching responsibilities. She had asked Kanae to take over several pupils seeking entrance to music school. And via another route, Kanae was about to become a part-time instructor at a certain Tokyo conservatory. In other words, the same background that was a dime a dozen in New York was still a boon in Japan, so that before Kanae quite knew what had happened she was settled in an unexpectedly good situation.

"Remember how she used to say she had no interest in going back to Japan?"

I remembered.

"The level of playing is completely different between Japan and America," Kanae would say. "Not technically, but musically.

But then the piano is a Western instrument to begin with, so you could hardly expect otherwise. Once you've been exposed to piano playing on this side of the Pacific, all you can do is stay here and try to get better." So she had kept on practicing, leading a quiet life apart from messy entanglements with a succession of boyfriends. Then one day she had phoned Nanae, sounding crestfallen: a Japanese female pianist—someone famous in Japan but unknown in the States—would be holding a recital at **Carnegie Hall**, "the same **Carnegie Hall** where **Horowitz** plays!"

Nanae, easily roused, had phoned me right away, still fuming. **"What nerve! Who's ever heard of her in New York? Maybe she plays better than Kanae. But that doesn't make her good enough for Carnegie Hall, you know.** Nobody's going to go to hear her play except people from the Japanese embassy, plus expats and their families, that's all. **And maybe her dear American friends.** Who else would attend a concert by some nobody? **Of course, with the Japanese yen—oh, the almighty yen—it's nothing for her to rent the hall. She can send out as many comps as she wants.** And in Japan, she can say she played Carnegie Hall. She'll be 'international.' **Well, that's what she wants and that's what the Japanese public wants. Let them be married happily ever after. The whole thing has nothing whatsoever to do with music.** Argh."

Nanae's voice over the phone now was subdued. "Now she says she's glad she went back. That it's not easy, but she's still glad."

I pictured Nanae's long, tawny fingers. If she had continued to play, she too could have supported herself with the piano in Japan. If she could return to Japan any time she wished, the conversation I had to have with her today would be far easier for me.

"Tokyo's heaven, she says."

"Huh."

"Not a bit cold even in December."

"Huh."

"Even without a car, you can go wherever you want on the train, and most of all she loves being able to walk alone at night."

"Huh."

"Hard to imagine, somehow."

When Nanae graduated from conservatory, our parents had bought her a **Steinway**, saying she was a now professional musician—only to see her give up music after her suicide attempt in Japan.

"Such a stupid thing to do—like a page from a trashy novel!" When Mother got the overseas call at dawn from Uncle Yokohama, who had rushed Nanae to a hospital, she was more indignant than worried. "It's a farce. Imposing on her aunt and uncle this way, never stopping to think what this would do to me! After all the trouble I went to, building up my relationship with them . . . Staging all this drama because her boyfriend left her just goes to show she's as much of a damned fool as her grandmother . . ."

I was living in my own place then, but I had to rush back to **Long Island** to calm Mother down.

Knowing that Aunt Yokohama was about to return home, Nanae had swallowed a bottle of sleeping pills. She was taken to the hospital, had her stomach pumped, and even after returning to "Yokohama" remained in a stupor for nearly a week, but her life was never in danger. As Mother and Father were discussing whether one of them ought to fly to Tokyo to be with her, Uncle Yokohama had telephoned to say that wouldn't be necessary. Farce or not, the suicide attempt was not only a way for Nanae to get back at her boyfriend but also an attempt for her to justify herself to Mother. She had of course wanted to marry the guy, but her feelings had been inextricably mixed with those of Mother, who'd been determined that the marriage take place.

That year, around the time the first winter winds began to blow, Nanae had shown up at **Kennedy** looking like a ghost. After resting for a while at our parents' house, she'd begun giving piano lessons, mostly to children of Japanese expatriates. Far from hiding her low spirits, she'd worn a morose face for all the world to see. That went on for about a year, and then Mother suggested that Nanae start taking lessons again. Out of the blue Nanae had responded by declaring that there was no point in her continuing with the piano, that she felt miserable about all the money that had been spent on her music education already, but really *she* was the one who had always wanted to study art. This last bit was a dig at me, as I had already quit art for French literature.

"No matter what, I'll never be good enough to be a concert pianist. **I am not good enough, you know. I don't have the technique, I don't have the character.**" That was her explanation. She was right—but Mother hadn't had her study piano in order to make a concert pianist of her in the first place. She had wanted her to play professionally in one way or another, but had no knowledge of the actual life of a concert pianist and couldn't possibly have imagined a future for her daughter that involved flying around the world from city to city and spending the better part of every year living in hotels, with her schedule booked solid for the next three years. Nor had Nanae been working toward that goal. For her to give up piano because she couldn't become a concert pianist sounded reasonable but was in fact no reason at all. Besides, her piano playing had been too central to our family for her to give it up so easily.

Mother had understandably been furious. But in the end she had yielded. After all, her daughter had suffered emotional trauma.

Nanae pleaded her case: "I want to go to art school in **Manhattan**. I'll scrape up the tuition myself by going on teaching piano here if you'll let me, I promise." For her, this was a proposal of such maturity that no one could take exception. Thus Nanae had ended her career in piano, some ten years ago. Semester by semester, her time taken up by new boyfriends and other diversions, her laudable intention to pay her way through art school was shunted aside. Mother and Father picked up the tab.

I asked the question that I had never asked in all these years: "Do you wish you had kept up with your piano?"

"Mmm." Her response was hard to read. "I dunno. I really liked the piano, as far as that goes."

Back when she took up sculpture, she had insisted that she'd never liked the piano to begin with.

"Yes, you did. Unlike me, you always did."

"Yeah, I suppose so." She sounded thoughtful. A short silence followed.

Art can be taken up at any age, yet the chances of making it as a professional artist are low. As a child, Nanae would become engrossed in folding origami, kneading clay, or making paper cutouts—anything that involved handwork. Later, when I was attending art school, she would watch me sculpting a bust or something and comment enviously, "If it weren't for the piano, I'd have done that too." Just how much connection there might be between manual dexterity and professional success as an artist, I had no idea. All I knew was that, in the end, perhaps in part because she was commuting from home, she had never really taken to art school. She always felt out of place in a studio that looked more like a construction site, the floor littered with scrap metal and wood shavings, the air filled with machines whirring, shearing, sawing. She also felt out of place among art school students, who unlike the students of classical music came from every background imaginable.

If only she'd stayed with the piano.

Nanae sighed as if she had heard my wordless comment. "When Kanae went back, you know, I thought *Oh, she chickened out. Couldn't take the heat.* She said so herself, but when it comes down to it, what if she had stayed on here, kept trying? **She wasn't getting anywhere, anyway.**"

"No, she wasn't."

"She'd only go on getting older."

"True," I said cautiously, afraid that Nanae would rush to conclusions and retort, *I'm not getting anywhere either. I'm only getting older. What am I to do?* I would have no reply. Probably she didn't want to paint herself into that corner.

"Anyway, there comes a time when it really doesn't matter anymore whether you're in the center of things or not. Maybe that's when you see where you're headed. Remember, Kanae said she was going back because she was worn out. I think it's as good a reason as any . . . **That is, if you can. After all, you only live once.**"

"Very true."

"I'm worn out too, you know. **Really and truly worn out.**"

"Mm-hm."

"Though I'm not saying I want to go back to Japan."

I'm not saying I want to go back to Japan: the words stirred something in me—a glimmer of hope, maybe. I said them over to myself. I wanted to cling to them, but the more I tried, the emptier they sounded.

The overcast sky must have darkened still more; a gloomy shadow fell on the stucco wall in front of me. Snow was definitely in the air.

She had quit the piano, and that couldn't be helped. Her quitting the piano had made Japan recede further into the distance for her, and that couldn't be helped, either. But thinking about

Nanae and her music always rekindled the indignation I had felt as a child, indignation that soon gave way to despondency, then resignation.

Back in Japan when I was in kindergarten, one day out of nowhere a gleaming black upright piano had appeared in our house. This was before every middle-class family was bent on having a piano in the living room, and it must have cost more than our parents could really afford. A few days later Mother, dressed up in a kimono, had taken Nanae and me to call on her cousin at "Yokohama."

"Please teach my daughter the piano," Mother had said, bowing.

Two grand pianos stood side by side in the large drawing room, which looked like a set from a foreign film. The three of us sat on the sofa. Suspended from the high ceiling was a pendant lamp shedding soft light over all. On our right were built-in bookcases with glass doors, crammed full of books and musical scores. The vermilion covers of the collected works of modern Japanese literature that would later become so important to me must have been on display as well, part of Grandpa Yokohama's library, but at the time I had no eyes for them. All I could do was sit on the sofa in a daze, savoring the fragrance of polished wood. What set "Yokohama" apart was not wealth. While wealth surely helped to distinguish the family, what that house had was something greater, something far sweeter-smelling.

Mother must have yearned to have been born in such a house, must have herself yearned to study piano with her cousin, whose lessons were expensive and sought after; he was, I would later learn, a pioneer in the introduction of Western music to Japan. She leaned forward until we could see the embroidery on the back of her obi.

"Please teach my daughter the piano," she said again. "I'll see to it that she practices at home."

Heaped in a cut crystal bowl in front of Uncle Yokohama were shiny silver objects that looked as delicate as tiny seashells; I later realized that they must have been **Hershey's Kisses**, then a novelty in Japan. He picked one up and began peeling off the foil with long fingers. "All right, but don't ask me to start her from scratch."

He introduced us to a recent conservatory graduate, a lovely young woman who was his favorite pupil, and it was she who taught both Nanae and me the basics. But when Mother had asked Uncle Yokohama to teach "my daughter" the piano, she of course meant Nanae. After we had acquired the basics, Nanae alone went on to study with Uncle Yokohama. To me, Mother simply said, "You have your ballet."

True, Nanae and I had started ballet together, and now only I was continuing with it. But Mother never came to see my lessons—not once. For Nanae's piano lessons she would always change into a pretty kimono and accompany Nanae to "Yokohama." Her job with Aunt Utako kept her out of the house at irregular hours, but when she could she would without fail oversee Nanae's practicing. With her knitting in her hands, she would sit beside Nanae and lay a matchstick on the edge of the piano each time Nanae played a piece through, not permitting her to go on to the next piece until there were ten matchsticks in a row. Anyone who didn't know her better would have thought her a modern-day version of the Chinese sage Mencius's exemplary mother.

After we moved to America, we got a grand piano. When people from Father's office came to the house, Nanae would play piece after piece for them and each time be showered with applause and compliments, while I bustled back and forth between the living room and kitchen bearing trays of tea and beer. Eventually we got a second grand piano, placed side by side with the first one in our none-too-large living room. Not until much later did I recall that pair of grand pianos in the "Yokohama" drawing room.

As a child, I was naturally annoyed about Mother's fixation with "Yokohama" and Nanae's piano lessons, a fixation that I came to

understand had its origins in her difficult childhood. Those piano
lessons epitomized what she had dreamed of as a young girl and
what she had been denied, less for pecuniary reasons than because
Japanese society was determined to keep someone like her in her
place. Years went by before I could feel pity for her ardor, knowing
what her investment in those lessons had meant to her, and knowing that it had gone to waste.

Outside the window, the clouds hung so heavy in the sky that it
was impossible to know where the sun was. I stared at the gray and
began, without having planned out exactly how I would tell her:
"Anyway, I called because . . ."

"Oops! That's right, *you* called. Sorry."

"It's nothing earth-shaking," I said, and then told her that
whether or not my **main advisor**, whom I called **"Herr Professor,"**
would be able to preside at my orals, I had decided to take them
soon after New Year's.

"So, you're not going to wait for him to recover?" She was surprisingly calm.

"I guess not."

"Is he dying?"

"I don't know. Possibly."

Maybe he really was.

Nanae said nothing for a moment. "So, you're finally going to
go through with it," she murmured, and then as an afterthought,
asked, **"Are you done then with your papers?"**

"Long ago."

"What? When did that happen?"

"It's been a while now." It was after my coursework was finished
and there was no need for me to put in an appearance on campus
that I began shutting myself up in the apartment, seeing no one.

I would sit in front of the **computer** screen all day, day after day, struggling to finish my overdue **papers**. But living in isolation had deepened my depression until churning out a few lines a day of those papers that would never be published anywhere had been all I could do. I must have moaned to Nanae about my inability to make headway. "I think I finally wrapped them up sometime around the first of the year."

"Oh. Then you're not writing anything now." She sounded a bit stupefied. "So that's why you haven't been going on about how you're stuck."

"Right."

All the writing I was doing was in my diary, where as a self-imposed penalty for spending my days in idleness, every day I had typed the words **"Didn't do anything today either."** I also kept track of my phone calls with Nanae. Other than that, there was nothing worthy of note.

"So now you're preparing for your orals?" She seemed abashed at how little she knew of my life.

"That's what I'm supposed to be doing. But really I'm not doing anything. Can't."

"*C'est pas vrai*. Don't give me that, please."

"It's true."

"You're not studying?"

"Nope. I try, but I just can't make myself do it."

My days began and ended in numb idleness. I couldn't bear to sit at my desk, so in the morning I would lie on the mattress-bed on the floor, turn on the **Luxo lamp**, and try to read some of the required literature lying around in piles, not bothering to get up and get dressed. Random thoughts distracted me. Guiltily I would resolve to focus, and shower and dress, but while I dried my hair, the focus would evaporate. The afternoon mail would bring magazines and assorted **junk mail**, which I would flip through until eventually the afternoon had waned. After dinner I would pick up my reading where I had left off, but soon Nanae would call. Day after day went by this way.

I feared not only the oral exam but setting foot on campus. I stayed away from the library, but life had to be lived, requiring occasional trips to the bank, the post office, the supermarket, the liquor store, the **Oriental grocery**, the bookstore, . . . To get where I was going, I would take detours to avoid going by the campus; if I couldn't avoid it, I would walk on the other side of the street, holding my breath and leaning away so that I walked at a tilt. I didn't do this consciously, but I came to realize it was what I did. As soon as my errand was accomplished, I would head straight back to the apartment, like an earthworm needing to get out of the sun. Once home again, I seldom even opened the windows to let in fresh air.

"I'm not sure what's going on, but I think it's **depression**," I said, skipping the details.

"Give me a break. You? Depression? No way!"

"I'm serious."

I couldn't possibly tell Nanae how I spent my days. I had never acquired the habit of confiding in her the way she did in me.

Worst of all was when I woke up in the night. As my sleep grew shallow, all the anxieties I had warded off during the day would surface in my half-conscious mind, and I would awaken with my heart beating rapidly and not be able to fall asleep again. Bleakly, I thought of how much time had gone by; of having no home even in this country; of Father in the nursing home, lying in bed staring at the ceiling, not knowing Mother had left him; of Mother, who had flown to **Singapore** to be with a younger man; of what was to become of Nanae and me; of . . . Helpless, I would stare into the darkness, my head on the pillow, until I found myself weeping. The next thing I knew it would be morning, sunlight poking through the blinds.

"Anyway, it's time to bite the bullet and take my orals," I said, the words tumbling out. I stopped, then added, "Then I'll be free."

Nanae must have caught something in my tone. **"But you are coming for Christmas,"** she said immediately. **"You have to."**

There was something pitiful in her automatic attempt to stave off loneliness. Suppose I did manage to visit her in New York this Christmas? What about next Christmas and the Christmas after that?

"Yes, I think so . . ."

"But what?"

"I might not write my dissertation after all."

"You mean your PhD dissertation?"

"Yes." A beat. "I might write it sometime, but I don't want to right now."

"Then what will you do?" Her voice was stiff.

"Write a novel or something."

"A novel? **Jesus!**" I could picture the look on her face. "That figures."

That figures? What did she mean by that? Had she always thought her little sister wanted to be a writer? Or was she saying, *After going to all the trouble of taking graduate seminars and writing graduate papers, you're going to try to become a novelist and end up like me, a broke wannabe?* Or could she be sensing the possibility of being left on her own in America?

"A novel in English? Or in Japanese?"

I want to be a novelist.

Oh, yes? Are you going to write in English or in Japanese?

I had had this conversation more than once with others, in English; I hadn't expected Nanae to ask the same question.

"Japanese, of course."

"But can you even write Japanese?"

Back in **high school**, when Mother caught me saying something about wanting to be a novelist, she would dismiss the idea out of hand: "Someone like you who doesn't know Japanese can't be a novelist." She and Father used to laugh at my "funny Japanese," but since they were the ones who had taken me to live in another country in the first place, their reaction struck me as unfair and wrong.

My only other Japanese teachers had been books.

Nanae didn't wait for me to answer. "I know you love Japan and everything. **Boy, that's been your passion . . . or rather, your obsession for, oh, I don't know how many years. Japanese this and Japanese that and I never hear the end of it.** But writing in Japanese is another matter."

"My English is worse."

"Really?"

"Besides, I've been writing nothing but French recently. Rather rudimentary French."

"Huh." She paused a moment. "Your writing in English is very good." She used the earnest tone she always adopted when offering me praise.

Children have their own world, and in our world Nanae had always given me more encouragement than either Father or Mother, never hesitating to lavish praise on me. When I learned to count to a hundred, she had gushed, "You're a genius!"

"Yes, but that's academic English."

"So?"

"An academic paper isn't the same as a novel. The vocabulary is much more limited, and anyway Japanese is my native language."

"What about Conrad, Nabokov?"

. . . *Naipaul, Rushdie* . . ., I thought, mentally continuing the list. **Conrad** was in a class by himself. Most non-native Anglophone novelists had grown up reading English from a young age. I sighed. "All I ever read was Japanese."

Nanae was silent a moment, and then she sighed too. "That's for sure. You were always reading novels in Japanese."

As a **junior high school student**, I was miserable. I set off each morning, arms loaded with textbooks, vowing to myself that if

I ever had children, I would never uproot them from Japan. At the time, there was still a normal distance between Nanae and me, so what she may have been feeling I had no way of knowing, but her sullen expression was enough to tell me that she too was not enjoying herself, and this was a source of comfort. Maybe she felt the same thing about me. In those days, reading Japanese books was my sole recourse; when I was reading Japanese books, I forgot my misery. After school, unsure even whether or not I had homework, I had nothing else to do, so while Nanae practiced the piano in the living room, I would be shut up in my bedroom, reading and reading and reading.

Nanae too seemed to be remembering those unhappy days. "You always, always had your nose in a book!"

In the beginning, when English had sounded to me like the chirping of birds, I would read novels in Japanese not just during recess but even during class. One day I was so absorbed in my book that class ended without my realizing it.

> What was I doing standing in this place, what had I come here for? I had no idea; it was foolish. It was madness. I must go back—and leaving the darkness of the alleyway, she strolled along a busy street with a row of night stalls, the faces of passersby small, so small, even the faces of people she brushed up against appearing far off, almost as if the ground where she walked were high above them, the clamor of their voices just reaching her yet sounding like the echo of something dropped in the bottom of a well, their voices belonging to them, her thoughts to her alone—

As I read on, a voice chirped, **"What's the story like?"** I looked up and there in front of me stood **Robin**, a warm-hearted girl with curly brown hair. *She's asking because she thinks I'm lonely, reading books by myself like this during recess.* Confronted with **Robin's**

face radiating goodwill, I was at a loss. Who knows how much
I understood at that age of the sad story of a Meiji woman working in a brothel, but to the extent that I did understand, how
was I to explain it in my next-to-nonexistent English? I stared
at her dumbly. "Is it a love story?" she asked helpfully. *Maybe you
could say so*, I thought, and answered in relief, "Yes, it's a love
story"—only for **Robin** to call out girlishly to the classroom, "Hey,
Minae's reading a love story!" The other girls laughed the way girls
did—**giggling**, it was called—and in apparent girlish fun repeated,
"Hey, Minae's reading a love story!" as if they had found out my
secret. Their **giggles** made me realize that their idea of a **love
story** was the kind in paperbacks on prominent display in the
drugstore, books with gaudy covers of a beautiful woman, bosom
bulging out, clasped in a man's sturdy arms. It was my fault—my
stupid description of the book as a love story—and I started to
feel I owed the author, Higuchi Ichiyō, an apology. Then **Joshua**,
a boy of constant curiosity, came over and peered at the book.
"You read from top to bottom, right?" he asked and reached out
for the book. "Can I?" He waved it around for the class to see.
"They don't read from left to right. They read from top to bottom.
Hey, did you know that?" The book was passed from hand to hand.
"Lemme see. Lemme see." Then **Jim**, a stuck-up kid I had never
liked, pointed to the numerals at the bottom of the page and
announced in the tone of one making a great discovery, "But they
have English numbers. They use English numbers. Look. Look!"
By rights I should have put him in his place: "You ignominious
ignoramus. That's not English. That's Arabic. Not everything originated in Europe. On the contrary . . ." But I was meek and a coward
and such advanced English was beyond me, so I said nothing.
Even **Alice**, who was usually thoughtful, began saying ridiculous
things: "Maybe it's not just a love story, maybe it's a romance, with
a Japanese princess." Did she have in mind the scene from some

picture book about a Chinese princess waiting beneath a willow tree, singing a love song to her hero? My classmates' concepts of what I was reading were so far removed from the poetic melancholy of Ichiyō's prose, the sordid back alleys, the despair, that even if one day I should become totally fluent in English—unlikely as that was—I could not imagine myself being able to bridge the gap. I felt helpless.

"Sure, I always guessed you wanted to write a novel," Nanae went on. "You were constantly reading. **Even when we were in Japan, I remember.** But since we ended up like this, I figured you must have given up on the idea long ago."

"*Since we ended up like this.*" Those words were sad. Too sad. I tried to buoy my spirits by summoning the image of that set of books with worn vermilion bindings that I had first seen in "Yokohama" and that now, after the **Long Island** house was gone, occupied the top shelf of the tall oak bookcase in the living room of this apartment. Whenever I opened one of those books, mustiness wafted up like dust, the smell of old cloth and yellowing paper. Every time, I was drawn into another world, one more real to me than the world I inhabited. That set of books, the first collection of modern Japanese literature, had come out just after Mother was born, and before leaving Japan she had persuaded Grandpa Yokohama—Uncle Yokohama's father, who had a soft spot for her—to give her the set for her girls, who would be growing up in America.

"Well, have you ever written anything in Japanese?" Nanae asked.

It was true, I never had. No, not even in my diary. Even so, I had somehow never doubted that I could write in Japanese.

"No, but I'm sure I could."

"Is it possible to write without ever having done it?"

"I'm sure I can. I'm sure I can write like Sōseki."

"Jesus." A long pause filled with her exhaling smoke.

In the final analysis, did not literature arise out of the deep desire to do something wondrous with a language? In my case, it was a desire to be born once again into my language so as to appreciate and explore it anew. As I spent ungodly amounts of time assembling futile strings of words in languages that remained foreign to me, this desire had grown inexorably, year by year, until my craving to write in Japanese now seemed intense enough to move mountains.

"Jesus," Nanae said again.

"I was always obsessed with Japan, or the Japanese language, and that's where you and I are different," I said defensively. I may have wanted to believe that the intensity of my craving would absolve me of my sin—what I could only conceive of as my sin if I returned to Japan and left her to fend for herself.

After a short silence Nanae said, **"You know, that's not true."** She said it as if to set straight a long-standing misapprehension. "I wasn't hung up on Japanese the way you were, but I was desperate to go back to Japan."

The meaning of her words did not register with me at first.

"I always had the same dream, that I was back in Japan."

"A dream?" *A dream?*

"Yes."

"When was this?"

"All the time. In my dream I would be riding the train with my friends. 'Why didn't you ever come back?' one of them would say. 'You could have come back on this train.' And then I would gnash my teeth and wonder why I never thought to take that train before."

Not once in those twenty years had I imagined that Nanae might be having the same dream as I was. Now that I thought about it, we had never shared how we each felt about being torn from Japan.

"You had that dream over and over?"

"You bet! Over and over and over."

Behind her sullen expression, had Nanae's thoughts, like mine, been drifting to Japan all the while?

"Still, you *couldn't* have wanted to go back as much as I did." I searched my memory for impressions of her in those days. She had often seemed out of sorts, even as a child. For a time after we came to America, her face had worn a perpetual pout, but I never imagined what lay behind it.

"But I tell you that's not true," Nanae replied hotly. "It really isn't. Actually, I felt like I wanted to go back to Japan more than you did."

"Why?"

"You were littler than me, and you always looked happy."

"I wasn't a bit happy."

"But you looked happier."

"But . . ."

Whatever she said, she was the one who had aped American girls without the least shame. In our second year in America, or maybe it was the third, the day school let out for summer vacation she'd come home with a small brown paper bag from the **drugstore** and then slipped out again when Mother wasn't looking and sat under the blazing sun, her back to the house. I opened the front door and called, "What are you doing?" "Mind your own business," she growled. Afterward, I learned that she was doing what American girls did in the summer—**bleach** their hair blonde and turn their skin bronze. It seemed bizarre to me that any girl would want to rub her hair with cotton balls soaked in peroxide and slather her body with gooey **Coppertone Suntan Lotion**. Of course her hair didn't turn golden, and the **Coppertone** promptly turned her skin—already so dark it looked as if she baked it year-round under the **Florida** sun—a dusky hue beyond the tones of East Asian complexions.

But Nanae was undaunted. Every year from then on, she openly anointed herself with peroxide and **Coppertone** in a ceremony that marked the beginning of summer. At the same time, her attic bedroom, into which she had recently moved, took on the appearance of a typical American **teenage** girl's room. Colorful bottles of nail polish stood in front of her three-way mirror, a giant stuffed animal was enshrined on her bed, something called a **peg board** hung on the wall and, one after another, college pennants were pinned to it—where she got them I don't know. She started reading English novels. She developed a crush on a boy named **Scott**. Before her graduation, she pestered Mother into buying her a completely pointless **high school ring**. If she wasn't adapting to life in America better than I was, she was definitely making a determined stab at it.

When I listed all the things she had done in **high school** that had seemed to me, a little patriot, to go against the "Japanese spirit," she let out a yelp of embarrassment.

"All that stuff, **you know me,** I'm pretty silly when it comes to those things. I'm a follow-the-crowd type, you could say. Matter of fact, I tried to follow trends among Japanese kids at the time. You've forgotten. Remember that record?" She said the name of a male singer popular in Japan at the time.

"Oh, him . . ."

"I thought he was cool."

His record cover had horrified me. It was the first photo I had ever seen of a Japanese man cradling an electric guitar, as if he'd turned into an American. That album was a huge hit in Japan, and someone visiting from Tokyo had kindly brought a copy for us sisters. One such gift led to another, and before long we had a decent collection of 45-rpm records from Japan. Father was intolerant of popular music but powerless to stop its flow from across the Pacific. I never approved but eventually grew used to the sight of Japanese men embracing electric guitars, and I learned the words to songs I liked and sang along. Nanae, who naturally developed an interest in the opposite sex before I did, would study record covers of sleazy young female pop stars and then spend hours before her three-way mirror trying to copy their eye makeup. So each in our own way, she and I had tried to remain a part of our generation in Japan, but as our lives in America dragged on, eventually we had to give up the effort.

What a different era that was! To Japanese youngsters brought to New York by their parents now, our intense homesickness would come across as something as antiquated as tales of the Meiji era. Unlike us, they would be surrounded by peers, their numbers continually on the rise. Outside the home they could attend weekend language classes with students who looked like them, and every day at home they could watch the curiously chirpy news announcers on the public broadcasting station, NHK. And, what my adolescent self would have envied most of all, they could tread on actual Japanese soil nearly as often as they wanted. They would never know the anguish I used to feel on seeing Father at **Kennedy**, heading off on a business trip to Tokyo. I always wished, with a longing so deep it hurt, that I could fit inside his suitcase.

"Anyway," said Nanae quietly, "I really wanted to go back to Japan. Remember when Sanae came for a visit with Aunt Utako before starting college?"

"Sure."

"Remember how her mother bought her all those clothes at **Saks**?"

"Yeah, that was amazing."

"I wasn't jealous of her clothes, but it killed me that she got to go to college in Japan."

"Really." I was still unconvinced. "But after you went to Boston, you seemed to enjoy life there all right." A spiteful edge might have crept into my voice as I remembered the brazen way she'd looked and behaved after entering the conservatory, when Mother used to

call her "boy-crazy" or sometimes even "nympho." Her transformation had been shocking to me.

"Yes, after I went to Boston, life did get more enjoyable," she
said, not taking offense.

"You bragged that in six months you **dated** men of ten different
nationalities."

"Oh, come now."

"You did so! I remember. You ticked them off on your fingers—
a Dutchman, a Spaniard, a Brit—and I was impressed that one
was Chinese."

After making a long-distance **collect call** from Boston and going
on and on to Mother about whatever came to mind, she would say,
"Is Minae there?" When I picked up the phone, she would plunge
into topics she couldn't broach with Mother. She conveyed a world
filled with the heady excitement of flirty young love—a world
utterly unknown to our parents, free-spirited for their generation
but in the end, middle-aged people who had come of age in Japan.

Nanae giggled, sounding pleased.

"There was somebody from Okinawa too," I said.

"That's right! He was from Ryukyu University. **How come you
remember him?**"

"I danced with him once."

"Really? **I don't remember.** When was that?"

"Right after I went to Boston, at some party. You introduced us.
'This is my little sister,' you said."

"Did I?"

"Yes, and then I danced with him. He told me I was as light as
a feather."

"No way."

"Oh, but he did. In dead earnest."

"How about that." She was silent a moment. **"It's because you
continued to take ballet lessons, I guess."**

She said that not without a hint of resentment. While we both started taking ballet at the same time, Nanae's lessons had soon come to an end. At a recital where we both danced, on the way home Mother had said bluntly of her performance, "Honestly, that was absolutely wooden." And that put an end to her dancing career, while mine went on for another ten years, long after I dropped the piano.

"I don't think that had anything to do with it. It was an ordinary slow dance, which made the comment even stranger. It sounded so un-Japanese, the kind of sentence you find in a translated novel. 'You're light as a feather.' "

"You thought that at the time, that it sounded like a translation?"

"Of course not! I was flattered and embarrassed."

Nanae had taken me to that party right after I arrived in Boston. There were more Japanese men there than I had ever seen in America, all with black hair and black glasses. The Greater Boston area is chock-full of universities, and back then students from Japan were predominantly graduate students and predominantly male.

"We had scarcity value," Nanae murmured as if to herself, "so maybe it didn't matter which of us he was with."

"Yeah, right," I scoffed. "As if we were so alike he couldn't tell the difference."

Nanae repeated my words, also laughing. "Yeah, right."

What would a stranger have made of us back then? Nobody would have taken us for citizens of the same country, let alone for sisters. Even though we'd grown up together, once Nanae graduated from **high school** and left **Long Island** for the conservatory, we rapidly evolved into very different creatures.

After her freshman year, Nanae came home for summer vacation, and Mother and I went to meet her at the **Port Authority**,

the **Manhattan** bus terminal. **"Hiya!"** she exclaimed, as she stepped
jauntily off the **Greyhound** bus wearing a brightly colored dress
that showed off tanned, shapely, bare arms and legs, and a pair
of heeled sandals decorated with red, yellow, and pink flowers.
She looked **Hispanic** or **Filipino** or **Indian** or **Chinese** or **Vietnamese**,
anything but Japanese. All I could do was stare, goggle-eyed. She
blended into that boisterous crowd of people of different races as
if born to it. A proper Japanese young lady would give the impression of being alien to such an environment, her tense face pale
with powder, her collar tightly buttoned, her hair smoothed down.

"What has that child gone and done to herself?" Mother said to
me, appalled.

Since leaving for the conservatory the previous fall, Nanae had
amazed and entertained me over the phone with stories about dating boys from faraway countries—but I never suspected she herself would become this alien. Come to think of it, when she came
home for the holidays, it was always cold, and she'd been wearing
the conservative clothes and overcoat our parents had paid for.
Now summer was here, and for the first time she was able to step
off the **Greyhound** bus proudly dressed in inexpensive outfits she
had bought with her pocket money. She seemed to sense our reaction. As we walked along, keeping our distance, she strode ahead
as if leading a demonstration.

After that first summer, my eyes slowly grew accustomed to the
way she looked until, four years later, I would be shocked all over
again upon seeing her emerge from that crowd in Tokyo.

In Boston Nanae lived in a dormitory, surrounded by Americans
morning to night, while I, left at home with our parents, with-
drew yet further into the world of Japanese. Those two years had a
decisive impact on how differently we turned out.

I came home from school every day to an empty house. About
the time Nanae moved out, Mother began working at a Japanese

firm in **Manhattan**. "Pretty soon you'll be going off to college too, and your father's salary alone won't be enough for us to live like this anymore." Undoubtedly she chose to act on her aversion to sitting still because the one left at home was me, her low-maintenance daughter. Nanae used to say, "You know the kind of mother who puts out snacks the minute you get home from school? I always wanted one of those." Not me. From an early age, I never minded Mother's absence. I could just go on with my reading. It was far better than having her voice ring through the house with chores for me to do: "Fold the laundry!" "Set the table!" "Polish your father's shoes!"

In the blessedly silent house I devoured Japanese novels. As soon as I came home from school, I would throw down my textbooks and grab a **Coke** from the refrigerator, rip open a box of **Cracker Jacks** I'd picked up at the **drugstore** on my way home, then curl up on one end of the sofa with a book. I always sat downstairs in the living room, not up in my room, perhaps because I enjoyed monopolizing the space with Nanae no longer around practicing the piano. With one hand I would reach out absently to pat Della, who, lonely from having been left on her own all day, would come over and nuzzle me with her pointy nose. I never looked up. My spirit sought salvation in the world of the Japanese language; the outer world was not just unnecessary but a hindrance. The light coming through the **Venetian blinds** would gradually darken, but I kept reading, hardly noticing. Sometime after sundown I would become aware that the only light in the house was coming from the lamp on the **side table**. About then the telephone would ring, Mother calling to say, "I'm just leaving now, so put on enough rice for the three of us, will you? And wash some lettuce and make a salad." Shaking my head clear, still immersed in the life of the novel, I would go around the suddenly chilly house turning on lights and closing all the **blinds** before heading into the kitchen to start the rice.

The Japanese newspapers Father brought home from the office and the magazines that arrived at regular intervals from Japan were nearly unreadable to me, nor did I want to read them. All I saw were strings of complicated *kanji* connected by *hiragana*. But the musty books with vermilion bindings supplied phonetic readings alongside *kanji*, and the stories in those books were fascinating to a young girl like me. Though I didn't learn how to pronounce common business terms in the newspaper until I was in my twenties, I easily mastered all the colorful and arcane words that I encountered in those novels, words that only enriched my yearning for the true life I was sure I would live once I went back to Japan.

Someday, somehow, I will miraculously transform into a beautiful young woman with lustrous black hair cascading down my back. Picturesque scenes will unfold before my eyes. I will know a life of wealth. I will suffer poverty. Men will stand in line to have a glimpse of me. Each moment will be filled with intense anticipation . . . How dismal in comparison was the reality of my life as an American **high school student**! My yearning, I later realized, was a yearning for a world given shape by art; and as that yearning must be part of the universal human need to make sense of life—and in so doing to come to appreciate the inestimable gift of one's life—then all around me, right in my **high school**, there had to have been other girls engrossed like me in novels and driven by the selfsame yearning. But my obsession blinded me. In my mind the gap between my lackluster reality and a world shaped by art was translated into the chasm created by the Pacific Ocean.

Before long the Japan I yearned for was no longer the Japan I knew.

As I communed with the musty volumes of modern Japanese literature, my yearning focused on the Japan that had existed before I was born. Mother's old cloth-bound scrapbooks, which she had sentimentally included in the boxes shipped by sea, became my treasured possessions. They contained colorful illustrations she had cut from girls' magazines long ago when she was about my age, showing young women in a variety of outfits and activities: one in a white-and-indigo summer *yukata*, holding a round fan to her face; one in a smart black dress with a small matching hat, praying in church; one in a bright New Year's kimono, raising a lacquer cup to her lips; one in a cream-colored satin negligee, seated in an elegant chair, crocheting. As Mother must have done thirty years before, I painstakingly copied the old-fashioned illustrations and colored them.

And then there were the songs.

One afternoon, I noticed an unfamiliar box on the record shelf in the living room. It was a set of LP albums of Japanese golden oldies. Perhaps Father had picked it up on his last business trip to Japan. Had he been overcome by nostalgia? I wondered. Or did he consider the songs that had been popular in the age of the Victrola, back when that was a luxury item, to be more highbrow than popular music of our day?

That night I went into his study—the porch had been remodeled into a study for him—and asked, "Did you buy these, Papa?"

When he saw what I was holding, his expression took on a tinge of embarrassment. "Yes, I did," he said, then resumed clipping articles from the **New York Times**.

When my parents were out of the house, I put a record on the phonograph and was struck by an inexplicable sense of nostalgia myself. One record led to the next. Several were familiar to me because Mother sometimes sang them around the kitchen, humming when she forgot the words. Most of them I could never have heard before, songs sung in high-pitched voices to clunky accompaniments, and yet they moved me in unexpected ways. The selections ranged from postwar boogie-woogie all the way back to queer prewar songs with lyrics like "*We dance to jazz and drink liqueur all night"* and *"If the moon were a mirror, I'd look at it every night to find your reflection,"* sung in a warbling falsetto. And then, over a crackling recording, there was a song sung by a geisha—*"Growing up on an island, a girl of sixteen, falling in love. . . ."*—that brought on a rush of memories of my grandmother, who I was told had once been a geisha. She had known nothing of Western musical scales; had mispronounced borrowed words, saying "pus" for "bus" and "piscuit" for "biscuit"; and wouldn't touch butter, milk, or even ice cream, let alone beef or pork, because of the old taboo on eating four-legged beasts. More and more memories of that woman old enough to be my great-grandmother came to me through those antiquated sounds, making me feel that in her I might find the Japan that I longed for so ardently, a Japan untainted by impurities from the West, a Japan that had never existed, not even for her.

Eventually, I became so consumed by this imagined past that my own parents struck me as frivolously modern. Yet I myself never suspected how obsolete I was becoming; I simply thought I was being Japanese. I took considerable pride in it too. Japanese gentlemen of Father's age who visited the house all said the same thing: "Your daughter is very Japanese—not Americanized in the least!" Hiding my pleasure, I would offer them teacakes, my fingertips neatly aligned.

Meanwhile, Nanae was on a different path.

Upon graduation from **high school**, I had gone on to study painting in Boston. Nanae and I would share an apartment, it had been decided long before. We moved into a charming old brick townhouse. Nanae was in her junior year at the conservatory and could no longer stay at the dormitory, and our parents didn't want either of us to live alone. I didn't mind. From the time I was a little girl I'd never been physically strong, and the thought of sharing a dormitory room with robust American girls—and having to speak English to them—terrified me. However, I soon realized that I'd have been far better off having a robust American girl as a roommate than my sister. We each saw the other as weird, and for the two years we lived together we fought constantly.

"**You are so stuck-up. I hate it.**"

"Even Mother said she was embarrassed to be seen walking with you."

"**I don't care.**"

Nanae, knowing she was no match for me in a quarrel, would cross her legs on the black vinyl couch, lean back, and blow smoke toward the ceiling. Her legs, fresh out of her boots, practically gave off steam. Winter in Boston was far harsher than on **Long Island**. A ten-minute walk through snow-piled streets would leave your fingers and toes numb, and then the moment you entered a heated room, you felt your blood start to circulate, as if you had stepped into a hot tub. Seated primly on the **ottoman**, I would glance at Nanae and sigh loud enough for her to hear. She would continue to blow smoke at the ceiling.

Looking back, I would say there was something eminently youthful about her way of smoking then, something self-conscious and rebellious. These days she smoked like any woman smoker.

Why did I think living with her would be easy? No matter what household chore I asked her to do, "I'll do it later," she would say from the piano bench. When she was done practicing, she would make up her face with care, spending easily five minutes on mascara alone, before throwing on her coat and rushing off on a date. "Sorry, have to go!" The main thing I remembered about that time was my determination never to live with her again.

"Yeah, you're right. Those years in Boston, I did enjoy them," she said, reflecting. "But even then, I wanted to go back. I always did, always."

"Huh."

"The first time I went back, all I could think was, *Finally, finally, I'm back in Japan!* When I practiced in the annex at 'Yokohama,' I was near the street, and I could hear the call of the vendor who'd give you a pack of facial tissues in exchange for old newspapers. It reminded me of how tofu vendors used to call out in the morning when we were kids."

"I remember. With their bugle."

"That's right. When I heard that call, it would hit me. I'd think, *I'm really in Japan*, and break down sobbing. Someone unsentimental like you might not be able to understand."

I let that pass. "So around then, you didn't especially dislike Japan."

"No."

"You wanted to go back."

"Yes."

"So it was after that . . ."

After that summer, she'd stayed away from Japan for a long time. Later, as I became increasingly aware of how long our parents had stretched out our time in the States, I saw that summer as the turning point in our family's history. If things had gone differently that summer, a more normal fate might have awaited us.

I sighed.

"What's wrong?"

"I can't help wondering how we ever ended up like this."

"What's that supposed to mean? **Are you blaming me or something?**"

"No."

It was water under the bridge. I did not wish Nanae were the sort of person that her boyfriend's family would have approved of, nor did I wish our parents had raised her to be that sort of person. It was just that thoughts of how our family went off the rails always brought to mind that disastrous first visit back to Japan.

"I only meant if things hadn't happened that way, everything would have been different . . ."

"Well, of course." Her voice was still sharp.

I hastened to add, "Not just for you, I mean for the whole family." If soon after that summer we'd all gone back permanently to Japan, everything would have been different. That might have been wishful thinking on my part, but it was an idea I could not shake. A steady diet of Japanese food might have kept Father's diabetes in check; concern about what people would say might have restrained Mother so that she merely had an extramarital fling. They might have ended up an old married couple in a Tokyo suburb, watching a big bright television together. "One thing's for sure. If we'd gone back then, we'd have a house in Tokyo now."

"Yes, a house." Her voice suddenly changed, became wistful. "That's right . . . Back then a house in Tokyo would have been affordable."

"Yes, it would."

Oh, how I had wanted a house in Japan!

If they'd sold the **Colonial** house on **Long Island** back then, they could have at least afforded a house in Tokyo much like our old one, complete with garden. An authentic Japanese house was what I had wanted—one where you passed through a latticed gate and under the branches of a pine tree and then through a garden with shrubs before arriving at the sliding front door. That's what I had always wanted, but my parents would probably have chosen a boring, vaguely Western-looking house painted white, possibly with bay windows. Even that would have been something. As long as we had a house in Tokyo, then instead of hopping from one American college to another I could have gone quietly back to Japan and probably eventually married. Or, content in the knowledge that I had a home there to return to whenever I chose, I might have been freed of my quixotic longing for Japan and taken a more rational look at my options.

"Think how different it would have been if they'd had a house in Tokyo," I said. Even now, how much easier this conversation would be if I knew that Nanae had a place to go home to.

It was her turn to sigh. "How crazy is that, to come to America and lose our house. **Don't you think?**"

"Absolutely."

Twenty years ago the dollar had seemed unassailable. The money from the sale of our Tokyo house lost value when it crossed the Pacific, turning into barely enough for a down payment on the house on **Long Island**. We accepted this stoically, the yen-dollar exchange rate seeming to us an eternal truth. But one day the dollar began to fall precipitously, and, at the same time, Japanese land prices began to soar beyond all reason. Soon the sale of the New York house surrounded by greenery wouldn't fetch enough for a decent-sized condominium—known by that peculiar misnomer マンション *manshon*—let alone a Tokyo house, where the neighbor's kitchen is right under your nose. Moreover, our parents, who equated a dollar-based pension with a life on easy street anywhere in the world, had set aside little or nothing for their old age. One reason Mother left Father without hesitation was surely that their plan to spend their golden years in Tokyo had gone up in smoke.

Nanae heaved another sigh.

In any case, if her life had taken a different turn that summer, the two of us wouldn't have ended up living abroad, our "marriageable years" (twenty-five was the decent upper limit for Japanese women) slipping away while we carried on interminable long-distance conversations over the phone.

"**Punka baby**, you're so lucky. You don't have to worry about a thing. You've got a good mommy."

The female cat had evidently climbed onto her lap. Wagahai, the tom, did nothing but beg for food, and **Punka**, his sister, did nothing but beg for affection. Did female cats in general tend to be that way, was it **Punka**'s individual personality, or had she taken after her mistress? There was no way of knowing, but Nanae would often ask my opinion.

"Our parents were pretty strange to begin with," I said. *Time to hang* up, I was thinking, yet I couldn't bring myself to end the conversation just yet.

"You said it!" Her tone was bitter. She paused to light another cigarette before going on. "How dare she call me a nympho? **What nerve! Look at *her* now."**

I had said "our parents," but Nanae only had Mother in mind. In revenge for having been called a "nympho" in the past, lately she had taken to turning the word against her.

"Indeed." It had been galling to see her leave our nearly blind father on his own at home while she stayed out late after work, becoming oddly young, as if her aging process had reversed. But that wasn't what I had wanted to say.

"That's not what I meant, though. I meant that they weren't in any hurry to go back to Japan. You don't find many Japanese in their shoes willing to prolong their stay the way they did." After that fateful summer, they made no effort to return.

"No, you don't. Definitely not. They were different. **That's why we ended up like this."**

"You know?"

"You're right. They weren't like other Japanese. The Murakamis have been here a long time too, and they're also a bit different. That makes them easier to get along with, though."

In retrospect, our parents' decisiveness in leaving Japan—selling the Tokyo house, distributing household goods among acquaintances, shaking the dust of Japan from their feet—was the decisiveness of people not coming back anytime soon. Their infatuation with America was shared by almost all who had lived through the

postwar period in Japan, though in varying degrees. But also intertwined with their decisiveness was the sense of liberation they
must each have felt on shedding the shackles of their past. Their
memories of their homeland bore the weight of the past going
back generations on both sides, childhoods that had been far from
happy, and a marriage greeted not with blessings but with out-
rage. The one person who would have welcomed them back with
unconditional joy, my grandmother, had died a few years before
we pulled up stakes. There was nothing left to lure them back.

After a brief silence, I said, "Sometimes I think if we'd been
boys . . ."

"Boys?" You've got to be kidding, her voice said. "**No thanks.
I have no penis envy, thank God.** What about you, sweetums? **Huh?
I hope you don't have any either, Punka baby.**"

"Who does?"

If I didn't know what country I would be born in, what race
or class I would belong to, or what talents I would or would not
have, then, given the choice, I would definitely choose to be born
male. Yet having been born a girl in an urban middle-class Japanese
family, I hadn't suffered any hardships to make me curse my fate.
When I was a child, the hunched shoulders of men hurrying home-
ward at dusk had seemed sad and dreary, and little as I was, I had
thanked whomever one thanks that I wasn't expected to work like
them in the future. But Nanae's and my being in constant touch
on the telephone like this was sad in its own way, and inseparable
from the fact that we were sisters and not brothers.

"But if we'd been boys," I continued, "I'll bet they would have
sent us to college in Japan." Mother used to say it was a good thing
we were girls so we didn't have to go to college in Japan. "Then
they'd have had to go back too, like it or not. I think they kept
putting it off because in the back of their minds they thought
they'd go when one of us got married."

Nanae thought this over before replying. "You're probably right."

Because we were girls, even in Japan they had raised us with little concern for our grades in school. We were only expected to become "women of accomplishment" and marry, preferably right after college.

She continued sarcastically, **"Well, they should be very happy then. They ended up staying here almost forever. Father's still here . . . whether he likes it or not."**

"Right."

"One thing I'll never forget." Resentment filled her voice again. "When I went to Boston, Mother told me to find myself someone proper. She meant, you don't have to graduate from a Japanese university, but at least marry a proper Japanese. **Too bad. Things didn't turn out the way she wanted."**

Japanese expats had always automatically gone along with Japanese social norms. Parents, if their stay in America was extended, had a clear choice. Their sons they would send back home for high school to prepare them for Japanese university; to be employable, sons had to be groomed to become full-fledged members of Japanese society. Their daughters, on the other hand, they could keep with them and send to local schools, intending someday to marry them off to well-employed Japanese men, here or there. Even in the rare cases where a daughter ventured farther away, once the father was ordered home they would take her back with them, often over her protests. If she insisted on staying, they had no compunction about making up a story that she was living with a family friend or in some fictitious all-girls' dormitory. The extent to which they conformed to the dictates of Japanese society ultimately determined their daughter's fate, and often by extension theirs as well.

Our parents, content to keep putting off their return to Japan, never bothered to bring us up in conformity with those dictates.

Perhaps Father had read too many foreign books. Perhaps Mother had seen too many foreign films. Even though they took it for granted that their daughters would marry Japanese men, they were generous, lenient, and even obtuse regarding our gradual deviation from Japanese norms. Moreover, they had not considered the fact that Nanae was highly impressionable and quick to take on the coloring of her American surroundings.

"**Too bad**," Nanae repeated. "**I tried. But it didn't work out.**"

That was definitely true. It definitely hadn't worked out.

I thought of Nanae after she went to Boston. The Nanae who in her high school days had aped the girls around her with peroxide and **Coppertone** had still been the Nanae we'd always known, shy, withdrawn, and often cross. Her transformation into someone we barely recognized, the transformation that first became shockingly apparent to Mother and me at Port Authority, began after she moved out of the house. In the dormitory she spoke English day in and day out with her **roommate**, an aspiring opera singer named **Cindy** who had bright **bleached** hair that she did up in curlers every night. Nanae's English improved dramatically. And, whether or not speaking English more fluently had anything to do with it, as her English improved, she became more emboldened to express her young womanhood. Her miniskirts got shorter and louder in color, her makeup heavier; she took up smoking; she even let her nails grow a little, very daring for a piano major. The Nanae I remembered from elementary school days, who would skin her knees climbing trees like a boy while I stayed fearfully on the ground, was long gone. She dated a merry-go-round of men. I prudishly disapproved of the sudden changes, thinking she had turned vulgar. Mother too was displeased—"That child is completely Americanized!"

Even so, and rather unfortunately for Nanae, she wasn't all that Americanized. Perhaps in a superficial way she was, but not in any deeper sense. Her adolescence had begun in Japan, for one thing. And for another, she was and always had been a clinging vine. What became clear when she left home, ironically, was how tied she was to Mother, how much she needed her approval, even for a Japanese daughter. She had a colorful array of admirers, but the ones she became serious about were always Japanese, and she brought them home for weekends and holidays, knowing Mother would be pleased. She had moved to Boston in September, and at **Thanksgiving** and **Christmas** she came back with a fellow piano major. The next time it was someone else, and then someone else, and so on. Each new beau was welcomed by the family, and mother and daughter would get together in private and assess him. Nanae seemed happy.

Not long after she and I began to share an apartment, Nanae met the guy who would be the source of all the trouble. On weekends he would show up with his violin and a bottle of **California red wine** tucked under one arm, having taken a bus across the **Charles River**. He was a student at **Harvard Business School** and had been first violinist in his university orchestra in Japan; he and Nanae bonded over music. I was sick unto death of Nanae's practicing, but I would listen, wineglass in hand, as they went over Brahms's Violin Sonata no. 1 again and again.

"He thinks his English is so good, it kills me!" Nanae said to me. "What's so funny is he rolls his 'l's. He goes **Harrro. Harrro! . . . Oh, I wish he wouldn't roll his 'r's . . . or 'l's, rather. But as for his violin, now, that's a totally different story. I'd say he's quite good. His bowing** is very professional," she pronounced, as if she were an expert.

Though flashy in appearance, her citizenship outwardly impossible to tell, Nanae was as devoted to **"Harrro"** as any Japanese girl in love could be. She knitted him a woolen scarf, laughed at all his jokes, and even gave him a **wake-up call** every morning after he claimed that alarm clocks didn't do the trick. Never mind that she herself was a perennial late sleeper, as Grandpa Yokohama had

noted; Mother used to say, "You couldn't pry that child out of bed
with a crowbar." Somehow she made herself get up early every
morning and telephone him. "Good morning," she would chirp.
"Time to get up!" and then go back to sleep. My bed was next to
hers, so I would be rudely awakened and forced, while she was
back getting her beauty sleep, to start my day out of sorts. I complained, but she paid me no mind.

Harrro seemed fond of her. "Of all the girlfriends I've ever had,
you're the prettiest," he once told her within my earshot—a lame
and tacky compliment that nonetheless pleased her. He must
have been receiving a substantial allowance from his parents since
he took her out to dinner regularly, often at Japanese restaurants,
the two or three that Boston boasted at the time.

I didn't much like him. She wasn't in love with everything about
him either. He was good-looking enough but had a stocky build,
whereas her ideal was the **willowy**, *fin de siècle* poetic type. **"I don't
care about his height. I just wish he looked more delicate, more
sensitive, you know."** It also seemed to bother her that he had no
interests apart from music. **"I also wish he read more. Literature
and stuff."**

Yet, most importantly, he got along famously with Mother.
As soon as he and Nanae became involved, Nanae brought him
home. Father, his face flushed from one beer, would tell the same
old stories—causing Nanae to glance at me as if to say *Oh no, not
again!*—and flush redder with pleasure, happy just to be conversing with a Japanese man who had yet to turn into a company
man. In truth, he was no fonder of this grinning fellow than any
of the others he had met. Nanae wasn't concerned about his reaction, anyway. It was Mother's reaction that counted, and as I said,
she and **Harrro** got along exceptionally well. The first night, he
praised her cooking, the way young men do when they know they
can endear themselves to a woman by praising her cooking and

having second and third helpings. He also engaged her in conversation and listened to all she had to say. From then on Mother was so gone on him you'd have thought he was *her* boyfriend. Nanae looked on with a mixture of happiness, pride, and jealousy, but in the main, seeing how Mother took to him seemed to intensify her devotion to him.

From then on, she would bring him home at every school break, however short, and he would eat, sleep, and even have his laundry done at our house, departing with an air of benevolence as if he were the one who had conferred a favor on us. Soon the word "marriage" was popping up with even greater frequency in Nanae's conversations with Mother.

Our parents could hardly have asked for more. He was genuinely Japanese, he had graduated from a prestigious Japanese university, and he had a place in Japanese society. Moreover, once he got his Harvard **MBA**, he was planning to spend two years at a major American accounting firm before returning to Japan to work in his father's firm. For our parents, who wanted to see Nanae married but weren't eager to have her leave right after graduation and who wanted to prolong their own American stay a little more, he was a godsend. In two years I would finish art school, so the timing was perfect. He was understanding and supportive of Nanae's music. He spoke English. His future was secure. His family seemed well off—a good deal more so than ours. Studying abroad was a rare privilege in those days, and while the other young men Nanae had brought home to Mother, even the musicians, had also been almost too good to be true, none satisfied every possible requirement in a husband quite the way he did.

In May, when Nanae graduated from the conservatory, **Harrro** got his **MBA**. Early in June he went back to Japan for a visit, in part to pay his respects to clients of his father's firm, and she followed him to meet his parents. The meeting could not have gone worse.

"They don't want a daughter-in-law who smokes, they said, and that turned him against me too," Nanae explained after coming back, puffing on a cigarette. "**Well, tough! I'm not going to quit smoking just for them!**"

On seeing her pinched, drawn face, I thought it was only natural if his parents didn't want a daughter-in-law who looked so fox-like, but on second thought I realized it was only after the breakup and the suicide attempt that she started looking like that.

"Argh. They couldn't have been more *petit bourgeois!*" As she told it, his CPA father often received gifts from clients, and the living room was packed not just with golf trophies but with brand-name porcelain ornaments and glassware, all brightly lit by a fluorescent chandelier, of all the inelegant things, with the whole collection crowned by a huge color television, bigger than any she had ever seen in America, planted squarely in the front of the room. In other words, I inferred, the house, though large, was a typical postwar Japanese house, tacky and overflowing with stuff. "**Everything about it was gaudy and cheap. Oh, the curtains, the carpet. . . . And you think they had better taste when it came to Japanese rooms? No, sir. What do you see in the** *tokonoma*? A shiny, brand-new Seiko clock! In the *tokonoma*! **Think of it! Not even an antique!**" She was bitter—and hurt—and once she got started, which was often, she could not stop. Her aversion to the house had been almost visceral—a mirror image of the reaction she must have evoked in **Harrro**'s parents.

He was a cad to disappear after reaping all the advantages of a young woman's affection, not to mention free piano accompaniment and generous hospitality from her family. Yet it was true he never had made a promise to marry her. He had only agreed to introduce her to his parents. "Nanae, you're so American," he used to say, less because he had no wish to marry her, I thought, than as a roundabout way of preparing her for what might lie ahead. What became of him after they broke up, no one knows.

After this fiasco, when Nanae came home to **Long Island** in shame, Mother made no attempt to hide her fury and her disappointment. However, beneath her reaction lay a troubling realization, which helps explain why she acquiesced in Nanae's decision to give up the piano. Seeing a Japanese man flee from her daughter had changed everything: getting Nanae married, which had always seemed a matter of course to her, now loomed as a challenge. And for that reason, it manifested itself to her as the one thing she must somehow achieve, especially because, in the term used by her generation, her daughter was now "damaged goods." The target of her passion shifted from Nanae's music to Nanae's marriage. She had always had it in mind, but now she fixated on it. Nanae needed to be recast as a proper young lady and decently married off to a Japanese man.

The discord between Nanae and Mother only grew deeper after Nanae began studying at a **Manhattan** art school, a place that attracted outlandish libertines from around the world and that to many Americans might as well have been Sodom and Gomorrah. Mother had no inkling of just how far removed such a place was from concepts like "damaged goods," "a proper young lady," and "a decent marriage"—concepts that were rapidly becoming *passé* even in Japan. Nanae developed an allergy to Japan that ebbed and flowed, and it was several years before mother and daughter gave up on the idea of "a decent marriage" a time that was filled with tears, abusive language, and, finally, resignation.

Nanae was no doubt conflicted, on the one hand wanting to make the kind of marriage her mother planned for her and, on the other, not wanting her life to go at all as her mother planned. By the time she left home and began living with a German photographer named **Karl**, Mother was willing for her to marry any decent man, not necessarily a Japanese man. **Karl** at least included doctors and politicians among his family. But in time Nanae broke up with him too, and continued to go out with a hodgepodge of men. Though professing annoyance at Mother's interference, she would telephone home whenever she got a new boyfriend and talk for hours, continually raising Mother's hopes only to dash them again. When she felt like it, she would bring her boyfriend home and, no wiser for all she'd been through, feed him Mother's home cooking. By the time she fell in love with a Japanese cellist, someone I got to know fairly well, she was nearly thirty. He was the second son of a wealthy family in Tokyo. Mother poured a terrifying amount of zeal into their relationship, and when it ended, she lacked the spirit to get angry. That was it for her. After that, as if she'd finally come to her senses, she showed no more interest in Nanae's love life—or in Nanae.

And so, on the verge of thirty, Nanae finally learned to confront men on her own terms.

The intensity of Mother's fixation on getting Nanae safely married was a source of constant amazement to me. It involved something beyond my ken: the love-hate relationship between a mother and her firstborn daughter. It also involved Nanae's clinging disposition, which only served to intensify the messiness of that relationship. Then there was Mother's own limitation that did not allow her to picture any future for Nanae except marriage; there was also the broader limitation set by the era she'd grown up in. Having to marry off a daughter who was half-Americanized only raised the stakes. Yet none of those things was enough to explain the fierceness of her fixation. There must have been something larger than herself at issue, something not even she understood. How much that fierceness had to do with her difficult childhood, I could not tell. All I knew for sure was that it somehow reflected a desperate need to reassert herself as a woman vicariously, through Nanae: Mother's sudden indifference toward Nanae's love life coincided with a resurgence of her own.

During all those years, as I moved from place to place, I was never left in peace. Wherever I might be, I found myself listening to their grievances over the telephone, caught up in their endless feud. I consoled myself thinking I was fortunate not to have been born first, knowing that Mother would have been sure to meddle in my love life too—though not as much, for unlike Nanae, I didn't have it in me to share such things with her.

"Do you think I'm wrong?" Mother would say over the phone, her voice raised. I could picture her eyes flashing. When she calmed down, she would speak in a worn voice. "What makes that child the way she is? Who does she take after?"

"It's because you spoiled her."

"No, I didn't. I brought you both up the same way. Some people are just born like that."

My phone conversations with Mother were relatively short, but as soon as I hung up, the phone would ring again.

"She called you up, right? What did she say?" Nanae's voice would be low and aggrieved.

I lived in California for a while and had to beg Nanae not to forget the three-hour time difference, or she'd be waking me up at the crack of dawn. I didn't have the wit to unplug the phone, or perhaps telephones back then didn't unplug. The three of us had become stiflingly close, as if we lived on a desert island.

Father was on the outside of all of this. He had a childlike quality—or, to put it another way, a kind of softness—far removed from destructive drama. None of us wanted him involved in this interminable feud. It seemed too sordid for him, and we knew that even if we turned to him, he wouldn't be any help. While Mother and Nanae went at it over Nanae's behavior and receding marriage prospects, he read the paper and watched television in solitude, and whenever he caught sight of Nanae or me on a visit home, he would simply say, "Get to bed early, now."

After giving up on Nanae's marriage, Mother proceeded to dump her own husband. The process that led up to this took a few years. Nanae and I never realized how far things had progressed until her lover was relocated to Singapore and she announced to us that she was following him there. Father's health was declining, and she took advantage of one prolonged hospital stay to take action. She had him whisked from the hospital to a nursing home, put the **Long Island** house on the market, and, as soon as a buyer appeared and signed the papers, took off. For some time Nanae and I were dazed, unable to absorb what had happened.

I lied, made up ridiculous stories to tell Father as he sat on the edge of his bed. "Mother wants to work in Japan. She says she'll be back soon." He didn't answer. That his hair was only half gray made me ache more. It was just as well that the long hospitalization had dulled his mental powers.

Nanae was right: *things with the family didn't turn out the way Mother wanted.* Then again, they didn't turn out the way anyone wanted.

Meanwhile, over the years, Nanae and I had grown steadily closer. She made the changes that were necessary if she was to make a life for herself. She got over her allergy to Japan and, partly because she lived in **Manhattan**, saw more Japanese people on a regular basis than I did. She still didn't look very Japanese, but she no longer affected a style that raised Japanese eyebrows. I too started to accept America. And, though separated geographically, we were increasingly bound together by the phone line.

I suddenly became aware of how long we'd been talking. The phone bill was mounting, Nanae had to go out soon, and I needed to tell her much more but couldn't. I felt the weight of everything on me. Switching the hot receiver to my other ear, I glanced out the window and saw tiny snowflakes in the air—the first snow. "Sure enough, it's snowing," I said, but Nanae wasn't listening.

"You know what I think? I think she should have told us *why* we were supposed to get married. She just kept harping on it, so I couldn't think **rationally** about marriage, and somewhere along the way I started to rebel against the whole idea."

"You mean she should have explained that unless we got married we'd have to support ourselves?" Having grown up without any notion that we needed to work, this perfectly ordinary fact had not occurred to either of us until recently. But it had probably never occurred to Mother either as she brought us up. She worked because she wanted to, not because she had to.

"**That's right.** If I'd realized something so basic, that being single meant supporting myself, I think I'd have been more serious about finding a husband."

After all Nanae had put us through, I didn't know what to say to this admission.

"Either that or I'd have gotten serious about finding a way to support myself. One or the other."

"Uh-huh."

"Even with the piano, **you know, I gotta earn my dough**—maybe I should have approached it with that in mind."

But neither of us had understood this. We thought the point of all our lessons had been to make us "women of accomplishment" and nothing more.

"**Juilliard** is full of **Orientals** now, you know," she went on. "Girls, all of them, too."

I had just been reading a magazine article about that very topic. Asian and **Asian American** girls . . . My first thought was, *Their mothers are living out their dreams through them.*

As if reading my mind, Nanae then said, "**Asian mothers** are really something. **They're worse than Jewish mothers, I hear.**"

Asian mothers . . . I pictured Mother, tall, slender, and elegant in a pretty kimono, accompanying Nanae to "Yokohama" for her piano lesson. Washed by the waves of time and wrapped in the mantle of words in musty books, my memory of her tall, slender, kimono-clad figure had taken on a poetic aura, touched by the lingering scent of a youth full of hymns, hilltop views of the harbor, and innocent romance. That lingering scent was somehow more quintessentially Western than anything I ever encountered after leaving Japan.

Maidens' voices raised in song came soaring across spacious blue skies:

> *Kono michi wa itsuka kita michi*
> *Aa, sō da yo*
> *Okāsama to basha de itta yo*

> *This road I've traveled once before*
> *O yes! I remember*
> *Carriage rides with Mother*

How far removed those poetic images were from the drabness of the expression **"Asian mothers"**! Nanae, it seemed to me, was entirely unmindful of the fact that her own mother was an **Asian mother.**

"Good thing you quit piano early," she said.

"I never liked it."

"You weren't that bad, you know."

"I never liked it."

"Well, you also quit taking ballet lessons, which you liked."

I didn't reply.

"I used to drive you there all the time, remember?"

"So you did, whenever I was late." *And somehow without complaining*, I added in my mind.

"You know, I wasn't such a bad sister after all."

"Thank you," I said in a hurry and slammed the car door, then flew down the narrow concrete steps. I quickly changed from my street clothes and entered the **studio**, where class was already under way. One wall was a floor-to-ceiling mirror, and fluorescent lights shone brightly down on the dozen or so neighborhood girls in leotards at the barre. A Chopin etude, the exercise music, was being dutifully played by a quiet brunette woman on a piano in the corner. The instructor, a Russian man—elderly, bald, and probably a Jewish defector—called out our steps with a heavy accent. The quality of my ballet lessons was, naturally, several notches below that of Nanae's piano lessons in **Manhattan**, but I well knew I lacked aptitude, so that was fine with me.

Our instructor's movements were still very precise; he must once have performed on a stage bathed in dazzling white light, and here he was keeping body and soul together in a basement like this with pupils like us—even as a child, I found it sad. After our exercises at the barre, as I shyly hid behind the other girls for the center floor practice, the instructor would motion to me and say, **"Minae, please,"** holding out one hand and bowing from the waist, his gestures as polite and graceful as if he were extending an invitation to a lady at a ball—and for a moment, the basement studio of painted concrete would be transformed into a Romanov palace hung with splendid brocades and lit by flickering candles.

One of the ballet pupils was a tiny Chinese girl a full head shorter than me who wore her hair in long braids and was always accompanied by her mother, a stout woman in a worn gray overcoat. The mother, who we somehow knew had fled Shanghai before her daughter was born, looked as if she belonged in a **Chinese restaurant** or **Chinese laundry**. So it was fascinating how, when the instructor talked to her, he always switched from halting English to fluent French, which she also spoke. They would talk in an undertone, almost secretively, with an air of buoyant excitement. Often from a corner of the room we would hear the intimate, seductive laughter of an old Russian man and a Chinese woman no longer young, laughter that contained the solidarity and knowing resignation of fellow survivors. The rest of us, unable to join in, stared at our reflections in the mirror and sensed the hopeless smallness of our lives.

I had just started learning French, and those conversations were my first exposure to the genuine spoken language. At the same time, in a way that conversations between two native speakers never could have, they afforded me a glimpse of the lost glory of French, the lingua franca of the past. The whispered exchanges between those two exotic beings left a lasting impression on me, perhaps implanting the idea of a perfect way to escape English later in life.

"Sure, I liked ballet, but there was just no point in going on with it."

"Not with your physique . . . **oops**. Well, you know what I mean."

I didn't take offense. I knew my head was way too big, for one thing.

"I'm glad I quit painting too." I had gone to art school to study oil painting, but only as a means of avoiding the English language, so it was little wonder I never felt committed to it.

"That's right, you studied painting too. *Mein Gott. Mon Dieu, mon Dieu*, we've covered almost all the branches of art."

"Yes, how ridiculous. . . ."

"I even took some violin lessons, remember?"

"Really ridiculous."

The path behind girls like us was littered with the detritus of lessons that had never come to anything, like heaps of the dead.

Unexpectedly, as if to balance the picture, up from the recesses of my mind came a memory of happiness. It must have been after a piano recital that Nanae and I were both in as small girls. *Ooh, it tickles! The bobby pin on the ribbon in my hair. Nanae's ribbon is just like mine—so wide and pretty, white with red and pink roses. Our skirts are the color of honeydew, and when we twirl on our toes they billow*

out. *We both have a big bouquet of flowers too—freesia, somebody said.*
Papa's taking our picture! Click, click. *The spring sunshine feels so nice,*
and Mama's laughing. Happiness almost too great to bear.

"It would've been fine if we'd been in Japan, I think. Taking all
sorts of lessons, then getting married . . . like Sanae." Nanae's voice
now bore a faraway quality.

The precious, gemlike child of wealthy parents, our friend
with the rather common name 早苗 Sanae had been guaranteed
every sort of happiness from the day she was born; our less common names, 奈苗 Nanae and 美苗 Minae, were variations on
hers and had been given to us in hopes that we might somehow
share in her happiness. She too of course had studied piano and
ballet, and by the time she attended her coming-of-age ceremony
at twenty, dressed in a *furisode* kimono with long flowing sleeves,
she also had certificates of mastery in tea ceremony and flower
arrangement. Now she was married, living happily on the remodeled second floor of Aunt Utako's house, not with a pair of cats
but with a husband and two children, a boy and a girl, having
gone straight from being a proper young lady to being a proper
young wife.

"Somehow we got off track after coming to America. Now here
we are, forced to pay our own way." Nanae's voice had come down
to earth.

I always wondered why Nanae had picked sculpture of all
things, surely the art form least likely to provide a living wage.
Mother used to let off steam to me—"What could that child be
thinking!"—and, in the next moment, make excuses for her: "But
then, you know your sister. She can't think ahead." I would cry out
in frustration, "She can't think ahead, or she's just plain stupid?
What's the difference?"

"You're in good shape, anyway," Nanae was saying. "You wised
up and quit all those lessons, and now you'll be able to support

yourself doing what suits you. **Punka baby, your aunt is real smart after all. Not a dummy like me.**"

"Yeah, well, . . ." I said.

After hanging around a couple of college campuses, I had somehow landed in this Ivy League university and then continued on to graduate school. That was a felicitous development that neither my parents nor I had ever envisioned. Thanks to the disciplined academic environment here, French had turned into something more than another idle pursuit. Now all I had to do was pass my orals and I would have enough credentials to teach in a Japanese university. No need to take a job at half a man's pay. If someday I decided I was not destined to write novels, I could try writing a dissertation instead. However severe my **depression**—or just my procrastination—I had no intention of leaving this college town without taking my orals; I could think ahead better than Nanae. And yet I did not want to earn my living by teaching unless I absolutely had to.

"The thing is," I said, "I don't want to remain in academia. I want to write a novel."

After a bit of silence, Nanae asked a simple question: "Well, if you write a novel, what will you write about?"

No way could this phone call go on any longer, I thought, as I looked at the lightly falling snow.

"That's just it."

The snow seemed to be coming down a little harder.

Nanae mused aloud, as if talking to herself. "What could you possibly write about if you were going to write in Japanese? I mean, you haven't lived in Japan for eons."

"I know. But I don't want to write about life in America." My life in America had always seemed unreal. Words I learned from old Japanese novels evoked a world far more real to me: 味噌こし *misokoshi*, "miso strainers," 黒縮緬 *kurochirimen*, "black silk crepe," 軽井澤の白樺 *Karuizawa no shirakaba*, "the birches of Karuizawa." . . .

She absorbed this, then quickly added in a comical tone, "You can't just turn your back on it either, though. How about something like *My Insane Youth in America*. **Write something that'll be on the best-seller list. Be famous.** Who knows, maybe my artwork will sell in Japan too. 'Oh, you're the artistic sisters! But I see the elder sister is the beauty of the pair,' *tee-hee!*" She mimicked the fawning voice of a housewife.

"I couldn't possibly."

"Why not?"

"I don't have anything to say."

"Ho-ho! **Aren't you a prude!** You've had your share of adventures."

"Nothing that would make a novel." Who would want to read the tragicomedy of a young girl living in America whose ideal image of a man was someone straight out of a Meiji novel wearing a square college cap, a black cape, and two-inch-high wooden clogs, drunkenly singing the "Dekansho Ballad"—that amusing tribute to Descartes, Kant, and Schopenhauer? "Japanese today wouldn't be interested."

"Well, you make something up. Something the Japanese would love."

"Impossible."

"Oh, come on. Say she's like, you know, living in **Harlem.**" Now she was imitating the speech of a young Japanese girl, wherever she might have picked that up. "There's like prostitutes and pimps and **junkies**, all kinds of scary people like right in her apartment building, and every now and then they have a shootout. *Bang! Bang!*"

Drawn in despite myself, I suggested she could have a black lover.

"Thaaat's right. With a big, big you-know-what."

"Listen to you."

"Why not? Clichés always work. The girl is pretty . . . just like us, you know. *Ha ha.* **And she's also our age."**

"Sorry. I'm sorry but that wouldn't work. **We can't possibly make her our age. She's got to be younger. Otherwise the story won't sell.**"

"**Okay, she's in her mid-twenties.**"

"**No, younger.**"

"**Why would you want to make her younger?**" Nanae sounded offended. "**I don't like young girls. They're not interesting.**"

I feared it would be pointless in present-day Japan to write a novel that didn't have young readers in mind. On my occasional visits back, the entire country seemed to have turned into a kindergartener's paradise. At the same time it seemed even more pointless to write one that did have young readers in mind.

"**Well, we'll make her very pretty.**" Nanae plowed ahead. "**Good figure and everything. What does she do?**"

"She's in **Harlem**, but she can't possibly do **hip-hop** or whatever you call it. I guess she should do **jazz**, don't you think?"

"**Jazz, huh. Then voice would be better than piano. It's more sexy. She sings in clubs.**"

"They've still got them in **Harlem**?"

"I wonder. Well, whatever. You can always look that up."

"She has a white friend who's **gay**."

"**Yep. Someone who'd listen to all her troubles. He's gotta be Jewish. Lives with his mother.**"

"Of course."

"**Dying of AIDS?**"

"Too contemporary. I don't think I'm up to it."

"**Okay, then he's tested HIV negative. Someone who doesn't sleep around. Real straight. 'Straight'** might not be the right word. **Anyway, let's see. We still have to give the girl a name.** What names are popular now? Is Masako too old-fashioned?"

"Nothing wrong with old-fashioned. But I don't think she should have grown up in America the way we did."

"I thought returnees were big now."

"Not extreme cases like ours."

"You mean we've gone overboard?"

"Yes."

"How sad." She sounded genuinely let down.

"I think having her finish **high school** here and then go on to college for two years or so would make her the most **marketable**. After that she works for a while in Japan, but an ultra traditional guy falls hopelessly in love with her and rejecting him out of hand would be too painful, so she runs back to America."

"She ends up in New York and then meets someone like us at a party in SoHo. They only know pidgin Japanese. '*Konichiwa*. I am America long time.'"

"Seriously?"

"Well, whatever."

"Then by sheer coincidence she runs into her first love from her high school days in Tokyo, right here in New York."

"Some kind of an artist. Real cool guy. Very tall for Japanese."

"They have a dramatic encounter on a street corner."

"Wow-ee!"

"This is sounding more and more like a stupid drama I saw on TV back in Tokyo one summer."

"Excuse my language, but what's the fuckin' difference it if sells?"

Strangely enough, from the time he lands in America the guy gets along great with his lousy English. By the time he's been here three weeks, he's high-fiving black guys in **Harlem**, going arm-in-arm with them and having intimate conversations till dawn, the kind of conversation Tono with his American **PhD** couldn't pull off if his life depended on it. A too-good-to-be-true novel ignoring the vertiginous chasm that separates the Japanese language from English as well as the American reality where most people see you not as some individual but as Asian or Other.

I did want to write in Japanese, but I didn't know if I could write anything that Japanese people would want to read.

"It's really coming down now," I said.

"Yeah, I've noticed."

Nanae too must be looking out the window, receiver in hand.

There was nothing nice about the snow falling from an ashen sky. It lacked nature's power to comfort you or take you out of yourself. All it did was fall mechanically from sky to earth.

"*'Où sont les neiges d'antan?'* Wasn't that it?" Nanae asked. "*'Where are the snows of yesteryear?'*"

"That's right. From the poem by **Villon**."

こぞ *kozo*, the archaic Japanese equivalent of *"antan,"* I knew from having read the poem in translation: *Kozo no yuki ima izuko.* Would Japanese people today know the word? I was certain that Nanae, for one, did not. One day several years back she had squealed, "I want to learn French too!" and took up the language for a while. A woman of many lovers, she had predictably had an affair with the teacher, a Frenchman. Yet for some reason, she spoke French with a strong American accent.

"Are you going to take your orals in French?"

"Half French and half English."

"Oh. **You know you're going to pass, right?**"

"I suppose so. They don't usually fail people."

"Just don't flip out like **Rebecca Rohmer**."

Nanae had met **Rebecca** a couple of times before I graduated from **high school**, and once when I mentioned she was coming to spend the night, she had remembered her as "the pretty girl with straight dark hair and red glasses."

"She didn't make it this time around either."

"What? She failed again?"

"Never came in the spring to take her exams."

"**She never showed up?**"

"That's right. I think she got spooked."

"*Oy gevalt*. Really? The poor thing." Nanae sounded genuinely sympathetic.

"Yeah."

"You always said she was so brainy."

"Too brainy, maybe."

"Well, you're pretty tough—you won't flip out."

Silence. I watched fine white snow fall and fall outside the window. Nanae's **loft** was a converted factory building with a row of big windows along one wall many feet long. She had to be staring at snow out her windows too.

At this rate the day would end with the two of us still attached by telephone. "Isn't your rice ready by now?"

"More than ready. **I think it's totally cold by now.**"

"Then go make the rice balls to take to Father."

"Yeah, I will," she said. "I don't feel like going in this snow. Just getting to the **parking lot** is a haul."

I felt sorry for her, having to trudge fifteen minutes just to get to the car and then drive on the highway in this weather, two hours round trip. But who knew when the weather would improve? When she first bought the **loft** she had rented a space in an underground garage nearby, but later switched to a farther spot that was cheaper. Just owning a car in **Manhattan** was a burden, and I knew it wouldn't be long before the added burden of going to see Father would be too much for her. How could I entrust the remainder of his life, which might be years, to someone who could barely manage her own life? Something had to be done.

"Life is such a drag," she said. "Nothing good ever happens."

"No, nothing."

"Nothing, nothing!" After a short silence, she asked, "Have you heard from Mother lately?"

"No, not since the last time I told you." I said nothing more. Even with her new life in **Singapore**, Mother was unwilling to cut ties with her daughters—after all, she might need looking after in her old age. She wrote from time to time to let us know what was going on in her life, sending the letters not to Nanae but to me.

"**Well, I guess I better get my ass movin',**" Nanae said.

"Bonito flakes or pickled plum?"

"What, the rice balls?"

"Yeah."

"Lately it's always pickled plum. If I choose bonito flakes, the little ones start pestering me the moment they hear the crinkling of the cellophane."

"Oh."

"I'm going to make some for myself. **Babies**, Mommy's hungry too. . . . You know something? Rice really tastes good to me these days. See, I'm Japanese after all."

A poster I'd seen one summer in Tokyo sprang to mind. An ad for an agricultural cooperative, it had showed a young woman distinguished only by impeccable cleanliness holding a bowl heaped high with white rice. The caption read, "I'm Japanese after all." Was the message "Eat Japanese rice" or just "Eat rice, not bread?" What about us, eating California rice? Were we "Japanese after all"?

"Well, give my love to Father."

"Sure. **Wish me good luck. You know how my car is.**"

"Yeah. Be careful."

Exhaling heavily, I replaced the receiver and then reached out to turn the bedside clock around. Loath to watch the steady progression of the hands around the dial, today at some point I had turned its face to the wall. As I'd guessed, it was just past one-thirty. Over the past few years I had become expert at estimating how long our phone calls had gone on. I felt disconnected from reality, the way you do when the movie ends and the theater

lights come on. My arm ached. I looked at the clock again. I had
talked about all sorts of things I usually didn't go near, but had
barely touched on the one topic that was the reason for the call.
Oh well. All I need to do is call again after she gets home tonight. If
the snow got any worse, I'd want to call anyway to make sure she
got back safely. Besides, after her visits to Father I usually called
to thank her for her trouble. If I failed to do so because we'd
already spoken at length in the daytime, she'd be sure to call me
with a full report that was never good. **"Oh, I'm so depressed. I
can't stand that place."** And **"Boy oh boy oh boy,** he's more senile
than ever now." By this evening I would have a clearer idea of
how to let her know my decision. Usually she didn't give things a
lot of thought, but surely now as she drove through the snow in
her beat-up car, the significance of my decision to take my orals
would occur to her.

I left the bedroom, went into the living room and, drawn by the
falling snow, stepped over to the window with a view of the street,
the one I always gazed through. The snow was nondescript. Still,
it had an energy that told me we were well into winter now. Day
after day it would be cold, so cold it was as if all the misery of the
world had descended on us, and the memory of spring sunshine
would fade irretrievably. At East Coast universities, student sui-
cides peak in February, weeks before spring.

The old white vagrant I always saw around was poking through
the steel dumpster beside the **University Cabaret**. In the last few
years the vagrants in town seemed to have rapidly increased in
number. Did he have somewhere to sleep when it snowed like this?
After guiltily watching the grizzled old man walk away from the
dumpster empty-handed, I crossed the living room and sat in
the red armchair. The window in the back looked out on a desolate parking lot, but sunk in the armchair, all I could see out that
window was white sky and white snow.

I needed to contact the two main supervisors who would attend my orals. I had already made the first move, so I didn't need to contact them today. The beginning of next week would do, Monday or Tuesday—all I really needed to do was get in touch with them before Christmas vacation. There was still plenty of time. I kept telling myself that I could put it off a little longer, but I knew that the more I put it off, the more terrified I would become that I might end up trapped forever in this apartment. *Better call today. Better yet, make the call now, this instant.* . . . Even as I told myself this, I remained glued to the armchair.

In the silence, a sense of dull helplessness smoldered. It was a feeling of frustration close to rage, but I couldn't tell what exactly I might be frustrated at. The joking conversation I had had with Nanae about the dumb Japanese novel I might end up writing lingered in my ears, depressing me. Was I angry at present-day Japanese people for being so clueless about anything and every-thing, as if they lived in a cocoon? Or at present-day Japan for not living up to my vision of what it should be? Or was I angry at myself for something that had been bothering me for quite a while, something so troubling that I preferred not to think about it? At least not today—or not right now, not when I had finally started to make the critical move. . . .

Whatever the answer, one thing was certain: my frustration was not directed at America. After twenty years, I was finally able to see clearly how kind this country had been to me.

America is the land of opportunity.

America had welcomed our family with open arms. I was under no illusion that this country would welcome all people with open arms, but to us, a Japanese family of comfortable mid-dle-class income that had moved to a comfortable middle-class neighborhood on the East Coast, the most broad-minded section of the country, people had been extraordinarily kind.

"Give me a hug!" Uncle Jesse would say, crouching down to my height and opening his arms wide. He did this every time I saw him. English made no sense to me, but children know when an adult likes them, and I used to shyly bury my face in his burly, ex-boxer's chest, which always gave off the earthy smell of his wool vest and the sweet smell of leaf tobacco. When I pulled away, he would point to my face, gripping his ever-present pipe in his right hand, and say **"She's so cute!"** After hugging Nanae, he would point to us: **"They're so cute!"** Turning to Father, he would then ask, **"How come you have pretty daughters like these, Phil?"**

"Phil" was the name our father had chosen for himself—perhaps mischievously, fully aware that pronouncing it would be a struggle for most Japanese—back when he worked for the American Occupation and had to have an American name.

Uncle Jesse was considerably older than Father, but somewhere along the way they had become friends and then neighbors, as it was he who suggested we settle in the town where he lived. He referred to Father as his lifelong friend and held him in high esteem, often saying that Phil Mizumura was the finest man he had ever known. Looking back, I would have to say that **Uncle Jesse** had him beat. **"I'm your American uncle."** That's how he introduced himself. In the beginning when we were bewildered, scarcely knowing up from down, he would look after us, invite us to his house and sometimes take Nanae and me to **Howard Johnson's** to treat us to American-sized **scoops** of **ice cream**. He radiated a kind of **goodness** that words like "nice" or "decent" don't begin to express.

Uncle Jesse's wife—whom for some reason we called **Rose**, and not **Aunt Rose**—was the same way. Mother spent an entire year trying to get her driver's license, finally succeeding after three failures, and that whole time, with never a look of annoyance, week after week **Rose** drove her to the supermarket so she could do her grocery shopping. **Rose** spoke slowly and carefully so even Mother could understand, and in all that time only once hinted at the difficulty of having spent the last twenty years living with **Uncle Jesse**'s Russian mother. Mother soon became comfortable greeting her with a cheery, American-style **"Hi, Rose!"** and also began to dress more flamboyantly, but **Rose** was the soul of consistency, always wearing a staid blouse monogrammed with her initials, **RW**, and a gray skirt. Despite her own plain wardrobe, at birthdays, graduations, and other occasions marking our growth, she always gave Nanae and me expensive gifts that we dimly understood were in excellent taste. All this even though her younger brother suffered from aphasia as a result of the Pearl Harbor attack—carried out by **"sneaky Japanese,"** I had often heard—and was in and out of mental hospitals, unable to lead a normal life. When she introduced him to us, **Rose** flushed with seeming embarrassment, almost as if he were the one who had wronged us and not the other way around.

The neighbors were kind too. The day we moved in, the **Berlin** family, who lived across the street, brought over a white box containing a chocolate cake decorated with the words **"Welcome to Colgate Road!"** After they left, Father translated this as "Welcome to Toothpaste Road!" and made us laugh. The white box was printed with **"Mayflower,"** the name of a pastry shop where we later often would go, located next to the **drugstore**. Then, a couple of weeks later, **Mrs. Weinberg**, who lived on our right, asked if either Nanae or I would **babysit** her little son, **Bill**, which we were happy to do. This made our whole family feel part of the community and gave us sisters another glimpse into American family life, beyond our acquaintance with **Uncle Jesse** and **Rose**.

When spring arrived and new leaves came out on the trees, neighborhood kids, mostly younger than us, would come over, vying with each other to invite us out to play: **"Hey, let's play ball!"**

They had big, colorful plastic orbs the likes of which we had never seen in Japan. We would play in the middle of the tree-shaded street. On the rare occasions when a car came along, the first one to spot it would yell at the top of their lungs: **"Car, car, C-A-R!"** Then all the kids would immediately stop and stand at the side of the road till the coast was clear. Once we started playing, we would stay outdoors till dark. Although Nanae and I were in junior high, these kids accepted us with enthusiasm, rather enjoying our ignorance of English.

And there was **Mrs. Gregory**.

"Columbus discovered America in 1492."

Of all possible introductions to the world of written English, this sentence was the first line in the first book of English I ever read in America.

One afternoon, I was sitting at a round table in a little room at school, side by side with **Mrs. Gregory**, whom I had just met. In front of me was a thin picture book for children. My English was limited in the extreme. In **Hawaii**, never having spoken to a foreigner in English, I had stared, round-eyed, when Mother tossed off phrases like **"Three vanilla ice creams, please."** The school dealt with Nanae and me, two Alices in Wonderland, by assigning a pair of classmates to be our guides and also by hiring as a twice-weekly tutor **Mrs. Gregory**, a white-haired former grade-school language arts teacher whose appearance was distinguished by a total lack of chin.

Mrs. Gregory was as kindhearted as she looked. Unusual in our predominantly Jewish town in being a **WASP**, she was given to exclaiming **"Oh dear!"** or **"Dear me!"**—old-fashioned, lady-like expressions to which she gave a most feminine intonation. What sort of lessons Nanae may have had with her, I couldn't say. **Mrs. Gregory** and I read the story of the conquest of the New

World. I did no preparation or review and stopped to look up every word in the dictionary, so our progress was slow, but she never lost patience. The lessons always ended with her exclaiming good-naturedly, "**Dear me! It's already two o'clock. How quickly time passes. Oh dear!**"

Even after the school dispensed with her services as tutor, she would invite our whole family over for dinner and serve meals so delicious—apart from the oddity of always beginning with **shrimp cocktail**—that they even impressed Father, who like many a Japanese gentleman fancied himself something of a gourmet. In the springtime, their yard, by no means big by American standards, would fill with all sorts of birds, and as one kind or another perched on a branch, her husband, a retired high school English teacher, would get out binoculars and comment: "**That's a blue jay. That one is a robin.**" As my knowledge of birds was limited to sparrows, crows, and pigeons, he would open up an illustrated guide and do his best to point out the rich avian variety around us. During summer vacation, we learned to play croquet on their lawn. And during the winter holiday, their lanky, unmarried daughter **Kate**, around thirty years old and **six feet tall**, would be there too. She taught English at a succession of U.S. military bases in Asia and liked to travel, taking photographs of places she'd visited. With logs burning in the fireplace, presents around the **Christmas tree**, and a feast laid out on the table—all in a room as full of warm happiness as the one the little match girl peered into before she froze to death—**Kate** would entertain us with slide after slide of Indian weddings, Korean street scenes, and other marvels. Though chinless like her mother, she was leggy and stylish, her bare feet encased in Chinese slippers with pretty embroidery.

When we learned about **Kate** and discovered that she had for a time taught English in Japan, we began to understand why her parents extended to us, the only Japanese people around at that time, such extraordinary hospitality. Yet not even that could fully explain their abundance of goodwill. The entire family apparently took English teaching as a mission, whether at home or in far-flung places abroad, but their warmth toward us never smacked of missionary arrogance. It was courtesy extended toward guests from afar, pure and simple, without any suggestion that they anticipated the reward of even self-satisfaction.

Now, twenty years on, both **Mr. and Mrs. Gregory** were dead. **Uncle Jesse** too. At least he was spared having to see Father the way he ended up.

Nanae and I had begun our lives in America wrapped in the warmth of these people, having not the foggiest idea what was what. Certainly no amount of goodwill could have prepared us for the relentless reality of life in a foreign country. That reality was yet to hit us, however, and so we had gone on groping our way blindly as through a dense mist, getting used to the feel of America.

I pledge allegiance to the flag of the United States of America and to the Republic for which it stands, one nation under God, indivisible, with liberty and justice for all.

Mounted in a corner of the classroom was the American flag. The American school day began with everyone standing at atten-tion, right hand over heart, reciting the **Pledge of Allegiance.** As a junior high schooler, I learned I had to take notes not in thin notebooks as I used to do in Japan but on what was called "**loose-leaf paper**," which had to be kept in a ridiculously big **binder**, on top of which I had to pile ridiculously thick textbooks, car-rying it all in my arms. If anyone had shoved me from behind, I would have toppled forward like a brick. I learned about lockers, a marvelous novelty; in Japan you only had a peg for your coat and

a cubbyhole for your other stuff. And I learned that in America, the world map divides Eurasia mercilessly in two and puts North and South America smack in the middle. World history was thoroughly pro-Britain till just before the Revolutionary War, when the British redcoats suddenly turned into bad guys. School rules were almost nonexistent. I could cross my legs during class without getting scolded, and the teacher herself conducted class perched on her desk, legs crossed. In Japan, going home straight after school was mandatory, but here once school was out we were free to do whatever we wanted, go drink a soda or hang out in the park. Nobody saw anything wrong with such behavior. Smoking was prohibited on school grounds and on the sidewalk adjacent to the school but not on the sidewalk across the street. School authorities showed no desire to interfere in our lives beyond the perimeter of the school grounds. The scary term "juvenile guidance official," which Nanae used to mention frequently in Japan, quickly fell from our vocabulary.

The hyperfeminine, even sexual, air of American girls my own age was another revelation. To begin with, there was nothing scandalous about having a boyfriend; it was rather something to be proud of. Girls never wore a wristwatch or carried a well-ironed handkerchief, the way everyone did in Japan, but they all had a smart-looking **pocketbook** that they brought to school packed with cosmetics—unthinkable in Japan, where all you could carry was a frumpy leather book bag. During breaks they would flock to the restroom and plant themselves in front of the mirrors, chattering noisily with their friends while combing their hair and fixing their makeup to the last second before the bell. I imitated them by having Mother get me a nice **pocketbook** too, and I learned to wear not just stockings but garters and even a brassiere, not that I had the least need of one. I learned to shower in the morning and do up my hair in curlers; a hair dryer, an item that I had thought belonged in beauty salons, turned out to be a necessity of life. **Deodorant**, an item then nonexistent in Japan, perfumed the air around **gym** lockers, where the precociously developed bodies of my classmates were bared matter-of-factly before my eyes; still, deodorant was for me totally unnecessary.

I learned too that wealth in America was beyond my imagining. It turned out that the town where we lived had once been a retreat for wealthy Manhattanites who had glorious **estates**, until large-scale development divided each **estate** into dozens or even hundreds of lots, one of which became ours. Even so, a mere ten-minute drive took us to the tip of the peninsula, where there remained a vestige of the exclusive neighborhood that had been the setting for *The Great Gatsby*, with houses that looked to me like the stately mansions of British nobility or the lavish homes of Hollywood stars—many of them my classmates' residences.

One time a few months after we arrived, a boy from my school who lived in that rarefied enclave invited me to his **bar mitzvah**, whatever that was, and Mother, sensing that it might be a special occasion, sent me off dressed up in a kimono. Outdoors, the property was so huge I was half afraid I might get lost; indoors, guests were ushered into a room that faced the garden and was big enough to hold a hundred people. The boy's mother said, **"Today the weather is so nice, I decided to use this parlor"**—astonishing me at the thought that there possibly was another parlor just as big. Another time, a girl living in one of those houses invited two other girls and me to a **slumber party**. The basement was big enough to play ballgames in, with ample room besides for four beds, one for each of us. After **Monopoly** and **Scrabble**, followed by **girl talk**, which I couldn't keep up with, we got ready for bed. I assumed that meant lights out and sleep, but no—that meant a **pillow fight**, a free-for-all, everyone whacking everyone else with pillows till the air was thick with feathers. Everything was so new to me that I was in a constant daze, and without knowing what I was doing I tried to do what the others did.

Nanae and I also went to summer camp in the mountains. Plenty of our classmates went off to luxurious camps offering a daily routine of horseback riding, tennis, and yachting, but our parents couldn't afford such retreats and instead sent us to a low-cost girls-only camp run by the **YWCA** where there was little to do but swim in the lake. There we encountered yet another America. Some of the girls stood morning to night in front of the mirror with a transistor radio, swaying their hips to the beat of the music. Others screamed themselves hoarse at baseball games and acted unabashedly masculine. I remember a pair of beautiful twins from Colombia who would **tease** their hair half the day, and another pair of Japanese sisters who were so unsociable I never heard them utter a word of either English or Japanese. There was also a pair of fairylike American girls with waist-long hair who kept everybody at arms' length and often went off on their own.

Something ethereal about those last two puzzled me, and I turned for an explanation to one of my cabin-mates, a girl named **Melanie** who came to the camp every year and was something of a doyen. She laughed in scorn.

"They're just hippies."

I had never heard the word. "What's that?"

"It's difficult to explain. They're not normal people."

Not normal people? What was that supposed to mean? Had they inherited some physical trait such that even if they ate the same food as the rest of us, a special chemical change occurred? In fact, they were as delicately lovely as if they lived on the nectar of flowers.

"Not normal?"

"You know, different. Not like you or me."

I was chagrined to be only normal.

There were lots of black girls at camp. Back in Japan, I'd never seen any black people outside of television and movie screens, or, if I had (there were still plenty of GIs around when I was born), I'd been too little to remember them. Encountering a handful of real-life black kids in school had been a new experience; mingling with so many at camp was an experience of a different order. **Eva**, whose hair was streaked blonde, was nice and would read books aloud with me. **Alice**, my partner on hikes, was big, easily weighing more than 200 pounds and standing as strong and tall as the warrior monk Benkei, while I at less than 100 pounds was even more delicate in build than Ushiwakamaru*—yet when we had to carry our gear, she refused to carry more than me. One girl was nicknamed **Snora**, she snored so much. She had darker skin than the other girls, yet daily she would look intently in the mirror and say, "**I think I got tanned,**" provoking wry smiles. **Candy** was the first and only possessor of **ESP** I had ever known, yet she made light of her gift and was devoted to ballet. Thanks to a financial aid program, several girls from **Harlem** were able to attend the camp. They formed a clique and walked around with a swagger behind their leader, a short-haired girl with a boyish face who strutted like a gang boss. To my astonishment, she never used the third-person singular "s" on any verb, and every other thing she said was "**It don't matter.**" One day she and her followers got on stage and sang a slow, enchanting song a cappella, after which I regarded them with awe and admiration; but apparently to the others, girls from **Harlem** singing with professional aplomb was as unsurprising as giraffes having long necks.

One other major experience I had at camp—one that I had not expected at all—was my first kiss. The culmination of eight weeks

---

* Childhood name of the famous samurai Minamoto no Yoshitsune (1159–1189), who defeated the giant Benkei in a duel while still a boy of around twelve, according to legend.

of camp was a grand dance party that **seventh graders** and above could attend and that boys from a boys' camp were invited to. The boys' camp was on the other side of the lake, where a trumpet sounded every morning and evening, military style, impressing the boys' presence on us daily. And so it became clear why, in addition to *x* many pairs of shorts, *x* many pairs of long pants, *x* many pairs of socks, and so forth, we had been required to pack a dress. Not knowing what to expect of this dance party made me anxious, but the other girls could not wait, counting the days to the big event, showing off their dresses to each other, debating whether to wear their hair up or down, and, if down, whether to curl it in or out. They let their nails grow. Shower days were allotted by age, but on the day of the party the schedule allowed everyone to shower. Dinnertime was moved up and, that day only, eating with curlers in your hair was allowed.

On the day of the party, toward evening, busloads of boys in suits and neckties began to arrive. They too appeared nervous and flushed. The fifteen- and sixteen-year-old girls, transformed by wearing dresses and stockings and putting on eye makeup and lipstick, looked surprisingly mature; to me they were breath-takingly beautiful and sexy. They all found dance partners in no time—tall, broad-shouldered, strapping young men with freshly shaven jaws, striking in their young manhood. Though every-one was meeting for the first time, when the music started up and people paired off, each boy's positioning of his palms and each girl's tossing back of her head was less like dance than fore-play, and while there was almost no conversation, hushed low tinklings of laughter rose here and there around the room, the atmosphere so frankly sexual that I wanted simultaneously to avert my eyes and stare in fascination. I stood with my back to the wall, my sticklike body wrapped in a dress with a ribbon on the bodice, in a daze.

Then my cabin counselor came by, smiling. **"Maybe you two can get along."** She had brought with her a small pink-skinned boy with blond hair and blue eyes whose voice had barely changed. Summoned back from a dream world, I felt embarrassed, as if my childishness had been held up to me in a mirror—embarrassment that intensified when I realized he must have felt the same way on seeing me. We danced a few numbers together, then left the building and stopped by some trees under the stars.

"Shall we do as expected?" said the small pink-skinned boy.

While being kissed, I worked out the meaning of what he had said, repeating *"Shall we do as expected?"* in my mind until the literal meaning came to me—but the shyness, panache, and cleverness in the words went over my head. *What a funny thing to say*, was my only thought then.

Several days later, a bulky letter arrived. **"Sealed with a kiss"** was written on the envelope, words that made no sense at the time but that later I realized may have been intentionally corny, the product of excessive self-consciousness. Whatever the small pink-skinned boy may have whispered under the stars that night, I had understood only bits and pieces and parted from him without any notion of what sort of person he might be; but if he was someone capable of pouring out his heart on paper to a girl from a foreign land who scarcely knew any English, then perhaps he and I shared a similar flair for the literary. In any case I was the only one in my cabin who received a letter from my dance partner. The other girls sat cross-legged on their bunks and took turns reading out loud the long letter written in a typically male, hard-to-read scrawl, howling with laughter and pausing every so often to try to explain the contents to me. There was no way I could possibly respond to a letter I couldn't read, and so the first love letter of my young life went unanswered.

Nanae, who had also experienced her first kiss that same night, stayed in bed the following day from the shock.

The following year, we were sent back to the same camp and reunited with **Melanie** as well as other familiar faces, once again swimming, playing softball, and singing around a campfire. All the activities were exactly the same as the year before. And then came the start of another school year.

In time, life in America grew less strange, and little by little my fog lifted. The novelty of all things American wore off, and once I stopped being a newcomer, people no longer found me an object of curiosity. It was around then that I began to be aware of a gulf in my life, a gulf that I have continued to feel in some measure ever since.

It was not a gulf between me and America. It wasn't that I existed and America was somewhere outside my existence, separate from it. Before I knew it, I found myself living in America's embrace. I had an everyday niche, a place where I felt I belonged. I developed relationships—few, to be sure—with people who familiarly called me **Minae**. So the gulf was not between me and America. It was something more like a gulf between myself and my American self, or between my Japanese self and my American self—or, to be still more precise, between my Japanese-language self and my English-language self. My Japanese self did not disappear just because I had come to America; it would continue as long as I spoke and read Japanese. And I was convinced that my Japanese-language self was my real self and I could only be true to it by one day going back to Japan; my English-language self felt utterly beneath me, alien.

At some point, I no longer recognized myself.

Am I really this girl? Aren't I supposed to be a girl with every advantage? With parents anyone would be jealous of? A tall, beautiful mother who wears stunning kimono and a father who—all right, maybe he isn't handsome—but who speaks fluent English and is a man of culture, and

the souvenirs he brings back from America are the envy of the neighbor-
hood, and I have tons of friends who are smart and nice and good-looking,
and boys who talk to me act shy and even when they're mean it's just
because secretly they like me—and most of all, more than anything, look,
I got to come to America!

Coming to America had definitely elevated me. But at the same
time it had caused me to fall precipitously—mainly, of course,
because of my inability to speak the language. **"I don't understand
English"**: how many times had I repeated this when I first arrived?
"My name is Minae": how many times did I say this and then feel
my mind go blank? Still, I hadn't felt any urgent need to acquire
English. For one thing, unlike the way it is now, and possibly to my
detriment, learning English did not seem like a universal imperative imposed on all humanity; and for another, our parents saw us
as mere children, bound to pick up the language with no difficulty.
I took advantage of this parental indifference to be supremely
lazy, so that even after I kept on hearing the words **"because"** and
"however" in school, I never bothered to look them up in the dictionary. But they kept popping up, and one day I finally asked
Father what they meant. Far from scolding me, he said, "What?
You don't know those words? How can you get along without
them?" and explained, cheerful as always when it came to any discussion of English, so that at long last I was able to attach meaning
to what had until then been mere noise. That's how lazy I was. And
yet, Nanae and I were fast leaving behind the stage of life when
such laziness was no barrier to mastering a foreign language.

We were young enough to be invited out to play ball with neighborhood kids, but not young enough to play ball all the livelong
day. Even if I played like a child in the daytime, at night I would
immerse myself in novels meant for adults. My classmates too were
entering the adult world, a merciless place where one's social status
hinged on one's linguistic skill, or lack thereof. My mathematical
achievements being high, thanks to the Japanese educational

system, my classmates probably did not see me as retarded, but my inability to ever say anything remotely interesting made me virtually indistinguishable from a mental defective, and so, inevitably, I was consigned to the lowest social stratum. Once my initial novelty value wore off, I had to accustom myself to living in relative isolation. I grew used to being as ignored as if I were invisible, and turned into a person of such low standing that this treatment seemed only natural. All the same, I remained absurdly stubborn. Not for one minute did I ever feel roused to improve my standing in the world of English. Rather, the more miserable I was in that world, the higher my pride soared, deepening my conviction that my American self had little to do with my true self.

Day after day, the moment I left the house I became an empty shell. The two conscientious classmates who had been assigned to me were now busy with their own lives. Having no friends worthy of the name, I began to spend time with a girl named **Linda** who took the same route home from school as me. How it happened that we started walking home together down the tree-shaded street, each clutching her armful of books, I can't really say. All I remember is how interminable the way seemed as I trudged unwillingly alongside her. Eager to get home and dive into a Japanese novel, I tried to avoid her, but as soon as I left the school grounds she would pounce.

   Linda too was friendless, an outcast. I soon realized why this girl whose only outward flaw was a tendency toward being overweight had no friends: she was utterly uninteresting and unpleasant. **"Hey, listen, Minae,"** she would begin, but her conversation never strayed from the limited realm of topics available to a girl of limited intelligence awakening to her sexuality. The unpleasantness of her character was such that she frequently turned the boring topic into something nasty. But that was not all; as I gradually found out, she was odd. I would half listen as she talked, murmuring an occasional word or two, and the conversation would taper off. Then all of a sudden she would pepper me with questions to which an inscrutable "Oriental smile" seemed the only possible response: "Hey, Minae, do you think I'm pretty?" "Do you think I'm sexy?" "Do you think I'm too fat?" "Do you think I look Jewish?" "Do you think I'm crazy?" On top of the silliness of a not-so-bright teenager, there was a repellant insistence in her manner. The barrage of questions seemed to point to layers of impenetrably thick curtains that barred her from reality and behind which there seemed to lie dull misery. Desire and fear undoubtedly warp the reflection of reality in the mirror of the soul, but what was reflected in the mirror of Linda's soul was not a warped version of reality, it seemed to me, but a barrier cutting off all paths to reality. I tried to imagine the barren landscape of a mind with no way in or out.

One day, after declaring she would tell me a secret, Linda whispered in my ear: "I killed my little brother."

I knew she didn't have a little brother.

"No!"

"Yeah!"

"But you don't have a brother." I was sure of it. All I knew of was a pair of twin sisters, still infants.

"I did. Long time ago. I drowned him in a bathtub."

The word "drown" was one I knew, since at camp we had gone swimming every day. I turned and looked incredulously into her light brown eyes.

"Yes. Yes," she said, nodding her head in seeming glee.

"No . . ."

"Yeah. Like this." She released one arm from the pile of books she was holding and gestured as if shoving her brother's head underwater "Hee-hee."

"No, you didn't."

"I swear I did. Long time ago."

Suddenly it hit me that for **Linda**, such a thing was not outside the bounds of possibility.

Perhaps seeing a change in my expression, she abruptly pulled away and let out a high-pitched laugh. **"I'm only kidding, Minae."** Her mouth was smiling but her light brown eyes were not. **"Don't tell anyone I told you this. Especially my mother. She'll get real upset."**

The story of her having murdered her little brother sounded strangely real. It was a world away from her usual talk about how she'd finally lost three pounds or was trying to decide whether or not to cut her bangs or thought her **dentist** had a crush on her. Besides, she had already told me she was adopted and that seemed to fit in somehow.

Her being an adopted child was another secret that she had confided to me alone.

"You think we look alike?" The first time I went to her house, as soon as her mother left the bedroom **Linda** asked me this.

"No."

"My mom is short and dark. I'm tall and light. Right?"

She sounded triumphant. Being **tall and light** seemed to be a *sine qua non* of beauty in this country. While **Linda** wasn't exactly tall, she was definitely taller than her mother, who was even shorter than me. Linda had fair skin and wavy hair that was almost blonde. Her mother, by contrast, had dusky skin and jet-black frizzy hair. When I first saw her, I had been surprised at the dissimilarity.

"Well, I'll tell you a secret, Minae. She's not my real mother. I'm adopted."

Perhaps I only imagined it, but after that whenever I saw that mother whose daughter resembled her not at all, she seemed enveloped in despair, as if quietly enduring the fate that had led her to make such a wretched human being her child. She never responded to **Linda**'s provocations by raising her voice. The tiny twins, who had dusky skin and jet-black frizzy hair, and who were and weren't **Linda**'s little sisters, remained in their stroller as she jollied them.

Not long after I heard **Linda**'s account of having killed her brother, I went to her house for an after-school snack. "**Oh, just for half an hour, please, please. . . .**" I gave in to her pleadings and reluctantly went to her house with her. Her mother and the twins sat with us around the kitchen table.

"**Remember what I told you about my little brother?**" **Linda** interrupted the conversation. She looked at me and nodded insinuatingly.

"**Hey, Linda, stop.**" Her mother's remonstrance was gentle, but her furrowed brow indicated deep concern. She turned to me. "**Minae, please don't pay her any attention.**"

"*Hee-hee.* **Mom's afraid.**"

Without intending to, I turned my gaze on the twins, who were sitting not in the stroller today but in high chairs placed side by side. As I stared, two pairs of dark eyes exactly like their mother's looked back and forth from her face to mine, wide with puzzlement.

"**Mom's afraid. She doesn't know what to do with me now that the twins are here.**"

I tried even more to stay away from **Linda** after that. It was awful to think she might really have killed her brother, and if she hadn't, it was just as awful to think she would make up such a story. I couldn't ask anyone else at school for fear of spreading gossip, and also I was afraid people might laugh at me for taking anything she said seriously.

After summer vacation, my former **junior high** classmates all enrolled in the **high school** on the same street. **Linda**, however, wasn't there. When day after day went by with no sign of her, in relief I decided that the family must have moved. Then one day I received a phone call from a girl named **Sophie**.

"**Linda's in the hospital.**"

"**Oh, really?**"

"**Yes, in a mental hospital.**"

"**Oh.**"

Apparently fearing that I might not understand the words
"mental hospital," she added, "That's where they put crazy people."
"Uh-huh."
"Her mother wants her friends to go and see her. Do you want to
do that together?"
"Oh yes."

I didn't know **Sophie** at all well, but we had a class together so
I vaguely knew who she was. What stood out about her was that
although she seemed nice enough, like **Linda** she wasn't the sort of
person that anyone went out of their way to befriend. She too was
an outcast—more than anything, I first thought, because of the way
she looked: she was short, fat, and her legs were different lengths.
The shorter leg was bowed and, even though she wore shoes of
different heights, dragged when she walked. This might not have
mattered if she'd been at all nice-looking, but the poor thing had
a face like an owl. To keep from attracting attention, she stayed
quietly to herself.

And so runty, pudgy, lame, owlish **Sophie** and I boarded the bus
and rode out to visit crazy **Linda** as her only "friends."

Apparently **Linda** was not violent, as the room we were shown
to was unlocked. I had feared we might find her in a cell-like space,
but her room was spacious and had a window looking out on the
courtyard, with colorful curtains obviously designed to appeal to
a girl. There were stuffed animals on the chest of drawers. She was
sitting cross-legged on the bed, wearing short-sleeved pajamas. In
the short time since I'd last seen her she'd put on enough weight
to rival **Sophie**, and whether from lack of exercise or medication,
her face was hideously puffy. Her once-rosy cheeks, her sole charm,
were now the color of fatty chicken meat. But to my relief, she
was full of energy. As soon as she saw us, she shouted a boisterous
"Hurray!", threw a pillow at the ceiling, and then, as if she felt she
needed to do more to welcome us, heaved herself up and started

bouncing on the bed. I soon forgot what the three of us talked about. All I could remember was my irritation when for no reason she interrupted the conversation to get off the bed, go stand barefoot in front of the mirror in the middle of the room, and launch into the same old litany: "**You think I'm pretty? . . . You think I'm sexy? . . . You think I'm too fat? . . . You think I look Jewish? . . . You think I'm crazy?**" Only after I went home and some time had passed did it occur to me to pity her.

That was the last time I ever saw **Linda**. What might have become of her, I never knew. I never even knew whether she was hospitalized because of something she had done or because of something they were afraid she might do. There was no gossip about her at school, or maybe it just never reached my ears. I felt no inclination to visit her mother and ask questions. I never did find out the truth about her, including whether or not she had committed fratricide, but later I learned that adoptions sometimes go awry and came to think that her birth mother or father might have had some strange genetic defect or suffered from addiction, as sometimes happens.

For a while **Sophie** and I stayed friends. Her disability was not her misfortune, I soon realized. Her misfortune lay in her lacking intelligence sufficient to make people think her disability an unjust fate; rather, her physical handicap seemed emblematic of her mental slowness. But **Sophie**, who never spoke ill of anyone, was good-hearted and, unlike **Linda**, pleasant company. She was taciturn, ashamed of her slowness, and when she did speak her voice was low and hesitant. She tried her best to get to know me. But on the day when I accepted her timid invitation to visit her house, I was miserable.

The house where she lived was far fancier than I had expected. On the outside it looked ordinary, if big, but indoors were whitish rooms flooded with sunlight affording glimpses of pillars, sculptures, classical wood furniture—a space of unusual luxury, like something out of a movie. Years later, looking back, I felt sure that it was meant to recreate the atmosphere of a Mediterranean villa.

Sophie's perfectly coiffed mother came clattering over the marble floors in sandals with five-inch heels and greeted me in a husky, strongly accented voice: **"Hi Minae, nice to meet you."** Then, switching to what sounded to me like Spanish or Italian, she began talking rapidly to **Sophie**, who responded in monosyllables— *"si"* and *"no."* Still, I was stunned to discover that she knew another language. When we were alone, I asked her about it. The surname **Contini** was Italian, it turned out, and her parents had emigrated from Italy just before World War II. They were unusual in our neighborhood, where the great majority of residents were second- and third-generation Eastern European Jews.

After addressing **Sophie**, the mother turned again to me. **"You like pizza, Minae?"**

"Yes." I was being polite. **Pizza** was a dish that I had never seen or tasted before coming to this country, but it had soon become all too familiar and lost its initial appeal.

"Okay, we'll order a pizza."

Sophie and I sat in the luxurious marble kitchen and ate **pizza** slices from a white box with our fingers. I wondered if the grown-ups would have a proper meal later, in the dining room. **Pizza** required minimal table manners, since all you had to do was eat with your fingers, wipe your hands and mouth on the **paper napkins** that always came with the order in amazing quantity, and **gulp** fizzy **Coke** from **plastic cups**. Still, we were now high school students after all, and I couldn't see why we should have to eat food like this at such an early hour, all by ourselves. **Sophie**'s mother, however, seemed to think it natural to treat **Sophie** and me like children.

Having never had a real conversation with **Sophie**, I had no idea what sort of inner life she might have, nor was I particularly

interested in finding out. After finishing the **pizza**, we went to
her room, where the nature of her inner life, or rather her lack of
anything resembling one, became apparent. It was the room of a
little child, full of dolls, games, and picture books. By then I was
fifteen and, through novels in Japanese, experiencing the full range
of adult emotions as my own, so the sight of someone my age playing with pull-toys was bizarre and distressing. To entertain me, she
handed me a variety of games and oddities of all colors and shapes,
explaining what to do with them. Try as I might to be responsive,
I couldn't help feeling more and more depressed.

"**I am sorry I'm so dumb.**" She looked on the verge of tears.

"**It's okay.**" Only after the words left my mouth did I realize
I should have said, "**No, you aren't dumb.**"

There was a brief silence, but **Sophie** wasn't mad. "**You met my
sister Margie, right?**" Her eyes began to shine. **Margie**, two years
her elder, was out somewhere that day, but I had met her at school.

"**Yeah.**"

"**You like her?**"

"**Yeah.**"

"**Well, she's real smart.**" **Sophie** said this with evident pride.

"**Oh yeah?**"

"**Yeah. She gets straight A's.**"

At that point in my life, I was perhaps at rock bottom. There was
nowhere to go but up. However stubbornly I turned my back on
English, my comprehension did improve and so did my grades.
At the same time, I began to walk home down the tree-shaded
street with girls from a different circle. Eventually I realized that
Sophie, self-effacing as always, was staying away from me, and as
we had no classes together she dropped out of my life. Nor did
thoughts of **Linda** much trouble me. By the time graduation rolled
around, I was walking home with a pair of honors students who

lived nearby: scholarly **Rebecca Rohmer**, with dark straight hair, red-rimmed glasses, and an ever-present armful of books that often included Goethe in the original, and artistic **Sarah Bloom**, with waves of chestnut hair spilling down her back.

Rebecca and **Sarah** were the best of friends. **Rebecca**'s father was an **editor** at a publishing house and **Sarah**'s father was a **lawyer**, but their families lived nearby in a regular house like ours, so neither of them came from wealth. In our town where so many *nouveau riche* families lived, the disadvantage of not being wealthy translated into a sense of superiority in having parents in intellectual professions, and the two of them were, I think, further bound in shared disdain for classmates who spent their weekends clothes shopping and their vacations on **Vermont** slopes or in the **Caribbean**, returning tanned from snow or sun. Occasionally I went to **Rebecca**'s or **Sarah**'s house and found it overflowing with books, an environment that surely made them more open-minded and contributed to their willingness to walk home with me, an inarticulate Japanese girl. I mostly listened to their rapid chatter as we walked along and was generally odd person out. When they each got into their first-choice college, I wasn't at all envious, glad to have been accepted to the art school of my choice. However, as the years went by, events conspired in such a way that I found myself studying at a university no less elite than theirs. Then as more time went by and I moved on to graduate school there, who should I run into on campus in the very first week but my old friend **Rebecca Rohmer**.

"I was going to get in touch with you," she said, apparently having seen my name on the list of new graduate students entering the French department. As usual she was carrying an armful of books, and as usual she talked fast. She had continued to be interested in German literature and was already in her third year of the doctoral program, preparing for her orals. I was in my first year. I had to head for class, and our conversation lasted only a couple of minutes. **"We really have to get together sometime, the three of us, you know,"**

she said before parting and jotted down **Sarah Bloom**'s phone number on a scrap of paper for me in her distinctive left-handed scrawl.

Again and again during class my eyes strayed to the number on that scrap of paper. What could **Sarah** be doing now? What would she think if she knew I was still in this country—and that I had been reunited with **Rebecca** here, on this venerable campus?

America is the land of opportunity.

Even though I isolated myself in America, the country kindly and insistently reached out to me until finally, before I scarcely realized it, I possessed a passport to the higher echelons of American society. But however high I might rise, never again would I enjoy the status I had had in Japan, nor was my imperfect English the only reason. Even if I could have written in the style of **Virginia Woolf**, I still could not have attained anything like my former status. As the fog of my confusion gradually lifted, I was forced to realize something that had never before entered my mind: I was Asian. In this country, a Japanese girl of privilege was above all Asian. To remain a Japanese girl of privilege, I would have had to stay at home on the Japanese archipelago, insulated from the rest of the world. In the wider world, only white people could be truly privileged— people who, if they were thoughtful, might bear a sense of guilt over their unearned privilege or at least feel it to be a burden. Someone like me, who by her mere presence might awaken others to their unearned privilege, could not possibly be truly privileged herself.

I was sitting in an almost too-soft sofa in her **family room**, a room with fireplace that looked out on the backyard, when a friend of mine said to me, "You know, people like us can't fall in love with just anyone." The daughter of the New York branch manager of a major Japanese trading firm, she had transferred to our school in my senior year and was a year behind me. Drawn by the novelty of having another Japanese person at school, I had begun to frequent the spacious house she lived in, which was owned by the firm.

"I suppose not," I said, though I myself had never looked at my future love life from such a perspective. The toy poodle in my lap was wagging its tail furiously, the way small dogs do. Back then, collies and poodles were all the rage in Japan, and just as we had brought our collie Della over with us, her family had brought a gray toy poodle from Tokyo, complete with opal-studded collar.

"Even if I met someone and thought he was ever so nice, it couldn't go anywhere. People would talk."

"Right."

"Anyway, once he found out who my father was, his whole attitude would change."

Knowing who her father was would certainly make it harder for a young man to approach her.

"I can see that."

The toy poodle jumped off my lap and went over to where she was sitting.

"Don't you find it awfully depressing?" She scooped up the frantically wagging dog and put it on her lap.

I nodded. "Your sister is lucky."

Her older sister was attending a Manhattan university with strong ties to Sacred Heart, an all-girls' school in Tokyo, and also she was going out with a young Japanese diplomat.

"Well, a friend of Father's introduced them." She pursed her lips slightly.

Someone called her name from the kitchen in a thin, high voice.

"That's Mother. Wait a moment."

She returned shortly, carrying a tray of tea and rice crackers. "You like these better than cookies, don't you?" Her voice was beautiful, high and clear as a bell. She was a gifted singer.

Later, one day just after New Year's, our mothers had us each dress up in colorful formal *furisode* kimono, the tightness of the obi making it hard to breathe, and we set off for **Manhattan** in her father's chauffeured black car. I was excited, having never been in a chauffeured car before, and as we chatted along the way, I kept glancing at the navy blue cap in front of me and the ruddy neck beneath, hoping the driver wouldn't sense my excitement. The son of the Japanese ambassador had an apartment on **Manhattan's Upper East Side** and was hosting a party for the children of Japanese branch managers and vice-managers, to which my friend had invited me.

There were some thirty people present, and introductions went along these lines: "Sumitomo here." "I'm Itochu." "She's JETRO." Names of everyone's father's company swirled about the room. Girls all wore *furisode* kimono like ours, with long flowing sleeves. Some of them put on grown-up airs, their delicate, crane-like necks arching above collars pulled back to reveal the nape; others were vigorously animated and often collapsed in giggles, pressing their long sleeves to their faces. Boys were few in number, as most of them had been sent back to Japan. Around each of the few boys present there formed a cluster of girls, their merry laughter rising and falling in waves. It was the high-pitched merriment of girls who knew themselves to be privileged in every way. Several had arrived like us in a black limousine. What did they make of the other personae they were forced to assume in their respective American **high schools**?

After we arrived in America, before **Uncle Jesse's** wife **Rose** began taking us regularly to the supermarket, Mother, Nanae, and I had to walk to the store to buy groceries. Once it snowed for two days. By the afternoon of the third day, the sidewalks had been shoveled, and so the three of us set out, walking single file with Mother in the lead, picking our way downhill. "Going is easy but returning is scary": the line from the old song seemed made for this situation, as, on our return journey, toting heavy grocery bags uphill was treacherous. On top of that, it started to snow again.

Then from behind us a large, shiny car pulled up alongside. A woman in her mid-thirties with an air of chilly refinement lowered her window and said brusquely, **"Get in. I'll give you a ride."** Was it embarrassment at offering help to strangers that made her so brusque? A pretty little girl around ten years old sitting next to her was looking at us curiously.

Following Mother's simple directions—**"Go straight, turn right, oh here here!"**—the car brought us home in a matter of minutes.

"Where are you from?"

"Oh we are from Japan!"

"Uh-huh."

That was the extent of their conversation.

"Now, wasn't that a kind lady?" Mother marveled to Nanae and me as she put away the ruby grapefruit we'd purchased. "And her little girl was just darling!" Nanae and I took issue with this last pronouncement as we laid our wet mittens and scarves on the radiator to dry. "She was okay," said Nanae. "Not that great," I said. Mother only paused, grapefruit in hand, and laughed.

Our antipathy to the privileged American girl was instinctive, probably arising from the self-image we still had as privileged Japanese girls. Mother's reaction too was naive, but grounded in her Japanese identity. She deeply regretted that her poor English had kept her from thanking the lady properly for coming to our rescue, evidently equating the incident to, say, forgetting a shopping bag in the ladies' room of Mitsukoshi Department Store in the Ginza and then having someone hand it to her—"Pardon me, madam, I believe this is yours?"—only to slip away before she could offer effusive thanks: "Oh, how extremely kind of you," etc., etc. Nanae and I sensed something different, something disturbing, in the incident, but we lacked the intellectual circuitry to bring it to consciousness. That evening when the story was brought up at dinner, Father nodded appreciatively and said, "How nice."

Years later, I reimagined the experience from the other side, as the woman driving the large, shiny car. Ahead I would have seen three black-haired figures, seemingly Asian, plodding hatless through the snow laden with armfuls of grocery bags. In the United States at that time, lack of a car was a sure indicator of poverty. Not being white was another. The three figures on foot would have fit both categories.

A mother and two kids. Poor souls! Walking in this snow! Who are they anyway? Is there a new dry cleaner's in town? A new Chinese restaurant? Anyway, they really shouldn't be out walking in this weather. I'll give them a ride. It'll be a good lesson for my daughter. No car—they must really have it hard.

In the car, the mother said they were Japanese. But the house that she indicated in her broken English—**"Oh here here!"**—was a perfectly fine house in a perfectly fine neighborhood, though not grand enough to require live-in household help, so she couldn't work there. When the car pulled up, she said, **"Thank you very much"** and smiled, and all three got out and went in through the front door.

What? They live here? Can this be their house?

Then as the woman drove on her way again, I imagined her daughter looking up and asking, **"Mommy, was that their house?"**

"I don't know, honey. Maybe."

"They aren't poor, then."

"Maybe they aren't."

"How come they don't have a car?"

"Oh, honey, I really don't know."

This was before anyone would have assumed that Japanese people were rich.

What might be called my first awakening to who I was from the American perspective—and from the perspective of the wider world—came shortly after that.

From the car window I saw a red phone booth with something like the reddish-orange roof of a Taoist temple. As I was taking this in, I realized that the street was overflowing with the names of banks, restaurants, and beauty parlors all written in familiar *kanji*: 中國國貸公司, 海鮮菜館, 東方電波髮之家. We had entered the foreign enclave known as **Chinatown**. One of Father's Japanese friends had driven us there for dinner, declaring confidently that the Chinese food there was far superior to the kind made to suit American taste buds, and that various Asian foods that could not be found elsewhere were available here. We left the car in a parking lot and picked our way through cluttered streets. The scene before my eyes was like nothing I knew, yet strangely familiar, and hence embarrassing.

People and things were crowded together with a density I had seen nowhere else in America, and shops spilled out onto the sidewalk, blurring the line between private property and public thoroughfare. Trampled Chinese cabbage leaves and bean sprouts littered the ground, mixed with water-soaked newspaper scraps. Red paper lanterns were hanging in souvenir shops, their shelves jammed with cheap ceramics and plastic knickknacks posing as ivory and jade. One shop added a Japanese doll to the mix. Some times the musty smell of incense would come wafting through the air. Magazines from Taiwan or Hong Kong, I couldn't tell which, were displayed in the windows of dilapidated shops, the cover girls smiling smiles that struck me as old-fashioned. As we walked

along, a flood of Japanese memories came to me: the busy street
by the station, crowded with small shops . . . my grandmother's
bent back . . . the rental bookstore where with Mother's permission
I used to borrow comics when I was little . . .

This of course was not Japan. It wasn't even a vision of how
I remembered Japan used to be. Most of what I saw was exotic
even to me. And yet many things bore a surprising resemblance
to Japan.

The grocery store was bustling. Naked Peking ducks hung
by their feet in the window, their skin a shiny red, and below
them was a row of severed pigs' feet. The sight unnerved me. But
behind that, a pyramid stack of steamed buns stuffed with bean
jam reminded me of the fluffy softness of the treat and though
I didn't have a sweet tooth, I felt like reaching out and cradling
one in my hand. Sunflower seeds and pine nuts were unfamiliar—
how did people use them?—but dried shrimp and ginger we had
in our kitchen. There were barrels of pickled vegetables that
I could almost taste. Blocks of tofu were immersed in water, just
as in tofu shops in Tokyo. Mother bustled around declaring how
much cheaper everything was compared to the lone Japanese
food store in **Manhattan**. She was full of energy, loading Father's
arms with all sorts of goodies for our family. Whether the energy
was unique to her or typical of housewives in bargain heaven
I couldn't be sure. I tagged along, ricocheting between curiosity
and something resembling nostalgia, never dreaming that as an
adult I would move from place to place in America and wherever I went find a store marked **Oriental Foods** run by Chinese
or Koreans where I would buy Chinese tofu and Korean dried
shiitake while exclaiming, exactly like my mother, how cheap
everything was. The air was filled with the heavy scent of spices
unfamiliar to me, punctuated by the sharp smell of soy sauce,
deeply and unsettlingly familiar.

◀ Souvenir store in Chinatown

温哥華大蟹
龍蝦
VOLUNTEER
POLICE DEPARTMENT
CITY OF NEW YORK
0.50 LB
1.10 LB
1.20 LB
1.80 LB
VEGETABLES
1.80 LB
1.60 LB
1.40 LB
好世界
好世界
California VEGET
1 X 44 LBS.
PRODUCT OF CHINA

And everywhere I looked, there were of course ideographs—what I knew as 漢字 *kanji*.

"Wa yu wan?" the Chinese waiter asked, all but yelling. His way of asking was so abrupt, it was almost as if he had been specifically trained never to say anything ordinary like **What would you like?** or **May I take your order now?** Yet he was neither unkind nor surly.

When Father's friend asked in English for a Chinese menu, the waiter responded **"Yu Japanese, right?"** and quickly complied. Then the grown-ups, able to read strings of Chinese characters, began pointing at the menu and discussing what to order. The waiter got into the act with periodic comments: **"Japanese people like dis."** Once the order was complete, he repeated it in accented English (**"soft-shell crabs wiz oyster sauce"**) and then used a stubby pencil to write it down in a small notebook. His characters looked superbly calligraphic to me. I recalled that the woman in the **Chinese laundry** near our house would write our last name on the receipt as 水村, not **Mizumura**, and treated Mother with special friendliness.

The bewilderment I felt upon seeing the flood of familiar *kanji* in Chinatown was soon replaced by a certain realization and, eventually, enlightenment. One day an American classmate said, **"Japanese people use Chinese characters too, right?"** That simple question made me realize for the first time that our word *kanji* literally meant **"Chinese characters."** Gradually it sank in that ideographs had indeed come to Japan from the Chinese mainland by way of the Korean Peninsula, knowledge that was no longer a bit of history picked up in school but something impressed deeper and deeper on my heart. There was such a thing as a Sinosphere, a cultural region bound together by Chinese characters that included not only China but also Korea, Vietnam, and Japan: this fact, common knowledge around the world, finally became part of my own mental furniture.

◀ Grocery store in Chinatown

Yet this fresh awareness did not by any means give spontaneous rise to a sense of solidarity with the Chinese. That we ate the same sort of food and used the same sort of writing system—that our cultures were closely intertwined—I found, if anything, disturbing. And the unyielding fact that Japanese and Chinese people were outwardly indistinguishable I found beyond disturbing—it was unforgivable and hard to accept. Later I would develop an interest in all things Chinese that took me from watching Hong Kong martial arts movies and dating a Taiwanese man to obsessing over Chinese tea, collecting affordable Chinese antiques, and ultimately taking Chinese lessons in Paris—but any solidarity I felt with Chinese people owed its beginnings to my forced awakening in America.

I was still far from such solidarity when, around a year later, on the way into the classroom I held the door open for the girl behind me and she said, **"Thanks, Cathy."** For a moment I didn't understand. Seeing my surprise, she realized her mistake: **"Oh, I meant Minae. I'm sorry."**

Cathy? Cathy who?

Naturally it was neither **Cathy Bradley** nor **Cathy Rosenthal**. It could only be **Cathy Tang** from the other **Chinese laundry** in town, the one a bit far from my house. I thought her an eyesore. *How on earth could anyone mistake me for her? She looks nothing like me! She's taller, but not nearly as nice-looking! And poor as poor can be! Her hair is cut so badly it can't have been done in a beauty shop, and she wears oddball clothes from who knows where.* But if my classmate could mix up the two of us, it could only mean that to her, **Cathy Tang** stood out first and foremost by being Asian.

Why would I blush to my earlobes and feel humiliated at being mistaken for someone Chinese? Was I not Asian myself?

Until not so long before, Imperial Japan had sought equality with the West by looking down upon and attempting to colonize the rest of Asia. Was it a vestige of that wrongheaded era that led present-day Japanese, myself included, to somehow think of ourselves as not Asian? Or was it possible that all people everywhere more or less identified with Westerners, given that in modern times Westerners had come to represent a universal image of humankind?

Awareness came slowly, in bits and pieces. Experiences piled up, telling me that I was as Asian as any Chinese or Korean, but for years I didn't get the message. Or perhaps I did not wish to understand those experiences, preferring to remain in the dark. Time worked patiently on me until finally I was dragged into the light. The same must have been true for Nanae.

One memorable event during this time was the episode of Nanae's **blind date**—an episode that always reminded me of the supreme beauty of spring in that town where we grew up. One day the falling snow would have a different quality. Snowflakes from a clear blue sky would glisten in the sunlight, floating in midair like tiny, transparent shards of glass, and vanish. That would be the last snow of the season. The sunlight would turn cheerful, a harbinger of spring. Then grass sleeping beneath the snow in our yard would put out new shoots as soft as cat's fur, and tiny leaf buds would appear on the trees. Soon flowers everywhere were in bloom, and by the time squirrels scampered from branch to branch, all around would be swathed in a frothy green so deep it was overpowering. The harshness of winter made us eager for spring, and when spring finally arrived it seemed a taste of heaven. After moving away, every spring I would return to feast on the season's beauty, even though the memory of anguished school days kept me from fully appreciating it. Only when I no longer had reason to go back to the town was the full

glory of spring there revealed to me; only then did I also see that a little drama like Nanae's **blind date** was marked more than anything by the excitement and surprise that are the prerogative of innocence and youth.

That spring, Nanae was seventeen and had just gotten her driver's license. She soon grew very comfortable behind the wheel and instead of being annoyed by highway driving, as she would later be, whenever she got upset she would leap into the car, speed off, and not come back till the middle of the night—to be scolded by Father, who always waited up for her. I got my license two years later, but after crashing into a neighbor's hedge backing up on the very first day, I hardly dared to take the wheel—so in this respect too Nanae was more suited for life in America than I was. Soon she was driving herself every Saturday to her piano lesson at her teacher's apartment on the **Upper West Side** of **Manhattan**, with me riding along in case there was some sort of trouble. Our parents evidently didn't worry about the possibility of losing both daughters at once; with the entire household revolving around Nanae's piano, no one, least of all me, questioned the wisdom of having me ride along. Although I could have stayed home reading, I never protested having to accompany her and in fact rather looked forward to the excursions, no doubt as a relief from the monotony of my life.

One Friday, the night before her piano lesson, as I was just about to change into my nightgown and crawl into bed, I caught an aroma from the kitchen. I went downstairs to find Mother standing in front of the gas range stirring a pan with long cooking chopsticks. This was before she had started working outside the home, as she used to in Japan, and before she apparently began wanting once again to be appreciated and admired as a woman; she was enjoying the abundance of life in America and contentedly cooked and sewed, devoted to her role as homemaker. I knew from the aroma that she was simmering daikon in a broth with soy

sauce, the commonest dish imaginable in Tokyo but a special treat here since daikon was scarce, available only in Asian food stores. In America, salmon was fancier than steak, rice crackers were rare imported items, and ordinary cod roe was as expensive as caviar; our eating habits were topsy-turvy. The prospect of getting to have simmered daikon thrilled me.

"Let me have some of it for lunch tomorrow before we leave for her piano lesson, all right, Mama?"

Mother glanced at me as I scooped up some of the broth to taste. "The lesson got moved to Sunday, remember?"

This was news to me. "Why?"

"Tomorrow she has a date. Didn't you know?"

"I most certainly did not."

"I thought she told you."

Nanae had already gone up to her third-floor attic room even though it was a weekend night.

"She doesn't care about me or my plans."

Mother didn't take my complaint seriously, murmuring "Now, now," while transferring freshly washed and quartered cabbage leaves to a bowl. Then she stepped into the little **pantry** adjacent to the kitchen, where on the floor she had arranged enamel containers of fermented rice bran for pickling vegetables—cabbage and mustard greens, mostly, since Japanese cucumbers, eggplant, and turnips were hard to come by.

"She doesn't care about me or my plans!" I said again, louder this time.

One reason the slight bothered me so much, even though I had no plans to speak of, was jealousy. Nanae was going out with a Japanese man named Suzuki who was a dozen years older than her, a bureaucrat temporarily stationed at the Japanese embassy in **Washington, DC**. He was as ordinary as could be in looks as well as in name. Introduced to us by a friend of Father's,

Suzuki would stay with us when he came up to New York for the
weekend and, on the pretext of paying back our hospitality, take
Nanae out for dinner at very expensive restaurants in **Manhattan**.
He was memorable only as the first in the astoundingly long line
of men who would hover around her over the next ten years. That
she felt free to bring assorted boyfriends home from Boston later
was undoubtedly aided by the precedent of Suzuki.

Nanae was still too young for a serious relationship, and the
gap between our family and his seemed insurmountable—Suzuki
being the first Japanese man from a distinguished family that we
had personally encountered in America—so even Mother didn't
see much hope of a match; but, just in case, she went out of
her way to welcome him. When he came for dinner, instead of
eating in the **breakfast nook** we would sit at the **dining table** covered with a tablecloth. He was pale and had markedly narrow
shoulders; he didn't look good in casual wear but was slightly
more presentable when he escorted Nanae somewhere in a business suit. He wasn't interesting enough to be a high school girl's
first crush, but I think he liked Nanae, who already looked the
part of an adult. He amused us by addressing Mother and Father
with the affectionate upper-class honorifics *obahama* and
ojihama, and he was nice to me too, but Nanae was the one he
took out to dinner.

I poked my head into the **pantry** where Mother was bending
over, stirring the rice bran. "Is he staying the night?" I asked. If he
was, I was going to ask him to join me in a round of two-ten-jack.

"Is who staying the night?" Mother looked at me, somewhat
surprised.

"Suzuki."

"It's not Suzuki," Mother said. "A friend from **high school**
invited her out. The idea seems to be that you go out on a date

without knowing who your date is going to be." She pulled herself up. "It's beyond me."

Instantly I understood why Nanae had seemed restless the past week. I understood too why she had not told me anything and why she had shut herself up in her room so early tonight: she was indulging in her endless solitary **daydreams**, avoiding the teasing and meddling of her annoying little sister. She had persuaded Mother to let her use the attic as her bedroom because it gave her privacy. Being out of sight also made it easier for her not only to sleep late but to get out of helping around the house—although as the piano-playing daughter she did precious little of that to begin with. I, in contrast, was known in the family as "a good helper," and now at Mother's request I obligingly washed some dishes and cleaned the sink before bounding up to Nanae's attic room. I was less miffed than full of curiosity.

In the low-ceilinged hall, yellow light leaked from under her doorway. I opened the door and stuck my head into her room. "You're going on a **blind date**?"

"What do you want? I was just going to bed."

She was sitting in front of her three-way mirror wearing a robe over her nightgown. Whatever she might have been doing the second before I came in, now she was coolly holding a set of **vocabulary cards**.

Nanae's bedroom was all in pink. The three-way mirror, dresser, headboard, and nightstand were a matched set, pink with white trim. Mother knew we envied our friend Sanae her set of imported bedroom furniture in Tokyo, so when Nanae moved into the attic room she had bought her this set. The carpet and curtains were pink too, as were the walls and the slanted ceiling. Like Mother, neither Nanae nor I had peaches-and-cream complexions and pink was not our color, but at the time we all thought a girl's bedroom should be covered in pink. My room had pale pink floral wallpaper.

Nanae innocently lowered her gaze back to the **vocabulary cards** in her hands, shuffling them. She had a diligent streak and unlike me was not put off by English, so generally she stayed up late studying; but on weekend nights like this she would usually be either sitting at the piano or chatting with Mother and me.

Was she trying to increase her English vocabulary to murmur words of love?

"Who's your date? You must have some idea."

She didn't look up.

"Come on." I sat on her bed, pressing her for an answer. A summer dress was laid out on top of the pink plaid bedspread, and next to it was a wire hanger and plastic bag from the **Chinese laundry**, the bag rolled up. She had been trying the outfit on in front of the mirror.

"Is this what you're going to wear?"

"Why not? It's spring."

It was a white dress with chartreuse **polka dots**, the outfit Nanae thought was the most flattering to her.

"Come on, tell me, who do you think it is?" I was not about to give up.

"I have no idea."

She shuffled the **cards** some more. I waited, sensing she wasn't cross. She looked up and made a face at me in the mirror.

"What do you want me to say?"

"Tell me more."

"All I know is he goes to a **prep school** in Connecticut." Ill-concealed pride bloomed on her cheeks.

The words **"prep school"** sent a tremor through me. We attended a public school and I had no idea what a **preparatory school** might be like, but the words suggested a world of refinement controlled by old money and even more so by tradition, a world far away, beyond our reach. Gothic-style stone buildings covered in ivy; a library with shelf upon shelf of well-worn books, gold lettering on their spines; a carillon with sonorous chimes . . . It was an exotic, rarefied world that recalled the volumes of foreign literature then gathering dust on the top shelves of the built-in bookcase in my bedroom—books in Japanese translation for children, abridged and/or rewritten. Back in Japan, before my love affair with the books with vermilion covers, like so many other girls at that time I used to pore over works by authors whose names in *katakana* became part of my childhood: ドーデ Daudet, シュトルム Storm, トルストイ Tolstoy, デュマ父子 Dumas father and son, ブロンテ姉妹 the Brontë sisters, ジョルジュ・サンド George Sand . . . The world evoked in their works represented the West to me. In a **prep school**, there would be boys like the young men in those books, who took long solitary walks, loved wildflowers, and turned bright pink with embarrassment at the slightest provocation—in a word, boys not at all like the ones in my **high school**, whose nonstop consumption of **hot dogs, hamburgers**, and **French fries** had wiped all sensitivity from their genes. For me, America was as relentlessly cheerful and devoid of poetry as an ad for **Kodak** color film. That Nanae, the one who bleached her hair and slathered herself with **Coppertone**, should get to go out with someone from a **prep school** was simply not fair.

"Really. **A prep school?**" For once I responded with real admiration.

Nanae said nothing, only shrugging her shoulders. She had not yet picked up the habit of freely mixing English into her speech, but her body language was becoming steadily more Americanized.

"Who **arranged** it?"

"**Amy. Amy Forman.** You don't know her. Two of her friends, **Carol** and **Gail**, and I are going to her house. We're all meeting there. **Carol** and **Gail** have **blind dates** too, and **Amy's** boyfriend is coming."

"Huh. I didn't know you had friends like that." In fact, this was the first I knew that Nanae, who seemed like me to be leading an isolated life at school, had friends—and ones nice enough to set her up on a **blind date**.

"We just have **history class** together."

"I'm going to tell Suzuki."

"Go ahead. I couldn't care less."

I went back to my room feeling decidedly put out.

The next morning Nanae sat plunking the piano, pretending to practice, but when Mother came back from the supermarket with a trunkful of groceries and honked the horn twice in the **driveway** the way she always did, meaning, "Girls, come and help me!" Nanae took the opportunity to close the piano lid. After lunch she stayed in her room doing something or other. Whenever Suzuki took her out, she always set up camp at Mother's dresser till the last minute, the two of them chatting away while she did up her hair and put on makeup; but that day she came down only to take a shower and kept to herself, as if talking to us would somehow jinx the evening. When **Amy**'s car pulled up in front of the house, we heard her come clattering down the stairs, say a hurried goodbye, and slam the door behind her.

At dinner, Father noticed Nanae's empty seat and asked where she was. Out with some high school friends, Mother told him, and left it at that. She may have thought revealing anything more would only cause him to worry unnecessarily, but actually she herself seemed scarcely interested.

While we cleaned up the kitchen after dinner, she talked about other things: The **sprinkler** system wasn't working right. She was thinking of using one of last year's *Vogue* patterns to sew Nanae and me a pair of outfits in contrasting colors. Sunday after next she had to go see our next-door neighbor, **Mrs. Weinberg**, in an amateur opera production—if only she hadn't mentioned taking singing lessons as a girl! Ordinary, everyday topics.

When Nanae was out with Suzuki, the conversation always gravitated toward the topic of marriage: one difficulty was that he came from altogether too good a family, another that he and everyone in his family had the annoying airs of bureaucrats. On the other hand, his being so much older than Nanae might make him a perfect match for her, she being such a child. And so on. The America that Nanae and I inhabited, where **teenagers** went on **blind dates**, was incomprehensible to Mother; she shut it out of her mind so completely that it might as well not have existed.

I made a cup of green tea for Father and carried it to his study, where as always he was cutting out articles from the *New York Times*.

He looked up. "Nanae's not back yet?"

"No, but it's still only nine." At such times I habitually stuck up for Nanae to keep her from being judged by the standards of fathers in Japan.

Mother and I stayed in the **breakfast nook** chatting until we finished our tea and then drifted separately upstairs. After a while I heard Father come upstairs as well.

On most nights I would sit at my desk with a heavy heart and try to dispatch my homework, but on Fridays and Saturdays I climbed into bed early to savor the pleasure of returning to whatever Japanese novel had absorbed me during the day. I would change into my nightgown, pat my two feather pillows, and arrange them just so against the headboard. Then I would slide into bed and nestle my head on the fluffy pillows, open the musty book and instantly be transported to another time and place, a world where time moved on a different track. That night I got into my customary position and opened the covers of my waiting book, but although my eyes ran along the print, my mind did not follow.

Real time, usually so quick to disappear, crept back out of nowhere, and before I knew it I was listening for sounds outside my window. This room, which had become mine when Nanae moved to the attic, had a window just above the bed overlooking the street, so I knew immediately when a car went by—all the more so because our street had very little traffic.

Because the Japanese language was my staff of life, I assumed with the obstinacy of the young that an unbridgeable gulf separated my innermost soul from anyone incapable of appreciating the myriad things and feelings evoked by Japanese words. Desire for romance with an American boy who could only babble in English was the furthest thing from my mind. Yet that evening, Nanae's **blind date** weighed on my thoughts. Captive to the spell of Japanese, I had turned my back on everyday reality, but what if I freed myself from that spell and turned instead to face reality—the reality of America and Americans, people who lived knowing nothing at all about Japan or the Japanese language? What then?

A vision of Nanae in her **polka-dot** dress kept appearing in my mind . . . *I bet she wore her hair in a pageboy too. I wonder what shoes she wore. The white ones Mama bought her last fall on sale, the ones with heels? She said they aren't **broken in** yet, that they hurt when she walks in them, but they make her look so grown-up. She's not the only one with pretty things, though. Mama bought me that moss-green dress at the same time, and it looks great on me too. The way the sleeves puff out like tulips makes me feel like a medieval princess. If her date goes to **prep school**, then he must be getting a classical education. Can he recite poems by **Ovid**? In Latin? If he writes **sonnets**, then maybe he and I would have something to talk about after all. Oh, but what if he isn't like that, what if he's one of those **jocks** the girls here go wild over, boys with shoulders three times as wide as mine? Then we wouldn't have two words to say to each other. He'd think I was the most boring girl*

*ever. I guess to get along in America you have to at least watch football
on TV. I look like I'm in grade school anyway, so he'd never take me
seriously . . .* I definitely did not want to see Nanae come home
looking as if she had enjoyed herself. Then I might be forced to
acknowledge that life free from the spell of the Japanese language
had its own enticements, but even if it did, I could not imagine
ever wishing to be set free. . . .

A little after eleven, I heard an approaching car slow down and
then stop in front of our house. Peering through the blinds, I was
just in time to see the door open and a shadowy figure emerge.

I hopped out of bed and flew down to the front hall.

The light had been left on for Nanae. She glanced at me, a
baleful look on her face. White pendant earrings I had never seen
before—*when did she buy those?*—dangled from her ears.

"Was that a **Lincoln Continental?**" I asked. I could recognize a
few cars: **Volkswagens**, **Cadillacs**, **Lincoln Continentals**.

Nanae didn't respond. She pushed me aside, crossed the front
hall and clattered up the stairs, then down the upstairs hall and
on up the stairway to her room, leaving me to stand dumbly in the
empty front hall. Gentle, cool spring night air that she had let in,
fragrant with dogwood, enveloped me.

I went upstairs, knocked on the door to my parents' bedroom,
and opened it. Father was watching television with the volume
turned up, and Mother was sitting at her dressing table with her
chin thrust out, applying night cream in front of the mirror.

"Nanae's rather late, isn't she?" Mother said.

"She just got back."

"Oh, really!" She looked at me, her face white and shiny with
cream. She was wearing a floor-length black polyester robe over a
negligee; this was before people looked down on polyester.

"How did it go?" She was looking again at her face in the mirror,
rubbing in cream.

"I don't know. She was in a bad mood."

"Hmm. That child . . ." Mother never took her eyes from her reflection. She sounded a bit upset that Nanae should have let her disappointment get the better of her. "Is she still downstairs?"

"No, she went up to her room."

"Without saying a word to us!"

I shut the door. For a girl to come home without properly greeting her parents was a minor scandal, and Mother was not pleased.

After Nanae went up, there hadn't been a peep from her. I knew that wouldn't be the end of it. I went back to my room, climbed into bed, and picked up the book I'd been reading. Sure enough, soon I heard Mother calling Nanae's name in the hall. There was no way Nanae couldn't hear her. She was shouting up the stairs: "Nanae!"

Whenever I heard Mother shout, I was always struck by how well her voice carried. She really should have gone on with her singing lessons and had a career. If she had been born in more privileged circumstances, she might have done just that. Then she wouldn't have married Father, and we sisters wouldn't be here, but perhaps that would have been better for someone who wanted so much from life.

"NANAE!"

There was the sound of shuffling feet overhead, then Nanae's voice. "What?" She had reluctantly come to the top of the stairs.

"When you come home, don't just go off to your room by yourself. Be civil and let us know you're back!"

"I was just about to." She could not possibly have sounded more sullen if she had tried.

Mother switched to a more conciliatory tone. "How was your date? Did you have a good time?"

"I don't know."

"You didn't have a good time?"

There was a short silence.

"I don't know."

I laid my open book flat on my chest. No way was Nanae going to get away with this. Sure enough, Mother's voice took on a sharp edge.

"You 'don't know'? What is that supposed to mean?"

"I don't know."

"Is that any way to talk to your mother?"

Uh-oh. I slid out of bed.

"What difference does it make?" Nanae's voice was low yet piercing.

Mother's high and piercing voice overlapped with hers. "What did you just say? Don't you be smart with me, young lady!"

The sound of wailing brought me out of my room. I stood next to Mother and looked up the stairs at Nanae. She was bawling with her elbows stuck out and her fists in her eyes, like a little child. Below the **polka dots** her young, strong legs stood firm, slightly apart.

"Honestly, the child falls apart at absolutely nothing." Mother now sounded defensive.

Before being summoned, Nanae must have been lying on her bed, crying. She was still wearing her earrings and party clothes, and her heavy dark hair was sticking up as if disheveled from sleep. She looked pathetic and ridiculous. I felt a pang of guilt in having hoped she wouldn't have too good a time.

"Hey, Nanae, don't cry, it's okay," I said, looking up the stairwell.

We fought constantly, but when she got scolded it was my job as her little sister to act as mediator. The sound of my voice set her off all the more. She was howling with all the stops pulled out. That she would be turning eighteen the next year seemed

unbelievable. Around then my attitude to her was undergoing a
change: I had always just thought of her as my big sister, but more
and more I saw her for what she was—someone I could not possibly
depend on.

"Now, now," Mother chimed in, "don't cry. Look at you, you're
too big to cry." Nanae's hysterics had effectively evaporated her
anger. "There's no need to cry . . ." The words hung hollowly in
the air. Changing tactics, she said gently, "Get changed and come
downstairs. We'll all have a nice cup of tea."

Nanae's crying gave way to hiccupping sobs.

"Did you eat dinner?" Mother asked, an ordinary, maternal
question.

Nanae nodded, still woebegone.

"You've got room for grapefruit, don't you? We didn't have ours
yet either, so let's all have some together."

After a pause Nanae nodded again, more slowly. "Okay."

There were no more grapefruits in the kitchen, so I went down
to the basement to get some from the spare refrigerator. There
was only a naked bulb to light the space that also held, aside
from two sealed tea chests containing Mother's kimono, other
large appliances that we would never have dreamed of owning
back in Tokyo and that symbolized for us the abundance of life
in America: a **GE** washer and dryer and an old oblong freezer big
enough to store a body in.

As Mother and I began to section the grapefruit halves, Nanae
came downstairs wearing a bathrobe. She crouched in front of the
refrigerator and peered inside.

"I thought you said you had dinner."

Mother's voice was the cluck of a mother hen worrying over her
chick—a tone she hardly ever used with me. Was it because I was
a grandma's girl? Or did she sense that I didn't need the kind of
coddling Nanae required?

Nanae pulled a **Tupperware** container from the recesses of the refrigerator. "Yes, but it was **lasagna**."

"**Yuck**," I said.

At one point I developed a yen for sweet stewed tomatoes, and once I was teased not only by my parents but by the waiter in a French restaurant in **Quebec** for ordering ketchup with my meal; yet a bit of tomato-y **lasagna**, gloppy with cheese, was enough to take away my appetite. Except for the **Gregorys**, I was pained to note, Americans were sure to serve you this yucky **lasagna** if they had you over for dinner. At the time, even in an affluent New York City suburb, the custom of people outdoing one another in preparing sophisticated meals had not yet taken hold.

"Only **lasagna**? Nothing else?" I was always interested in food.

"Lasagna and salad. And **ice cream** with **chocolate fudge** sauce on top." Nanae licked her fingers, opened another **Tupperware** container, and pulled out the simmered daikon.

Mother laid down her grapefruit knife. "Honey, if you're hungry, I'll get you something to eat, so you come over here and finish cutting these for me, all right?"

I finished the grapefruit half I was working on and sprinkled it with a pinch of sugar. "I'll take this up to Papa," I said, getting a little fork out of the drawer.

"Oh, would you?" said Mother. With a topic like "how was your date" looming, Father would be out of his depth; it was better for all concerned that he stay upstairs.

In the dim, lonely bedroom upstairs, the television screen gave out the only light.

"She's home, is she?" He glanced at his watch. "Awfully late to be getting home." He had heard the ruckus. I set the grapefruit plate down and didn't say anything.

When I got back to the kitchen, Nanae had finished cutting up the rest of the grapefruit; with her nimble fingers, she was better than any of us at tasks like this. Usually she made do with pearly pink nail polish out of fear of being scolded if she used anything brighter, but today for once her short nails were painted red. Last night had she been about to apply the polish when I poked my head in the door?

Mother set out some leftovers from dinner in front of Nanae. As Nanae picked up her chopsticks, seeming self-conscious about having cried, I asked nonchalantly, "So what kind of house was it?"

Bit by bit she began to talk. **Amy**'s house, which she had visited for the first time that evening, wasn't terribly big, but the yard was huge, with a grove where you could take a walk; in the basement they had played **pool**, a game of billiards that was new to her. She had felt embarrassed because she hadn't known how to hold the cue. They played **darts** too, she said, and when Mother expressed mystification she explained that **darts** was a kind of indoor arrow-throwing game.

"Oh, that," said Mother. "I've seen it in the movies."

Overenthusiastically, as if making amends for her previous behavior, Nanae said, "Oh, really? In the movies?"

Seeing Nanae start to open up filled me with relief; she must not have had such an awful time after all. Mother evidently felt the same way. She bustled around the kitchen chiming in as Nanae spoke, her earlier wrath now seemingly forgotten. Finally she set out some pickled vegetables and a fresh pot of tea, untied her apron, laid it over the back of her chair, and sat down.

"My date was **Korean**," Nanae spat out as if on cue. Her face was scrunched up as if she might start to cry again.

"**Korean?**" Mother sounded puzzled as she reached for the cup of tea I'd poured her.

"Yes."

"What was?"

"My date."

"You mean he was from Korea?"

"Yes, **Korean**." Nanae repeated the word in a low voice and sighed.

I meanwhile was so stunned at this surprising turn of events that I could only stare at her.

Mother took a sip of tea before asking, "But there were other boys there too, weren't there?" The concept of a **blind date** eluded her.

"Yes, but the one who was my date was settled from the start."

"And he was a Korean boy?"

"Yes."

"The others were all Americans?"

"Yes. Because the other girls were all Americans too." Slight irritation at Mother's denseness crept into Nanae's voice and expression. She turned to me. "They didn't have to go and pick a **Korean** for me, did they?"

Utterly sympathetic, I shook my head.

"I mean, after all, I'm Japanese!"

I nodded in agreement.

"**Amy**'s mother is a loud woman with a **Brooklyn accent**, and while we're eating our **lasagna** she whips out two pairs of big chopsticks she must have picked up in some **Chinese restaurant** somewhere and says, '**Let me see you two use chopsticks**.' Just unbelievable."

"What did you do?" I asked.

"What else could I do? I showed her how to use them. Just a little."

She said this with a superior air, but our family was united in condemning Nanae's way of handling chopsticks. Mother looked at her with barely concealed amusement. I made a noncommittal sound.

"You can't imagine how awful I felt. **Carol**'s date was tall and really handsome. Maybe not **Jewish**, from the way he looked. He had **hazel eyes** and **dirty blond** hair. A fantastic **pool** player. But Carol is so shameless, while his back was turned you know what she said? 'The guy already has such a crush on me, he'd jump off a cliff if I told him to.'"

Mother broke in, bewildered. "What is that supposed to mean?"

I translated: "He's so crazy about me he'd go through hell or high water for my sake."

"If it was me," said Nanae enviously, "he's so good-looking, I'd be the one who was crazy about him."

I would never have said such a thing, but she would and did. Her eyeliner, eye shadow, and mascara had dissolved in her crying jag, leaving her eyes ringed with black smudges.

"The Korean boy wasn't good-looking?" I asked timidly.

"He was short, fat, greasy, and had no neck," she answered immediately, as if she had rehearsed the line.

I visualized the squat, dumpy Korean among the three tall Americans. I felt Nanae's shock as if it were my own. I knew that Koreans, perhaps even more than Chinese, were looked down upon in Japan, a prejudice from Japan's imperial past; yet having grown up in Tokyo, where people were supposed to be more enlightened, and having parents who prided themselves on being liberal-minded, I had never felt that either of us was particularly prejudiced—at least, that's what I'd always believed.

The three of us were silent, each absorbed in our thoughts. After a bit, Mother said, "I suppose when you come down to it, Koreans and Japanese are all the same to Americans." She sounded at once surprised and accepting.

Nanae glanced at her and made no comment. I too kept my mouth shut. Mother's remark showed how remote her experience was from ours. To her, the fact that Americans made no distinction between Koreans and Japanese simply reflected the reality of the United States as a foreign land, but Nanae and I had to find our place in that reality.

Had the Korean boy assigned to Nanae that night been good-looking with a slender, graceful neck and limbs, then doubtless she wouldn't have fallen apart the way she did, and had he been a smarmy ladies' man, then—knowing her—he might well have become her first love. Even then, she could not have escaped being hit over the head with the disturbing reality that in American eyes she was another Asian, no more.

"Was he **Korean** or **Korean American?**" I asked.

Nanae said his English was good but he went back to his parents' house in Korea every year for Christmas and summer vacation, so he was probably **Korean.**

"They must be rich." I was jealous that he could go back and see his homeland twice a year when I could not.

"Filthy rich, apparently. They say that to get into his **prep school** takes more money than brains, and he's one of the richest boys there, but I don't think that would ever make him popular with girls."

"That **Lincoln Continental** was his?"

"Yes."

On the heels of Nanae's response, Mother said: "My, he brought you home in a Lincoln Continental? Well, well!" She sounded impressed, then added with finality, "But if he's not Japanese, then that's that."

She picked up a pickle with her chopsticks and popped it into her mouth.

She was sitting on the kitchen chair with her feet tucked under her and her bottom resting on the soles of her feet, as if she were on a tatami mat in a traditional Japanese house. When had she started to perch on chairs that way? From as far back as I could remember, we had always sat on chairs back home in Tokyo, not on tatami; but as she grew older her body, accustomed from childhood to life on tatami, must have rebelled and reverted to the familiar posture of old. When she used a sewing machine she would sit normally in a chair, humming, but when she sewed by hand she sat on the carpet with her legs tucked under her—the way she would have sat as a girl just learning to sew. She looked vaguely like my grandmother, who always sat on tatami, bent over alongside an old-fashioned sewing box with a vertical wooden arm and a pincushion on top, squinting as she stitched. She also resembled Grandma in the way she had of touching the needle to her short black hair. Then one day as I was reading a musty volume from the set of modern Japanese literature, it hit me: that was the same gesture with which women used to apply hair oil pomade to their needles. When she saw me reading Tanizaki's novel *A Fool's Love*, my mother, who affected all things Western, would exclaim, "You know what? When I was young, people said I was just like Naomi!"* And yet her connection to the world of modern Japanese literature, that world I yearned for with such passion, lay not in her resemblance to a fictional character but rather in the everyday habits and preferences she exhibited unawares. Watching her pop another pickle into her mouth, I thought about how much she loved plain, quintessentially Japanese meals like white rice with dried fish, vegetables boiled in soy, and pickles, so much so that soon after we first arrived in New York, she declared "I'm dying!" and rushed off to a Japanese grocery to buy a rice cooker, rice, and pickled plums, then brought them back to the hotel and surreptitiously made hot steaming rice in our room. Unlike us sisters, who could get along fine without Japanese food for weeks or even months, Mother was, after all, Japanese through and through.

---

* Naomi, the beautiful antagonist of the ironic 1925 novel by Tanizaki Jun'ichirō (1886–1965), is raised Pygmalion-style to be the ideal modern (Westernized) woman, but in the end comes to completely dominate and manipulate her would-be master.

All three of us, led by Mother, munched on the pickles. Then she started on her teeth with a toothpick, a typical middle-aged Japanese woman. "Did that Korean boy speak Japanese?"

Nanae and I exchanged puzzled looks.

"Of course not," Nanae said. "Why would he?"

Mother seemed unable to fathom our surprise, having grown up taking it for granted that Taiwanese and Koreans, as former subjects of the Japanese Empire, could get around in the Japanese language.

"Well, a Korean wouldn't do in any case. When you went back to Japan, he'd suffer discrimination."

Her mind seldom strayed far from the question of whom Nanae was to marry.

Mother used to tell us in some embarrassment—unusual for her—of her youthful dream of romance with an American. During World War II, while Japan made an enemy of almost the entire world, she, as an ordinary Japanese, was not unpatriotic and certainly did not wish for the empire to be defeated. But secretly she spent odd moments between unaccustomed farmwork dreaming that a B-29 would crash and a soldier come parachuting down to the bamboo grove behind her, someone as handsome and strong-armed as Gary Cooper. He would be injured, and when she found him she would pull out a white handkerchief from the pocket of her work pants and minister to his wounds; then, after hiding him in an abandoned shed, she would sneak him food and water from the house, and so their love might blossom. Whether her daydream went any further I don't know, but as soon as the war ended, over the protests of her family she took a job with the occupying forces, perhaps hoping to run into an officer who looked like Gary Cooper. Things played out rather differently. In no time she fell in love with a married man she met at the base: it was Father, a man with a round nose and round spectacles, as Japanese-looking as any man could be.

That night when I went into the bathroom to brush my teeth before bed, Nanae was there removing her smeared eye makeup with cleansing cream. She confided a little more about her evening: her date had said, **"Shall we go out for a walk?"** but she had managed to talk her way out of it. She went on dabbing at her mascara with soft, moist tissue.

The next day, in the car driving to **Manhattan** for her piano lesson, she was in better spirits, though every so often she would make an aggrieved allusion to the previous evening's disaster. On either side of the wide highway stood trees covered in new leaves, shimmering in the warm sun.

At the time, I sided unhesitatingly with Nanae and had sympathy only for her disappointment, but looking back, it was terribly presumptuous of us to give no thought to the feelings of the Korean boy who was her date. We assumed that he had been selected for the evening with her in mind, but in retrospect I could see that we were unrealistic to suppose the other girls would set up a **blind date** on their own initiative for someone who still had trouble speaking English and with whom they weren't even close, someone who led a solitary life at school.

It made far more sense to look at the situation from the other side. Surely the boys at the **prep school** had asked, **"Hey, do you have any Oriental girls in your school?"** so their Korean friend wouldn't be left out. The girls had then replied, **"Yeah, we have a Japanese girl in our history class,"** and so Nanae was picked, no questions asked. How did the no-neck, pudgy, rich Korean boy feel when the date who materialized in front of him turned out to be a Japanese girl with straight black hair like his own? What if he too had been expecting to date a "typical" American girl? Worse yet, as a Korean he might easily have harbored deep antipathy for Japan. Yet he had seemed to enjoy himself when he was with Nanae, had even said the sort of thing a boy was supposed to say—**"Shall we go out for** a walk?" He had certainly handled the situation with more grace than she had.

Which would offend Koreans more, to be lumped with Chinese or Japanese? Rather than the Japanese, who were known derisively as "dwarf people" in ancient times, would they prefer to be associated with the Chinese, who had boasted the world's greatest culture through the centuries? Or could there be some modern Koreans who chose rather to be associated with Japan, a well-to-do country where young people spent ridiculous amounts of money on a haircut without thinking twice? And what of the Chinese, what would they say about it all? Not until later would such thoughts occur to me. This, after all, was a time when I was shocked to learn that a Japanese American couple wishing to adopt a child would be told by the agency, **"We've found a wonderful girl for you"**—and be handed a Chinese baby. Gradually I came to understand that an American would be surprised to know that Japanese felt any shock at being lumped with Chinese and Koreans in the first place.

Later, in my sophomore year, I became friends with a girl named **Judy**, who happened to be blonde, a rarity in my school, and we took to visiting each other's houses. One day, apropos of nothing, she said, **"Hey, look, Minae. We'd make a perfect picture for the UN."** Her eyes were fixed on the mirror. Sure enough, there in the full-length mirror in her bedroom were the two of us: her with her waist-length yellow hair, and me, sitting beside her, with my thick, shoulder-length black hair. We might have been posing for the cover of a UN pamphlet to be entitled **"Teenagers around the World."** In that moment, I got the uncomfortable feeling that **Judy** saw me as representative of teeming Asians on the other side of the world.

The gradual discovery that I was Asian wasn't shocking in and of itself. The shock I felt came from being lumped together with people whom Westerners regarded as Others—as did I, a Japanese.

To be lumped together with those whom in some hidden corner of my mind I had always blithely congratulated myself on being distinct from was worse than shocking. It was humiliating.

The discoveries did not stop there.

One year on the first day of the fall term, the corridor was thronged with students trying to find their new classrooms. I pushed my way through the crowd, arrived at my art class, and took a seat. Other students milled noisily around, hoping to sit near their friends. The teacher had not yet arrived, but pacing around at the front of the room was a black man who I assumed was the janitor, there to erase the blackboard or empty the wastebasket.

When the bell rang, signifying the start of class, the man went over to the door—but instead of leaving, he pulled the door shut. For a moment I was stunned, caught off balance. Everyone else must have been taken aback, too. The man then walked back to the front of the room and looked at us levelly. "I'm Mr. Shields. I'm your art teacher." A hush fell over the room. A black man was our art teacher? Until that moment he'd been a faceless janitor, had barely existed in our minds, but suddenly he had taken on the contours of a human being. I now realized that he wasn't wearing a janitor's uniform; he was wearing a suit.

As much a surprise as he was to us, Mr. Shields was not the first black teacher at the high school. Mr. Jenkins, who taught chemistry, had been the sole black member of the faculty until then. Other teachers were often made the butt of jokes, but Mr. Jenkins was respected and admired. He was also one of the few teachers with a doctorate, almost as if he had been deliberately hired to demonstrate the unfortunate reality of American society that a black man, even with PhD in hand, was often barred from teaching in a university.

Our school tried to keep current with vital issues of the day, including the messy issue of race in America, and **outside speakers** were often invited to give lectures to us. One of them was **Mrs. Jenkins**, a black woman who taught at another school and was married to our **Mr. Jenkins**. Speaking with perfect command of white people's English (as did he), she put the issue of inadvertent racism in terms that our school's affluent, overwhelmingly white student body could understand. We could do one thing right away to make a difference, she said: **"Stop referring to the maid in your house as Betsy or Betty and call her Mrs. Johnson or Mrs. Jones, just as you normally would when speaking to any woman older than you. Use her last name. Show her respect."**

There were eight black students, four girls and four boys, in the class of five hundred. I wondered what they thought. A white girl timidly raised her hand and protested: **"But she's like a member of our family."**

"No! She is *not* a member of your family!" Mrs. Jenkins's retort was so sharp we all sat up straight. Mrs. Jenkins caught herself and resumed her previous calm tone. **"Whatever you may think, she is not a member of your family."**

The existence of these not-a-member-of-your-family maids was impressed upon me not long after our arrival in America. One evening, Nanae and I rode the train back from **Manhattan** and found ourselves among white men in tailored suits on their way home from work, reading the ***New York Times***. When a train passed us going in the opposite direction, I saw that car after car was packed full of black women. I nudged Nanae, and she too gaped. After a bit it dawned on us that these black women were probably maids, also on their way home from work, just going the other way. After that, I began to understand who these black women might be who were waiting at bus stops in town. Sometimes in the evening I would see them sitting in a corner of the train station, chattering away with bursts of loud laughter; if a leisured white woman came on the scene, fresh from the beauty parlor with her hair puffed up, high heels clattering on the floor, they would often lower their voices in seeming deference.

Compared to black women, black men were far less visible in town. They were mainly the sanitation workers who came riding to our house on a big truck early in the morning to pick up our garbage, disappearing before I could see their faces. I don't remember many others. For most of my classmates it must have been the same—and so our first day in **Mr. Shields's** art class was a real eye-opener.

By the end of that first class we knew **Mr. Shields** was a force to be reckoned with. Unlike the courtly **Mr. Jenkins**, who was the same as any white gentleman in all respects but for the color of his skin, **Mr. Shields** belonged to a new generation of blacks and had a different sort of pride. He seemed to revel in his black English, and he would scoff at our naive, sheltered views of life, almost flaunting his rough-and-tumble background. He called us by our last names, without benefit of any **"Miss"** or **"Mr."** Years later, I could still hear the crisp way he used to say my name: **"Mitzu-MUra."**

His teaching methods were unorthodox. Believing that art had to be seen firsthand to be experienced and appreciated, he immediately organized a field trip to **MoMA, the Museum of Modern Art** in **Manhattan**, initiating us into a world of art that was at once unsettling and fascinating. (It was he who instilled in me—walking anachronism though I was—a lifelong habit of frequenting that museum.) He had us write a long paper on **"The Validity of Contemporary American Sculpture,"** knowing we were clueless about what modern art was, let alone contemporary sculpture; he rejected any late project; he required weekly drawings that took half a day to complete. Art used to be considered an easy A, but not three students in our class of twenty-five got an A for the semester.

And the things he assigned us to sketch! One week it would be a roadside ditch, the next a car bumper, followed by kitchen garbage. We couldn't help being flustered, unknowingly accustomed as we all were to the *beaux-arts* tradition of the previous century. Mother would come out and comment, eyebrows raised, as I sat pencil in hand before a pile of half-rotten garbage spread out on the lawn: "That's a funny thing to be sketching."

No wonder the other art teacher and even the two I studied with before **Mr. Shields**—former beatniks, I'd thought—were suddenly diminished in our eyes. The students may have felt uncomfortable with **Mr. Shields's** approach and muttered about it in private, but face-to-face with him we were overpowered by his energy.

Like **Mr. Shields**, many black people of that era were full of the sort of vigor that propels a man uphill in no time. Soon after I graduated, he left the **high school**, and I fully expected him to make a name for himself as an artist—at least to live his life as an artist and not **"sell out."**

I was **Mr. Shields's** pet.

"Mitzu-MUra, roll up my sleeves."

Before my eyes he would hold out two dark brown arms, the arms of a sculptor. One hand would be holding the piece of wood or metal or whatever material he was working on and the other a tool of some kind—an electric saw, say, or a torch. Every time he got himself into a bind like that, unable to do what he wanted for himself, he would come to me, hold out his muscular arms, and have me roll up his sleeves. Sometimes the whole class would look on in silence. **Mr. Shields** had just gotten a graduate degree in art and was in his late twenties. I was seventeen or eighteen. The moment was so sexually charged, I felt embarrassed, but I pretended this was nothing and struggled to make sure my fingertips didn't come into direct contact with those arms.

Mr. Shields would often single out my works for praise, and one of the rare A's he gave out was sure to be mine. Anybody could see he was partial to me.

His partiality was easy enough to account for. Only two students were to attend art school after graduation: a cheeky white boy and me, a sweet Japanese girl. The other students surely understood this. But they also saw something else, something that would never have occurred to the sweet Japanese girl I was, and Mr. Shields undoubtedly didn't mind if they did. They saw a solidarity between two people who had been assigned a negative racial value—a link between two people who weren't white. I alone didn't see this. At the time I thought of black people and myself as farther apart than the African continent and the Japanese archipelago.

Several incidents could have enlightened me if I had not been so innocent—so dense. The first took place soon after summer camp, when I was thirteen. One day Uncle Jesse's wife Rose turned to me with eyes full of good intentions and asked, "Were you more comfortable there, Minae?" We'd been talking about how for the first time in my life I'd lived with black girls. Looking at her elegant face framed by ash-brown hair, I was stumped for an answer. Camp life with black girls, something I could never have imagined back in Japan, had been unusual and interesting, but why would that make her think I might have felt "more comfortable there"?

"No." I contained all my bafflement within the single word.

Then there was the incident later, sometime in high school, in the locker room after gym class when I overheard two girls talking: "No, those are Annie's. Not Nancy's." Two white girls changing clothes were apparently referring to a pair of sneakers on the bench. Then one of them said, "Oh, hell. What's the difference!", and they both laughed. When they saw me looking at them, they seemed to laugh even harder. I scarcely knew Annie and Nancy, who were both black, but I was indignant that they could be treated as interchangeable. That I myself had been seen as interchangeable with **Cathy Tang** did not occur to me at that time.

A more educational incident took place close to graduation. The storm sweeping college campuses around the world had no direct effect on our peaceful **high school**, but one day the **outside speakers** brought before us were leaders of a group of black revolutionaries. In uniforms that made them look like guerilla soldiers, they lined up in front of the microphone and spoke passionately in fast black English that I could understand only in bits and pieces. Then there was a question-and-answer session that again I could not follow, during which the topic shifted to the bogged-down war U.S. forces were fighting in Asia. I did catch one of the scary speakers saying he sympathized with the enemy **"because those people are colored, too."** Those last words resounded clearly in my ears. Until then I had been listening vacantly, but all at once I felt the floor give way beneath me. As someone who never voluntarily looked at English books, magazines, or newspapers, and who watched no television, I had no sense of the depth or breadth of the word "colored" and had always taken it simply as a word referring to black people. I already knew, however unwittingly, that the people wearing triangular bamboo hats in that far-off country were Asian like me, but what could it mean that Asians were **"colored"**? The little-used Japanese equivalent, 有色人種 yūshoku jinshu, for "people of color," did not come to mind, and I drifted between bewilderment and the sensation of having hit a brick wall.

That Americans found it nearly impossible to distinguish Japanese people from Chinese and Koreans made sense. But to identify Japanese as **"colored"** like blacks struck me as purely conceptual, like saying that women and the moon both belong to the world of yin. It was years before I could look back on my response

at that moment as an example of the blissful innocence of someone from a country where the notion of race was as abstract as the
notion of winter for people living near the equator. As my stay
in America dragged on and I began seeing the world with more
American eyes, I lost that innocence. So did Nanae.

And then one day, Nanae appeared to me for a second like a
total stranger.

It was a spring day full of sunshine, and I took the train to
Manhattan for the first time in a while, on my way to meet Nanae.
In one of our interminable phone conversations she had urged,
"Why don't you come up? It's already spring, you know," and we'd
made arrangements to get together. **Henryk** was then unemployed
and hanging out at her **loft** in **SoHo**, along with a cousin and com-
rade-in-arms from their **Solidarity** days, so we decided to meet at
the corner of **Madison Avenue** and **East Seventy-Fourth Street** by
the bus stop.

My train was late, as often happened, and the bus uptown
crawled along. Nanae was at the corner we'd agreed on, as promised; I could see her standing there as the bus drew near. Perhaps
she had grown tired of waiting, for she didn't notice the bus, only
staring vacantly at the flow of people in front of her. For a second
I saw her as a total stranger—an Asian woman past the bloom of
youth, with the long black hair typical of Asian women in America.
Though bathed in bright sunshine, she looked somehow bleak,
frowning as though she'd been cast off by the world, thin and cold
as if she stood alone in howling wind. Perhaps abandonment by
her mother had translated in her mind to abandonment by her
mother country; the air of loneliness that engulfed her belonged
not to an Asian American woman at home here but to a rootless woman without a country to call home. I was wearing slacks,

but she had on a long skirt. An image of her in childhood, **shy** yet a tree-climbing **tomboy**, flashed through my mind before vanishing.

Nanae looked up in seeming wonder as I walked toward her.

"Sorry, I'm late!"

"The train, I guess."

Her upturned eyes were outlined with jet-black eyeliner, though she no longer wore layers of eye shadow the way she used to. She held a cigarette in her right hand.

"Right. That train's never on time."

"Ah."

"Also I had to go to the bathroom at **Grand Central**."

"Oh."

Though her replies were curt, pleasure at seeing me showed in her eyes. The displaced woman of a moment ago was gone, leaving only my familiar sister. Her habit of hiding her pleasure under a pout was unchanged from childhood. From close up she appeared younger, and she even had the glamorous aura of a young woman stepping out after having taken a bit of extra care with her appearance. Still, the desolate image of a moment before was imprinted on me like a shadow darkening the spring.

"Remember this?"

Nanae fingered the heavy silk shawl she had bought at **Liberty** on a family trip to London a lifetime ago. It was smooth and lovely, possessing all the chic of twentieth-century Western civilization, although from the bus, against her long black hair and dark skin, it had seemed rough in texture, the kind of thing a Tartar woman might throw around her shoulders.

I touched the shawl and felt its softness once more. "I remember, all right."

"From the good ole days." For the first time, she smiled.

A year after having been cut off by Mother, Nanae no longer brooded or wept. With the companionship of her cats and **Henryk**,

and steady part-time work at the architectural firm, she seemed
set to make a go of life. Yet I couldn't help feeling uneasy. With
our family dissolved and the family house gone for good, I worried
about what would become of her. One reason our spring outing
was to linger long in my memory was surely that my worries, hazy
until then, stood out in sharp outline that day.

She took a last drag on her cigarette before dropping it on the
sidewalk and extinguishing it with the toe of her boot—her manners were execrable. She looked up again. **"Where shall we eat?"**

I glanced around. **Madison Avenue** stretched out before us, busy
with many shops. **East Seventy-Fourth Street** at right angles to it,
was lined on either side with trees and apartment buildings that
had entrance canopies stretching out over the sidewalk. A doorman in a navy blue uniform was strutting back and forth. Across
the street, a young woman in summery white shorts was being
dragged along by her dog, an 秋田犬 *Akitaken*, the breed known
as **"a-KI-ta."** The scene was peaceful. Beautiful, with the peculiarly
urban beauty of cold, inorganic stone and concrete set off by the
leafy green of street trees. The fragrance of wealth was almost
palpable in the tranquil spring sunshine.

"So pretty."

"Well, what d'ya expect? This is the Upper East Side, hon."

What a contrast from the noise and smell and chaos I'd made
my way through at **Grand Central Station**, which now rose before
me almost like a vision of hell. . . .

Shoved out onto the underground platform into the hot air and
the acrid stink of rusting iron, I felt my body grow tense. I climbed
the stairs, people on all sides bumping into me, and entered the
station, where fluorescent lights shone garishly and everywhere
I looked there were vagrants. As I walked straight ahead, avoiding
scum on the floor that might be mud or mucus or blood, stag-
gering toward me came a young black man, something about his

bloodshot eyes not right; possibly he was a crack addict. I went up more stairs and pushed open first one, then another iron door marked **"ladies,"** to find an elderly white vagrant woman standing by the mirrors next to **Hispanic** girls chattering in rapid-fire Spanish, their navels visible as they fixed their makeup. The woman, bags filled with all her worldly goods dangling from her arms, was reaching over the sink as she attempted to fill a plastic bottle with water. On her feet were oversize men's shoes—probably taken off the body of someone who didn't make it through the winter. I went into one of the toilet stalls, where the chicken-wire-like netting installed above and below the partitions as a guard against purse-snatchers only made me feel less secure. On emerging I fled as quickly as I could out the doors, across the station and onto the street, only to encounter a white man slumped on the sidewalk, legs stretched out, with a cardboard sign around his neck that read, **"I have AIDS. Please help me get back to my home in Nevada."** At his feet was a paper cup with coins people had tossed in. A string of threatening *kanji* flashed in my mind: 貧困殺人強盗強姦失業売春麻薬疫病孤独絶望—"poverty murder theft rape unemployment prostitution drugs epidemics loneliness despair." Every ill known to humanity was present in the college town where I lived, but the sheer density of misery here was overpowering. The more fortunate **Manhattan** residents walked with great strides, eyes straight ahead, seeing and not seeing the horror.

"So where shall we eat?" Nanae repeated, in Japanese this time. The same spring sunshine that shone upon the beautiful neighborhood cast its tranquil light across her face. I smiled for no reason.

We were standing on a corner near the **Whitney Museum**. There were any number of smart restaurants in that neighborhood, so we had figured on having lunch somewhere around there. After that, our plan was that I would accompany her to a **Donald Judd** exhibition at the **Whitney**, and then she would accompany me to

the Kinokuniya bookstore at **Rockefeller Center**, after which we
would see a **Cary Grant** screwball comedy at a **Greenwich Village**
cinema devoted entirely to old movies and end our day with a late
supper of Thai food, which was just then becoming popular. This
meant we would take the **Fifth Avenue** bus straight down the island
of **Manhattan** from **uptown** to **midtown** to **downtown**—a plan perfect
for us, since neither of us had any sense of direction.

Nanae motioned toward **Madison Avenue**. **"I saw a rather nice
place a few blocks down the road. Kind of European,"** she said, seeming eager to go there. Ordinarily people living in **SoHo** looked
down on **uptown** as it smelled of establishment, but Nanae liked
uptown just fine.

"Sure, let's go there."

"But it may be a bit expensive." Perhaps she was strapped for
cash, as usual. Hesitation showed in her face and eyes.

"I don't mind," I said bravely. "We're having Thai food for dinner, and that will cost a lot less. Anyway, **I've got money.** That
interpreting job I had yesterday, showing a group of architects
around—it paid really well." It had also been the first time in a long
while I had acted as tour guide. The college town where I lived was
a mecca of modern architecture, and from time to time Japanese
architects on field trips came through to take a look.

"Really?"

"Yeah. They were from the design department of some big construction company that paid all their expenses. And they were
thinking in yen when they paid me, so I got a bundle."

"Lucky you!"

We began walking briskly along. The heels of our boots made
pleasant, dry clicks against the smooth sidewalk, delighting us
with the realization that the snow and ice were now gone.

"But you know, Japanese men like that are awful," I began. "We
had dinner at a sushi place . . ."

"There is one?"

"Two, actually. So there we are eating sushi, and one of them says, looking right at me, 'Yes, a woman under thirty is the best.'"

"No! How rude!"

"Oh, he meant it as a compliment. They're all drunk by then, so they start chiming in. 'You said it! Women in their thirties are over the hill!'"

"Huh!" Nanae's heels started clacking heavily. "Didn't it occur to them that you might be over thirty?" She was outraged.

"Apparently not."

"Besides, what's the difference between twenty-nine and thirty? I'd like to know!"

"They weren't thinking. They were just drinking and living it up. They'd spent the whole day walking around town, so in the evening they thought they could cut loose at a Japanese restaurant."

"And show their true colors."

"Exactly."

"Were they young?"

"Hardly. **In their fifties.** Maybe some of them were in their late forties."

"**What nerve!** Look who's talking, you should have said. Makes you think we should never go back to Japan, doesn't it?"

Our footsteps seemed to sound even louder.

The expensive-looking "kind of European" restaurant was on a corner. It was French. Tall windows with elegant dark blue awnings. Behind a door inlaid with art nouveau stained glass stood a tuxedoed **maître d'**. Nanae glanced at me, hesitant. With a show of confidence, I stepped up, placed my hand on the curved brass handle, and pulled the door open.

"*Bonjour, mesdemoiselles.*" The handsome French **maître d'** greeted us, swept up two leather-covered menus, and held them against his chest. Obviously, the more expensive a restaurant, the better-looking the waitstaff. **"Smoking or nonsmoking?"**

Nanae, no longer hanging back, gave him the wide, sweet smile she always used on such occasions. **"Smoking, please,"** she said, avoiding my eyes.

"Then this way please, *mesdemoiselles*," he said, ushering us, sure enough, to the back of the room, a shadowy area where there was no day or night. Not only that, it was one step below the main room of the restaurant.

I took my seat, looking longingly at the sun-drenched tables in front. "Why don't you give up smoking . . .?" Nanae was still standing, removing the silk shawl from her shoulders, and didn't say a word. "At least during mealtimes?"

"Calm down, it's okay."

As the antismoking movement gained steam, we'd been having more and more such conversations, largely because every time we ate out, we got stuck in dark corners. I started to argue the point, but the memory of those fateful words from a decade ago—"*We don't want a smoker for our son's wife*"—made me bite my tongue.

Now seated, Nanae peered at the menu. "The prices aren't too bad after all."

"You're right. The *Plats du Jour* are a bargain."

"And no tourists around." She was glancing discreetly around the room, on her best behavior.

On our table were red and pink carnations in a cut-glass vase that seemed like something you could get for **$2.99** at **Woolworth's**. Neither the vase nor the carnations could have looked cheaper, yet in this high-ceilinged, classic-style restaurant, they oddly belonged.

"It's been a while since I came to a place like this," Nanae said, sounding happy.

"There are lots of nice places in **SoHo** too, at reasonable prices. Even more in the **Village**. You and **Henryk** ought to go."

She muttered something noncommittal, seemingly reluctant to pursue the topic. Restaurants in **SoHo** and the **Village** were trendier, staffed by brisk employees whose haircuts and dress were provocatively avant-garde. Probably they weren't to her taste.

"What are you going to have?" I asked.

She said she was on a diet and chose *Salade César* from the *Plats du Jour*. I wavered before finally settling on *Poulet à l'Orientale*, whatever that was. In a restaurant this elegant I assumed it wouldn't be gooey and sweet like **chicken teriyaki**, a staple of Japanese restaurants here, but would be marinated in a soy-based sauce. Both our selections came with *Soupe du Jour*.

"Shall we have something to drink?" I asked. "I mean, shouldn't we?" As long as we were having lunch in a place with starched napkins, I looked forward to lingering over the meal and felt like treating myself to a glass of wine. I didn't suspect how long this lunch was going to go on or how it would eventually affect me.

"**I'll just have a Diet Coke,**" Nanae said.

"**A Diet Coke?**"

"**Uh-huh.**"

"In a place like this?" I frowned.

She shrugged. "**I like it.** Can't help liking something."

"**No alcohol?**"

"**No.**"

"**Not even a glass of wine?**"

"**You know, I happen to live with a person who drinks twenty-four hours a day.** I can't bear the sight of alcohol anymore," she said with a touch of pent-up resentment. She had complained about how much **Henryk** drank, but I hadn't known he was a drunkard. "But you go ahead. Don't mind me."

"All right then, I'll just have a **beer**. But it's going to be **Heineken**."

After a young waiter no less handsome than the **maître d'** took our order, Nanae laid her big shoulder bag in her lap and drew out a **pack** of **Virginia Slims**. I recalled her carrying a leather cigarette case in the past, but perhaps those had gone out of fashion—or perhaps since she became a heavy smoker it was just too much trouble fitting a new pack into the case all the time.

"**Caesar salad** reminds me," she said. "I had dinner with **David Zuckerman** the other day." She lit a slender cigarette with a click of her lighter.

David Zuckerman was a friend of Nanae's going back to her conservatory days. For whatever reason, they had always remained just friends, but for a time he had been Kanae's boyfriend, while she was at **Juilliard**.

"Oh? How's he doing?"

"Fine, fine. He called a little while ago, but with **Henryk** out of a job and lying around the house, I couldn't just leave and go off and see **David**."

"Why not take him with you?" This was sarcastic of me, I knew.

"**You** *know* **they have absolutely nothing in common**," she said. "And now we've got his cousin **Wojtek** freeloading off us too." The previous week, **Henryk** and this cousin had been invited to the **Brooklyn** house of a friend from their **Solidarity** days. Nanae had been invited too, but she told them she was going to take the opportunity to see her old friend **David** instead. "Getting back to **Caesar salad**," she went on, "I did something awful. You know there are **anchovies** in Caesar dressing."

"No kidding? So that's what gives it such body."

"**Don't tell me you didn't know.**"

"Well, I didn't."

"**I thought everyone knew.** And I said it to **David**, of all people."

David Zuckerman was a vegetarian, she explained, not for the sake of his health but rather because of what he himself called

"**Bambi syndrome**," an extreme pity for animals that also kept him from wearing a leather jacket or belt or even carrying a leather wallet. They had gone to a Japanese restaurant, and David, on finding a white crescent-shaped object floating in his soup, pink along the edges, had picked it up in his chopsticks and asked her what it was. She had explained it was a slice of *kamaboko*, fish cake, and from there the conversation moved on to foods that unexpectedly had meat or fish content. David mentioned several of them and, thinking of course he would know, she brought up **Caesar dressing**.

"He didn't know."

"Right. '**Oh well, so now I have to give up Caesar salad,**' he told me, with this really sad look on his face, and I felt like I'd done something awful."

When Nanae talked about David, she imitated his way of speaking, using a whispery, shy voice of delicate refinement. His personality, as she conveyed it, perfectly matched that soft-spoken voice, making her telling of the story curiously real.

"On top of it all, there he is sipping his soup right in front of me. I couldn't bear to tell him that it was made with bonito stock. I mean, there's only a **teeny-weeny bit** of bonito in it. **I couldn't very well take all his food away, you know.**"

"If he's that die-hard, he won't have anything to eat."

"I know."

"Is he terribly thin?"

"Not at all . . . **to say the least. I wonder what he eats. Maybe he's a Cookie Monster!**"

David had never seen Nanae's **loft**, so on that evening she had taken advantage of **Henryk**'s absence to show him the place, and when Wagahai and **Punka** came along, mewing hungrily, she'd opened a can of **cat food** and asked him if he would take over while she made tea—only for him to beg off, almost in tears, as she was getting out the his-and-hers teacups.

"He said, 'Oh, Nanae. You know I just can't feed one animal with another animal.'" She artfully imitated the trembling, sensitive man's voice. She was on her second cigarette by now.

"Huh." I poured some **Heineken** into my glass. "Is he still a member of what-do-you-call-it? **Children of Alcoholics**, was that it? Or was it **Children of Alcoholics Anonymous?**"

"I'm not sure what it's called either, but I think he still goes. He's so earnest."

David's mother had died when he was young, and his wealthy father was an alcoholic.

"And listen to what he told me—it's really crazy." Nanae was grinning.

"What?" I took a sip of my beer, the first I'd had in a while. It tasted very good.

"He's also in **group therapy** for **spendthrifts**."

"There is such a thing?"

"Apparently."

"He wasn't joking?"

"Nope. He's not the type to joke about things like that."

"What's it called, I wonder. **Spendthrifts Anonymous?**"

"Yeah, that or **Compulsive Shoppers Anonymous**."

"It's hard for me to imagine **David** as a compulsive shopper, though," I said. With the abstemious way he lived, according to Nanae, what could he possibly be buying?

"I can't imagine it either. **Maybe he just thinks he's got a problem. He's obsessed with his problems, you know.**" With one hand on the straw in her **Diet Coke**, Nanae looked up at me with raised eyes. Her long hair was in the way, so she swept it back with her other hand.

"Maybe he's got too much money," I said. I knew from Nanae that since he couldn't make a living from the clarinet, his college major, he had become a recording engineer, but every year his father gave him several tens of thousands of dollars in a lump sum as a tax dodge and he lived mostly off that.

"Maybe so. **Yeah, I guess so.**"

"He still goes to see **Pamela**, right?"

"**Yep.** Diligently."

Pamela was a psychotherapist—a **shrink**, as people commonly said—and at **David**'s introduction Nanae too had gone to see her for a while, back when she was constantly battling with Mother. The notion of Nanae being psychoanalyzed in English by an American struck me as peculiar: weren't her childhood memories, supposedly crucial in understanding her problems, engraved in Japanese on her brain? But she used to go quite happily for therapy sessions. Once she began seeing **Pamela**, our father's insubstantial presence in her life began to take on an overabundance of meaning. Whether because of Freud or *Oedipus Rex*, Westerners seemed to be perversely obsessed with father figures.

"Still goes to demonstrations too," she added.

David participated year-round in **antinuke, prochoice, gun control**, and other such demonstrations, even spending money on airfare to get there.

"For a marriage partner, he'd be a bit **too much**, wouldn't he?" I said.

This observation was pointless. Shortly after splitting up with Kanae years before, **David Zuckerman** had married, divorced, and was apparently now in a good marriage with his second wife.

"That's right." Nanae blew cigarette smoke in the air, her lips affectedly pursed. This was her public smoking style. "But he doesn't push his beliefs on you, so it might not actually be too bad. **Gloria** isn't a **vegetarian**."

Gloria was David's second wife and, according to Nanae, **nowhere near as attractive as Kanae**.

"Well, at least he's rich," I said.

"Yeah, and he's really smart."

"Too bad he's married," I said jokingly. I had only drunk a little of the beer, and already I could feel it taking effect.

"Yep, too bad," Nanae laughed back. With one last drag on her cigarette, she crushed it out in the glass ashtray. Then she looked at me and said, "Is there any guy out there that's reasonable? Somebody decent?"

Her tone was facetious, and yet there seemed to be something behind her words. Knowing I thought she and **Henryk** had no future, was she playing up to me, or after several months of living with him, had she reached the same conclusion? I couldn't tell.

I looked back at her. "No, not likely."

"I don't mind a nice-looking Japanese guy."

"Even less likely."

She sighed. "I'd mention that it's all gay men, everywhere you look, if it weren't such a cliché."

For women living in **Manhattan**—especially women traveling in anything resembling artistic circles—this was the consummate cliché.

Green asparagus soup was set before us.

"You've heard this, right? '**There are only two kinds of good men in this world.'** " She looked up as she picked up her soupspoon. Her mouth was in a half-smile as she prepared to tell her joke.

"No, what are they?"

"Married men and homosexuals."

I laughed out loud. **"David Zuckerman and David Zimmerman."**

"You said it, baby."

David Zimmerman, another friend from Nanae's days in conservatory, was a gay man who had been living with his lover for a decade. He lived in **Manhattan** too, and when she occasionally saw him, she would mention his name to me over the phone.

"Have you seen **Zimmerman** lately?" I asked.

"Yes, after **Passover,** I think it was. He was telling me about his parents' inviting him and his boyfriend to their house."

A table loaded with Passover delicacies, and in the center a pair of tall candlesticks. Seated around the table would be aunts, uncles, and cousins of all ages, and in their midst, two men on intimate terms. I pictured the scene.

"I wonder when his parents decided to accept them?"

"I don't know. He says it was difficult for everyone when he came out. **Very trying for them all.**"

"Well, good for the parents for coming around."

"I agree. **I met them once at a concert.** They were as nice as could be."

"Is his work going well?"

David Zimmerman too had given up the piano.

"Uh-huh. He's a good businessman."

Somehow, by whatever route, he had ended up involved in the production of musicals.

This conversation differed very little from the sort of conversations single middle-class women were having all over **Manhattan.** The luxury of dining out in the daytime with a close female friend at a nice restaurant with starched napkins was a small festival to enliven the monotony of everyday life, and such small festivals gave American women strength to face the next day—but we were not American women. The two of us, enjoying our lighthearted conversation, were not close friends but two sisters who had grown up together on foreign soil. Two foreigners in this country who had never formed any friendships closer than their own sisterhood. In some people around us, Americans, we glimpsed a loneliness that was chilling, but the loneliness we sisters shared was of a different order.

That day, it occurred to me that all Nanae's American friends were people from the dorm where she had lived while at the conservatory. In the past ten years or so, ever since giving up the piano, she had devoted all her energy to a succession of romances and her unending feud with Mother and done almost nothing to find a place in American society. And now, having come to the point where she needed to make her own way, she had taken up with a man who was even less rooted in America than she was, whose English was shaky, who didn't even have a bank account in his own name, let alone a steady job—a man with nothing at all going for him. Whatever friendships, whatever human connections she had for support were fraying before my eyes.

"You know something?" Nanae began, changing the subject. "It would be awkward coming to a place like this with **Henryk. You know, he would feel very uncomfortable.**" An expression akin to mortification crossed her face.

"Would he?"

The sun must have gone behind a cloud, for the area by the windows suddenly darkened. The furnishings around us stood out in bold relief, and I realized that many of the tables were now empty.

"Yes. You know the kind of rundown **bar** with posters for beer in the window—what they probably mean by an '**Irish bar**'?"

"Maybe. I don't know." I imagined the sort of dim place likely to be found in any town in America. A television in the corner with a football game on, and drunk men making a racket as they cheered and jeered. Empty beer bottles on tables. No men in suits. No women. The sort of place I never had the nerve to go into, though I was sometimes tempted.

"That's where he feels most **comfortable**."

"Oh. You go with him?"

"Only to places where women go. With loud music banging away."

I kept my eyes on her face as she went on.

"Back when **Henryk** was in **Brooklyn**, we used to go to places like that all the time."

"You did?"

"And anyway . . ." She hesitated before starting up again. "And anyway, when I do go someplace nice with **Henryk**, the waiter's attitude is always different. It's like he's looking down on us. Like he's waiting on us only because he has to . . . Because **Henryk** gives off a certain kind of vibe."

I pictured **Henryk**'s face. For some reason hard to pinpoint, it didn't look American. With shoulder-length brown hair and eyes that seemed to convey spiritual tension, he looked almost like an ascetic monk from a medieval painting. Watching him recite Polish poem after poem written to shake the spirit of Slavic lands awake, Nanae had been totally captivated. But his face was also bony, his expression rather seedy. Moreover, even though he was a gourmand as well as a drinker, he was quite thin and even looked half starved, owing in part to his missing teeth and the way he dressed.

"**He has no manners.**"

"That *would* make bringing him to a place like this hard."

"Yes, it does. He doesn't see why I would even want to come somewhere like this. '**You are such a princess,**' he says, and it's no compliment. He says it when he's irritated."

"Hah!" I laughed. "**A Japanese American Princess.**" Not a **Jewish American Princess**. A JAP of another sort.

Nanae ignored my quip. "**He says I'm too bourgeois,**" she scoffed.

"He uses the word '**bourgeois**'?" For someone who had fled socialism to criticize a person who grew up in the West as "too bourgeois" was too too predictable, and also absurd.

"Yes, even though his English is limited, to say the least. Words like that must be **international.**"

"Internationalism" had of course played a key role in the spread of Marxism, but Nanae, I felt sure, was using the word in ignorance of this bit of history.

After a moment she sighed loudly. Then lit another cigarette. Service was slow, so I wasn't sure if we would be able to do all we had planned, but, if not, I didn't really mind. Nanae probably didn't give a hoot about **Donald Judd**'s sculptures either. But I also had the nagging feeling she had something on her mind, something she wanted to say but couldn't get out, so she was talking around it in circles. A familiar weariness came over me. When would this sister of mine ever stop casting all her woes onto me? The exuberant mood we had had on entering the restaurant was fading.

Nanae's **Salade César** was set in front of her, but she went on smoking. Next came my **Poulet à l'Orientale**. She motioned for me to go ahead and then began to talk again.

"Remember Mitsui, that ultra-Japanese guy?"

"Oh, Mitsui! How is he doing?" Lately there had been no mention over the phone of the man, so I'd been curious, but I avoided asking out of fear that she was feeling abandoned. "Is he coming back this way?"

"Not any time soon."

Mitsui was an elite businessman. In Nanae's colorful array of boyfriends, he fell along the lines of Suzuki, the bureaucrat who used to take her out to classy restaurants when she was only seventeen. She had met Mitsui when he was posted to New York several years before, and at one point he had sworn he would divorce his wife and marry Nanae, but whether that had just been talk on his part, or whether Nanae herself had gotten romantically involved with someone else, eventually he went back to his family in Japan. He still seemed to have feelings for her, however, and whenever he

returned to New York he would invite her out to dinner. When
that happened, she always sounded rather pleased. I hadn't heard
her rather-pleased-sounding voice in some time.

"A while ago he called me from Tokyo. He says he's as busy as ever."
Her voice was tinged with annoyance, but less than I had feared.

"Mitsui" was not the man's real name. He was so proud of
working for the conglomerate Mitsui & Co. that "Mitsui" was
how she referred to him—behind his back. His pride was no
run-of-the-mill variety. His family had a close association with
Mitsui's arch rival, Mitsubishi, going back decades: his grandfather had been on the board of directors of Mitsubishi Bank, his
father was an executive at Mitsubishi Heavy Industries, Ltd., and
his younger sister in her single days had worked for Mitsubishi
Corporation. He himself possessed sterling academic credentials
that amply qualified him to join their ranks, yet he had flouted
family tradition by going to work for Mitsui & Co. This was the
source of his pride. He saw himself as quite the rebel—all the
more reason, perhaps, that he liked to go to Japanese restaurants
accompanied by a peculiar Japanese woman, one who did not
look quite Japanese, so that waiters sometimes addressed her
in English.

"He's like a robot in a suit, you know? Always strutting around."

I laughed and nodded. "You could have him bring you to places
like this."

"The places he takes me to are on a different level." Nanae drew
in her chin and looked at me with a faint, pitying smile.

Whenever she went out with Mitsui, she always called the next
day to report where they had eaten and how much it must have
cost—her estimate often surpassing a month's food bill for us. Most
of those almost criminally expensive restaurants were Japanese,
patronized by expatriates on company budgets who casually spent
a small fortune on their meals—a Japanese custom that Americans

found incomprehensible. When I was younger, I too had been escorted to such restaurants, but as Japan grew richer and Japanese people developed a taste for rare delicacies, even consuming gold leaf in their pursuit of the last word in fine dining, our connection with that nouveau riche Japan grew more and more distant. In **Manhattan**, we could only afford the sort of Japanese restaurant frequented by cost-conscious Americans.

"Next time he comes I'll invite you."

"Okay."

No telling when "next time" might be. As if she had read my mind, Nanae murmured, "Though who knows when that might be . . ."

For a while we plied our knives and forks in silence.

Mitsui was the last of Nanae's boyfriends to belong to Japan's elite. I had met him a few times, and each time he was dressed in a perfectly tailored three-piece suit (it always looked too tight-fitting to my eyes, but that was the way Japanese businessmen dressed). He gave the impression that if he walked down **Wall Street**, Tokyo's Marunouchi business district might waft into being behind him. He saw Nanae as a young thing dependent on her parents and full of extravagant grievances, and so he went on indulging and pampering her.

If Mitsui dropped out of her life and then I did too, what would Nanae do? Though not very money-minded, she was snobbish and spoiled by the privileged upbringing we had enjoyed, especially after coming to America; it was unlikely that she would now settle for a Japanese man of the sort known as a "New York drifter," someone changing jobs aimlessly, not sent over by a company, not a student. Yet hadn't she remained too Japanese to go on living in this country without some connection to Japan?

Suddenly Nanae spoke up, the hand holding her fork arrested in midair. "These days I feel less and less able to fit into American society. . . ." Her eyes were fixed on my face. She had the same bleak air I had glimpsed out the bus window. "As if no matter how long I'm here, I'll never fit in. . . ." She set down her fork and stared at me again. "We're not white."

The word "white" took me by surprise. My hand too froze in midair.

"I mean, we're just not," she said.

"No, we're not."

"The longer I'm here in America, the more Oriental I feel . . ."

I looked at her blankly. The Japanese word for "white person"—白人 *hakujin*—sounded strange, coming from her lips. I realized that though I used the English word without compunction, I too hardly ever used *hakujin*, and certainly not with Nanae. Japanese people basically had no need for such a race-specific word. When Europeans first reached Japanese soil from the southern sea to conduct trade or spread the gospel, the term 南蛮 *namban*, "southern barbarians," came into use, following Chinese tradition; then as Japanese people saw more Europeans with their own eyes, they called them 紅毛碧眼 *kōmōhekigan*, "the red-haired and blue-eyed." Finally, after the country opened its doors to the world, the notion of the West, 西洋 *seiyō*, was introduced, along with the word 西洋人 *seiyōjin*, "Westerners." That word took some root in the language, but a simpler expression became common in speech: 外人 *gaijin*, "outsider." The word for "white" never caught on, probably because the country escaped Western colonization and so the Japanese never had to deal with rulers who were white. The word always sounded foreign, like a direct translation of a sociological term. Yet that day it was to come up again and again between us, as if a taboo had been lifted. Our repeated use of the word might have suggested our avoidance of it until then.

A brief silence settled on us. Her eyes began to smolder. She blurted out, "Tell me something. Does this ever happen to you? You're walking down the street and you get the feeling you shouldn't be there, because you're not white, that you really have no right to walk down the street, or at least not as much as white people do. You ever feel like that?"

It sounded less like a question than a confession. "Sure. I feel that way sometimes."

"You do?"

"Yeah. Sometimes."

"With me, if the **doorman** or the **hairdresser** is white, I often get the feeling I have no right to accept their service. The thought goes through my mind."

"I know the feeling."

"Even in a restaurant like this, I wonder if it's all right to sit back and enjoy my food this way. Somewhere inside, I wonder."

The few customers still at tables in the restaurant were all white. Even the waitstaff was white. In most restaurants, busboys were likely to be black, or Puerto Rican, or Arab or Indian or Asian—many of them immigrants—but not here; still, it seemed likely that nonwhites would be found in the narrow kitchen, out of sight, working long hours. Such situations were common in America. The finer the restaurant, the more likely that servers in the public eye were not just good-looking but white.

"When did you start feeling that way?"

"I don't know."

"Recently?"

"The longer I'm here, the more it feels like I don't **count** the way white people do . . ."

I looked at Nanae's face, now stiffened, and thought back to the peculiar fear that had haunted me growing up in America. Sometime after we arrived, the childish innocence of the fears that used to come over me walking in the Ginza with Nanae—*What if I get lost? What if I lose the money Mama gave me for the train?*—was underscored by a new, far more chilling fear: *What if*

I get murdered? Making this fear worse was the vague awareness that even if I were murdered, American society wouldn't care. I took to wishing my father were a diplomat, because then surely in the event of my murder America would be forced to sit up and take notice—a point that would hardly seem to matter once I was gone. I must have dimly sensed that my life in America had but the limited value of an Asian life. All the more so since this was before America began paying court to a newly rich Japan. **"All men are created equal."** Perhaps. But all lives did not have equal value. This was true in all societies; everywhere, people were sorted into groups and were assigned greater or lesser value by various markers—the way they dressed, behaved, spoke. Yet here in America where people gathered (or had been made to gather) from around the world, race, in its most loosely defined form, was a marker that superseded all others.

In a crowd, Mitsui, the quintessential Japanese elite, would be barely distinguishable from an illegal Chinese immigrant, and a young government official from Africa would likewise be barely distinguishable from a black delinquent. The death of a social nonentity was a mere statistic. The early fear implanted in my heart evidently ran deep, for I recall that later, after I was accepted into an Ivy League university, I let out a sigh of relief: now if I were murdered, the **New York Times** was sure at least to run a small article under the headline **"Japanese Student Shot on Campus."**

"Remember how Father used to take Della for walks all the time?" Nanae was saying. "Now that I think of it, I bet some people didn't like it. I mean, realtors even use the expression **all-white neighborhood**, don't they?"

"Yeah."

"Right? Mother could dress up all she liked to go to the **Metropolitan Opera**, and for all we know the whole time people were looking at her and thinking, *Oh dear, here's another Oriental,* *ruining the atmosphere."* I opened my mouth to speak, but Nanae went on. *"How would that woman know the first thing about opera? But you know, I think the same thing when I see an Oriental."* She looked down at her **Caesar salad**. And then sighed. "Just thinking about it makes me feel rotten, sitting here in a place like this. . . ."

I peered at her. "Did something happen?"

"Not really."

"Something between you and **Henryk?**"

"Not really. We're fine."

I was silent.

Nanae shrugged. "When I'm with him, I get treated like an Oriental."

I remained silent, waiting.

"He gets looked down on, for starters. Because it's so obvious he's an immigrant laborer. **A Polack.** So when I'm with him, people look down on me too."

"So something did happen."

She was staring hollow-eyed at her salad.

"Tell me."

"It was nothing. No big deal." She flicked a glance at me. "We got thrown out of a **bar**."

"Thrown out? You got thrown out of a **bar**? How did that happen?"

"It happened, that's all." She sighed again and began to talk rapidly. "A perfectly nice **bar**. Close to **Lincoln Center**. It looked really stylish from the outside, and I'd always wanted to go in. The other day we went to see that **Andrzej Wajda** film at the **Regency**, remember? So since we were in the neighborhood, afterwards we stopped by. I got him to go in with me. **It was Saturday night and the place was full. The only seats available were at the counter.** Maybe **Henryk** was nervous or something, but he got drunker and drunker . . . and then he kept trying to kiss me. Even though I didn't want him to."

"Oh, no."

"I didn't want people to look down on me because I was with him, so I was dressed carefully, and when I placed my **order** I used proper English. I was sitting up straight and everything. And he just got more and more aggressive. **"No, Henryk. Please,"** I'd say, but he wouldn't stop. **He just wouldn't listen and wouldn't stop kissing me."**

"Uh-oh."

"Pretty soon the **bartender** had had enough. He came and stood in front of us and said, **'Will you two behave yourselves or will I have to ask you to leave?'** He didn't say it just to **Henryk**, mind you. He said **'Will you two,'** meaning both of us. **'Will you two behave yourselves?'** I was so humiliated I just blanked out. I took **Henryk** by the hand and started to leave, but he was drunk, so he yelled back at the bartender in his awful English and wouldn't move. Then the **bartender** got mad and said, **'Hey, look, I just don't think you two belong in a place like this.'** In a tone of utmost contempt. Everybody there must have heard him. I was mortified, and so I left **Henryk** there and ran outside. After a while he came out looking deflated. He always just shrivels up."

"Was the **bartender** white?"

"Of course he was white."

"An **actor** or a **dancer**? Lots of them tend bar, you know."

"He wasn't that type. **Just a plain-looking white bartender.** Middle-aged."

"An unpleasant kind of guy?"

"Not especially. Just an ordinary guy. But a **bartender**! How do you think it felt to have someone like that come up to you and say, **'I just don't think you two belong in a place like this'?"**

I could imagine the insult. At the same time, part of me marveled that we sisters had lived over thirty years without ever being spoken to in such a way before, either here or back in Japan.

"Something similar could have happened even if I were white. We were at fault, after all. But having a thing like that happen to

you really makes you aware of being Oriental, you know? If I'd
been a white woman, that **bartender** wouldn't have been so rude.
At least not to my face. If I were white, he would have seen I wasn't
enjoying it. He would have drawn a distinction between **Henryk**
and me. **Because it was so obvious.** But because I'm Oriental, he
just couldn't see the difference. People of his **class** have no idea
there are all sorts of Oriental people. I mean, he never even looked
at me properly in the face. When I came in, all he saw was an Oriental woman with long hair. Then when things started to get out
of hand, he assumed that both of us were to blame. **And you know
what's worse? I realized that it wasn't just Henryk who made me look
cheap. I made him look cheap too, because I was Oriental. To some
Americans—I wouldn't say all, but to some Americans, a guy who
hangs around with an Oriental girl is already a cheap guy.** Although
to **Henryk,** I'm a princess. To that **bartender—what was I, I wonder.
Maybe not much more than an Oriental whore . . .yeah, that's right.
I wasn't anything better, I tell you, than an Oriental whore.** I felt
really, truly miserable that night."

Her eyes were moist and her mouth was trembling, the corners
downturned, but she didn't burst into tears. I was relieved, having watched on countless occasions as she started to cry, her eye
makeup dissolving so that black tears streamed down her cheeks.

How must Nanae have felt as she and **Henryk** set off after that
horribleness, the wintry wind sharp and cutting? On their way
home, she must have quarreled with him, her voice tearful and hys-
terical—and all in English. After five minutes of walking through
muddy snow, her legs would have felt frozen from the soles on up,
making her more miserable. Once in the **loft,** what went through
her mind as she changed into her nightgown? Had she already
wiped off her ruined eye makeup with a crumpled tissue on the
way home? What expression did she wear as she slid between the
sheets? In the old days, no matter what happened she always slept

soundly, but lately she would sometimes say, "Maybe I'm getting old; sometimes I lie in bed wide awake and can't get to sleep," so perhaps she had lain with her head on her pillow, staring at the ceiling. Or perhaps she had turned and looked through the big, still-uncurtained window at the dark winter sky . . .

"It's your fault for being with **Henryk**," I said after a considerable pause.

"I know, but . . ." She struggled not to cry. "That night it hit me." Her voice was hoarse. "I realized that unlike me, **Henryk** . . ." She stopped, then started again. "I mean, he was treated terribly that night, but in the end, he's white."

Looking on **Henryk**'s angular face as he lay drunk and dead to the world beside her that night, had she said to herself, "In the end, he's white"?

"In time he'll fit into American society better than I ever will."

"Sure."

"Like **Karl**."

The German photographer **Karl**, the boyfriend who had provided the pretext for Nanae to leave our parents' house once and for all, had been so favorably disposed to America that in a short time he was thoroughly Americanized, to the extent that once on a **Lufthansa** flight home, a compatriot had complimented him on his "excellent German." He had moved to the Midwest, married a German American woman with roots in Bavaria, his homeland, and fathered a child. At some point Nanae had told me, "I ran into him by chance. He said he was in **Manhattan** on **business**. He looked more American than ever, in a yucky plaid **jacket**."

"Or **Claudia**, for that matter. Or **Janos**."

"Right."

Claudia was the Italian friend who sometimes woke her up with her "*tatahta tatahta*." **Janos** was a Hungarian who had defected years ago—whether he had ever been her boyfriend, I wasn't sure.

Europeans like them eventually blended into American society, which seemed logical enough given that when all was said and done, the United States as a nation had been created by men of European descent.

"Whereas we'll always be Orientals, however long we stay." Her voice still sounded hoarse.

Where we lived, being Asian never caused us any particular difficulty, but neither could we ever forget that that's what we were. It was less an awareness than a sensation. The moment I crossed the threshold on the way out of my apartment, the sensation came over me like a clinging shadow.

A tall figure silently approached our table.

"How is everything, ladies?"

"Oh, very good."

Nanae swallowed and gave him the flirty smile that was second nature to her. I smiled too, tardily. The handsome young waiter with styled hair showing the tooth marks of a comb nodded at each of us and then left, as silently as he had arrived.

"It's not quite at the level of '**very good**,'" I said.

Nanae shrugged. The smile of a few moments ago lingered on her face. I set about carving up what remained of my *Poulet à l'Orientale*, which at least was not too sweet. Nanae reached for her pack of **Virginia Slims** and with a flick of her wrist removed a cigarette, letting her long fingers show to good advantage.

From a distance, the waiter was watching.

I recalled the change in Nanae after she went off to college, a change that had driven Mother to call her "boy crazy" or a "nympho." Even then, I had the vague sense that it had something to do with her not being white. A girl's interest in attracting the opposite sex was an animal instinct, but at the same time it was something political, a mirror of social hierarchy. Mother used to lament how "Americanized" Nanae was, but white American girls generally felt no need to affect a flashy, loud appearance the way Nanae did; they knew without thinking that as members of the dominant group in America, they were the natural objects of male desire. Other young women had to either give up on the whole business or take pains to play up their femininity, going to two or three times the lengths of white girls to make themselves alluring. Nanae's efforts had paid off handsomely in Boston, a college town full of young men open-minded or curious enough to be attracted to someone like her.

I found myself sighing.

Nanae looked up at me. "What?"

"Nothing."

She now looked pretty normal, compared to those days. Still, just as she was giving up heavy makeup, she had started letting her sleek, black hair grow long, which I had mixed feelings about. When she was working on a piece of art, she tied it up, but when she went out anywhere, as now, she let it tumble down her back. Undoubtedly many a white guy with flyaway hair like dandelion fluff had told her, **"Oh, Nanae! Your hair is so beautiful!"**, making her preen. She still sometimes wore the stilettos known, wryly, as **fuck-me-heels**.

What will she look like when she grows old?

A lineup of Japanese women with surly faces came to my mind. We occasionally encountered them, women who had come to America soon after World War II and were much older than us but who had been proper young ladies in their time. One played the piano, another painted, another was the wife of a wealthy white American. They had lost their gracious air as vague discontent set in. Japanese war brides on their way to becoming grannies had the careworn faces common to aging women of every race and nation, but those highborn women were a different breed, their proud faces dried up and hard-set.

What a contrast between them and the young Asian American women appearing on **campus** in increasing numbers every year! The daughters of second- or third-generation immigrants, most of them had undoubtedly lost their ancestral language; at a glance, it was impossible to distinguish the Japanese Americans from the Korean and Chinese Americans. With the hardships of their forebears relegated to history, the surging Asian economies gave them new confidence, and thanks to the introduction in academia of what was called "multiculturalism," they seemed to count among their own virtues the ancient culture of their ancestral land. They walked about the campus with a self-assured swagger, as if they belonged.

"If we'd grown up in **California**, things would be different," I said, imagining how the large Asian presence on the West Coast would have made us feel less isolated.

Nanae raised her head and looked at me. She seemed calmer now, more like her usual self. **"California?"**

"Yes."

"No thanks. Who wants to grow up in California?" she said with typical East Coast scorn. **"It's way too far from Europe!"**

She picked up the saltshaker and, almost on cue, began salting her salad in what she called the **"European way,"** which was to tap the shaker with her index finger lightly. This began when she was going out with **Karl**, and when I used the saltshaker by shaking it, many a time she would tell me bossily, **"That's the American way, you know. The Europeans do it this way,"** and demonstrate accordingly, her pinky extended affectedly. When we first arrived on the East Coast, she seemed bent on assimilating; how had she become such a snob? Asians often borrowed European manners to look down on America, and since I myself was majoring in French literature I was perhaps no one to talk. Still, Nanae's affinity for all things European had developed rapidly after she met **Karl**, and around the time she was demonstrating the "proper" way to use a saltshaker, she was making stained-glass art she said was inspired by medieval churches she'd visited in Germany. Since she herself was a foreigner, it was perhaps only natural that she should have friends from other countries, but most of them were European.

What if we *had* grown up in **California**? I now wondered for the first time.

Nanae put the saltshaker back next to the carnations and glanced up. **"I'm perfectly happy I grew up in New York, aren't you?"**

"Yes, but if we'd grown up in **California**, think how much more easily we could have blended in."

She said nothing.

"By now we might have been Americans."

"I don't especially want to be an American, and you always wanted to stay Japanese much more than I did." After a pause, she continued, "In any case, you and I can never be Americans. **We'll only be Japanese Americans."**

"I know."

"Or Asian Americans."

But nearly half the population of **California** was already made up of non-European immigrants. And statistically speaking, the entire country was predicted to resemble **California** in the not very distant future. When I pointed this out, Nanae said·

"I know this sounds terrible, but I don't know if I want that to happen. That's not my image of America."

"But if it does, it won't matter so much that we're Asian."

"I suppose not. **I guess that's true."**

"We could walk down the street with a lighter heart."

"Yeah, I guess so." She ate her salad, using the tines of her fork to move the croutons to the edge of the plate, seeming at a loss to imagine this new America.

*You wouldn't have to bawl your eyes out because you thought you'd
been insulted in a bar either,* I added silently.

For the last half hour or so there had been only a few couples in
the restaurant, engrossed in conversation. They seemed, like us, to
have all the time in the world. The sun had come out, and in the
afternoon light the pavement outside was a dazzling white. Inside,
the languid air of a spring afternoon pervaded the room, reaching
even our dim corner, inviting us to linger longer.

"The last time I went back to Japan," Nanae began, holding her
fork in midair, looking as if she was summoning a memory from
afar, "I felt really at ease there. Being in my own country."

"Of course you did."

"To walk somewhere nearby, I could go out in flat sandals, no
makeup, my hair a mess, and not be bothered. It was so nice."

"Nobody would pay you any attention."

"And I didn't care if they did. People looking down on you for
how disheveled you look is different from them looking down on
you for your race."

"That's very true."

Nanae let out an exaggerated sigh.

A black-and-white photograph emerged in my mind. A scene by
the Tamagawa River—Nanae, early in middle school, being yanked
along by our dog Della, Nanae's legs at an angle, bracing against
the pull, a wide smile on her face. A young girl yet to blossom, not
sulking for once, caught in a moment's delight. I always liked that
photo. It contained the innocence of girlhood, nothing more, and
yet as an adult I came to see in it the innocence that might have
been possible for us both had we stayed in Japan.

Naturally, we could never regain that innocence even if we
went back to Japan. But would we have been better off if we had
remained blissfully sheltered, unsuspecting of what awaited anyone
who stepped out of the archipelago? Shouldn't Japanese people at

least be aware of what the West thought of us historically—as much as the West had ever bothered to think of us in return? Wouldn't we then no longer be so self-deluded, telling ourselves that we, unlike other Asians, were essentially Western?

Nanae finished her **Caesar salad** and dabbed her mouth with her napkin, deftly avoiding smearing her lipstick. I had long since finished my meal and was waiting for her, sipping my now-flat beer. Nanae's cigarette smoking meant it took her that much longer to eat.

"Hey." She seemed to realize my thoughts were far away.

"What?"

"Who we were in Japan is basically the same as who we are now, right?"

I nodded, thinking not about me but about her.

"That's what's so strange to me. Because doesn't it seem like there's a huge **break** between before and after coming here? Like we entered a different world."

"Absolutely."

"And yet I'm still the same. **The same old me.**"

She was always **the same old Nanae**. "Yes, you are."

Nanae folded her napkin and laid it on the table. It was so well starched that even folded, it did not lie flat. "It just seems so strange. **You know what I mean?**"

"Yeah."

"Despite all that's happened."

"Yeah."

Apparently content to leave it there, she reached for her shoulder bag. "Mind if I go to the powder room?"

"Be my guest."

"Want to come?"

"I'm fine."

"Well then, **excuse me.**"

The waiter followed her with his eyes as she walked across the room, her long black hair falling to her narrow waist.

When we were in Japan, the East had been much farther away than the West. The country wanted to forget its disastrous overture in Asia and felt the need to become more enlightened, turning its back on the East and becoming, or trying to become, Westernized. I myself played with blue-eyed dolls, drew pictures of princesses wearing long flaring beribboned skirts, and read girls' novels written by foreign authors with main characters who had foreign names written in *katakana*. When I heard we were moving to America, my main thought was that now I would be sitting at school next to a freckled blond boy like the one on the imported box of **Kellogg's Corn Flakes**. The prospect pleased me. I was more than happy to leave behind Japanese boys, who were already throwing around rough, uncouth male talk. A freckle-faced blond boy was bound to be much more civil and would surely later turn into a true, refined gentleman. It wasn't only me; the whole nation was impatient for Japan to transform into an enlightened society, as it had been determined to do in the Meiji era at the dawn of its modernity.

And how that Meiji era lived on in the professor's office in the tall Gothic building on campus!

Every time I pushed open the arched wooden door to the office and stepped inside, I was overwhelmed at the sight of row upon row of Japanese books, their spines aligned on floor-to-ceiling shelves interrupted only by a pair of small windows with artisanal glass. Here amid the dust of old paper, the smell of tobacco, and the glow of dark reddish-brown sherry, the Japan from a hundred years ago lived quietly on. The astonishment of the Japanese upon encountering Commodore Perry's Black Ships and the astonishment of Westerners upon encountering wood-and-paper houses—the two astonishments that marked the Meiji era— were somehow evoked in equal measure here. "**Big Mac**," the professor whose inner sanctum this was, sat in the armchair at one end of the room and seemed himself to be the living embodiment of those bygone days; from personal experience he knew well how one could encounter faraway cultures in unexpected places.

"And Europe was there, right there in the midst of Kobe."

Born in Kobe to a Scottish father and a Japanese mother—she died when he was only two—**Big Mac** lived in Japan until his late teens, when the outbreak of war forced him to leave and go to Scotland with his father. Though young, he was soon recruited to work for Allied intelligence in Washington, DC, because of his knowledge of Japanese. When the war ended he returned to Scotland, finished his studies there, married a Scottish woman, and eventually landed with his wife at this East Coast university, where he lived while immersing himself not in Americana but in the worlds of prewar Kobe and early modern Japanese literature. **Big Mac** was a small man with a round, full face that suggested to students what **McDonald's** was famous for, hence the unlikely nickname, but his manner and way of speaking were as imperious and intimidating as if he were a member of the English aristocracy. For all that, he spoke of Natsume Sōseki with a reverence that I found moving, and his awe for the writers of Meiji and Taishō Japan was infectious.

Since the French department allowed its graduate students to take some outside courses, for the second consecutive year I had enrolled in **Big Mac**'s weekly graduate seminar on modern Japanese literature, which met here, in his office. His taste in literature was refined, and he had no compunction in assigning long old novels with little plot to speak of, novels that not even elderly Japanese read, let alone the younger generation. **"It has no plot!"** fresh graduate students were known to naively complain. When a hush fell over the room and **Big Mac** glanced at them caustically over the top of his glasses, the imprudent remarks stopped.

We read little of Akutagawa Ryūnosuke, two of whose clever short works had combined to inspire the Kurosawa film *Rashōmon*. **Big Mac** had no use for such stories with a definite structure. However, after a young woman in the seminar published a paper on a different Akutagawa short story, he had her tell us about it one day as the seminar was nearing its end.

"Shall we start pouring some sherry now?"

With this prompt, seminar members got up from their seats and retrieved paper cups from a shelf as **Big Mac** proceeded to open a bottle of sherry. We would then pass the bottle of slightly sweet, dark reddish-brown liquid around the table. It was a luxury possible only because the seminar was so much more intimate than any in the French department. As the afternoon sun was waning and we had finished our discussion of the assigned writer for that day, all that remained was sherry and **Christina**'s presentation.

Christina began nervously, while on my lap sat a book opened to that very short story, one I had read many times in that musty set of vermilion-covered books. A young woman dressed entirely in rose pink was ascending, on the arm of her father, a staircase at the Rokumeikan, "Deer Cry Pavilion," the grand French Renaissance-styled structure that symbolized the pinnacle of Meiji Westernization. The rose-pink girl had been taught French and ballroom dancing, and tonight was her very first ball.

I took a sip of the sherry and felt it warming me immediately.
Christina's stiff, monotonous voice filled the seminar room.
Amid the languor of the moment I looked absently down
at the pages of the book. Strings of elegant words and
expressions no longer in use beckoned me back to
the fragrant dawn of Japan's modern era, and
before my eyes I saw . . . dancing and
pirouetting pirouetting and dancing
dipping and gliding in an enchanted
waltz a maiden with a single pink rose
in her hair clad in a rose-colored ball
gown her feet shod in dainty rose
dancing slippers, all in rose from
head to toe save for the light-blue
ribbon encircling her slender neck.
Her beauty is so expressive of the beauty
of a maiden of Japan's Enlightenment
that it surprises the Chinese officials
with long queues as well as the count
with his graying beard and the
countess attired in Louis XV
style, all of whom can but sigh
with admiration. All around
the ballroom are silver and
gold chrysanthemums, white
shoulders, and swallow-tail
coats. Lace and flowers and
ivory fans move in noiseless
waves and the smoke of cigars
wafts slowly upward like dreams.
The other maidens are clad in
evening gowns of light blue

and rose pink, and they twitter like
birds. The strains of the beautiful
Blue Danube Waltz fill the
air. The young man who
invited her to dance is
a French naval officer with
a thick mustache. He leads
her expertly, weaving through the
crowd and now and then whispering
gallant words of French in her ear.
The maiden responds to his sweet
words with smiles of embarrassment.
The naval officer wonders—does
a young lady so beautiful live
like a doll in a house of
paper and bamboo?...
With slender metal
chopsticks does
she convey
grains of
rice to
her small
mouth
from a palm-sized
bowl decorated in blue
flowers? ... The gay
orchestral melody bubbles
like champagne. Borne on the
breeze of the music, the delicate
dancing slippers slide ever more lightly across
the floor dancing and dancing and dancing ... The
French naval officer accompanied Akiko to one of the
tables, and together they took spoons for ice cream. She was
aware that the whole time, his eyes were drawn now to her hands, now to

her hair, now to the light-blue ribbon that encircled her neck. Of course she found this by no means unpleasant, yet she entertained a moment's feminine doubt.

When a German young lady passed them by, a red camellia tucked into her bosom of black velvet, to resolve her doubt Akiko murmured these words of admiration: "How beautiful Western ladies truly are!"

The naval officer shook his head. "Japanese women are beautiful too. Especially you—"

"That is not true."

"Yes, it is. I do mean it. You could attend a ball in Paris as you are. Everyone would be captivated. You are like a princess in a painting by Watteau."

Akiko knew nothing of Watteau, but the naval officer's words evoked romantic visions of the past—a fountain in a shadowy forest, fading roses—that vanished without a trace the next moment. But she was a very astute young woman, and she did not forget to pursue her lingering concern:

"I would love to attend a ball in Paris."

"Oh, a ball in Paris is no different from this." The naval officer glanced around the room at the waves of people and the masses of chrysanthemums, and then a weary smile seemed to stir deep in his eyes. He held his ice cream spoon in midair and added, half to himself, "Not only in Paris. Balls are the same everywhere."

"This is basically an exercise in style," Christina was going on. Akutagawa's short story "The Ball" was an exercise in style that could be traced back to Mori Ōgai's "Dancing Girl" and on through Mishima Yukio's "Rokumeikan," an exercise in borrowing traditional Japanese expressions to describe the Western or Westernized world in new language, she contended, a style that took full advantage of the refined grace of pseudo-classical Japanese . . .

I listened, abstracted, as my eyes retraced the words on the page: " . . . and added, half to himself, 'Not only in Paris. Balls are the same everywhere.'"

Balls everywhere are the same?

The young French naval officer, weary of the vanity of city life, did not merely offer the gallant opinion that Japanese ladies are fully as beautiful as Western ladies, but also said that there was little to choose between Tokyo and Paris. What could Akutagawa possibly have intended by this fairy tale?

Because this naval officer was based on the very man who, in real life, soon returned to France and wrote mockingly not only of Rokumeikan—"looks like a casino in one of our hot-spring resort towns"—and the balls held there, but also of the Japanese people who, quick to modernize their weapons, were equally keen to turn themselves into civilized and enlightened beings by imitating the West: "Such servile imitation, while naturally amusing to foreigners passing through, shows that the people have no taste and are totally lacking in national pride." Of the gentle sex in Japan: "How ugly they are, these poor little women of Japan! I prefer stating that brutally at first and then softening it with a bit of kindness by speaking of their charming wit, their wonderfully tiny hands, their face powder made of rice, their rouge, their lips dusted with gold, and a host of other artificial decorations." The truth was, he could only think of Japanese people as creatures utterly different from himself: "The yellow race and ours are at opposite poles of humanity." This very man went on to become a novelist whose power of description and exquisite style would eventually earn him a seat in the Académie française.

I had no intention of attempting to express my swirl of confused emotions. This was after all a literature seminar. As it turned out, **Big Mac** himself lit the fuse. **"Yes, I agree that this is an exercise in style,"** he said to **Christina,** **"but what do you make of the denial on the part of Akutagawa?"**

"The denial?" She didn't seem to understand.

"Yes, the denial—and the wishful thinking."

Christina looked troubled. Glancing at her, **Big Mac** took a sip of sherry.

"You know who this French naval officer is?"

"Yes. Pierre Loti."

"Well, then you must know how absolutely contemptuous he was of the Japanese people. Akutagawa must have known it too, at least to some degree."

If he weren't half-Japanese, **Big Mac** might not have spoken so bluntly. But then, as if a dam had burst, the sort of discussion that never happened in our seminar took off. The other students all had spent time in Japan and seemed perplexed by the wishful thinking that seemed to permeate people's minds there.

"This can't be mere ignorance," said **Big Mac**, looking around at our faces.

Paul, who often had something worthwhile to say, spoke up: "I call it selective ignorance."

I repeated the words "selective ignorance" to myself, relishing the cleverness of the expression. Unlike "denial," "repression," or "suppression," it didn't sound accusatory, as if to say "you fear the truth." It actually had a touch of humor. His coming up with it so smoothly seemed a sign that he had participated in discussions where the matter had come up before.

"Selective ignorance—I like that phrase," said **Stephen**, expressing just what I was thinking.

"You people are being very polite. Maybe too polite." Big Mac roared with laughter. A bit of sherry always made him jolly.

Nanae's voice sounded in my ear, bringing me back to where I was sitting in the restaurant. She had returned from the powder room.

"Guess what! **Couldn't believe my eyes!** It's exactly the same."

"What is?"

"The **wallpaper** in the ladies' room. It's the same as in your bedroom."

"The design by **William Morris**?"

"Yes. The exact same pattern!"

One summer vacation several years before, Nanae and I had thrown ourselves into the task of repapering walls in our **Long Island** house. We worked up a sweat, wearing bikini tops and shorts, by first making buckets of liquid starch in the basement. Then, as if to sweep away our family's jejune taste, I replaced the childish pink wallpaper in my room with a brick-colored William Morris pattern suggestive of the Victorian era. Little did I know the house would soon be sold.

"It really took me back," she said, sweeping freshly brushed hair over her shoulder with her right hand.

"Well, what a coincidence." I had been fond of that wallpaper.

"**Yep. Quite a coincidence.**" Nodding, she reached for her pack of cigarettes for the umpteenth time. "**Why don't you go and take a look at it?**"

"I should." But the beer had taken effect, making it an effort to move. Nor did I have any desire to deepen the sense of loss. "Maybe later."

"Okay." She glanced at me and then sighed. "I looked old in the mirror, middle-aged."

"You look fine."

"I don't know, I'm just so tired." It was around then that she began saying this. "**Worn out. Real worn out.**"

She exhaled smoke, holding the cigarette in her left hand. On her ring finger was the narrow silver ring that **Henryk** had made for her, unbeknownst to his boss, at the jewelry shop where he used to work. That narrow band of silver looked good on her finger, but it made me wonder once again, *What will become of her?*

"What in the world do you suppose will become of us?" It was as if she had read my mind, but she said it with a lilt. Perhaps Nanae's greatest strength was her inability to anticipate even the foreseeable perils of life.

"Anyway," she said, "I'm just worn out."

After removing our dishes, the young waiter once again handed us menus. The dessert offerings were at the bottom. We both settled on **Mousse au Chocolat**; I ordered tea, and Nanae asked for **cappuccino**.

"Tono liked **cappuccino**," I said after the waiter had gone. I wanted to change the mood—the way a news announcer on NHK, after relating news of civil strife, fires, and murder, would switch to a cheerful voice as if to say, "Now, on a more positive note . . ."

"Oh?" There was a bit of an edge to her voice. She had liked and approved of Tono, who had always treated me well, and she felt hurt in her own way that he had gone back to Japan. We had scarcely spoken of him since his departure at the end of the semester, back in December.

"But whenever he said, '**A cappuccino, please**,' they would always bring him tea."

"Tea?"

"Yes. Apparently the way he said '**a cappuccino**' sounded like '**a cup of tea**.' And maybe they figured he's Asian, probably likes tea, wouldn't order anything so European, anyway."

Her expression changed from a frown to a smile of delight. "**Please . . . You gotta be joking.**"

"**No, I'm not.**"

"**Oh, this is so funny . . .**" She howled with laughter as she waved away the cigarette smoke from in front of her face.

I could tell she was happy to go on talking about Tono like this. For a long time, we had enjoyed teasing him for being the quintessential Japanese male that he was. He himself had enjoyed our teasing. We told **Tono jokes** the way Americans told **Polish jokes**. To stop telling them just because he had left us to return to Japan seemed altogether too sad.

"It's true. It didn't happen just once or twice either."

"I can imagine. A Japanese man's English can be pretty horrible." She always said this.

"Yes, but he was here such a long time." I always said this. Indeed, some Japanese women had the uncanny ability to chatter away in near-native English after only a couple of years in America, so what ailed Japanese men?

"You know China's Cultural Revolution?" I said.

"Yeah."

"If there was ever something like Japan's Cultural Revolution, Tono would be a prime **target**. Having a **PhD** from an American university and all."

She laughed. "The **Red Guards** would string him up, figuring he was a traitor. They would beat him, because of course they'd think he spoke fluent English. **Think of it! A crime he could never have dreamt of committing. Not in his wildest dreams. I bet he'd be very flattered.**"

I laughed. "He'd be walking on air."

"Then they might say, 'Go on, say something in English!'"

"The second he opened his mouth, they'd let him go."

"Or, no, when he said something, it would sound so bad they'd think he was doing it on purpose and beat him up some more: 'Wise guy! Who do you think you're kidding!'"

Nanae's spirits were now completely restored.

After that we did all the things we had planned to do. We went to the **Whitney**, where Nanae had wanted to see **Donald Judd**'s sculptures, breezing past the pieces without comment. I followed around after her, unable to tell if she was so used to visiting museums that she always zipped through them, or if she had already seen enough of his work. Then we took a bus to midtown, got off at **Rockefeller Center**, and peered down at the courtyard that would turn into the ice skating rink in winter, before stopping into the Kinokuniya bookstore. In the second-floor section with collected works of Japanese authors there were only a few customers, graduate students by the look of them, while downstairs near the entrance Japanese people clustered around magazines with garish covers. From there we took another bus to the **Village** and watched *My Favorite Wife* in a **revival house**. Nanae laughed hard and, just as when she was sad, she shed tears that left black rings around her eyes. When the movie ended it was almost nine. The Thai restaurant we went to for dinner was the polar opposite of the **Upper East Side** restaurant where we'd had lunch, crowded with people of every description including many so outlandish I had no idea what to call them. It struck me, looking around, that people like Nanae and me with parents of the same ethnicity might well soon be the exception rather than the rule. Here, where the crowd did not diminish as the evening wore on, the waiters were narrow-hipped Thais who worked briskly. The food was too spicy for Nanae, and she ended up shedding yet more tears.

By the time I caught a **cab** and headed for **Grand Central Station**, it was nearly midnight. Nanae, alone on the sidewalk, kept looking at me and waving as the **cab** drove off. Thinking how Americans didn't share this custom, I in turn stared at her slender figure and waved back. Soon she was swallowed in darkness, and her voice from that afternoon sounded in my ear: "**Remember?** We used to come here every year at Christmastime, the whole family." "Here" was that skating rink at **Rockefeller Center**—where we had been earlier and which in spring had become an open-air café. "Here" she had turned to me and uttered those words.

More than a year and a half had passed since that **Manhattan** outing.

A dozen years before, at the time of Nanae's suicide attempt—the incident Mother dismissed as "a page from a trashy novel"—young as I was, I'd vaguely sensed that someday my sister might end up my responsibility. That day I began to understand that responsibility for her had indeed come to rest on my shoulders. Mother's abandonment of her was real and clear. The bleak image of Nanae looking like a total stranger on that street corner in spring had continued to haunt me ever since.

I had been sitting in the red armchair staring vacantly at nothing for I did not know how long. The radiator and pipes were quiet. The room was getting cold. Nothing moved except the snow falling outside the windows. It was picking up in intensity, definitely turning into a snowstorm.

My body was stiff from lack of movement. The chair was capacious enough that I could easily have curled up to make myself comfortable, but I stayed immobile, loath to move, as I felt gloom and weariness building up further inside me. The flow of my memories, I realized, was now propelling me in a direction I didn't want to go—a direction that had nothing to do with Nanae. Perhaps I worried excessively about her just to prevent this from happening. I especially didn't want to go in that direction today, having finally emerged from my lethargy and taken a first step. I looked up at the ceiling. I let my eyes wander from corner to corner. I listened to the silence. Nanae's becoming my responsibility was an eventuality I had dreaded but was prepared to take on in the end. What I had not been prepared for was this nagging feeling, a feeling that had been weighing on me for quite some time . . .

Was I wrong all these years to turn my back on English so obstinately? Should I have spent my time differently? Have I have been colossally stupid?

During class in seventh grade on **Long Island**, often I would find myself writing these vertical lines on a sheet of **loose-leaf paper**:

東 東 東 東 東
京 京 京 京 京
都 都 都 都 都
世 世 世 世 世
田 田 田 田 田
谷 谷 谷 谷 谷
区 区 区 区 区
船 船 船 船 船
橋 橋 橋 橋 橋
町 町 町 町 町
六 六 六 六 六
九 九 九 九 九
番 番 番 番 番
地 地 地 地 地

How many times did I write those lines of *kanji*, which signified no more than our old Tokyo address? As I sat, disconsolate, through yet another lesson in English that I could not understand, my pen would start moving of its own accord. I wrote partly out of nostalgia for our modest wooden house back in Tokyo. But more than that, I would be swept with desire to write *kanji*, even though no other *kanji* than those of our old address came readily to my hand. Thanks to the musty set of books from Grandpa Yokohama, I was acquiring a large reading vocabulary, but writing *kanji* was a different matter. I was rapidly forgetting how to write even the ones I had learned in grade school. Learning *kanji* used to strike me as a pure nuisance, unlike the multiplication table, the usefulness of which was obvious; but on entering a world containing only the **alphabet**, I had discovered that *kanji* were an inalienable part of me. Writing out my old Tokyo address over and over, I felt like a monk in a temple, his body freezing in the bitter cold of winter, copying a sutra by candlelight: 南無阿弥陀仏南無阿弥陀仏. *Namu Amida Butsu Namu Amida Butsu.*

Sometimes I wrote *hiragana*. Then I would feel like a character in *The Tale of Genji*—the Lady of the Paulownia Court seated behind a bamboo screen, wrapped in layer upon layer of perfumed silk robes, a lady "not of the highest rank but beloved of the emperor."

や　　　や　　　や
よ　　　よ　　　よ
ひ　　　ひ　　　ひ
の　　　の　　　の
そ　　　そ　　　そ
ら　　　ら　　　ら

And other times I wrote a mix of *kanji* and *hiragana*.

美　　　美　　　美
し　　　し　　　し
い　　　い　　　い
花　　　花　　　花

The rounded soft loveliness of *hiragana* was like the shape of a beautiful woman now reaching up, now bending down as she went about her work in the home. The simple elegance of the *hiragana* し *shi* in particular enthralled me beyond reason. I took solitary pleasure in writing し stretched out extra long, as if I were an avant-garde calligrapher. When *kanji* were mixed with the phonetic *hiragana*, their essence as ideographs stood out commandingly.

The graceful vertical lines of *kanji* and *hiragana* interspersed evoked a world so unlike that of the **alphabet**, where letters crowded tightly together in horizontal rows like tiny black ants.

Even as incomprehensible lessons surrounded me daily, the act of writing in Japanese transformed me from someone who was a dimwit at school, a second-class *homo sapiens*, to someone with knowledge of a rarefied world conveyed through the mix of different writing systems, knowledge inaccessible through English.

But years later the question kept coming back to me: why, oh why had I always rebelled so vehemently against English and clung so passionately to Japanese?

In eighth grade in our **Long Island** school, unlike schools in Japan, students could choose from an array of electives, and in ninth grade the number of electives increased still more. For everything from science and math to foreign languages, we were free to select the level of difficulty we felt was right for us. For English, however, we were streamed according to our grades and ability. This came as a surprise: *Is it okay to label students so blatantly?* Most students were in a regular class, but those whose language skills were judged to be exceptional were put in **honors classes**, and those on the opposite end of the spectrum were put in one of the **remedial classes**, known commonly among the students as "**dumb classes**."

Students each followed a different schedule throughout the day, and so who was in which class was not fully clear. Besides, my American classmates demonstrated a laudable quality: rather than putting down a dimwit, they preferred to offer exaggerated admiration to anyone who excelled, so that while I often heard people say that so-and-so was a genius, I never heard anyone call someone

a moron behind their back. Perhaps that is why those assigned to a
dumb class in English were not particularly embarrassed about it.

I knew all this for a very good reason: I myself was put in a
dumb class.

Our teacher was **Mr. Keith.**

Aagh, I'm a genuine dummy: the thought went through my mind.
But the class turned out to be fun. It was the first class where
I understood everything the teacher said. The class was based on
dialogue. We would take turns reading a story aloud, and then
Mr. Keith would ask what we thought: Was the main character right
in what he or she did? Would they now be happy? What would we
have done in their shoes? This Socratic method of instruction was
possible since there were fewer than ten students in the class. The
story was always an illustrated short story from our thick textbook;
to help students with sadly little imagination identify with the
characters, the stories were all set in modern America, and mostly
the protagonists were ordinary American **teenagers**. I could only
assume that the stories had been written expressly for the textbook.

One such story was about a family with a salesman father who
had recently been diagnosed with late-stage cancer and had less
than a year to live. The father had only a small life insurance pol-
icy, but instead of working like a demon in the time he had left and
earning money to support his family after he was gone, he decided
to quit his job and spend time with his family. If he chose to work,
he would have to be constantly on the road. The time with his wife
and children was rewarding, but his small savings quickly dried
up. There was an illustration of a middle-aged man sitting on a
bench in his backyard, staring straight ahead with hollow eyes.
The children he would leave behind were of course a boy and girl
of approximately our age.

When we had finished reading the story in class, **Mr. Keith** posed
the same question to each of us, one at a time: **"Do you think the**

father made the right choice?" Other students answered "**Yes**" or "**No**" and offered their explanations. I worried about what to say when he called on me.

"**How about you, Minae? Do you think he made the right choice?**"

"**I don't know.**"

"**Tell me what you think.**"

I constructed an English sentence in my mind before answering. "**I think it's difficult to answer such a question.**"

Mr. Keith's face brightened. "**Yes, isn't it? It's difficult to say either yes or no in a situation like this.**" He let the matter rest there.

Did **Mr. Keith** want to make the point that there are problems in life that have no easy answers, and literature is there to point them out? Refraining from drawing any conclusions himself, he simply encouraged us to engage with the stories and think. Perhaps he wanted students already estranged from books so early in life to understand that the written word was not irrelevant to them.

One day, as we were discussing something or other, **Mr. Keith** looked around the class and shrugged his shoulders. "**It's very frustrating, don't you think, when you know for sure that the author you're reading is less intelligent than you.**"

An author less intelligent than me? How is that possible?

In my family, stepping over a book was considered a sign of disrespect, so to me the printed word represented truth, goodness, and beauty, and the author behind it was a sage dwelling in a sacred realm I could never hope to glimpse. What right did any of us, including a mere junior high school teacher, have to look down on an author? But **Mr. Keith** only sounded a bit fed up and not at all arrogant. In that moment I understood how childish I had been in putting all writers equally on a pedestal. And yet for him to say such a thing to us members of the **dumb class**—the more I thought about it later, the more interesting **Mr. Keith** was to me.

About a month into the fall term, as I was gathering my things at the end of class, **Mr. Keith** called out to me. **"Do you have a moment, Minae?"**

"Yes."

I went and stood in front of his desk, holding my books in my arms. The smell of his tweed jacket reminded me of **Uncle Jesse**; I wondered, did **Mr. Keith** smoke a pipe too? He leaned forward in his chair.

"Is this your lunch hour?"

"Yes."

"Good."

Students had their lunch break at different times, so I guessed he meant that if I had had a class in the next period, I'd have to dash off. Maybe he wanted to talk about something. This was all new and strange to me. I glanced out the window, and the green expanse of lawn struck me as a typically American scene.

Mr. Keith looked at me, his gray eyes contemplative.

At the time I never gave any thought to the age of middle-aged people, but he could have been in his late forties, an age that I would later see as the height of maturity, far from the sillinesses of youth and old age. He was short and had a lusterless complexion, the skin beginning to go slack with wrinkles. I suppose he was a bit on the unattractive side, but I liked him and found his face pleasing, full of good humor informed by confidence and generosity.

"You know, Minae, I read your composition to the students in my honors classes and told them that *this* **is an A composition."**

That was the first time I heard that **Mr. Keith** also taught the **honors classes**. But what was **"an 'A' composition"**? The kindness in his look and voice told me I was being praised, and then it hit me—**"an 'A'"** could be the letter grade—**"an A"**! *I got an A on my composition! That I wrote in English!*

Think of something you like and write about it: that had been the assignment, chosen no doubt to stir interest in writing among those in the **dumb class**. With summer over, the leaves on the **maple tree** in our front yard were turning yellower by the day, and the apples on the tree in the backyard were starting to fall. With my chronic nostalgia, I had chosen as my topic a memory of how, as I was picking autumn flowers in the paths between paddy fields back home, dusk would creep up and slowly turn the sky a fiery red, filling me with loneliness.

The title of my essay was **"My Favorite Moment in Autumn."**

"You were the only student who didn't write about things . . . physical things, you know." Mr. Keith chuckled and then smiled at me.

I was so elated at having a composition of mine praised for the first time since coming to America that I could have stood on my tiptoes and twirled. Memories of school life in Japan came back to me. *That's right, I was good at composition. My teachers used to read my compositions aloud in class!*

I had dreaded writing in English, but the more I wrote the more engrossed I'd gotten.

Was that my first-ever composition in English? Or did it just stick in my mind because the teacher praised it?

In describing the gradual deepening of the sunset colors, I had written that they turned **"from red to crimson"**; how did I happen to know the word **"crimson"**? he asked, and when I explained that I had searched my father's heavy Japanese-English dictionary, he nodded and murmured **"Aha,"** before asking what other words I had looked up.

"I liked it an awful lot." Mr. Keith repeated his praise, then added, **"There's one word that bothers me a bit."** I had ended the essay by writing that, **"though I am smarter now,"** in every returning autumn that same loneliness came back. In his Socratic way, he said, **"But Minae, do people really become smarter?"**

So the English word **"smart"** referred narrowly to intelligence; it did not also suggest depth. I realized I should have written **"though I am wiser."**

"I didn't tell the class who wrote it. But they might have guessed from the 'paddy field.'"

That was a phrase I had found in the dictionary. Naturally, I hadn't seen any paddy fields since coming to America. But then, even around the Tokyo suburb where I used to live, they had all but disappeared.

I was the daughter of two people who wouldn't know a stalk of rice from a stalk of wheat, a girl whose grandparents and perhaps great-grandparents very likely had known little about cultivating land, yet in spring I used to walk between paddy fields and pick milk-vetch, braiding it into wreaths while watching sideways to see how my nimble-fingered sister did it, and in the autumn I would carry home armfuls of wild chrysanthemums, knotweed, and golden lace to make pressed flowers. All this had been possible since I used to play by far-off paddy fields. Our house happened to be next door to the one remaining patch of farmland in the neighborhood. The family was wealthy, the owners of several apartment buildings, and when the father was out working in the field and Mother and I happened by, he would pause to wipe the sweat from his brow with a narrow towel around his neck and smile self-consciously. He only kept on working in the field for his health, he said. The family had three daughters about our age, and in summertime when the wind blew in their direction and they could hear Nanae practicing the piano, all three would come traipsing across the field and stick their heads in our window. They were pretty, red-cheeked country lasses who took after their mother. Sometimes they would invite us to play in their paddy fields farther away.

That I thought of writing about paddy fields based on such meager personal experience may have had something to do with

my native tongue, a language where the harvesting of rice is invested
with an overabundance of meaning, going back to a famous sev-
enth-century *waka* poem attributed to an emperor. Reflection on
the seasons, moreover, is central to Japanese literary tradition,
autumn being associated with dusk as spring is with dawn. That
composition **Mr. Keith** praised so highly might well have been a
mere string of Japanese platitudes. Could commonplace emotions
and unoriginal expressions—the manifestation of a banal literary
sensibility—transform into something more remarkable when rendered in a different language? The question kept coming back to
me in later years whenever I remembered that happy afternoon.

Mr. Keith asked how long it had been since I came to America,
how much I understood in my other classes, and then:

"Do you read a lot at home?"

"Yes."

"Well, what do you read?"

"Novels."

"In Japanese?"

"Yes."

"What kind of novels? Japanese novels?"

"Yes, Japanese novels." Even if I told him the names of Japanese
novelists I liked such as Ichiyō and Sōseki, he would not understand. This was well before some American bookstores started
carrying works by the authors who became America's favorites:
Mishima, **Tanizaki**, and **Kawabata**.

"Well, Minae, do you read anything besides Japanese novels?"

I thought hard and mentioned the names of some Western
writers I had read at home. I didn't know how to pronounce their
names properly, but it brought a smile to his face.

"Who do you like best?"

I said **Dostoevsky**, the name that seemed the most impressive—
and hardest to pronounce. I had just finished struggling through

without understanding *Crime and Punishment* in a thick edition that my father had bought in his student days.

"**Good.**"

I was headed toward the door when he said, "**Oh, yes,**" and added, as if he had forgotten to mention it before, "**do you have any friends here at school?**"

This threw cold water on my elation. Should I tell him that I had **Linda** as a friend—**Linda** the possible killer of her little brother, who was then following me around and would later be confined to a mental institution? But answering "**No**" seemed just too sad.

"**Yes.**"

"**What's her name?**"

"**Linda Gladstein.**"

"**Linda Gladstein? I don't know her . . .**"

I went out and closed the door without explaining.

At that point I had not understood the unique position **Mr. Keith** occupied at school. He was the head of the **English** department, but apart from the respect accorded someone so wise and cultured, he was apparently on a par with the principal in the way he was treated. He taught our **dumb class**, which must have been a challenge, and the **honors classes**, which must have been a pleasure. Soon after that conversation, the school office notified me that I was to attend both the **dumb class** and an **honors class**.

And so I began to move back and forth between two very different worlds. The **Mr. Keith** in charge of the bright students was not the **Mr. Keith** I had previously known. There was no Socratic dialogue and no discussion of life. It was a fast-paced lecture class, and suddenly I had no idea what he was saying. Instead of a childish textbook, he handed me a **paperback** copy of **Robert Graves's** *The Greek Myths*, with discouragingly small print. Every day he would assign a certain number of chapters as homework, and at the beginning of class the next day there would be a **quiz**. This went on day after day.

The class learned story after story from the Greek myths, and I did my best—which often didn't amount to much. After myths, we moved on to **The Iliad** and then **The Odyssey**. After **Homer** came **Shakespeare**. The bright students seemed to relish the challenge of reading something new every day and committing it to memory. They never complained and upon entering the classroom would without being told set their books and notebooks at their feet, lay a sheet of paper on their desktop, and grip a ballpoint pen in hand, waiting eagerly for **Mr. Keith** to pose the first question. To the Old World, America may have symbolized crass ignorance, yet in that corner of America the English literary canon was being celebrated, taught with dedication and learned with enthusiasm.

Mr. Keith's priorities were clear. Students' views on the meaning of life, the meaning of death, the sorrows of love, the thin line between good and evil, and questions like "Where did I come from and where will I go?" concerned him not at all. It was as if he knew we could deal with those matters at some later date, as we pleased. When the time came, we could criticize the English literary canon, deny the central importance of **Shakespeare**, or even take up arms against the English language itself for all he cared. But right then was our time to quaff the water of life from the wellspring of English literature. He showed utter disregard for our opinions and absolute confidence in our abilities. He knew that if invited to write about life, students even in the **honors classes** could only produce twaddle, but that if led to the riches of English literature, they could absorb them with nearly effortless ease and so possess a lasting treasure.

Though **Mr. Keith** loved the classics, he was not a classicist. Nor of course was he a believer in the supremacy of Western civilization. Far from it—he was a revolutionary teacher who, long before multiculturalism came into vogue, strove to implant in his students interest in, knowledge of, and respect for other cultures. When we studied Greek mythology, he had us write reports on the myths of other civilizations, and he took advantage of having a living representative of a distant culture in class by asking me to read Japanese poetry aloud, conducting a class on **haiku**, and assigning haiku composition as homework.

That's the sort of teacher **Mr. Keith** was, and that's why one day he said these words to me: **"Don't forget your Japanese."**

Naturally, I did not forget my Japanese. But could he have imagined that the girl he said that to would go further and spend the next twenty years doing everything she could to escape English? **Mr. Keith's** advice was based on the assumption that English would eventually become my first language, and over the course of that year he tried to speed me toward that goal, assigning me a special tutor and handing me extra grammar books. I liked him very much. I think I even loved him—with the deepest gratitude for him as a teacher and respect for him as a human being. But, unable to respond to his warm solicitude, I never did more than temporize, and guilt over my inability to respond distanced me yet further from English—and, alas, from him.

After starting **high school**, I spent my free time in school drawing and my time at home, when not reading Japanese books, working away on French, so much so that Nanae rolled her eyes in disbelief. The **junior high school** and **high school** stood next to each other on the same broad street, so stopping by to see **Mr. Keith** on the way home would have been easy to do. Both **Rebecca Rohmer** and **Sarah Bloom** were fond of him and did just that. They continued to talk about him right up to the end of senior year. Although my English couldn't help improving, I was ashamed of my failure to live up to his kindness and faith in me, and so I refrained from ever setting foot again on the grounds of the **junior high school** that was only a stone's throw away.

Outside the windows, the snow was falling faster, harder.

Had Nanae taken that old heap of hers on the highway and made it safely to **Long Island**? Father, lying in bed with his eyes trained on the ceiling, might not even realize there was a snowstorm, this winter's first. Or, with his earphones in, had he been listening hazily to news reports of the snow over the radio? Either way, even if Nanae came in smelling like snow, with drops of melted snow glistening on her hair and eyelashes, unless she called his name and shook his thin arm he probably wouldn't realize it was his daughter standing there. He certainly wouldn't be remembering that twenty years ago this day, his wife and daughters had boarded a plane to join him here in America.

Was the snow to continue falling all night? It possessed a strength that suggested it could keep on going well into the dawn and even beyond. A harbinger of the long harsh winter to come.

Twenty years ago, such snow had been a curiosity to me. During our first winter in the house on **Long Island**, on nights when the snow gradually picked up in intensity, unsatisfied by peering out through my **Venetian blinds**, I would sneak out of bed, tiptoe downstairs so my parents couldn't hear me, and open the front door. Withstanding the blast of cold wet air, I would raise my eyes and see snowflakes dancing a mad dance in the darkness and the silence. For a moment I would have the illusion of being swallowed by the snow. Those were rare and precious times when reality surpassed imagination.

Even when it snowed all night, generally by the time I woke up in the morning the snow would have stopped. The piled-up snow shone dazzling white in the sun, and my sister and I, eager to tramp around in it, would run out into the backyard with Della. One such morning the snow had drifted against the garage door, making a small hill, and Nanae and I took turns pressing our faces into the bracingly cold smooth soft surface, making detailed 3D imprints.

"Look! What a beauty!"

"Mine's better."

Soon our faces were stinging from the cold. When we went inside and looked in the mirror, my cheeks were swollen and red.

Nothing of the sort for Nanae, who had done exactly the same thing in the snow as me.

"It's because you're thick-skinned," I told her, as I applied the **Johnson & Johnson baby oil** Mother got out for me.

"That has nothing to do with it."

"Does too. Nah nah, you've got thick skin."

Nanae, then slow of tongue, only glared at me without a retort.

We had snowball fights and made snowmen and snow houses. As the years went by, we got used to snow; by the time we lived in Boston and had to do our grocery shopping without a car, it had ceased to be anything but a nuisance. Would I spend next winter somewhere in Japan, never seeing snow like this?

The big empty apartment was enveloped in too-early darkness. It seemed to grow with every passing moment and plunge the room into further gloom.

I felt with mounting urgency that I needed to telephone the professors on my committee. Today was Friday, and they might not be on campus; even if they had gone in earlier, they would have left in advance of the storm. I could call them at home later tonight, so I still had a few hours before I'd have to pick up the receiver and start dialing. But when I pictured them relaxing after dinner, only for the phone to ring, I thought again. The hands on the kitchen clock, which I could see from the red armchair, pointed almost to four o'clock. Annoyingly, now was the perfect time. *Go ahead and get it over with*, I told myself. Still, I had been lost too deep in reminiscences and could not bring myself to act. The radiator pipes were going *clang* again.

I got up and headed toward the kitchen. My nerves were on edge, and I wasn't really hungry, but I hadn't had anything to eat since breakfast. I decided to fortify myself.

My eyes, used to the shadowy interior of the living room, were momentarily blinded by the white linoleum when I switched on the light. I felt around in the freezer for one of the rice balls I kept on hand, took one out, and set it on the radiator. Since the door of the freezer compartment was missing, nothing froze very hard, and if the radiator was crackling with steam, as now, a half-frozen rice ball placed on top of it would defrost in no time. If the radiator was off, I poured hot water directly over the **Saran Wrap** covering. Back when Mother sold the house on **Long Island**, Nanae had taken the microwave, leaving me to continue defrosting my rice balls by these primitive means.

Indeed, compared to Nanae, who made an effort to lead a middle-class life with modern amenities, I had continued to live the bare-bones life of a student. When Mother was emptying out the house, Nanae had carted off so much stuff we called her "greedy granny" after an old folktale, but except for books there had been nothing I wanted. I was content to go on using the old pots and pans, dishes, towels, and sheets Mother had provided for our apartment in Boston—things Mother had bought when we first came to America twenty years earlier. My life in America had had its share of excitement and joy, but the stubborn belief that this was not the life I was meant to live had stealthily permeated every aspect of my existence, down to the way I defrosted rice balls.

I found half an onion along with carrots and a stalk of celery, chopped them up finely with some canned olives and added them to the rice, then mixed in **canned tuna, olive oil, wine vinegar**, and a dash of salt and pepper to make *la salade du riz*. This recipe for rice salad was something I had invented during my second stay in Paris as an easy substitute for *chirashizushi*. Perhaps as a reaction to my prolonged indolence, normally when I went into the kitchen I turned into a different person, totally focused on cooking and setting right to work, but today as I prepared my meal my head was still hot and heavy and my arms and legs seemed to belong to someone else.

A quarter of an hour later when I sat down to eat, I realized there was no new magazine for me to thumb through. Ever since Tono's departure, I had taken to spreading one open during meals—a sad habit that left me at loose ends when none was at hand. Today the snow would probably delay the mail, but even so by now there ought to be some magazine or other—at least a mail-order catalogue—in the mailbox. I felt a sudden urge to go down and check but fought back the urge and forced myself to raise my fork.

Today was the day when I must face up to the reality of time passing. If today I retreated and did not make those phone calls, then tomorrow and the day after I would retreat a step further, then further, until the prospect of taking any action at all would once again terrify me. What if I missed my chance, and next year when the thirteenth of December rolled around I was still here?

The rice in my salad was still partially frozen. As the iciness of the grains registered on my tongue, suddenly I was transported to the moment, exactly twenty years ago to the day, when for the first time in my life I tasted something called **"rice pudding."** When the plane took off from Haneda, the stewardess in a *furisode* kimono with a design of scattered flowers was the most beautiful person I had ever seen outside of photographs or movie screens, but before I knew it she had changed into a smart navy-blue uniform and was graciously distributing meals on trays. The amount of food was more than my twelve-year-old self could eat, but even so I was gluttonous, eating everything until the only food untouched was the square, creamy substance in the upper left corner of the tray. I guessed that it was some sort of dessert, and when I tasted it, my mouth filled with spicy aroma and sweetness. But the instant I realized that the substance on my tongue was in fact rice, I felt my throat constrict.

"Mama, this is rice!" I pointed to the bit of goo on the tip of my fork.

"Rice?" She too applied her fork to an edge of the square dessert. "You're right, it is!"

Nanae, sitting by the window, followed suit and lifted her fork to her mouth. "Weird," she said, making a face.

"I think this is what they call rice pudding," Mother decided.

Where did Mama learn that? From books? Movies? Since she said she used to work for the Americans right after the war, maybe that's where. Rice boiled in milk with sugar and spice had the usual feel of rice, but that made the experience of eating it all the stranger. Watching the beautiful Japanese stewardess remove our trays, I wondered if she was someone so sophisticated that she could eat this funny food without a qualm. She seemed even more remote.

The shock of that first encounter stayed with me. I never was able to get over it, and I was never able to abide **rice pudding**.

Nanae was the same way. She had gone with **Karl** to visit his family in Munich, and for dessert she was served, of all things, **rice pudding**. The family was a veritable picture of domestic bliss and decency, and to welcome her son's exotic foreign sweetheart, the mother had been hard at work in the kitchen all day. The crowning touch to her home-cooked dinner was the **rice pudding**.

"**Dis is my vife's specialty**," **Karl**'s father had announced with pride, Nanae said, imitating the man's German accent.

"'**Oh, wonderful!**' I said, all the while thinking, *Oh my God! How am I going to eat all this?* **It was huge, humongous!** I tried to wash it down with **sips** of water, but my face was stiff and I guess they could tell how I felt. It cast a pall over the meal. Afterward I told **Karl**, '**I'm sorry, but I couldn't help it.**' He said, '**No, I'm sorry. I should have warned my mother that Japanese people don't eat rice that way.**' Quite decent, isn't he?"

She had been crazy about **Karl** at the time.

That at one time the only way of consuming rice in most of the West had been to boil it with milk and sugar was something I learned on my own first trip to Europe. The cheerful woman who headed the household on the outskirts of Paris where I stayed, a marvelous cook, laughed and told me that when she was young, she couldn't imagine eating rice that hadn't been sweetened: *"C'était quelque chose d' inouï!"* —it was unheard of. The Bretagne region where she'd grown up was far removed from Mediterranean culture with its cuisine of paella and risotto. It was shocking to find that people were shocked by the idea of non-sweetened rice.

But culture was not an island unto itself.

Time went by and, eventually, as restaurants featuring Southeast Asian cuisine spread in **Manhattan** and elsewhere, I came to realize that **rice pudding** was not a strange invention that Westerners had come up with on their own, but rather a variation of a dessert that even I enjoyed: glutinous rice cooked in coconut milk. The dish must have originated somewhere in Asia and through foreign trade crossed the seven seas to the West. In time, non-sweetened rice dishes also gained wide popularity in areas in the West that only grew wheat. By now, even in my small college town, the shelves of the local supermarket stocked rice and other Asian essentials—soy sauce, tofu, bean sprouts, Chinese cabbage, shiitake mushrooms, instant ramen—as well as the requisite **Diet Coke** and **Special K**. More esoteric items were available at the **Oriental food store**, whose Korean owner was rumored to have fended off a gang of local black youths using karate, and where non-Asian shoppers frequently roamed the aisles. And besides the ubiquitous Chinese restaurants, sushi places had begun springing up in town before my eyes quite recently, Indian and Vietnamese restaurants too.

The acceptance granted to rice was extended to chopsticks. When I was growing up in America, the word "**chopsticks**" carried an undertone of scorn, like the "**chop**" of **karate chop** and also of **chop suey** (a dish that, like **chow mein**, no self-respecting Asian would ever touch); like "**Chink**," referring to a Chinese person (or, really, any Asian), and "*ching chang chong*," nonsense words mimicking, and making fun of, the Chinese language; and like **Charlie Chan**, the pidgin-speaking Chinese detective in old Hollywood movies, always played by a white actor. But at some point chopsticks fell out of that category. Being able to use them skillfully became a mark of cosmopolitanism similar to being able to read a menu in French. Chopsticks were now seen as a great cultural convenience and even in some cases as works of art, and anyone boorish enough to eat Japanese or other Asian food with a fork had to be a neanderthal.

Around the same time, a flood of items of all colors and shapes produced in factories on the other side of the Pacific Ocean began to inundate the market in America. The change in America taking place before my eyes seemed to epitomize the "fall of the West"— and so perhaps it was symbolic, though unfortunate, that **Herr Professor** should be wasting away.

Herr Professor was supposed to be my doctoral adviser. It was a long time since I'd seen his stoop-shouldered figure around **campus**, always carrying his worn leather bag. He had been in and out of the hospital with liver cancer since the year before last, and that was the ostensible reason for my having postponed my orals three times. As he was born in a small European country, his native language was neither English nor French nor German. Nevertheless, he used all three languages with consummate skill, and his colleagues were in awe of his keen mind and the depth and breadth of his knowledge. He was European intellectualism incarnate.

Herr Professor's office was in a corner of one of the oldest buildings on the ivied campus. When I timidly visited him there, he would open the door with one hand and, lowering his stooped shoulders even more, gesture with the other for me to come in. His movements were those of a man in early old age with stiffening joints, yet they retained a suggestion of such disciplined grace that I wondered fleetingly if perhaps as a child he had been made to

take dancing lessons. In this unmistakably American college town where, off campus, loud music blasted from the open windows of passing cars, he could not have been more out of place, giving off as he did the air of the Old World. When I came in, he would indicate the sofa and say **"Please,"** and then, once he had seen that I was settled, sit down, lean forward, and say in his heavily accented English, **"Vat can I do for you?"** He wore a greenish-brown jacket that matched his eyes, eyes that for whatever reason were always smiling. No one knew all the whys and wherefores of how he had arrived in America; in his mysterious past we sensed something like the darkness of European civilization, a darkness that many people preferred to keep under wraps. Speculation was rampant.

So it was in a way symbolic of the fall of the West that the flesh housing his spirit should be attacked by cancer cells. People with prewar classical educations were rapidly disappearing from academia. Western literature was being taught by people with no knowledge of Latin or Greek, and the spread of multiculturalism meant that introductory courses in literature now included as compulsory reading whole sections of *The Tale of Genji*. A nation's literary taste was linked, evidently, to its diet: just as the birth of modern literature in Japan had occurred in tandem with a surge in appetite for the once-taboo meat of cows and other four-legged beasts, so in the West *Genji* had become compulsory reading in tandem with the growing acceptability of rice. Yet in all this there was one important caveat: the fall of the West did not correspond to a fall in status of the English language. Far from it.

It happened after I left **junior high school** and moved on to **high school**. As I was bent over a painting in the art room during my free time, I heard a voice say, **"You know, you should be working on your English."** My English teacher had come in on some errand or other. Holding a brush in my right hand, I raised my head from my watercolor painting and glared at him, hot all over with rebellion. *I'm perfectly fine as I am. I have no wish to become American, thank you. I have no need of English.* America was extending to me the same educational opportunities it offered to the children of immigrants, and there was no reason for me to get upset. Yet I felt unreasonably indignant. It may have been the teacher's tone of voice. I somehow was certain that he would not have spoken in the same way if I were a French or German girl. Something told me that, for him, my language from faraway Asia was utterly unimportant—so inconsequential, in fact, that I would have been better off just forgetting it and devoting myself to learning English, the key to a better world. But my indignation must have gone deeper. What was the point of my learning the language if as an Asian girl I could have no legitimate claim to it? The children of Italian immigrants eventually became heirs not of **Dante** but of **Shakespeare**, but someone like myself could not be heir to English in the same way—so I must have believed somewhere deep down, however nebulously. I didn't so much believe it as sense it.

The sweep of history stands verities on their heads without compunction.

Perhaps he shouldn't have used such a tone of voice. Perhaps he should have shown a little more respect for my language—even a tenth of the respect **Mr. Keith** had shown in urging, **"Don't forget your Japanese."** But as the years went by, and especially as my determination to write in Japanese grew, I began perversely to see how prescient that teacher's words actually had been.

The sweep of history brings about unexpected—and often unwanted—changes that affect us all. Some are alert to these changes, while others remain in a blessed stupor until time renders the changes all too apparent. When I finally awoke from my blessed stupor, I saw what the English language had turned into. After centuries of increasing domination, it had at some point ceased to be a mere national language of English-speaking countries and become dissociated from the speaker's blood or country of origin. It was a language that millions around the world could read and choose to write in. A language that even a non-native could choose to inherit—and to pass on in turn to future generations. A language that anyone who dreamt of making writing their vocation, of touching as many souls as possible with their own words, should gladly embrace.

And the Japanese language? Certainly it had a long literary tradition; it still had many people speaking it; yet in the end, it was used almost solely by the Japanese people and in the Japanese archipelago. It did not even belong to a major linguistic group. It was indeed an inconsequential language.

Kicking and screaming, I was eventually forced to admit that the troubling feeling that sometimes overwhelmed me could only be called remorse: I had realized my stupidity too late. I thought of all the chances I had been given . . . but by the time I realized what an incomparable privilege I had passed up, I had gone too far down a road from which there could be no turning back.

Sarah Bloom, prospective novelist, of course wrote in English.

I had known her since **high school**, but she and I became close only after **Rebecca Rohmer** failed her orals. After **Rebecca** gave me Sarah's number, I had made sure to enter it in my address book, but then, not knowing what to say when I called, I had done nothing further until I heard indirectly about **Rebecca**'s failure. Then, happy to have common ground to start a conversation, I dialed the number.

Sarah sounded gratifyingly happy to hear from me. **"Oh, Minae!"** I remembered her as an artistic **teenager**, and now her rich alto voice conveyed a gracious womanliness. She'd heard from **Rebecca**

about running into me on **campus**, she said, but there had been no further word and she'd been wondering what had happened.

Containing my surprise, I told her that **Rebecca** had gone off the rails and blown her orals.

"My goodness! I can't believe it!" After a moment, she said with unexpected calmness, **"Come to think of it, I *can* believe it."** She added that over the past few years it had been increasingly difficult to carry on a normal conversation with **Rebecca**. They had gone on to different colleges, and eventually grown apart. It occurred to me that while over the past decade Rebecca must have devoted herself to her studies, I couldn't imagine **Sarah** leading such an ascetic life.

In **high school**, I used to see **Rebecca** more often because she lived only two blocks away, but I somehow felt closer to **Sarah**, though I doubted if she knew. She would look straight into my eyes and speak in a quiet voice, nodding deeply when I said something, which made me feel appreciated. I assumed she would have plenty of friends now, so when I phoned her I wasn't expecting much more than to talk about **Rebecca**. However, rather than dwelling on **Rebecca**'s misfortune, she expressed unexpected interest in what I had been doing, and as I talked on, encouraged by her skilled listening, before I knew it I had told her that I wanted eventually to write a novel.

She burst out laughing. **"Oh, Minae, this is so interesting! As a matter of fact, I'm writing a novel myself."**

Sarah had always been so multitalented that I used to wonder what she would do in the future. After graduating from college she had thought about becoming a painter or a film director, but now she seriously wanted to be a writer and had just secured an **agent**. She was making her living writing short book reviews, proofreading for magazines, and the like.

I was surprised and elated at her words. Unlike the state of affairs in Japan, or France for that matter, few people in the US obsessed about becoming a novelist, as far as I knew; I had never before run across anyone here who wanted to write novels, not even in the literature department.

"We should get together sometime, the two of us," Sarah said as we were hanging up. I remembered that **Rebecca** had said something similar, only she had said "the three of us," including **Sarah**. A few days later **Sarah** called me, again urging "Let's get together."

And so one day when Tono and I went to **Manhattan**, while he watched one of those films with **European chic** that he had a soft spot for, I visited **Sarah**'s apartment in the **West Village**. She lived in an old building, and her small antique-strewn rooms had oil paintings and ukiyo-e on the walls. She had become a confident, graceful woman with an elegant carriage. Her chestnut hair, fuller than ever, still fell in waves down her back, and her conversation intimated the presence of men in her life.

From then on we saw each other fairly often, and I looked forward to our get-togethers. Tono was shy, but he often came along with me. She would greet him "Hi, Tono!" and plant a kiss on his cheek, which he accepted with seeming indifference, though I could tell he was pleased.

One time **Sarah** turned laughing to Tono. "It's amazing how much we girls are alike." She was referring to the actually quite classic taste in English literature that she and I shared. Both of us preferred works from the past and **Victorian novels** above all. Our favorite author was **Jane Austen**, and we of course liked *Pride and Prejudice* best. It also came out that growing up, we had read the same novels for girls.

Sarah smiled. "My favorite was *A Little Princess*, obviously." She was holding her teacup in her right hand, the saucer in her left.

I quickly understood that *A Little Princess* must be the book I knew as 『小公女』 *Shōkōjo*. What I couldn't understand was why she said "obviously."

"'Obviously'?"

"Oh, you know, the girl's name, Sara."

"Sarah?" I was struggling to reconcile my friend's name with the little princess's name in *katakana*, セーラ, which had always intrigued me because the sound came out like "sehra," which was also the Japanese pronunciation of "sailor."

"Yes. Sara, without the 'h.'"

So セーラ was Sara. Until then, that remarkable little girl had inhabited the world of Japanese in my mind, and now all of a sudden I sensed her switching over to the world of English.

After that, leaving Tono, who had grown up looking at illustrated encyclopedias of animals, plants, and minerals, out of our conversation, **Sarah** and I went through all the books we had read and reread in childhood. Discovering that the book familiar to me as 『小公子』 *Shōkōshi* was actually ***Little Lord Fauntleroy***, that 『若草物語』 *Wakakusa monogatari* was actually ***Little Women***, that 『あしながおじさん』 *Ashinaga ojisan* was actually ***Daddy-Long-Legs***, gave me a sense of satisfaction akin to that of reuniting lost children with their mother.

"But you know something?" Sarah said thoughtfully. "I always thought Japanese children read Japanese children's books—not English children's books."

"Yeah, that's the thing. That *is* the thing!" Suddenly excited, I began to talk about how the English language dominated the world. Languages, I told her, weren't like the row of flags in front of the UN building, all equal. Like the countries that the flags represented, they were subject to a relentless power dynamic. Therefore, as long as she and I wrote in English and Japanese respectively, as writers we would not share the same status. Writing in English exponentially increased your chances of being translated into the world's languages; even more important, it meant that people around the world could read you *without* translation. Writing in English was a damned privilege, I concluded with perhaps more heat than was warranted. I was just beginning to face up to my remorse.

Sarah said, a serious look on her face, "Huh. I've never looked at it that way, though I think you're quite right." Then she repeated, "I think you are quite right." And then in her rich alto voice she asked, "Well, then, why don't you try writing in English?"

"Me?"

"Yes."

According to her, to be a novelist nowadays, the more marginal you were, the better. "You're a woman. You're Japanese. You're perfect. You have all the necessary attributes."

"But I can't think of anything to write about in English." Never mind whether I was capable of writing in English or not.

"Oh, come on," Sarah replied instantly. "You can write about your grandmother."

She had a good memory. So was I supposed to write in English about the old woman who couldn't pronounce "bus" or "biscuit" and wouldn't touch meat? In my mind, my grandmother belonged to the world of early modern Japanese literature, where newly borrowed words mingled freely with centuries-old expressions and poetic allusions, invigorating the country's rich literary tradition that seemed somehow inalienable from vertical writing. I simply could not imagine her inhabiting the world of the English language, with Latin letters neatly aligned horizontally, left to right.

"And about your mother," Sarah went on. "And about yourself." She elaborated, saying I could write about how my grandmother had died a prisoner of Oriental ignorance and superstition; how my mother, having grown up resenting that environment, was liberated by the American Occupation forces; and finally how I, the third generation, had become even more liberated thanks to my having landed in America. "The Americans would love that, especially the feminists! Maybe you can strike a movie deal.

Oh, Minae, you'd be rich and famous!" With a wide smile on her face, she turned to Tono, who had been sitting, just listening. **"What do you think, Tono?"**

   "Oh yesu! Ritchi ando feimasu!" he exclaimed.

The plate in front of me was now empty.

   Having fortified myself, I had no more to do but make the phone calls. A glance at the clock over the sink told me it was just past five. The impulse to go down and check my mailbox seized me again, but I resisted. Slowly I stood up and laid the plate and fork in the sink. Then I turned out the kitchen light, stepped into the hallway, and walked past the bedroom, heading for my study. When calling Nanae, I always lay on the bed on the floor, but for formal calls I sat at my **writing desk**. I took out my notebook from the drawer. The numbers written on its white pages were swallowed in the half-light, making them difficult to read, but I dared not turn on the desk lamp for fear that my courage would desert me in the sudden glare.

   First I called my **adviser** in the French department.

   After the phone rang several times, **Mme. Ellman**'s accented **"Hello"** came on the line. Young, single, and handsome, she already had an impressive list of publications and was especially popular with female graduate students; we all imitated her French. Another source of her popularity was the sternness that now and again made her thunder at us. Rumor had it that she lived alone in a big house with a big dog.

   I informed her that whether **Herr Professor** could be there or not, I intended to take my oral examination as scheduled, at the beginning of the year. I added that I would be contacting another faculty member willing to replace him if it seemed unlikely that he could make it.

"Yes, I think you'd better do that," she said in a low voice. "I wouldn't wait for him if I were you."

"Is his condition that serious?"

"Yes, I don't think there's much room for optimism."

"I see."

So he was dying after all. My heart beat a little faster.

After a short pause, **Mme. Ellman** asked, "Are you still thinking of going back to Japan after you pass your oral examination?"

Was she using the word **"pass"** in the English sense or the French? In English it meant to receive a passing grade, but in French it meant merely to take an examination. This was one of the first things one learned when studying French in America.

"Yes, I think so," I said. I had been telling my professors that after "passing" my orals I intended to return to Japan, ostensibly to write my dissertation.

"I see." She paused and then said, "I don't know if it's ever a good idea to go back home."

I couldn't think how to reply.

After another brief silence she said, "Home is not a place to return to." **Mme. Ellman**, an Israeli with shiny black hair, piercing black eyes, and sensual, deep-red lips, had arrived in the United States fairly recently. She seemed to have no intention of returning some-day to her homeland, which her people now finally possessed after two thousand years of wandering. Many of them had put down deep roots there, while others, like her, were moving on to forge bonds elsewhere. How her family might have ended up in Israel, I had no idea. Her surname suggested that she was a German Jew, but she had once told me laughingly that her father could speak almost every European language but English, so wherever her family was from, they might not consider that place "home" in any true sense.

For **Mme. Ellman**, at least, America may have been a promised land.

One day I saw her standing in the entrance to a campus building talking rapidly in low tones with a woman of approximately
her age. The language they were speaking was totally unfamiliar
to me, and it took me a moment to realize that it was Hebrew,
her mother tongue and a non-Indo-European language. With
that linguistic background, neither French nor English could
have been easy for her to learn, but she conducted graduate seminars in fluent French, using straightforward theoretical terms,
and her English, barely serviceable when I met her, improved
with remarkable speed: one day we were talking in French, and
then, before I quite realized it, in English. Also, while she published books and articles in French when I first met her, she soon
was writing mainly in English. Such quick acquisition of yet
another foreign tongue probably did not come from conscious
determination to put down roots in a promised land. Rather, it
seemed to stem from a frame of mind nurtured by the collective
memory of the diaspora: you go to a new place, you learn the
new language. Period.

Thinking of **Mme. Ellman** almost always reminded me of
Mme. Lemoine, another professor at the university who was
about the same age but had grown up in the French country-
side and whose English never improved in the slightest as far as
I could tell. To the last, she would converse with me in French.
When I visited her office, she would complain about America in
a half-exasperated, half-joking way: Americans didn't understand
the virtue of understatement; during her job interview, when
asked about the reception in France of a paper she had published
on **Flaubert**, she had said *"Pas mal"* —not bad—and, to her cha-
grin, been taken literally. Americans gave **"parties,"** incomprehensible events where one was required to discuss topics with
strangers, which made it necessary to know what people were
talking about and thus to scan *Time* or *Newsweek* before going—a

total waste of time! And the worst: **Proust** was meant to be read at a leisurely pace, ideally taking years, but to her horror she had seen American students forced to rush through his enormous novel in a single semester.

Mme. Lemoine seemed to feel a bond with me as a fellow foreigner. She talked to me, a mere graduate student, about the difficulty of the act of writing: a sentence one thought brilliant under the spell of night would frequently lose its luster in the light of morning. *"Il faut tout recommencer, tout!"*—One has to start all over again! Uninterested in publishing short articles, she was writing a dense book about her beloved **Proust** in apparent *"il-faut-tout-recommencer"* fashion—the project was taking years. Unsurprisingly, she failed to receive tenure and had returned to France. I remembered the pair of silver flats she always used to wear; they looked like ballet slippers, which seemed out of character. She was a demure person of the sort I had hardly encountered in Paris, someone whose unpowdered cheeks were always flushed with shyness. At the same time, she was given to pronouncements that I found charming. She delighted me once by almost ferociously declaring that it had never—*"Jamais!"*—entered her mind that she might be less intelligent than men. Her old-fashioned father was against girls receiving higher education and it was only because her mother had threatened to leave him that she was able to attend university—a revelation that somehow made me like her even more.

Among the foreign faculty members striving to survive in American academia, **Mme. Lemoine** had been rare. I identified with her sense of alienation in America. But I did not have a homeland that I could easily return to, the way she had. Twenty years away was a long time.

After a brief pause, I responded to **Mme. Ellman's** remark about home not being a place one should return to: **"Well, I think I'd be quite lonely in Japan."**

◀ Gothic building

"**But you know, loneliness is the very condition of a writer.**" She spoke decisively. There was always a philosophical bent to her conversation. Given her theoretical approach to literature, this was perhaps to be expected; I also noted her tendency—common among intellectuals speaking in a foreign language—to come up with sentences that sounded a bit axiomatic.

I made sure of the date of the orals once more before hanging up.

Her words stuck in my mind like a tiny thorn: *Home is not a place to return to.* I took a deep breath and picked up the receiver again.

The phone rang and rang. I imagined the **English garden** tended carefully by **Big Mac**'s wife buried now in snow. They might have a fire going in the fireplace. As I was recalling the bright orange flames in their fireplace on the **Thanksgiving** the seminar had been invited to their home, **Big Mac** came on the line, his British accent even more noticeable over the telephone. If there was a hint of a Scottish burr, I could not tell.

I told him that I had finally decided to take my orals at the beginning of the year, and added after some hesitation that I might not start right in on my doctoral dissertation.

"**Oh?**" He sounded somewhat surprised. Even his way of saying "**Oh?**" was singularly British.

"**I want to do some creative writing . . . like writing novels.**"

"**Novels?**" I could tell from his voice that he was frowning.

"**Yes.**" I quickly added, "**In Japanese.**"

"*Ho-ho!*" He laughed heartily, out of surprise, and with a touch of raillery. Without attempting to hide his amusement, he asked, "**Can you write Japanese? I mean, good Japanese. After all, you weren't educated in Japan, Minae.**" He might have had a glass or three of sherry as an aperitif; I thought he sounded more jovial than usual.

"**I know. But I've been reading Japanese all these years.**" *And writing letters in Japanese*, I started to say, but thought better of it, realizing how stupid that would sound.

"**Well, I suppose you can give it a try.**" He then asked in a teasing way, "**Do you know what you'd write about?**"

"**I don't know yet.**"

"**Your experiences in America?**"

"**No. I think that'd be too boring.**"

Bracing myself for his laughter, I added, "**I do want to write like Sōseki.**"

"*Ho-ho!*"

Sure enough, **Big Mac** gave a belly laugh. I laughed too. Still chuckling, he said, "**Well, whatever you do, . . .**"

"**Well, whatever you do, try not to mix up your Japanese with English.**"

"**I'll try not to.**" After I said this, I found myself telling him about the remorse I'd been haunted by in recent years. "**Lately, though, I've been feeling a bit down. I don't know how to put it, but . . . I sometimes think maybe I should have put down roots in America and made English my first language.**"

His reply was immediate: "**Nonsense!**" He sounded firm. Now he was serious. "**You wouldn't be what you are now.**"

His words were comforting, which was as I had expected. I had brought up the question knowing that he would say something along those lines. Equally at home in Japanese and English, he knew that language shapes people—or rather, that it shapes one's world. A celebrated translator, he was not about to deny the possibility of translation. But, precisely because he worked within the bounds of translation, he knew to cherish the inherent, non-transferable qualities of language. Indeed, I sensed that he cherished English as much as he did Japanese.

The phone call ended.

I felt numb and drained, knowing I had finally done what I needed to do. Now the way was clear for me to take my orals and go back to Japan. Three short telephone calls—one to the department secretary and two to professors—was all it had taken. What had I been so afraid of? What was my problem? Why had I hidden myself away day after day in this brick apartment building, peering out on gray skies?

My apartment now felt even emptier than usual.

I went on sitting vacantly at the desk. Only the plaster walls loomed white around me while the rest of the room sank further into darkness. The radiator was silent. I realized the resident upstairs hadn't played the piano all day, though usually she practiced religiously for half an hour daily on her out-of-tune instrument.

Mailbox key in hand, I listened for footsteps in the corridor, not wanting to have to smile and say hello to anyone, then undid the chain. Outside was a wide landing and stairs with a classically curving bannister that spiraled all the way from the fourth floor at the top to the first. I was on the third floor. Apart from light that came through the skylight, the only illumination was from a small wall fixture on each floor, so at night it was as dark as a haunted house. I descended the shadowy staircase to the first floor and threw my weight against the heavy wooden door with a glass pane. Every time I opened that heavy door, I thought glumly that this country had been made for strapping six-foot-tall men.

The air in the entrance hall was cold.

With its row of mailboxes, the entrance hall was as far as I dared go without a coat, scarf, gloves, and boots. The hall ended in another heavy, glass-paned door, beyond which snow was falling thick and fast. The front light silently illuminated the falling snow. **George**, the building superintendent, must have gone home early. He had probably shoveled the steps before he left, but now the snow covered them in soft undulations.

A night taken over by snow was quietly underway.

I opened the mailbox and found a bright airmail envelope that seemed to be elbowing the other pieces of mail aside. Sure enough, it turned out to be a letter from my mother. Usually she wrote on a thin blue aerogram, covering every available inch of space, so the sight of the bulky envelope made me uneasy. Moreover, although the return address was in **Singapore** as usual, the stamp was Japanese. It was postmarked "Tokyo." When had she gone back to Japan? She wrote fairly regularly, so her recent silence had had me a bit concerned.

Mother's letters always came to me, even those that began "Dear Nanae and Minae." After her rift with Nanae, the daughter into whom she had poured such energy, she had come to rely on me, the daughter whom she had rather neglected. In her letters, I caught a discomfiting fear of creeping old age; her taking a younger lover and suddenly blossoming like an off-season flower must have been an escape from the encroachment of old age—but she apparently needed someone to whom she could confide her fears about the future. These fears seemed to grow as the affair stretched on, and when she had something more serious on her mind, the letter would be written only to me. A bulky envelope like today's was certain to contain one of those.

It could wait. I went back up the stairs, ripping open a bill from the telephone company with my finger. I could almost hear Mother fretting, "Heaven help me, child, *why* won't you use a letter opener?" For someone so freewheeling, she was the most methodical of any of us in her habits, always stacking her opened mail neatly on her desk, the ends slit cleanly with a letter opener. The bill, almost entirely for long-distance calls to Nanae, was high. Too high for a grad student, but then Nanae's bill had to be even higher. Whenever I worried about it, she would say, **"Hey, this is my only luxury. It's cheaper than paying a shrink."** I sighed to myself. *Poor Nanae. She'll have to start saving for a* **shrink**. I stuffed the phone bill back in the envelope as I mounted the stairs through the shadows.

Back in my apartment, I turned on the light and sank into the red armchair, Mother's letter on my lap. I hesitated to open it. Every time I read one of her letters with references to her lover— never by name—I couldn't help feeling some revulsion; but today I held back for a different reason. Why had she written? Why from Japan? Why? The weight of the letter bothered me.

When I finally ripped the envelope open, I saw that, sure enough, she had written only to me. Row after row of her familiar round writing covered the thin airmail stationery, eight pages in all.

Dear Minae—

How is everything? You must be busy preparing for your examination.

I am writing from Japan. It's now all but decided that he will be transferred back to Tokyo. I waited to write to you until I knew for certain, and that's why you haven't heard from me for a while. My apologies. We had an inkling this was coming, and so this time when he had business in Japan, I came along to have a look around before it was time to move. I am staying with Aunt Utako.

It was bound to happen. He will most likely start working in Tokyo next spring.

To get right to the point—if you are coming back to Japan to live, then why not bring your father back so that we can place him in an old people's home here? I remember your saying on the phone that after your oral examination is over you might come back and look for a teaching position at a university here. That was last year in late September or early October, I think . . . I've had that in mind ever since, and when talk of the transfer came along, I thought of having you bring Father back with you. I can't expect Nanae to look after him by herself. All I expect from

her is to somehow manage to live on her own — nothing more. I
understand that sometimes she goes to visit him on her way to or
from the Murakamis, but the Murakamis are not going to stay in
New York forever. And I know you already help out regularly by
giving her gasoline money to defray her costs. When you told me
that, I felt terrible. Nanae isn't strong, and although she loves her
father dearly, having to visit him without your support and also
to handle his financial affairs as you are now doing would surely
make her feel oppressed and miserable at being left alone in a
foreign country. Just thinking of it makes me sad. When Father had
his second operation, you did much more to look after him even
though you lived farther away. My conclusion is that both for his
sake and Nanae's, it's best to bring him back to Japan.

The year before last when the move to Singapore suddenly came
up, I had no choice but to put Father where he is now, but I would
like to do my duty, as far as conditions allow. I am no longer young,
but if you would share the responsibility with me, I am willing to look
in on him when I can, in an old people's home here. Even if I had
to leave Japan again, you have always had a good head on your
shoulders, and I know you would visit him and take over his laundry
and other concerns without any fuss. Somewhere off in Saitama or
Chiba there is bound to be a place that would take him in, don't
you think? It might not be as nice as where he is now, but he would
probably be more comfortable being looked after by Japanese staff,
and the meals might be more to his liking too, now that he's lost his
taste for rich, buttery food. Our savings are limited, and I have my
own old age to think of, so he'll have to go into a ward, but then he
is nearly blind, anyway.

Spending two years away from your father has softened my feelings
for him somewhat. I do not expect you or your sister to understand
the emptiness of living with a husband from whom I was growing
more and more distant, both emotionally and physically — he aged so

much faster than me. When you two are my age, you may be able to understand a little, but until then I won't expect you to.

Of course, Minae, if you decide to remain in America, I won't object. In that case, though, I'm sorry but I would like your father to stay for the time being where he is. When you have made your decision, please let me know. How much longer do you think your examination will be postponed?

Is Nanae getting along all right? I pray that she will not be a burden on you in years to come. Family ties — whether with a husband or a sister — are hard to break, and that can make life difficult. I no longer have the strength to manage her. If you come back to Japan, she may want to come too, but she's only just bought that nice place in SoHo, so please do whatever you can to persuade her to carry on alone.

When I think that in less than half a year I will be living in Japan, my mind grows restless and fidgety. The biggest problem will be finding someplace to live. It's awful to reach this age and have limited resources. I've been going around looking at notices in the windows of realtors by Ogikubo Station, and if those are any indication, prices have gone up since the year before last. Buying a place is out of the question. Even if we rent, it will be impossible to find an apartment as spacious as I would like. But unlike the old days, there are lots of attractive new places, so at least we won't have to live in squalor. It never does to set your sights too high. He is not a man of fancy tastes, so I doubt that he will complain wherever we end up.

Eventually I will ask you to send me the things in storage. The mahogany dining set and cabinet alone will fill a Japanese apartment, but I want to keep them as mementos of my life in New York. (The leather on the chairs is worn out, so I will have to have them reupholstered in Japan. Do you suppose anyone here knows how to put in studs?) Also I want the antique Chinese lamp and the rosewood stand it sits on, and the Satsuma-ware lamps. That's all the furniture I'll take. Nanae can keep the chandelier I've been letting her use. I'm sure she wouldn't want to part with it — once that child gets something, she doesn't like to give it up. She can have the Mizumura heirloom calligraphy too. She is the elder daughter after all, and her place is quite a bit larger than yours, and will be even more so if you come to Japan. As for the box packed full of your grade school essays, report cards, and old photos, as well as Grandma Tsukuda's old letters and Grandpa Mizumura's diary, dispose of them as you like. Oh, and please send me the tea chests packed with kimono. Aunt Utako says she will be happy to return both of the paulownia chests she's been keeping for me. I don't know what you want to do with the furisode kimono you girls used to wear. At your age you could never wear them again in Japan, but in America you just might be able to get away with it. (There are also two unlined summer ones that Aunt Utako gave you when she and Sanae came to visit us in New York that time.)

Living in Japan won't be so bad, I think. Unlike you girls, I am most comfortable here, after all. Aunt Utako took me grocery shopping, and the neighborhood supermarket has lots of prepared foods, which will be a great help. But the crowds and the stairs everywhere are dreadful. I'll have to shorten my long dresses. My Ferragamo heels will have to go too. It's a shame.

I haven't yet told Aunt Utako anything about our family situation. She's rather straitlaced, so she is very likely to disapprove.

Tomorrow I'm meeting Cousin Tsuyako in Kyoto, and I'll visit Grandma Tsukuda's grave for the first time. (Your Kyoto grandfather's family being the way they are, I won't be seeing them.) You'll have to come with me sometime. Grandma led such a sad life . . . These days when I'm alone I get emotional and begin to weep; the other day I went back in time fifty years and just sobbed like a little girl. I'm after all grateful for the mother I had.

*When I come back here, I want to take a writing class and
set down a record of my crazy upbringing, as you always tell me
I should, to leave a testimony. You used to sometimes say you
wanted to write novels. Can you imagine if we made our writing
debuts at the same time? If I worked at it for the next ten years,
I think I could publish a book by the time I was seventy. What do
you think? I certainly haven't got anything better to do. Perhaps
I should take a class in word processing too.*

*Every time I look in the mirror, I see how much I've aged, and
with every year that passes I realize that wherever one is, one is
essentially alone. I will phone you on Christmas Day. For Christmas
Eve I'm getting taken to Maxim's de Paris in Ginza (ahem). Will you
be at Nanae's place? I want you both to know that in my own way,
I love my girls. Take care.*

Mother

*P.S. I have such a terrible nasal allergy that I want you to get
two boxes of **Allerest** tablets and airmail them to Singapore as
soon as you can. We were given some terribly expensive Chinese tea,
but we don't drink it, so I'll send it to you if you would like it.*

P.P.S. Please sum up the situation to Nanae as you think best.

Midway through her letter, I felt a wave of some ill-defined
emotion, neither the aversion nor the love that family inspires.
When I had finished reading, I felt only mute helplessness.

I read the letter again.

So she had had the same thoughts as me about Father—and
about Nanae. I was surprised to find that our thinking ran so
much alike, but then again it seemed only natural. Who would
want to leave Father in Nanae's hands for however many years
of life remained to him? Yet this meant that when I returned to
Japan, both of my parents would be there too. I imagined our lives

in Tokyo: Father lying in some out-of-the-way old people's home, Mother setting up some wretched love nest with a middle-aged man, me living in some one-room apartment, hearing city noises through thin walls while trying to tap out a novel. Where in any of that was there the need to have spent day after day in America all these years? Just as our old house in Tokyo had vanished, so had the small happiness that as a child I used to pray might go on forever. Was that the intangible fruit of those twenty years—the complete evaporation of that modest happiness? The sole testament to our sojourn in America would be across the Pacific Ocean, in **Manhattan**, mothering her cats and smoking her cigarettes.

Outside it was now completely dark. From the windows in the cavernous room, through the curtain of heavily falling snow I could dimly make out the lights of the surrounding buildings. They gave off a dull, yellowish glow.

I picked up my mother's letter. As I read through it again, the Japan I had come to know as an adult appeared before me in all its insufferableness. Narrow, cramped streets. Jostling crowds on station stairs. Everything depressingly small and cheap. Was that what I was going back to? What sadness lay in that picture of ordinary life!

Then, as if by reflex, I saw in my mind's eye the curve of my grandmother's back as she knelt on the tatami floor, forever stitching and re-stitching her several old kimono.

My grandmother . . .

My grandmother, my mother's mother, Grandma Tsukuda, who doted on me, had died when I was seven. After she became jaundiced and took to her futon, she'd lain in the tatami room where Nanae and I usually slept, scarcely able to sit up. After the helper went home at night, it was my duty to take in her dinner tray and feed her. "She eats well when *you* feed her, Minae," my mother would say, flattering me. I would sit on the tatami by Grandma's pillow and with a child's seriousness convey to her mouth spoonfuls of rice gruel and vinegared *mozuku* seaweed, a delicacy she loved. As the end drew near, she became confused and would point to nonexistent canned goods on top of the paulownia chest opposite her futon, insisting that they be given to us children for supper—flustering the helper, who lacked the wits to brush off such requests by saying "Yes, yes." Two nights before she died, Grandma asked in an unusually clear voice that we be gotten up. Mother told her no, because we were asleep, and then in the morning she could no longer speak. Mother regretted not having granted her final request. I mourned when I heard the story, thinking she might have had some special message for me, her favorite. She lingered one more day, and then in the early morning she was gone. A white cloth was laid over her face.

My memories of the funeral are sketchy. A few relatives came from Western Japan, but I had no idea who any of them were. Afterward Mother tried to explain, but the connections were too complicated for a child to understand. Grandma's life had been colorful but messy and tangled beyond all comprehension. Yet the old woman I knew and loved had been a typical Japanese grandmother, always clad in a somber-colored kimono, her sparse white hair in a bun.

The day she died, I stayed home from school. Mother walked briskly toward the station on some errand, her face so grim that, tagging along beside her, I was afraid to speak. Rather than sadness over her loss, she might have been feeling irritation at the mountain of tasks that had to be completed following the death of any human being. Father was away on a business trip in America, but even if he had been in Japan he might not have been much help. It was mid-March, so I wonder—were there peach blossoms along the way? Had horsetails put out green shoots in the roadside field? Was Mount Fuji, visible from our second-story window, wrapped in spring mist that day?

My early childhood memories took on a mythical dimension as I mulled them over in America. I had not written them down, but writers had written theirs, in books that I read and reread until the line between their memories and mine blurred. Was I returning to Japan for the sake of memories that were not even my own?

I stood up, taking the remainder of the mail from my lap, and crossed the hall into the bedroom. I groped for the **Luxo lamp** on the floor, switched it on, and tossed the mail on the bed. Then I snuggled under the blanket, the day's task accomplished. *Now my bridges are burned*—as I said this to myself, one thought loomed: I had yet to tell Nanae. Would she be getting safely home in the snow?

The mail on top of the blanket gleamed in the light of the lamp: a card from the library asking for the return of a book; printed matter from a **computer** software company, addressed to Tono; a lingerie catalogue that I sometimes received for no reason. I flipped through the pages, taking note of the brunette and blonde models in stock poses wearing see-through undergarments, before switching to the staid *New York Review of Books*.

The hands on the bedside clock moved with painful slowness. I read this and that article, but time scarcely inched forward. I wanted to call Nanae, but it was still too early; she couldn't possibly be back yet. Besides, with snow turning into a storm like this, she herself was likely to call as soon as she got home to say, "**I'm home safe, honey.**" When the hands pointed to seven o'clock, I ran out of patience, rolled over, and pulled the telephone toward me.

Nanae's voice, with its suggestion of a Japanese accent, came over the line. "**Hello. This is two one two, five nine five . . . I can't come to the phone right now, so please leave a message after the tone. Thank you.**" However many times she had tried to record the message, she always got nervous, and her English came off sounding Japanese. I remembered she said it was especially hard to say the numbers quickly. I waited for the beep but hung up.

I crawled out of bed, went back to the kitchen, and ate the left-over *salade du riz* straight from the **Tupperware**. The radiators were on, but as I ate the cold food I felt a chill spread upward from my back to the nape of my neck. Turning, I saw through the window that snow was heaped up on the back porch. **George** would be busy all day tomorrow shoveling the fire escape.

I washed the dishes and wiped the counters, and it still wasn't seven-thirty. Thinking I might settle down if I went through the motions of studying, I boiled water at the old gas range that, like the refrigerator, was surely of prewar vintage, made a **mug** of Chinese black tea, and went down the hall. English and French dictionaries lined the shelf over the **writing desk**, and next to them was a pile of photocopied articles I had barely gone over.

I reached out and pushed the buttons on the phone.

"**Hello. This is two one two, five nine five . . . I can't come to the phone right now, so please leave a message after the tone. Thank you.**"

Oh, the loneliness.

The little desk lamp shed amber light on the **writing desk**, and beside it the clock ticked off the seconds with a cheap, tinny sound. I had bought this clock a while ago at the college co-op, a round alarm clock, primitive and classic in style, the sort you would have a hard time finding in a timepiece-developed nation like Japan. The clock always lost five minutes a day, and unless I wound it every night using the turn key in back, with its familiar grinding sound, it would soon stop keeping time altogether. As time had in a sense stopped for me ever since my arrival in America, this old-fashioned clock, like the old-fashioned apartment, was perfect for me. The hands pointed to a quarter to eight.

Would Nanae have eaten dinner with the Murakami family in this weather? The later it got, the more likely she was to be stranded on the highway if she tried to drive back. Already this first snowstorm threatened to be one of the worst in years. Back in **high school**, when it snowed heavily at night I used to peer outside in hopes that school would be canceled the next day. But as the night advanced and the snow fell with increasing intensity, school no longer mattered: the darkness and the snow would go on forever, the passage of ordinary time would change qualitatively—and a quiet terror would gradually possess me.

Tonight too the darkness and the snow seemed likely to go on forever.

How lonely it was, really. Could one possibly experience this level of loneliness in Japan?

I thought of the loneliness of the old ladies—the morose-sounding biddies who dialed my number by mistake. **"Is this Social Security?"** The caller's voice would be frail and gravelly, as if she were calling from the underworld. Perhaps for aged eyes the telephone numbers were harder to read, or trembling aged fingers lost their place in the **Yellow Pages**; in any case, the calls used to come in around nine in the morning, just as the Social Security office was opening. Until I got smart and learned to unplug the telephone, I was awakened by a cracked voice more than a few times. The voice was never male. Was that because men died younger?

I would not hide my annoyance at having been awakened: **"No! You have the wrong number!"**

"Oh." Most of the old ladies would add a grudging **"I'm sorry."** Others impressed me by saying **"Oh, I'm *very* sorry,"** in a gracious tone that led me to picture someone living bravely amid her loneliness. I saw short lace curtains at her kitchen window and beyond them perhaps a birdhouse hanging in a tree. She still drove a car,

still read the newspaper, perhaps even did some volunteer work. Her sons and daughters, scattered across the country, might only come to see her at **Christmas** and **Thanksgiving**, but she never complained to them about being lonely. She believed that to stay on an even keel amid one's loneliness was the natural duty of human beings, a duty she took pride in fulfilling.

Of course, some callers were different. Those without a remaining shred of the social graces would simply say an absent-minded "**Oh...**" and hang up. Such a woman would have fallen into a light sleep the night before, wrapped in nocturnal loneliness, and awakened early in the gray light before dawn. Not young enough to turn over and go back to sleep, she would have lain in bed staring at the ceiling, waiting for the Social Security office to open so she could complain that her check hadn't yet arrived. On a snowy night like this, she and others like her might lose their footing in the world of sanity and slip into madness.

The America that Nanae and I knew was a scary place. The suburban town where we had grown up was luckily violence-free, but once we left our parents' home and began living in cities, being alert to physical danger became part of everyday life. We learned to walk with eyes at the back of our heads, even in daytime. If a man was coming toward us, we automatically swerved to the left or right; in a parking lot, we looked around to see if the coast was clear before proceeding to the car; when boarding an elevator, we checked in the corner mirror on the ceiling to make sure no one suspicious-looking was lurking inside. When we went out, we made sure to carry enough cash to avoid being murdered if mugged, and when we came back, we locked the door with a deadbolt and a chain. It became second nature to take at least the minimum precautions to preserve life. We were not paranoid; we had experienced our share of violence: someone had smashed Nanae's car window and stolen items from within; her wallet had been taken at gunpoint; I had been punched, throttled, once nearly raped. But as great as the fear of violence was, it paled next to the fear of loneliness.

Urban loneliness was endemic to big cities, but the loneliness whose specter terrified me ran deeper. Something in American society caused many to live in isolation, I sensed, cut off from one another. Those who couldn't bear the weight of isolation slowly lost their mental balance and all too often fell through the cracks.

Nanae and I talked about it over the telephone.

"It's hard, isn't it?"

"Really hard."

"Oh, it's so hard, so hard!"

What comforted us was guessing that we were not alone.

"It's not only us. Americans look like they're not having it any easier."

"It's true. They aren't."

"Single women especially."

In fact, **Sarah Bloom**, the budding writer, also seemed to feel a wan aloneness. After Tono went back to Japan, I had less occasion to go to **Manhattan**, but last May **Sarah** had phoned me and urged me, despite my hesitation, to attend a party she was giving. **"You have to come. I only do this every few years."**

All that evening, a crowd of critics, scholars, and artists, those who had made it and those who were up-and-coming, had drifted in and out of **Sarah**'s small apartment. I felt lost in the throng. How many men and women had set foot in her apartment that night? I was stunned to discover that she had so many friends and acquaintances. I couldn't rid myself of the deflating thought that I was after all merely one among many to her. She was wearing a black velvet dress with lace trimming that I could tell at a glance was from a vintage clothing store; her long chestnut hair, arranged more carefully than usual, fell in soft waves down her back; and she was smiling at everyone with greater than usual elegance and charm.

Yet I knew that most of the time she felt abysmally alone. One day she had confessed that she would wake up in the morning feeling good, do her exercises, wash her face and get dressed, then water her plants and feed the cat—but that often by the time she sat down to breakfast for one, tears would be rolling down her cheeks. **"I feel so lonely—so desolate. I can't stop crying."**

I thought about this as I watched **Sarah** play the charming hostess.

The loneliness of such women built up gradually during the day, growing discernibly as evening came on and finally exploding in the hush of night, making those lucky enough to have a confidant reach for the telephone. In the middle of the night, the wires across America were filled with the voices of women whose struggle with loneliness had proven too much to bear quietly alone.

Over and over, Nanae and I comforted each other with the same words.

"It's so hard."

"It really is."

"But it's hard for Americans too, I think."

Yet were American women really as lonely as we were?

"Lonely but free."

The words sounded to me as if anybody could have said them, but Nanae insisted they were from Brahms. It would be nice to feel **lonely but free**, I agreed, but all I seemed to feel was **free but lonely**.

"Free but lonely."

Depending on which word came last, the nature of the loneliness differed. Someone like **Evelyn** would definitely call herself **lonely but free**.

I had met **Evelyn**, who was now nearly fifty but looked much younger, several times at parties given by **Uncle Jesse** and **Rose**. A conscientious couple who felt that merely by raising their own child they had not done their full duty by society, they took an interest in **Evelyn** when she was a young girl and every **Christmas**, **Thanksgiving**, and **Easter**, as well as summer vacations, they had her over from the orphanage where she lived. She continued to visit them on holidays even after she grew up, and that's how we came to know her. A pretty woman with a wheat-colored complexion and dark brown hair, she looked Italian or Spanish; I wondered how much she might know about her lineage. She would puff on a cigarette with her elbow stuck out, cast flirty sidelong glances, and laugh uproariously—traits that set her apart from her foster family, who lived quiet lives of simplicity and fortitude. As she was growing up she had started on the wayward path of a delinquent, I had heard, and I could well believe it, although by the time I met Evelyn she herself was a mother and had more or less settled down. When **Uncle Jesse** and **Rose** grew old, she cared for them as tenderly as a daughter.

I saw her for the last time at **Uncle Jesse**'s funeral. Maybe she had decided that I was now grown up enough to talk to, for she winked as she held a mug of coffee in one hand—**"I like it real strong!"**—and a cigarette in the other, puffing away with her elbow stuck out while she told me her life story. I knew that she had married in her teens and divorced after giving birth to two daughters, but it was news to me that she was now living with a younger man and that her daughters already had children of their own. That she was living with a younger man didn't surprise me, since she herself looked so young, but it was hard to believe that she was a grandmother.

"Do you see your daughters once in a while?"

"Oh, yeah. I sometimes drive up to see them."

◀ So lonely

"You do?" I remembered hearing that they lived near each other somewhere in the Midwest.

"Yeah. It only takes a few days." She spoke casually, as if it were nothing. She took along a big dog as bodyguard, she said, and slept in the car along the way. **"You know what's so wonderful about driving alone?"** With her trim, pretty face raised, her eyes shone as she related how waking up in the morning and stepping out of the car, she could watch the sun come up in a flaming red sky. **"I feel so happy! So totally free!"** She beamed, her arms spread wide to express her joy at seeing the horizon.

Evelyn, who had grown up not knowing her biological parents, found her greatest joy not in spending time with her daughters and grandchildren, her only blood relations, or in being with her young lover, but in standing alone, facing the horizon. Or at least she wanted it to be so. She wanted it to be so because she thought it *should* be so. Perhaps as an American she was prisoner of an ideology that placed freedom above all else. American settlers had left the fences of the Old World in search of freedom, making it imperative for them to accept loneliness as a basic condition of life. Perhaps more than an ideology, it was a faith. And what could fortify a human being against life's adversities better than faith?

I felt the acceptance of loneliness in this land most strongly each time I returned from Japan. When I arrived at **Kennedy**, I would climb into a van that made a misnomer of **"limousine service"** and go down the highway toward the college town I lived in. Through the dusty window I would see lawns and trees baked in the summer sun and, beyond them, mixed among ordinary buildings, ruins horribly exposed, their brick walls crumbling and their windows smashed. It would then become clear to me that I was back in America, where different rules applied. Japan, the land of busybody slogans like "When you leave home, let your neighbors know" and "If you see someone suspicious, dial 110 right away" was

◀ So desolate

far behind me. Inside the station wagon there would be a mere scattering of passengers, each with eyes staring straight ahead, locked in a private world. A loneliness I had forgotten while in Japan would sweep over me, and it would sink in again that I had left a land where anyone different from the rest stood out and entered a land where even the presence of an out-and-out lunatic raised little concern. Broken people, like broken buildings, were simply part of the American landscape.

From around the time I isolated myself in my apartment, I had made a point of adhering to at least minimal social norms by being awake in the bustling daytime and asleep when the streets were silent. I did not feel immune to the danger of slipping beneath the surface of sanity and drowning. When I did go outside, whether walking down the sidewalk, riding the bus, or eating in a **fast food** restaurant, I saw men and women who had gone mad, unable perhaps to tolerate their loneliness. They created impenetrable invisible walls around themselves, muttering in low voices, hunched over. The sight of them filled me less with pity than with relief that I had not yet lost my mind and made a public spectacle of myself. That I had not done so seemed something of a miracle.

But on the night of a blizzard like this, I could not help feeling the imminent danger of being engulfed in darkness and slipping into insanity unawares. It was not so much that I myself would do so as that all around me I sensed lonely soul after lonely soul, lost in the dark, crossing that fateful line.

The amber light of the desk lamp only made me more conscious of the darkness at my back.

Out of the silence the telephone rang. Even though I had been waiting for Nanae to call, the sound gave me a start.

"Hello, it's me. Just got back." She sounded out of breath.

"Oh, good. Glad you made it back okay." I glanced at the clock: just eight. She must have driven back without eating.

"Did you call me?"

"Yes."

"Twice?" She sounded happy. When I called and she was out, it proved that she wasn't the only one making calls. "There weren't any messages but I figured it was you."

"Yes. I didn't leave a message."

"The snow is really coming down. I was half afraid I might not make it home from the parking lot. The sidewalks weren't shoveled."

After their daughters' piano lessons, Mr. and Mrs. Murakami had urged her to spend the night because the highway would be dangerous, but she had declined, explaining that her cats would be waiting for her. "So Mrs. Murakami said, 'Wait, I'll fix you something to take with you,' and packed me a dinner in Tupperware. I left right after that, but it took a pretty long time to get home."

"Sounds dangerous."

"Oh yeah. I don't know how I survived. The visibility was terrible, but cars kept whizzing past me. I was scared to death. Lots of cars had pulled onto the shoulder."

I imagined her car skidding. As she swung around to the left, pivoting on her rear wheels, a car speeding in the next lane slamming into her . . .

Nanae's stock refrain went through my mind. "I know. I know. Nobody gives a damn if my car gets crushed by a truck or something and I get killed." She would say this reproachfully and then add, "But imagine! What's going to become of my babies once I'm gone? If scary Aunt Minae gets you, she'll cart you off to the vet and have you put to sleep. Poor souls! If I die it won't make any difference to anybody, but I would feel so sorry for you two . . ." Lately, Nanae was practicing safe driving for this reason.

"Hey, hey, babies, whatcha doin'? Ooh, so noisy! . . . Listen, can I call you back after I feed my babies? The light was flashing on the telephone so I figured you were worried and called as soon as I took off my boots and coat. **Jeez, this place is goddam cold."**

Since she paid the heating bill herself, Nanae turned the heat off when she went out. I offered to call her back.

"No, no. Let me call you back. Okay? You called me this noon when we had that long talk."

"It's all right," I said. "You've called me a lot this month. I'll give you a ring around the time you finish your dinner." I felt strongly that this call was one that I should initiate.

"Really? Thanks. **Then I don't mind waiting till eleven."**

If I sat around and waited until the rates went down, I was afraid this crucial call might end up no different from any of our ordinary talkathons. "That's okay. I'll call when you're done eating. **How about at nine?"**

"Oh, I'll be done in less. Make it a quarter to nine."

"Okay."

Even after I hung up, Nanae's excitement from her trek through the snow lingered in the air. Had she failed to deduce from my earlier call that I might go back to Japan? It bothered me that she had come home sounding so chipper. Perhaps she had merely set the disturbing prospect of my departure aside, as was her habit. Or perhaps my leaving America was beyond her imagination. I myself found it impossible to imagine in concrete terms. And yet it was equally impossible to imagine remaining as I was.

I reached up, pulled down a thin folder from the top shelf of the **writing desk**, and laid it open on the desktop. It contained references that I hadn't glanced at in months. I leafed through the pages in the amber light, so familiar yet so strange they seemed encrypted documents from some remote planet. Disconnected from meaning, the letters of the **alphabet** danced noisily on the page as if to reveal their nature as phonetic symbols.

I recalled a peculiar sensation I used to have during class—a sense that the classroom had suddenly receded, as if viewed through the wrong end of binoculars. It was as if my soul had wandered off somewhere. Indeed, what business did someone like me have inquiring into the relationship that *lux, luce, licht,* light, *lumière* and similar words from Western languages bore to the concept of "truth"? The French literature department was world-renowned for its cogitations on words, words, and more words, but whatever language those words might be from, they were certain to be Western in origin; therefore, the more protracted my graduate school life became, the deeper my sense of alienation. That I had taken up the study of French as a means of fleeing English seemed increasingly ludicrous. My desire to turn my back on the French language as well grew stronger as time went on. And yet I had ended up taking classes in ancient and medieval French literature, and during summer vacations I had studied Latin, Italian, and German, trying to learn inflections in each language, even though I was sure to forget them all right away. When it came to writing papers, an act seemingly as aimless as my presence in graduate school, I procrastinated and ended up producing pointless papers twice as long as those of other students in five times the amount of time. Remorse filled me to think I had squandered years of my youth in this way.

And the sin against my own life was not my only sin. Here I was taking up space in an august institution of learning when I had no intention of ever becoming a scholar. The library itself, open late night after night, symbolized all that I did not deserve. Resembling a cathedral, it was majestic outside and in, with vaulted ceilings and stained-glass windows. The real luxury, however, was its contents. The reference room alone, packed with rows of dictionaries, encyclopedias, and periodicals from around the world, bewildered me by the sheer magnitude of the accumulated knowledge on every

University library ▐▶

imaginable subject made available even before one got to actual books. In the reading room, where high-backed armchairs sat next to reading lamps, I could take as many books as I liked from the shelves and examine them; if I left them piled on the table, before long someone would come along and re-shelve them. In the maze-like stacks I had easy access to a bounty of books, some a century or two old, leather-bound volumes with gilt lettering—the sort that would fetch a pretty penny on the old-book market. I never did get used to those riches of knowledge, a banquet as sumptuous as any the ancient Romans gave without a thought for poverty in the streets. I never got over my guilt at having a seat at the banquet while others more deserving were shut out.

The place I occupied at the table was meant not for me, I felt, but for someone like **Rebecca Rohmer**.

On an eternal night of heavy snow, the memory of the misfortune of others returns like a ghost.

The previous December, after spending two days and nights with me, **Rebecca** was set to leave on the morning of the third day. In the kitchen, where gray morning light came in from the back porch, we ate a classic American breakfast of ham and eggs with toast and tea. I laid out two of the damask napkins I'd bought in France, which I had used occasionally when Tono and I entertained.

The time with **Rebecca** had exhausted me. She was not yet well, it was clear, and talked nonstop. I was glad that she would be leaving as soon as breakfast was over. My first American friend had been crazy **Linda**; I thought I had progressed from her to the honors student **Rebecca**, but now maybe **Rebecca** was going crazy too—there was something darkly funny in the thought. Although my spoken English was improved since **high school**, out of habit I mostly listened quietly, murmuring an appropriate response at pauses; perhaps that made me easy to talk to.

Rebecca wiped her mouth with the napkin and laid it on the table. **"Thanks so much for everything."**

In another fifteen minutes, I would call her a taxi so that she could make her train on time. I felt the need to say some sort of farewell.

"I guess I'll see you next spring, then." She had mentioned that was when she'd be coming to take her orals and had asked me to put her up again. **"I hope I can get through it this time. Well, I'll keep my fingers crossed."** She looked at me through her red-rimmed glasses. **"You know, Minae, there's one more favor I want to ask you."**

What else could she possibly want? Hiding my unease, I smiled. **"Well, what is it?"**

"You'll see."

She took a manila envelope from the heavy-looking bag at her side and drew out a sheet of paper. Then, moving her plate aside to make room for it, she began writing with a ballpoint pen. As I looked at her hair, streaked with gray, I recalled how back in **high school** when I was still reading *le Petit Prince* she had already been reading unillustrated books in German, and how envious and awed I had felt. Meanwhile, she went on writing with her wrist bent. *That's right, I remember now—she was left-handed.* I felt a rush of pleasure at the memory. It was good to know my memories of her could still be pleasurable.

Rebecca looked up and handed me the paper. **"I want you to be my first witness."**

"Your first witness?"

"Yes. I need three witnesses in order to donate my brain."

Donate her brain?

Rebecca went on, seemingly amused at my puzzled frown. **"So that the doctors can see what's wrong with it after I'm dead."**

They wanted to autopsy her brain after she died, and to do so they needed a document granting permission, with three witnesses guaranteeing that she was of sound mind when she signed it.

A cousin of hers had committed suicide, and if her medicine ran out she was at imminent risk of suicide herself, so she had decided to prepare the document now, she said. According to her doctors, there was a high probability that she had a genetic disorder.

Floored by the strangeness of the request, I said mechanically, **"And you want me to be your first witness?"**

"Yep. You're one of my oldest friends."

I accepted the sheet of paper covered with small print. **"Wow. I'm quite honored."** I didn't know how to react except to say this in a half joking way. **"Wait a minute, then."**

Reluctant to sign such a document with a ballpoint pen—was that because I was Japanese?—I went into the study and brought out the black fountain pen Tono had once given me for my birthday. I signed my name carefully: **Minae Mizumura**. The paper was divided into three equal sections, and I signed the top one as the first witness.

"How long have you been carrying this form around?"

"Oh, about a month, I guess."

If she had had the form for a whole month, I couldn't understand why someone like me, whom she hadn't seen in years, should be the first witness. Wasn't there someone else she could have turned to more easily? But then, she had recently quit her job as an in-house copy editor and was living on unemployment insurance, so perhaps she was as devoid of social life as I was. Her parents had sold their house in the suburbs some years ago and now lived in a cottage in the mountains of **Vermont**, she said. I did not know if the genetic condition in question was bipolar disorder, schizophrenia, or something else.

I called a taxi for her. She maneuvered herself sluggishly into the seat and drew in her swollen legs, once so athletic and beautiful. A numb pity overcame me, as snow began to fall. I stood in the falling snow and watched the taxi until it disappeared—something

I usually didn't do when seeing off non-Japanese people. That evening too the snow had gained force as the night drew on.

Rebecca hadn't come back to take her oral examination in the spring. When I called the number she had given me, the operator's recorded voice came on with the familiar words, "**The number you have reached has been disconnected.**" I thought of the enormous mental institution visible from the highway. The windows were barred, as in a prison.

When I called **Sarah Bloom** to thank her for the party in May, she said, "**By the way, I meant to ask you. Did Rebecca come back to take her orals?**"

I had grown used to the fact that the two of them were no longer close, but it still felt odd for her to be asking me for news of **Rebecca**. I replied that she had not and that her line was disconnected.

After a pause, she said, "**Life is quite terrible—so full of unknowns. Don't you think?**" Her voice was deeper than usual. "**I wish I were twenty years younger or twenty years older.**"

Since then I hadn't spoken with **Sarah** on the telephone. What would she be doing on a night like this? Where was **Rebecca**? I did not know even if she was alive.

The sensation of being engulfed in darkness that Nanae's call had interrupted slowly returned.

The bottomless night stretched on without end. Against the abundance of white snow falling outside, the blackness of the black night stood out all the more.

Silence reigned inside and out.

Before I knew it, the hands on the clock were pointing to the time Nanae had said to call her. Only then did I realize that I had been staring at it. My fingers moved of their own accord, dialing her number, and after only two rings she picked up.

"Thanks for calling back."

I was relieved to hear her normal, everyday voice. Had she had time to feed the cats and finish her own dinner? "You ate already?"

"Yeah. I'm a fast eater when I make up my mind to be. Embarrassingly fast."

"What did you have?" For once, the sheer pleasure of talking about nothing with her flooded through me. All too soon these daily conversations would be a thing of the past.

"What would you call it? Sukiyaki, I guess. Beef and veggies cooked in soy sauce and sugar. **It was a bit too sweet, though.** She's a good cook, but everything's a bit too sweet."

"Oh?"

"Not that I'm in any position to complain."

We had grown up on our mother's salty cooking. Mother liked salt so much that when she was a baby on Grandma's back, she used to suck on salt instead of sweets, the story went. Nanae and I always complained that our food was too salty, but we must have grown used to it.

With Mother's letter hovering in mind, I said, "Will the Murakamis be staying on in New York for a while more?" It was perhaps asking too much to expect them to stay put.

"I have no idea because they have no idea."

A couple of years had gone by since they first said they'd been in America so long, they expected to be called back to Japan any time. They lived not knowing when the order might come through. The girls, who took special Saturday classes in Japanese, still didn't know where they would be going to school next year. Nanae had heard the parents say, "It's a good thing they're girls. If we'd had boys, think what a huge problem it would have been."

"They don't know?"

"Nope. They laugh about it. 'It's our fate, Miss Nanae. We just wait and do what they tell us.' They're philosophical about it, or at least he is."

To avoid a similar predicament, our father had chosen to be taken on as a local hire, though in the end he hadn't had any control over his fate either.

"How was Father?"

It took Nanae a few seconds to answer; she seemed to be lighting a cigarette.

"**Oh, it's so depressing.** He's in more and more of a fog, and he doesn't seem especially happy to see me. **I sometimes wonder if it's worth all this effort to go and see him.**"

"Last time I went, he looked happy enough."

"He's slipped a lot since then."

"Did he eat the rice balls?"

"One."

"Did you tell him it's been twenty years today?"

"**No. I thought of telling him, but I decided not to.** I just couldn't bring myself to do it. When we first came to America, he was so full of hope, remember? It seemed heartless to remind him. Seeing him the way he is now, I just couldn't."

"Right."

After a short silence, I said, "A letter from Mother came today."

"Oh, did it now?" Her voice took on a sharp edge. "I wonder what she'd think of my going to see him on a night like this. She's probably lolling by the pool."

The incongruity of it hit me: somewhere on Earth, today was just another hot day. It also shocked me a bit that Nanae had immediately thought of the swimming pool. Some time ago Mother had written that she went swimming every day in the pool attached to the Singapore condominium, but I had forgotten.

"So what did the old dear have to say?"

"She's gone back to Japan for a little bit. Two weeks or so."

"Oh?" I could hear her vent her feelings by letting out a stream of smoke. "Well, sounds like she's living quite the life. **Don't you think?**" Her tone was acerbic.

"He had to go there, so she went too, she said."

"**Ay-yai-yai**. She can't get enough of him. That woman's got more hormones than you and me put together."

I explained that the guy was going to be sent back to Japan next spring. Nanae suddenly turned serious.

"Oh, he's going back. **Then they're going to settle in Japan after all.**"

"**Uh-huh.**"

"Quite a short stay then, in **Singapore**."

"Yes. Shorter than I thought."

"Huh."

I hastily added, "But she apparently thinks they might come back here sometime too." With my own as yet unspoken plans in mind, I wanted her to know that Mother's return to Japan might not be permanent, hoping that this might provide her some emotional support.

"Come back . . . **You mean to the States?**"

"Yeah."

"Well, still, she'll be living in Japan at least for a while."

"Right."

"Huh." Then she murmured as if to herself, "But even if she goes back, with the house gone she'll be pretty miserable."

"I know."

"What's she going to do?"

The idea of our parents having no money was hard to get used to. I thought of our luxury-loving mother and wondered—what, indeed, was she going to do?

"What about Kyoto?" Nanae asked all of a sudden. Mother's father and his relatives were in Kyoto, but relations with them had been strained beyond repair over the years.

"She didn't go there, apparently."

"**Jesus.** So she doesn't have a place in Kyoto either."

"No, she doesn't."

The house in Kyoto, which Mother always disparaged as "that hovel," was a typical two-story house with a token pine tree planted by the entrance. It was nothing special, but as I returned to Japan for summer vacations and saw firsthand the country being made new with modern housing and concrete structures springing up everywhere, I had grown fond of the traditional, weathered wooden house. Apart from the kitchen and the veranda with standard rattan chairs, every room had tatami, and meals were all eaten seated on cushions at a low table; to me the house conveyed vestiges of the world of early modern Japanese literature. Sitting sprawled in a rattan chair, I could look out on the garden, where instead of grass there were trees and shrubs carefully tended by Grandfather, all of them rarities to me. There was even a small Shinto shrine where he went every morning to pay respects, bowing his head and clapping twice. In addition to this fair-sized garden, the property had a good location, and if Mother, Grandfather's only child, could have inherited it, she might have parlayed it into a decent house in Tokyo. Then Nanae would have had a place to go home to when the time came. Perhaps it couldn't be helped, but I felt sad thinking about the way Mother lived, almost always casting aside those closest to her.

Nanae gave voice to our shared feeling. "What's she going to do when she goes back to Japan, with all her relationships shot?"

"I don't know."

"You at least know people **here and there** around Japan. You've dated Japanese men exclusively, after all, never tiring of them for some reason."

"Not *that* many," I said, allowing myself a little chuckle. Nanae had done as she pleased all her life, yet she was jealous of my little flings with Japanese men. I grew serious again. "She said she went to pay her respects to Grandma at the Tsukuda family grave."

"She did?"

"Yes."

"At the family grave?" She sounded surprisingly interested.

"Apparently."

"Where is it?"

"Somewhere deep in the hills of Kyoto."

After Grandma's funeral, her boxed ashes had lain on top of the paulownia chest, wrapped in a white cloth. I hadn't needed to be told not to touch the white package; the very air surrounding it had seemed forbidding. But who had taken it and how her remains had come to be buried deep in the hills of Kyoto, I had no idea. I pictured a gentle landscape of the sort conjured by the words "deep in the hills of Kyoto."

"So she was properly buried after all." She sounded moved.

When we were little, our paternal grandmother had also lived with us in the Tokyo house, and the reason Grandma Tsukuda lavished her affections on me and not Nanae, Mother used to say, was probably in deference to Grandma Mizumura. The vestiges of patriarchy dictated that a paternal grandmother had more right over the eldest child, the supposed heir. But Grandma Mizumura had died relatively early on, so only I had grown up a grandma's girl—which Nanae always said was the reason "you're so maddeningly stable."

It soon became clear why Nanae was so interested in the news of Grandma Tsukuda's grave, even though Grandma had never doted on her.

"You know, there's a grave in Japan for us too." Her voice had a lilt.

"Uh-huh."

Actually nothing came to mind. Father had long since declined to have anything to do with the Mizumura family, as they had offered no help when his father died, young, and yet had vehemently opposed his marriage to Mother; by extension, he rejected the family grave. "I'll be damned if I go in there," he used to say.

As children, Nanae and I had never experienced the tradition of paying respects at ancestors' graves several times a year. It was hard to believe that she would know any more about it than me.

"When I think that there's a gravesite waiting for me in Japan, I feel relieved. Just knowing that at the very end, I'll have a place to go. **The last haven, I suppose.** It's ours because we're the main branch of the family."

"Is that right?"

"Oh, yes. Plus it's in Tokyo." Her tone was increasingly proud. "Used to be quite big, they say. They moved the temple, graves and all, because of **highway** construction or **subway** construction or something, and in the process our plot got shrunk. **Isn't that terrible? You really shouldn't move graves around.** Even so, it's supposed to be twice the size of most family graves. **Did you know about all this?**"

"I think I did, now that you mention it."

Besides "I'll be damned if I go in there," all Father had to say on the subject was "I hate those money-grubbing priests." At the same time, he never troubled himself to purchase a gravesite elsewhere. Mother also would periodically comment that she didn't like the idea of being buried with the Mizumura ancestors, total strangers to her, but she too never made any other provision. Recently she had taken to saying, "I wasn't a good wife anyway, so if you just scatter my ashes in the Pacific Ocean, that will be fine with me." Now their daughter was boasting about a family grave she had never laid eyes on.

"We only get to be buried there if we haven't married out of the family, right?" she asked.

"I think so. If we want to be."

"Then, since it doesn't look like either of us is ever going to tie the knot, and we'd still be part of the family, we can both be buried there. We'll be together even after we die. **We're gonna be together forever and ever, baby. How d'ya like that? *Ha ha . . .*"**

"Whatever," I said. My heart ached to think that Nanae drew some kind of strength from thinking about the destination of her future remains.

"Listen, listen!" she went on, obviously having no idea what I was thinking. There was suppressed laughter in her voice, the way she always sounded before telling a joke. "Talking about graves reminds me—I bet you haven't heard this one."

"Go on."

"A guy was walking around a graveyard and he heard this funny sound." Then she sang, *"Da da da daaa, da da da daaa."* It sounded like the theme of Beethoven's Fifth, but on the final syllable her voice went up, not down.

"What's that supposed to be?"

"What do you think the sound was?"

"Something to do with Beethoven."

She giggled. "Yes, but what? Guess."

"I can't."

"You can't?"

"No."

"It was the sound of Beethoven *de*composing in his grave."

I laughed. "I get it. Funny!"

"Isn't it?"

"Where'd you hear it?"

"From David, the gay David. Quite a while ago." Cheered by her own joke, Nanae returned to the topic of Mother's letter. "Did she say anything else in the letter?"

"She said she's going to take a writing class once she's settled in Tokyo."

"A writing class?"

"You know, they have hundreds of what are called 'culture centers' in Japan now."

"So she's going to become one of those lah-di-dah culture ladies?"

"Sounds like it."

"God forbid! Maybe she'll write a book called *Once a Woman, Forever a Woman.*"

Sighing, I explained that I was the one who had suggested to Mother that she write something about her past and how she came to know she was a love child. It wasn't only because I wanted some-day to write a book about Grandma; I also thought it would be a good way for Mother to spend her time, now that she had quit work. I never imagined that she would consider writing a book for publication, let alone actually sign up for a writing class. As usual, her approach was eminently practical, while Father, though brainier, was never good at focusing on his objectives. Even when weeding the lawn, he used to sit flat on the ground like a kid in a sandbox and randomly pull weeds while listening to music on his earphones; a casual passer-by would have found it hard to tell what he was doing. Nanae and I both took after him to a certain degree. Mother, the only one in the family with a strong life force, was different.

"She's a powerhouse, so she might just get it published," I said.

"God forbid!" Nanae repeated and blew out smoke again.

To convince myself, I said, "Well, anybody can write a novel."

"Same here. Anybody can do sculpture. Nowadays."

The conversation came to a pause.

"Also, she says that if I go back to Japan, she wants me to bring Father back too." My tone was deliberately casual. I had talked about everything else to delay bringing up the topic of my leaving.

Nanae drew in a sharp breath. "If you go back?"

"Yes."

After a short silence, Nanae said, "Ah," in a low voice. I could imagine her face clouding over.

She intended to put him in a hospital or old people's home, I explained, somewhere off in Saitama or Chiba. Neither Nanae nor I knew the Tokyo area well, so the place names meant little to us.

Nanae did not hide her displeasure. "If she's not going to **take care** of him herself, then whatever you do, he ought to stay here."

"Doesn't look like she plans to look after him herself. It's more like she's getting on in years, so she'll look in on him if I'm there to help out."

"She'll only admit she's getting on in years when it's to her advantage." Her tone was bitter. Then she mused, "Which do you suppose would make Father happier, being here or in Japan?"

"Mother was more concerned about you than about him."

"Me?"

"Yeah."

"Fat chance! Why would she care about *me*?"

"Well, what if you ended up staying here all alone? She seems to think it'd be hard on you, having to visit Father and handle all the paperwork involved and so on."

"Oh yeah?" She sounded unconvinced.

"Admit it, you're the type that feels like everything's a burden."

"Am I?"

Couldn't she imagine how miserable she would be after I was gone, if for some reason she had to go see Father on a snowy day like this? How much longer would her old rattletrap hold out, anyway?

Still unconvinced, Nanae said, "You know, I really don't think she gives a damn about me."

"Why?"

"Well, because . . ." She hesitated and then spat it out: "She just doesn't want me back in Japan."

The meaning of something Mother had said in her letter now became clearer and hence crueler: "*I no longer have the strength*

*to manage her. If you come back to Japan, she may want to come too,
but . . . please do whatever you can to persuade her to carry on alone."*
She feared having to "manage" Nanae in Japan. Then the realization hit me: what Mother feared was what I secretly feared
as well.

"She thinks it would be a nuisance having me around."

"Hmm. Could be." I had no words of comfort. Since Nanae had
effectively been relegated to my care, perhaps it was me, even more
than Mother, who didn't want her back in Japan. But then I didn't
want Mother there either—nor Father, for that matter. If I were to
build my own life in Japan, family would only be a guilt-inflicting,
energy-depleting burden. I had no desire to start my new life in
the style of the "I-novel," that confessional exposition of, often,
too-binding family ties.

After a short pause Nanae asked, in what seemed as casual a tone
as she could muster, **"So are you thinking of going back to Japan?"**

"I might. I haven't definitely decided yet."

I heard myself utter those words and cursed my lack of courage.
If I could only come right out and tell her, it would all be settled,
but I couldn't bring myself to do it.

"To write novels, like you said? Seriously? It's a shame. You've
invested so much time working toward your degree." Nanae
sounded as if she had more common sense than I did.

"It's not a shame."

"Are you sure?"

"Positive." I then opened my heart to her with something
rare for me, a sincere confession. "My only regret is that it never
occurred to me to write in English."

"Oh." A pause. **"You know, you can still try."**

"Too late."

"You can at least give it a chance."

"No, I've made up my mind to write in Japanese."

After another short silence, Nanae asked, "But do you need to go back to Japan in order to write in Japanese?"

Of course I didn't. All sorts of refugees came to America and wrote in their own languages. But I felt I needed to get to know my native land as an adult if I was going to write in my native tongue. Besides, I could not give up my dream of living in Japan again, however disillusioning the reality might turn out to be.

"Not really . . . but I always intended to go back. You know I did."

"I always did too," she retorted. "Someday." The severity in her tone startled me. "I never made up my mind to stay on here, come what may."

"But you're a sculptor." I wanted her to remain in America. Or I may have needed to convince myself that she should. Words that I had often thought to myself came pouring out: As a sculptor, she was supremely fortunate to be able to live in New York, the mecca of modern art. Any budding sculptor who'd gone to a Japanese art school would look on her New York life as the stuff of dreams. She had a **loft** in **SoHo**, she had part-time work that allowed her to support herself while enjoying plenty of free time, she had a green card, she was fluent in English. I finished the litany with a cheery flourish: **"What more can you want?"**

"Yeah, I know, but . . ." She mumbled, unable to openly refute my superficial logic, yet unconvinced. It was hardly surprising if I failed to convince her, since I knew things were not as simple as I had made them out to be. Above all, just because she was making modern sculpture did not mean she could free herself from the sensibilities that formed her. No art, however abstract, was free from either personal or historical context. She would have to come to terms with what it might mean to pursue sculpture in America as a native Japanese.

Thankfully, she didn't dwell on the subject. "Then if you did go back, it'd be after you took your orals?"

"I guess so."

"When will you decide?"

Stories came to mind of Nanae as a toddler, following Mother around and howling and banging on the door if Mother so much as went to the toilet.

"It had better be soon, I think."

"Huh." I heard the click of her lighter as she lit another cigarette and then let out a long breath. "Japan treats women horribly, you know. **You think you can stand that?**"

"I don't know. I think I'd have to separate myself from all the nonsense that goes on in that country. Otherwise I'd go nuts."

Before my eyes there emerged a vision of ugly cities all alike and small towns dismal in their sameness. A nation that as it rose to become a major economic power had become more and more stunted in spirit; a nation without a soul; a nation of little people . . . or was my negativity toward Japan only defensive, a hedge against the predictable anticlimax of my return?

"Anyway, I need to be free of my **fixation**," I said.

"Then you've as good as made up your mind." I detected a note of anger in her voice.

"Not really."

"No?"

"A lot of things give me pause, you know." This, at least, was true.

"Yeah, I guess."

I realized that somewhere along the way I'd given up on the idea that this would be the crucial telephone call. My cowardice was beyond frustrating. Surely Nanae would rather be told straight out that I was going back. But I could not bring myself to lower the axe. For the first time in my life, I was forced to admit that although poles apart in personality—something I secretly congratulated myself on—we had ended up as close as twins: my guilt over leaving her bordered on the pathological.

I gave in to my cowardice. "Anyway, glad you made it back in one piece. Talk to you soon."

She sighed. "Life is such a drag." She seemed unwilling to let me go.

"Yep."

"Especially on a night like this . . ."

Her words deepened the gloom of the snowy night.

From time to time, one or the other of us would at night succumb to the sensation of falling into a lightless hole. The day after one such endless night, Nanae would call and announce, **"Guess what time I went to bed last night. Five! Five in the morning**, mind you. **How do you like that?"** Sometimes she would put off telling me for a day or two out of embarrassment. **"I listened to them all night—all night!"** By "them" she meant popular songs on old records or tapes she happened to have on hand. "Japanese **arrangements** are really **cheap**—all they do is follow the **melody. Even I could do better than** *that!"* And yet she must have been starved for those cheap melodies and even cheaper lyrics. I would imagine her opening a bottle of whiskey, sniffing and slobbering too, using up boxes of **Kleenex**; the reason I could picture this was because I sometimes turned, weeping, **Jack Daniel's** in hand, to a bedside pile of tattered girls' manga for solace in the night.

What happened in the daytime to send us into such nocturnal tailspins was uncertain. In my case it could be because the grocery bag I was carrying in my arms broke, sending oranges tumbling across the muddy sidewalk, or because the sun hadn't shone for three straight days, or because signs of spring, promising happiness, only made me sad. Whatever the cause, once I started down the slope, I just slipped farther and farther.

On such nights, not even the telephone seemed to offer any hope. Longing for bygone days when life was child's play, we let ourselves descend to a place as far removed as possible from our present predicament, a place where we sought to empty and forgive ourselves. To forgive all. Some might call this longing a desire to return to the womb, but I simply called it **regression**, repeating the word in tears as I lay flat on my back, eyes closed, tattered manga now scattered on the floor. By naming the process, I sought to accept my mental exhaustion and so find a way to crawl back toward the light. Was this ritual of descent and resurrection somehow necessary for all human beings? Was it twice as necessary for people like my sister and me, rootless and adrift?

I pulled myself back to reality. "Yes, but it's hard on everyone." It was the well-worn phrase we always used to comfort each other. Nanae obligingly took comfort.

"True. While I was on my way back from the **parking lot** I was thinking how nice it was to have somewhere to go home to. With these two **babies** waiting for me."

"For sure."

"In weather like this I'll bet lots of **homeless** people freeze to death."

"Yep." The word **"homeless"** rang in my ears with the shadow meaning of people lacking not just a house to shelter them but a homeland to return to. I tried again to hang up. "I'll let you go then. We'll talk soon."

"Okay." A pause. "Bye, then."

That would be our last phone conversation of the day. From habit I glanced at the clock, still marking off the seconds with its cheap, tinny sound. It was past nine-thirty. I turned off the lamp and went out through the hall to the kitchen, turned on the

light, and fixed myself a **Jack Daniel's**-and-water. Then I went back
out and sat at Tono's big desk in the living room.

I switched the **computer** on, and the screen glowed bluish-white.

Friday, December 13, 198X.
Alas! Twenty years since our—

※ ※ ※

8:45 p.m. The last call to Nanae.
I could not bring myself to tell her that I have already made
up my mind. I shall tell her tomorrow. Maybe the day after.
There's still time.

Oh, how silence reigns!
Whether all the sounds in the world were absorbed by the snow
or had simply disappeared, all I could hear was the low hum of
the **computer**.

*Everything's so still. What happened to that snowplow? Isn't it com-
ing back? And, oh yes, the siren . . . I wonder if the guy was all right. No,
maybe it was a woman. A reckless driver. No, a jaywalker. Maybe she's
dead. Then there should be a falling star, but tonight it wouldn't show . . .*

A night so long, it seemed as if the planet had left its orbit and
headed off into night eternal.

How long have I been sitting like this?
I had been typing a line, taking a sip of Jack Daniel's, typing
another line, and then letting my thoughts drift until I remembered what I was doing and started up again. The last call to Nanae
couldn't have ended more than an hour ago, but it felt as if a lifetime had gone by.

The ice in my **Jack Daniel's** had melted, and the condensation on the outside of the glass had been absorbed by the small cloth coaster. The whiskey gave off a warm, sour smell; the air around it seemed even more stagnant than in the rest of the apartment. I was thirsty. I wanted to go to the kitchen for a glass of cold water, but in the profound silence I felt chained to my chair. I reached out and switched the **computer** off. Then I immediately switched it back on. I felt there was something else to add to the diary, but what?

The low hum of the **computer** filled my ears again. It was a sound so faint it might have been an illusion. Yet in the absolute quiet, that faint sound gradually gained an eerie intensity.

I pushed back the chair, as if to break free from all invisible chains. I wanted to break free from family, from America, even from Japan—better yet, from life itself—and be engulfed by nothingness.

Before I knew it, I was standing in front of the tall oak bookcase on the opposite wall from the **computer**, looking up. On the top shelf was the set of books with vermilion bindings, untouched for a while. I reached up and pulled a volume down. I opened it, and the familiar musty smell rushed out. The past twenty years—and many more—were contained in that smell.

> **If I but could, I would travel to far-off Cathay or India . . .Oh, I hate it I hate it I hate it. How can I go where there are no human voices, no sounds, just quiet, such quiet that my mind empties and is free of anxiety? How much longer must I be held here, in this place so tiresome, tedious, irksome, dreadful, sad, and lonely? All my life? Is my life to be only this? Ah, I hate it I hate it! As if in a dream, she stopped by a grove of trees at the side of the road and as she lingered there, out of nowhere she heard her own voice singing: "I am afraid to cross, yet cross I must."**

I stood transfixed by the lines of writing on the page.

Those words belonged to a woman I had never met, a woman who had died long before I was born. It was uncanny how her words reverberated in me as if they were my own, giving voice to my ill-defined yearning in a way no other words could. And yet there was something else, something less personal but more profound and powerful that made me feel close to that woman, so close in fact that I imagined her standing right behind me, reading over my shoulder and sighing in delighted amazement that those lines she had written lived on . . .

I turned around, holding the book open, and of course there was only empty space and beyond that, the glowing **computer** screen. But I felt the presence of that woman, Ichiyō, in the room. The presence of a writer who had felt an unstoppable urge to write in the one language she knew and who had done something with that language that was wondrous. I felt her beckoning me to join her, to write something in that language and to do something wondrous with it too. And then I knew, in a way I'd never known before, that the act of writing was itself bliss. Any lingering remorse over my long obsession with a language of such little consequence dissipated in the musty smell floating upward from the yellowed pages. I carefully closed the book.

Destabilizing the darkness, the phone rang. I put the book back on the top shelf and went down the hall to the study to take the call.

"Hello? It's me." Nanae's voice was hoarse. Before I could speak, she announced, "You can go back."

Caught off guard, I couldn't find words.

"Back to Japan."

Silence stretched between us.

"I mean, you always wanted to and everything."

She got that far and broke down. I heard a hiccupping noise, and then all of a sudden she burst into tears. At that helplessly childish sound, an unbearable wretchedness filled me and before I knew it, tears flooded my eyes and I was choking with sobs. For a while the two of us, grown women, sobbed together like children on opposite ends of the line.

"But you'll be all alone . . ." Finally I got that much out. An image of Nanae standing in the valley between **Manhattan** skyscrapers, alone and lost, rose again before my eyes. She was thin and cold.

"That's just how it is!" Her voice was almost a shriek.

"Will you be all right?"

"Well, I'll just . . . have to be . . . won't I?"

She cried all the harder—the unrestrained bawling I had witnessed so many times. Drawn in, I cried harder. It felt as if I were split in two—as if the one in tears was a little lost child standing by the side of the road in utter desolation, a desolation incomprehensible to adults, and I was looking on helplessly, not knowing what to do, while at the same time I myself was that sobbing child.

I groped for a chair and sat down, then switched on the little lamp in front of me. The list of references for my orals came into view, letters of the **alphabet** like ants lined up in rows, blurring together till I was seeing double, then triple. "I'm so sorry," I said through my tears.

"That's just how it is, that's just how it is," she sobbed back.

"I'm so, so sorry."

Nanae continued to cry as I listened, gripping the receiver. But I felt myself in a trance, listening to nothing at all. Time went blank. For a while, all I could do was stare into the hollow in my heart. The next thing I knew, Nanae's sobs were quieting, growing intermittent, and then they were all but gone. Guilt at leaving her behind— guilt at cutting her lifeline—overwhelmed me. Scarcely thinking, I said, "Nanae, you know you can go back to Japan too, if you want."

Her reply was instantaneous. "I could never survive there."

"Of course you could."

"How?"

"You know English. You speak it. There's always a way."

Plenty of young women left Japan for English-speaking countries every year to attend language schools just so they could acquire enough English to earn their living. Nanae's English was beyond sufficient. Her nimble fingers made her a far faster typist than me, despite all the time I'd spent typing papers. Forgetting for the moment her late rising, frailty, indolence, snobbery, and romanticism, I pictured her striding down a sunny sidewalk some morning in Tokyo, her heels clicking on the pavement as she headed for a crowded commuter train.

"What about my sculpting?"

I didn't know how to respond.

"You never, ever take it seriously."

It was true. I could not take it seriously. *She can't give it up*. Not her art so much as the past, which allowed her to dream dreams, however vain. Ultimately she could not bid farewell to herself, to the person her past had shaped, and this was understandable. But until she was able to bid farewell to herself, to the person she was now, the day would never come when she could start life anew and stride purposefully down the street some Tokyo morning.

"Once you were making a living, by **freelance** interpreting or whatever, you'd be able to find time for it." I said this to convince myself. For her to reach that point in Japan would require many times over the resolve and energy she showed now, but in theory it wasn't impossible.

"It's not that simple. **I need a huge space to work and I can't afford one in Japan.**" She added, as if to comfort me: "It's all right. **I just don't feel there's a place for me there.**"

No place for her in Japan, or no place for her in her family going back to Japan?

"**I'll go back when the right time comes.**" She sighed and asked, "Do you think we were unlucky to have been brought to America?"

"I don't know."

I conjured the image of the Japanese housewife I frequently saw in my mind's eye, a housewife mothering not a pair of cats but a pair of children in grade school. Even Sanae, the picture of domestic happiness, must have had days when she longed to live a life limited only by her own limitations.

I corrected myself. "I don't think we were unlucky."

"No."

"I mean, there've been lots of good things too, haven't there?"

"Yes."

"Come visit me once I'm settled. I'll have an **extra** futon for you." I said this to lighten the mood. But as soon as the words were out of my mouth, I pictured with dismay Tokyo's cheap, nondescript buildings and their interiors cluttered with papier-mâché furniture. Traditional futon might not go with such a place at all. "Or at least an **extra mattress**," I amended. "The kind that folds up neatly."

"Remember those red futon?" Nanae summoned a nostalgic, far-off voice. "The silk ones we used to have for guests? They were so beautiful."

"Yeah, I remember. Underquilts of figured satin."

"Figured satin? Is that what it's called?"

"That's what Mother used to call it."

"They were so beautiful. So beautifully Japanese."

The set of underquilts had been made before the war. Their silk luster, deep carmine, and old-fashioned plum-blossom design had had a beauty that thrilled us. In our flimsy Tokyo house where everything else dated from after the war, those quilts alone had inhabited a different world—a world where things had seemed to have their proper place. When Mother told me they were "underquilts of figured satin," she also said the color had faded after they were washed and stretched on boards to dry, that they used to be even more gorgeous. She said that originally they came with matching sleeved coverlets and comforters.

"I wonder what happened to them," murmured Nanae, as if to herself.

"I'm fairly certain they went to Grandfather in Kyoto."

"Oh, good. They'd look perfect in that house."

But that house too was bound to disappear soon. Everything I remembered fondly in Japan was fast disappearing . . . I mourned not only for Japan. I mourned, I grieved, for the landscapes with distinctive faces—faces marked by the singularity of their histories—that were vanishing moment by moment from the Earth.

"Anyway, you can save up the **airfare** and come for a visit," I said. "And once there, you won't have to pay for a thing. We'll manage."

"I still owe you some money, remember?"

This was true. "No rush."

"And who's going to feed my babies?"

"You'll come for just a little while. You could find someone to care for them while you're away."

"Yeah, I guess so."

"We can celebrate New Year's in Japan."

New Year's in Japan. A time filled with traditions and festive Japanese words that I had only a passing acquaintance with: 門松 *kadomatsu*, an outdoor decoration of bamboo and pine branches; 鏡餅 *kagamimochi*, a pile of two flat rice cakes topped with a small bitter orange; 初詣 *hatsumōde*, the first shrine visit of the year; しめ縄 *shimenawa*, sacred Shinto straw ropes hung with festoons; お年玉 *otoshidama*, gifts of money tucked into decorated envelopes for children.

I hadn't experienced a real Japanese New Year's even when I was a child, though our family always celebrated Christmas, probably thinking it a more Western and therefore a more modern and enlightened holiday. Even when I was in Paris, I had gone home to **Long Island** at the end of the year and helped decorate the **Christmas tree**. What would it be like to replace that annual event with a real Japanese New Year's? If I could make my studio apartment look a little festive and have Father stay for the holiday, maybe we could bring back the ghost of family.

"Let's do it," I said, feeling sentimental, even excited. "New Year's in Japan. You have to come!"

"I guess so." She made no show of enthusiasm. "Are you ever coming back?" There was sober intensity in her voice.

"Well, of course I am."

"When?"

"I don't know, but sometime, for sure. I'm still registered at the university."

"So you are." Somehow I could see her staring hollow-eyed into space. **"I wonder what's going to become of me . . ."**

Her murmur resonated deep within me, words for which I could offer no answer. But she uttered them as if to herself, knowing well that I could say nothing. I remained silent. She spoke next with a slight shift in tone.

"You really don't think it was unlucky to come to America?"

"No, I do not."

"Are you sure?"

"Yes, I am."

"I'm asking about me, you know. You'd have been happy any-where, anyway."

"Of course I mean you too."

Nanae might someday cease clinging to the past and go back to Japan to start anew. Or she might make up her mind to put down roots in America. She might finally meet the right man and start a family. She might even wake up one morning and decide to become an American citizen, as millions of others had done.

I tried looking at the two of us with the eyes of an old woman facing death. Her eyes were a source of strength to others whose spirit had fallen so low it could fall no lower. Her eyes knew the emptiness of all things and, knowing this, knew also that life was bliss. The eyes shone from afar, across the sea, with a piercing, unearthly light. And through the old woman's eyes I saw the two of us afresh. We sisters, whom I had thought no longer young, were radiant with youth and possibility, entering the noontide of life. Seasons not yet known would roll around; time not yet born would unfold. This was a blessing.

"**Anyway,**" she said, "**you'll be here for Christmas.**"

"Right."

"I'll get a **tree**."

"Right. I'm looking forward to it."

"Yes, great."

After a short silence, she said, "The snow is really coming down." Her voice sounded different now, as if she had lifted her head up to look out the big window of her **loft**.

"I know, it really is," I echoed.

"I wonder if it's ever going to stop."

"Of course it will, sometime."

"**I guess it has to.**"

"Right."

There was nothing left to say.

"Bye then." Nanae was the first to utter words of farewell.

"Okay, good night."

"G'night."

I listened to the sound of her hanging up before setting the receiver gently back in its cradle. I switched off the desk lamp, padded down the hall, and stood at the bay window in the living room. Reflected faintly in the glass was the square, bluish-white glow of the **computer** screen on the big desk behind me, waiting patiently for my return. Outside, around the streetlamp that shed light on the darkness, powdery flakes continued to swirl and shimmer.

Far off in the distance, white fluorescent light still glowed through the windows of the imposing architecture building.

Snow was falling from the sky as if to wipe out all human sorrow and error and pain, falling amid a silence like death, falling in eternity. A sudden mad yearning for life coursed through me, and in that instant my ears filled with the singing of the *yamamba* mountain women as they danced out of their graves and went sprinting over the ridge and down into the valley, wild hair streaming in the wind.

Awaken, all dreams!
Awaken, all desires!

For the first time in weeks, I grasped the brass handle of the window in both hands and flung it open. Cold air rushed in, the stagnant air around me began to stir, and a breeze swept upward.

The End

◀ Snow

NOTE ON NAMES

Except for the name of the author, who has an established identity
in English, Japanese names are rendered family name first, as custom dictates in Japan.

BIBLIOGRAPHY

Akutagawa, Ryūnosuke (1892–1927). "Butōkai" ("The Ball"). 1920.
    Amazon kindle version. Originally published 1895.
Higuchi, Ichiyō (1872–1896). "Nigorie" ("Troubled Waters"). 1895.
    Amazon kindle version. Originally published 1895.
Loti, Pierre (1850-1923). "Un bal à Yeddo." In *Japonerie d'automne*,
    1889. Amazon kindle version. Originally published 1889.
———. *l'Exilée (From Lands of Exile)*, 1893. Amazon kindle version.
    Originally published 1889.
Mizumura, Minae. *The Fall of Language in the Age of English (Nihongo*
    ga horobiru toki: Eigo no seiki no naka de). New York: Columbia
    University Press, 2015.

All citations are translated by Juliet Winters Carpenter.